ONCE UPON A RIVER

After the violent death of her father, in which she is complicit, sixteen-year-old Margo Crane takes to the Stark River in her boat in search of her vanished mother. But the river, Margo's childhood paradise, is a dangerous place for a young woman travelling alone, and she must be strong to survive, using her knowledge of the natural world and her ability to look unsparingly into the hearts of those around her. Her river odyssey through rural Michigan becomes a defining journey, one that leads her beyond self-preservation and into deciding what price she is willing to pay for her choices.

BONNIE JO CAMPBELL

ONCE UPON A RIVER

Complete and Unabridged

CHARNWOOD
Leicester

First published in Great Britain in 2011 by
Fourth Estate
An imprint of HarperCollins*Publishers*, London

First Charnwood Edition
published 2013
by arrangement with
HarperCollins*Publishers*, London

A catalogue record for this book is available from the British Library.

ISBN 978–1–4448–1622–8

Published by
F. A. Thorpe (Publishing)
Anstey, Leicestershire

Set by Words & Graphics Ltd.
Anstey, Leicestershire
Printed and bound in Great Britain by
T. J. International Ltd., Padstow, Cornwall

This book is printed on acid-free paper

To All the Children Raised by Wolves

My home is on the water, I don't like no land at all.
Home is on the water, I don't like no land at all.
My home is on the water, I don't want no land at all.
I'd rather be dead than stay here and be your dog.

— 'SEE SEE RIDER,' TRADITIONAL

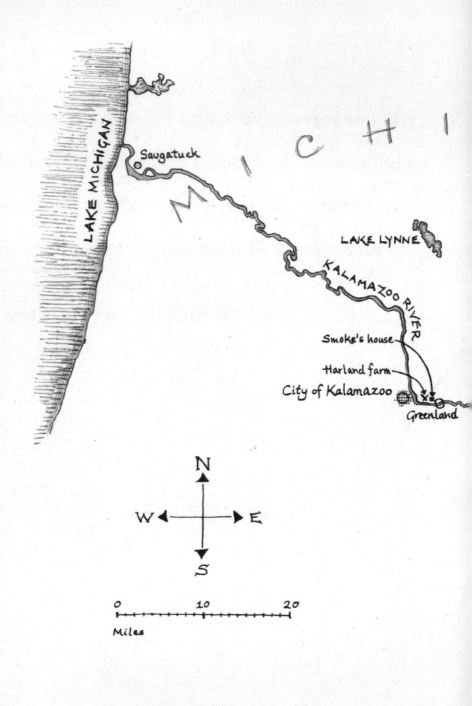

G̲ A N

big Murray house — marijuana house

Village of Murrayville ⊕ — Crane's house

Murrayville cemetery X

Murray Metal Fabricating plant

Pokagon Mound picnic area
dam X
STARK RIVER

Confluence ⊕

Michael's house

Brian's cabin on stilts ● — Heart of Pines ⊕ X Willow Island

KALAMAZOO RIVER

PART
I

1

The Stark River flowed around the oxbow at Murrayville the way blood flowed through Margo Crane's heart. She rowed upstream to see wood ducks, canvasbacks, and ospreys and to search for tiger salamanders in the ferns. She drifted downstream to find painted turtles sunning on fallen trees and to count the herons in the heronry beside the Murrayville cemetery. She tied up her boat and followed shallow feeder streams to collect crayfish, watercress, and tiny wild strawberries. Her feet were toughened against sharp stones and broken glass. When Margo swam, she swallowed minnows alive and felt the Stark River move inside her.

She waded through serpentine tree roots to grab hold of water snakes and let the river clean the wounds from the nonvenomous bites. She sometimes tricked a snapping turtle into clamping its jaws down hard on a branch so she could carry it home to Grandpa Murray. He boiled the meat to make soup and told the children that eating snapping turtle was like eating dinosaur. Margo was the only one the old man would take along when he fished or checked his animal traps because she could sit without speaking for hours in the prow of *The River Rose*, his small teak boat. Margo learned that when she was tempted to speak or cry out, she should, instead, be still and watch and listen. The old man called her Sprite or River Nymph. Her cousins called her Nympho, though not usually within the old man's hearing.

Margo, named Margaret Louise, and her cousins knew the muddy water and the brisk current, knew the sand and silt between their toes, scooped it into plastic cottage cheese tubs and sherbet buckets and dribbled it through their fingers to build sagging stalagmites and soggy castles. They hollowed out the riverbanks, cut through soil and roots to create collapsing caves and tunnels. If any kid stood too long in a soft spot and sank above his knees, he just had to holler, and somebody pulled him free. They spent summers naked or nearly naked, harvesting night crawlers from the mossy woods and frogs' eggs from goo in underwater snags. They built rafts from driftwood and baling twine. They learned to read upon the surface of the water evidence of distress below. Once, when Margo was eight and her favorite cousin, Junior, was nine, they rescued an uncle who'd fallen in drunk.

They all fished the snags at the edges of the river for bluegills, sunfish, and rock bass, though they avoided the area just downstream of the Murray Metal Fabricating plant, where a drainpipe released a mixture of wastewater, machine oil, and solvents into the river — some of the fish there had strange tumors, bubbled flesh around their lips, a fraying at their gills. On certain windy days, the clay-colored smoke from the shop wafted along the river, reached them on their screen porches, and even when they closed

4

their windows, the smoke entered their houses through floorboards and the gaps around their doors.

The Murrays were a stubborn tribe, and Bernard Crane was no less stubborn for being born the bastard son of Dorothy Crane and Old Man Murray during his bout of infidelity, forgiven in time by a wife who, despite (or perhaps because of) her forgiving nature, died young. The old man begged Dorothy Crane to give their child his last name, but she put on the birth certificate *father unknown*. Some said Dorothy was part Indian and that was why Bernard was so small, and others said that she had begrudged her baby sufficient milk at her breast because the old man would not leave his lawful wife, while others, including Cal Murray, denied that Bernard was in any way a Murray. Years later, however, when Bernard Crane, whom everyone called simply Crane, and his wife, Luanne, gave birth to a beautiful green-eyed daughter, a spell of reconciliation was cast across the river, and all the Murrays claimed Margo. The girl's mother even enjoyed the favor of the other women for a while. More often, they referred to Luanne as a 'free spirit.' They did not mean it as a compliment.

When the weather allowed, Margo and her cousins swam all day long. Even when drought made the river shallow enough to walk across, they swam to the big Murray farmhouse on the north bank, where Aunt Joanna was hanging laundry or baking bread and where Uncle Cal might let them shoot skeet with shotguns or plink targets with .22 rifles. Swam straight across to the heavily shaded Crane house, where Luanne was often lying flat in a reclining chair at the end of the floating dock in the only sun on the place, wearing an unfastened bikini. Luanne lay browning like one of Joanna's loaves of bread, lifting her head and opening her eyes only to drink the watered-down white wine she kept in a mason jar full of melting ice. Her scent of cocoa butter drifted out onto the water, and the boys could not take their eyes off her.

In the evenings, Margo rowed, swam, or floated home, and her mother woke up, anticipated the girl's return, and stood, perhaps unsteadily, on the dock, holding a towel for Margo, her favorite towel, oversized, with a pattern of jungle greens. Margo's teeth would chatter as her mother wrapped and hugged her. Only then would Margo smell the sweet breath of wine inside the cloud of cocoa butter. Luanne would say, 'Hold on, Margaret Louise,' as they made their way in an embrace down the dock, along the bank, and into the house. They checked Margo for bloodsuckers on the screen porch and doused any stragglers with salt. After they had both showered, Luanne might go to bed with her bottle of wine and watch TV, or begin her twelve-hour sleep, but Margo curled on the couch and waited for her father to get home from the second shift at Murray Metal Fabricating, sometimes thumbing through her book about Annie Oakley, whose somber face she never tired of studying. Annie looked so natural with her rifles and shotguns, and it seemed to Margo that any girl would want a long gun at her side. When she'd said that to her ma, Luanne had said tiredly that she didn't know how Annie Oakley could have 'fired so many times without killing anyone, without killing the whole damned lot of them,' and Margo hadn't brought it up again.

After a big storm or a sudden thaw, the river could become a passionate surge, dragging along debris from upstream: ill-secured boats or pieces of floats and docks that had been dashed against trees. All manner of stuff might be dragged up onto the riverbank — fifty-five-gallon drums, mildewed buoys on nylon ropes, animal carcasses. And the floodwaters washed away what the Murrays had not secured or could not secure: sand from the sandbox, pig shit from the half dozen pigs in the pasture, garden stakes and tomato cages left out from the previous summer, toys and dog dishes, thousands of shotgun shells and bullet casings from beside the barn. The yearly floods scrubbed the muskrat caves, drowned the moles, carried away burn barrels, wore away land, and swept clear portions of the earth. One February after an early snowmelt, the Cranes lost a whole cord of firewood that was stacked too close to the water's edge.

The death of Margo's grandpa, when she was fourteen, hit the whole family like one of those late winter floods, chilling everything, washing away that old generation and whatever invisible glue and strings had been holding the Murrays together. Margo had stayed by Grandpa's sickbed on the sunporch whenever they'd let her.

After the funeral, she went out with Uncle Cal, loaded his lever-action .22 Marlin like Annie Oakley's with fifteen long-rifle cartridges, threaded her arm into the sling, and took aim through the iron sights. After her first shot went awry, Cal suggested she sit cross-legged and pull the sling tighter. The following fourteen shots hit the paper target just left of center in a tight cluster. Twelve of the shots created a single hole a little more than half an inch across. 'What the hell was that?' Cal said, running his finger over the torn paper. 'I've never shot like that in my life. That's unholy.' Uncle Cal claimed credit for teaching her to shoot, but while Margo had felt his guidance, she had felt just as strongly the guidance of the gun itself. It held her steady, and then sadness perfected her aim.

When Cal Murray took over as president of Murray Metal Fabricating, he called upon his sons to work in the summers rather than exploring the river all day. At about this time, Margo's mother began to put on makeup and disappear for hours in the afternoons. She always returned home at dusk, until one July evening when Margo found herself alone at the dock. Her oversized minnow net contained a giant puffball, white as the moon, bigger than her own head. Margo rose from the river, stood on the dock holding the skull-white mushroom, which she would slice and fry for dinner. The Cranes' little house was dark. When she turned on the kitchen light, she found the note on the table. She read and reread it, but could not crack its code. So many times, Luanne had said she could

8

not bear living in this place, but there she had always been. Margo scratched her ankle and found a fat bloodsucker. She didn't have the patience to shrivel it with salt. Instead she took a butcher knife, smashed the end of the wooden handle into the creature's head, and twisted until the bloody pulp fell onto the kitchen tile.

Maybe the decline of Murray Metal Fabricating after Old Man Murray died and the resulting unemployment in Murrayville was inevitable, given the economic trends of the late 1970s, or maybe Cal's bad management was to blame. Maybe what happened with Uncle Cal and Margo the day after Thanksgiving was bound to happen, too. After Margo finished washing a second sinkful of dishes, her aunt Joanna kicked her out of the kitchen.

'Go out and join the party, hang out with the other kids,' Joanna said. 'Shoo.'

'Let me go change into jeans,' Margo said. She was wearing a long-sleeved dress, something Joanna made her wear when she went along to church, even if it was just to donate canned food. The dress was not bad on top, but it hung below her knees.

'What's wrong with dressing like a girl?' Joanna said. 'Go out there and tell your cousin Junior to stop playing rock-and-roll records. Give us some country music.'

The party was in full swing, and 'Smoke on the Water' was coming over speakers mounted on the trees. Joanna led her to the door, pushed her jacket into her arms, and sent her out into the cold. Margo hiked up her dress and folded it over at the waist to shorten it. This was the first party without Grandpa Murray, and Margo missed his big presence. She wandered across the frozen grass to her father, who was engrossed in a conversation about welding. She couldn't get his attention, so she moved to where the roast pig had been ravaged. The uncle that Margo had saved from drowning, Hank Slocum, was cutting away ribbons of pork and putting them in a big aluminum pan. Margo watched a long white bone appear as he trimmed the meat close. Hank Slocum lived with his wife and their six kids in a pair of camping trailers a half mile upstream on the Murray property. Julie Slocum, who was thirteen and still a tattletale, was flirting with their cousin Junior, who sat cross-legged at the record player, ignoring her. Billy Murray, a few months older than Margo, was bossing around some little kids, including his twin brothers, Toby and Tommy. While she watched, he instructed them to crawl on hands and knees to where the men were tossing horseshoes and to spit into their foamy draft beers. The men didn't notice, and each time one of those men tipped a plastic cup to his lips, Billy and the kids shrieked with pleasure. Margo was lying with the black Lab, Moe, having a conversation of growls and barks, when her uncle Cal nudged her rib with the toe of his boot. 'Hey, Sprite, if you want to go hunting, first you're going to have to learn to skin a deer.'

Margo stood and tugged the dress up at the waist again. Cal was known to compliment the girls if they looked pretty, so they all tried to.

'If you want to learn right now, I'll teach you.' He was slurring his words.

Though her father had told her to stay away from men when they were drinking — himself included — Margo followed her uncle Cal into the whitewashed shed. She smoothed her hair to make sure it wasn't sticking up. The woodstove had gone out, but the room was still warm, so Cal took off his jacket and tossed it on the dirt floor. She hadn't expected Cal to pull her against him, and when he did, she tripped and knocked him into the gutted carcass, making it swing, releasing a blood smell into the air.

When Cal kissed the top of her head, Margo pressed her face into his big chest, felt his thick flannel shirt against her cheek. She loved the leathery smell of him, though it was tinged with pork and beer. He reached down, tightened his arms around her, and lifted her whole body so she was in front of his face, something he might have done when she was a little kid. She had just turned fifteen.

'You want to come out hunting with me tomorrow? Five a.m.?'

Margo nodded, though she had seen the horror on Aunt Joanna's face when Cal suggested a few days ago that he would take Margo hunting on opening day rather than one of their five sons. Margo kicked her legs as though swimming.

While still holding her a foot above the

ground, Cal kissed her mouth. He whispered, 'How's that? Is that so bad?'

Margo swallowed a gasp. She had kissed a few guys in the stairwell at school and had kissed a friend of Junior's in the abandoned cabin upstream, had tried out all kinds of kissing — soft and hard, fast and slow. When they were sure Junior was passed out, Margo and that friend of his had undressed. Margo thought nobody knew she'd gone all the way with him, but maybe Cal knew. Cal moved her in his arms so he was carrying her like a bride over a threshold. He was the handsomest man — her mother had said it all the time. When Cal laid Margo down on his big jacket on the dirt floor, Margo tried to keep breathing normally. When Cal's hands were on her, she reminded herself of when he was first showing her how to shoot, adjusting her hands and arms, telling her to *press*, not *pull* the trigger. Firing the gun should come as a surprise to the shooter, he said, though everything he was doing was moving him toward it.

'You're so lovely,' he whispered. 'It's unholy.'

Cal was the finest man in this town, her mother had said, but where was her mother to explain what was happening now? Margo knew it was all messed up, and she knew her father would be furious, but she didn't say no. Saying no would be like releasing a bullet from the chamber — there would be no way to take it back. Shouting no was something she might practice, once this was over, but for now she would trust Cal. The jacket beneath her head

12

slipped, so when she turned to look at the door, her ear was pressed against the dirt. She smelled blood and mold and mouse piss as Cal moved on top of her. The golden light from the window to the west was warm on her cheek, and she saw a girl's face in the window. At first Margo thought it was her own reflection, but it was Julie Slocum. The girl's hand went to her mouth, and then she disappeared.

'That wasn't so bad, was it?' Cal said afterward.

She knew Cal didn't expect her to say anything. Nobody ever expected her to say anything. Not even her teachers. Before she could answer a question posed in the classroom, she always had to figure out how a thing she was being asked connected to all the other things she knew. She might answer hours later, when she was alone in her boat studying water bugs on the river's surface. It was easier to practice math problems in her head while she rowed, easier to understand how cells divided while she was underwater.

Had it been so bad? Margo slipped her underpants back on. She thought that if she didn't concentrate on her breathing, she would forget to breathe. She looked around to see what else had changed. Not the deer carcass, not the cobwebs or the blood smell. Uncle Cal smiled his same smile. She needed to get out of this shed, to look at it from outside and figure out what had just happened.

Then Margo's father burst through the door. Cal was getting up, buttoning his fly, when her father, barely taller than Margo, kicked open

13

the door and kicked Cal in the mouth with a work boot. Margo heard bones crunch, and two red-and-white nuggets — Uncle Cal's teeth — bounced on the ground. The half-brothers, famous for their tempers, growled at each other like bears. Cal punched Crane in the jaw hard enough that Margo heard a bone break.

Aunt Joanna entered the shed just after Margo's daddy head-butted Cal hard enough to crack a rib. A dozen or more people gathered and watched, some from inside the shed, others through the open door or the dirty window. Julie Slocum slipped in and rubbed her hand over Margo's hair. Margo could smell kerosene on her from the space heaters her family used in their camping trailers. Cal lay on the ground now, and Joanna's long spine curved over his body. She wiped blood from his mouth with a handkerchief and whispered something angrily to him. Then Cal whispered his defense to Joanna, but everyone went suddenly quiet. 'The little slut lured me in here, Jo, but I swear I never touched her.'

Everyone stayed still and quiet until Julie backed away toward the door. Someone coughed, and people began to murmur.

Joanna looked at Margo. 'Damn you,' she said.

Margo squinted at Cal, studied him as though over the Marlin's iron sights, waiting for an explanation or a wink, even, that would suggest he had not meant what he'd said. It had started with the death of Margo's grandfather in January and the departure of her mother in July, and now the severing was complete between Margo and all the rest of them. Even her daddy, bleeding from his cheek and mouth beside her, telling her to stand up, seemed far away.

———

In the front seat of the truck, her daddy demanded she tell what had happened, but she said nothing. He drove her to the police station parking lot and begged her to go inside with him. He briefly tried to drag her out of the truck, but she gripped the gearshift knob with her left hand and the armrest with her right and held fast. She had not resisted Cal, but resistance was a lesson she was learning quickly. At home that night, sleepless in her bed, she heard an owl call, *Who-who, who cooks for you?* She whispered in imitation. She imagined aiming and shooting the bird off its foolish perch in the cedars. From her window, she saw lights still shining at the Murray house across the way and heard music quietly playing.

The next morning, Margo awoke to her daddy moaning through the wall. She forced open his locked door with a butter knife and found him in bed, smelling of blackberry brandy, his face swollen and crusted with blood. He asked her to bring him a beer. Margo took his unopened twelve-pack from beside the refrigerator and kicked it off the porch and end-over-end into the woods outside his window until the cardboard busted open. She cracked one beer and let it foam all over her hand, took a big slug of what remained, and spit it out. She set the can on a stump. She put a second can, unopened, in the crook of a tree and paused to listen to a mourning dove coo from the frosted earth. Using its own sad call, she told the bird to go away. She placed a third can of beer beneath a cluster of barbed raspberry spears. She went on to set up all twelve cans in the woods. In one hand she had her daddy's twenty-gauge shotgun, and in her pocket she had a dozen shells. She stood a few yards away, loaded four shells in the magazine, chambered a round, pulled the trigger, and pulverized the first can. She absorbed the recoil without flinching. She racked the pump, jammed the butt tighter against her shoulder, fired again, and watched the second can explode. Beer foamed eight feet in the air. One by one, in the dim light, she blasted the cans of beer to smithereens, pausing only to reload. She inhaled deeply the sweetness of the gunpowder. Each shot echoed through the woods and across the water.

A light came on in her father's bedroom. She would get him to the hospital. As she waited for him to come outside, she listened to the water flowing beside her in its journey down the Stark, heading toward the dam at Confluence, beyond which lay the Kalamazoo River and, finally, Lake Michigan. Her ears were alive with her blasts. Her shoulder throbbed.

2

A year later, on the Sunday before Thanksgiving, Margo was kneeling between two cedars in the predawn dark, just upstream of her house, watching a six-point buck rooting for acorns in the frozen leaf litter. Margo had all the time in the world to study the creature, its dark hooves and slender legs, its dusky chest, wide as a man's, its heavy crown, white beard, and arrogant gaze. The buck lifted its head and flared its nostrils as it caught the scent of a doe. Margo lifted the shotgun to her shoulder, pressed her cheek against the stock. The river seemed to guide her arm and her eye as she aimed into the heart and lungs, touched the trigger, and *bang*. Only when she stood up did she notice her knee was wet and that ice was forming on the fabric of her jeans.

Her father's bedroom light came on. By the time he dressed and put on his boots and came outside, shaking his head and grumbling, she had dragged the buck on a sled to the swing set frame behind the house. Her third kill in five days.

'This is it. No more hunting, girl,' Crane said and then helped her saw off the legs and string the beast up with a chain around its neck. He sat on an oak stump on the riverbank and raked his butcher knife across a sharpening stone. The water below him was black and cold. 'You hear,

17

Margo, about no more hunting? Speak up. You're not mute.'

'I heard you,' she said, just above a whisper.

This summer and fall Margo had been taking 4-H shooting and hunting classes from Mr. Peake, and she had been relieved when he said her *quiet nature* would benefit her shooting.

'I'll get you whatever targets you want, but no more deer.'

Margo nodded, but she caught sight of something in the gray fog, an orange paper stuck up on the beech tree beside the driveway. Among the maples, oaks, and pignuts was one smooth-skinned beech on which Luanne had used a nutpick to carve lines and ages for Margo's height. Margo moved around the side of the house as stealthily as she could.

'The chest freezer's full, Margo. We've got more than enough meat.' Crane squinted hard upstream, as though suspicious of the pink at the horizon.

Though Margo stepped lightly, the frozen leaves crunched under her feet.

'Being sixteen doesn't exempt you from the law,' Crane said. He touched the edge of his knife blade to the edge of a pack of matches to test its sharpness and then dropped the matches into his pocket. He took a couple more swipes on the stone. Though he was a small man, his voice was strong, and it carried. 'That hunting license pinned to your jacket entitles you to one buck, Margo, not three.'

On opening day, Thursday, they had dressed out her first buck, spent that evening wrapping a few chops and steaks in pale green freezer paper, but turning most of it into burger with a meat grinder clamped to the kitchen table, mixing the lean venison with beef suet from the grocery where Crane now worked, earning half of what he used to make. They had gutted the second deer she killed, and, after a few phone calls, they put the carcass in the back of the pickup, covered it with a tarp, and delivered it to a man who had eight kids and had just lost his job at Murray Metal.

When Crane glanced behind him and saw Margo sneaking away, paying no attention, he stabbed the tip of the knife into the stump so it stuck, and he stood up. 'Goddamn it, girl. Even if you aren't going to answer, you've got to listen when I talk to you.'

Margo reached up, but the orange paper was stapled too high on the tree. Then Crane was beside her, looking up at the hand-drawn sign.

Murrays Annual Thanksgiving Weekend Reunion, Friday Nov. 23, it said and gave the address on Stark River Road, as though every Murray didn't already know it. There were simple line drawings of a pig, a turkey, and a pie, added by Aunt Joanna, no doubt — no one else would have bothered to decorate the invitations.

'Son of a bitch,' Crane said, and clamped his jaw so the muscle in front of his ear twitched. He jumped up a few times and grabbed at the paper, but couldn't reach it.

Margo figured this was the work of her cousin Billy, who was almost as tall as Cal now, with ears that stuck out more than an inch on either side of his head, and who made Margo's life at school hell. After he almost drove over her walking home a month ago — she had to jump into a ditch full of brambles — Margo put a road-killed woodchuck in the back seat of his Camaro in the school parking lot. For that, Billy had snuck up behind her in the hallway with scissors and cut off a good hunk of her long, dark ponytail. She'd lied and told her daddy she'd done it herself. Crane had shaken his head, and when she'd handed over the hank of hair, he coiled it around his hand and slipped it into his jacket pocket, same as he'd done with her mother's note.

Junior Murray used to look out for her at school, but the day after Cal had caught him smoking pot for the third time this summer, he packed him up and sent him away to a military academy out West. Before that, Margo used to sneak out and visit Junior at the abandoned cabin upstream that he called *the marijuana house*. On rare occasions Margo had taken a puff, but she didn't like the dull way pot made her feel. Sometimes on the way up to the cabin, Margo saw her cousin Julie Slocum sitting alone on the riverbank, singing along with a transistor radio. Margo thought of talking to her. But if Julie had minded her own business a year ago, nobody would have known about Margo and Cal, and everything could have stayed the way it was.

After Crane stomped away, Margo ran her fingers over the scars on the smooth bark of the beech. Before Luanne had left, she'd measured

Margo for age fourteen, and it turned out she hadn't grown any taller in that year, so Luanne didn't make a mark. 'I guess that's it,' she'd said. 'You're all grown up.'

Crane returned with his chain saw and yanked the starter until the motor roared. Margo stepped back just before her father jabbed the tip of the saw into the beech, thigh-high. Sawdust flew, and with one clean, angry slice, the tree was free from its roots. It had been taller than Margo realized, and the top got hung up on a big swamp oak before falling through and taking down one of the oak's limbs with it. When the beech finally landed between Crane's truck and the house, it smashed a spice bush that had always smelled sweet in spring. Crane put his foot on the downed trunk and cut a few stove-length pieces. When he reached the invitation, he shredded it with the chain. Margo was surprised how much shredding it took before the word *Murrays* was destroyed.

'Nerve of that bastard,' Crane said.

Margo swallowed.

'You got something to say, Margo, say it. I can't handle that earnest, wide-eyed look so early in the morning.' Crane sliced a half dozen more lengths of firewood, and then he killed the motor and threw the chain saw into the bed of his truck. 'You ready to talk about this yet?'

She stopped herself from shaking her head.

'Well, he's not going to insult us this way,' Crane said before climbing into the cab and slamming the door. When he pulled away, carbon spewed from the tailpipe, and the Ford's back wheels dug into the ice crust of their two-track driveway. After he was out of sight, Margo heard him kick up gravel on the road, and later she heard the truck's noisy exhaust as it crossed the road bridge downstream.

No, she wasn't ready to talk about it. And she wasn't ready to send her Uncle Cal to *rot in prison*, as her father put it. She wished Crane could be patient with her. If he hadn't gone crazy with the chain saw this morning, she might have stood in the stirrup of his two hands clasped, and he could have lifted her up to reach the paper. She would have tugged it down and burned it along with the kitchen trash. Now there were tiny bits of orange paper all over the place, and each bit would remind Crane of the invitation every day until the first big snow. And a few days after that, the construction paper would bleed orange into the snow, and pieces of it would still be there in spring when the snow melted.

Margo returned to the swing set, put her arm around her strung-up buck, and looked across the river. Maybe the invitation was not an insult aimed at Crane. More likely it was a suggestion that they forget about last year's trouble for one day and join together for food, drink, and fun. Margo would be glad to see Joanna, who'd taught her to cook as her mother never had — Luanne could burn water, Crane used to say. Joanna would already be making her pies for Friday: mincemeat, apple, pumpkin, and black walnut. The boys were good at cracking the nuts open with hammers, but right away they got

22

tired of digging nut meats out of the walnut-shell mazes, so that work had always come down to Joanna and Margo. Her cousins had been as good as brothers, apart from Billy, who would always be mad that Grandpa gave his teak rowboat, *The River Rose*, to Margo instead of to him. If Cal would apologize for what he had done and said, and if he would rehire her father as a foreman at Murray Metal, everything would be fine again. Her daddy could trade the aqua-blue grocery-store smock for his old shop uniform with CRANE stitched in red cursive on a white patch above the breast pocket, and they could afford to pay the dentist's bill.

Margo retrieved the sharpened knife from the stump and returned to her buck, the biggest of the three she'd killed so far. She'd already tied up the bung, and she wanted to hurry and get the first long cut behind her, because she knew this third time would be no easier than the first or second had been. She'd be fine after that initial cut, after she turned the deer from a dead creature into meat. It had come as a surprise that the killing was the easy part. Crane would help her with the gutting and skinning if she asked, but Grandpa Murray had stressed how important it was to do a thing herself. She reached up and stuck the knife about half an inch into the flesh below where the ribs came together. Pulling down hard and steady on the back of the blade, she unzipped the buck from sternum to balls, tore through skin, flesh, and corn fat, and then, as the guts sloshed into the galvanized trough, she closed her eyes.

A rifle shot yipped from the Murray farm across the river, and Margo dropped her knife into the tub of curled and steaming entrails. A second shot followed. The Murrays' four beagles began to bark and throw themselves against the wood and chicken wire of their kennel. The black Lab made a moaning sound that echoed over the water. Margo used to lie around reading with her back against that dog, used to row him in her boat and swim with him. This past summer, Crane had forbidden all swimming, as well as crossing the river for any reason.

A third shot sounded from the other side of the river.

Margo had feared this day would come, that Crane would kill her uncle. Then Crane would go to prison and she'd be on her own. Margo hadn't heard from her ma since she went away a year and a half ago. Her note, on blue paper with herons on it, left on the kitchen table, had said, *Dear Margaret Louise, I hope you know I'm not abandoning you. I want to bring you with me, but first I need to find myself and I can't do it in this place. Take care of your daddy and I'll contact you soon. Love, Mom.* Margo had feared that if she didn't handle the paper carefully, the dark blue ink would evaporate, the herons would flap off the page, and the paper itself would dissolve to leave only a puff of cocoa butter and a few drops of wine.

A fourth gunshot echoed over the water.

Margo looked into the hole she had dug in the half-frozen ground for burying deer guts. She knew she had to act fast to cover up her father's

24

crime by disposing of the evidence. She grabbed the shovel and bone saw, tossed them into the boat, and rowed to the other side. She tied off and climbed the riverbank. She got a sick feeling as she passed the whitewashed shed, but she kept going until she saw Cal's new white Chevy Suburban. It was all sunk down on flattened tires. Cal stood alongside, a tall, broad-shouldered figure, yelling at the banged-up back end of her daddy's departing Ford.

'Crane, you son of a bitch! Those were brand-new snow tires!'

Margo collapsed in relief against the shed.

Aunt Joanna stood beside Cal, wearing a dress with an apron and no jacket, holding an apple in one raw-looking hand and a peeler in the other. Margo would almost be willing to forgive Cal everything if it meant she could then sit with Joanna peeling apples in the big Murray kitchen with the woodstove going, listening to Joanna sing or talk about her 4-H cooking students, of which Margo used to be one.

Wednesday, the day before Thanksgiving, Margo was sitting on her side of the river watching the Murray place, when a buck came high-stepping down the trail beside the whitewashed shed, toward the river's edge. It drank and then looked downstream, presenting Margo with its perfect profile. Margo lifted her shotgun, got her sight bead on a spot just behind the foreleg, and then she aimed slightly high to adjust for gravity over the distance. She calmly fired the slug into the beast's heart and lungs and absorbed the recoil. She had not been sure she could hit at thirty yards, but the buck collapsed to its knees and fell forward onto the sand as though bowing. Margo waited a few minutes to see if any Murrays were roused by the noise, but no one came out to investigate. Margo carried the big knife across in the rowboat with her, dreading the prospect of finishing the buck off by slicing through the jugular — something Mr. Peake warned her she might have to do — but it was dead when she got there. Taking the buck meant Uncle Cal couldn't have it, and neither could Billy.

She wrapped her arms around the buck's chest and neck and tried to lift it, but it was too heavy. She was able to pick up the butt end of the deer and get it partway into her boat, but still she was unable to move the chest. She got the idea, finally, to crawl headfirst beneath the creature's torso. She wiggled beneath the body in the cold mud until she was squeezed on her belly all the way under the deer. She smelled its musk and urine; she smelled blood and earth and moss and sweat, felt its warm weight on her neck and back. When the deer was on her and the mud was in her nose, inside her jacket, down her pants, and in her socks, she thought she would smother. She remembered Mr. Peake saying to calm herself before shooting, by slowing her breathing and heartbeat. She gathered all her strength, lifted her head up under the deer's chin, and slowly raised her body. She got to her knees, so she was wearing the buck like a bloody cloak. And then she stood so that the buck slid off her back. It fell crashing across the prow of *The River Rose*. Two legs dangled in the water. On the way home, the weight made it hard to row against the current.

When Crane got home from work, Margo was dragging the warm, soft body of her ten-point buck by the antlers up onto the riverbank.

'What the hell?'

She stopped pulling and looked at him.

'You have got to stop this slaughter, child.' He shook his head. 'They'll fine us if you get caught, and I don't have the money to pay. Lord, I wish I could have a drink about now, just one goddamned drink.'

Margo resumed pulling, but one of the deer's hind legs was tangled in poison ivy roots. She tugged and tugged again, not wanting to let go of the buck, fearing it would tumble down the bank and she'd have to start all over.

'Listen,' Crane said. 'The Murrays could make one phone call, and if those state of Michigan sons of bitches show up and find the meat we already got in the freezer, we're in trouble.'

He didn't need to worry, Margo knew. Cal had not even reported Crane for shooting out his tires the other day. She couldn't expect her father to understand why she had to kill these bucks — she didn't understand it herself — but when she got one in her sights, she had to take it down as naturally as she needed to take her next breath.

When Margo tugged again, Crane jumped down the riverbank and pulled the hoof and leg

27

free from the roots. He shook his head as he pushed from below, helping her get the buck up onto the riverbank, and then into the air with the pulley.

'You are one hell of a hunter. I don't know where you got your aim, but you sure hit what you're shooting at.' He patted her back, wiped away some dirt, and rested his arm there. 'Did you wrestle this buck in the mud?'

Margo smiled at him. She thought it was the first time he'd put his arm around her since she won first prize at the 4-H Rimfire Target Competition last month. She'd been standing right there when Mr. Peake had told her father that her shooting was *uncanny*, and also it was possibly a miracle, considering she was shooting with Crane's old single-shot Remington 510 with iron sights.

'Don't you ever forget, Margo, you're the only reason I'm alive and sober in this world.' He sniffed at the air and then sniffed her jacket. 'You look like an angel, but you smell like a rutting buck.'

When he went inside to get his knife, Margo sniffed her sleeve. She saw, across the river, Billy coming out of the barn, dragging the heavy pig roaster by its legs over the frozen ground a few feet at a time. The roaster was made out of a 275-gallon fuel-oil tank cut in half. Margo had been lucky to get the buck home without anybody seeing.

Aunt Joanna, meanwhile, came out of the house wearing insulated rubber boots and a long plaid coat and dragging one end of an orange

28

extension cord. She walked out onto the oil-barrel float carrying a strand of colored Christmas lights that were already twinkling in her hands. Last year Margo had helped her screw in cup hooks around the edge of the float, so it would look festive after dark with the lights reflecting off the water. After the Thanksgiving party, the Murrays would pull their float up onto land and chain it to a tree to protect it from ice and floods.

'I know you miss your aunt Joanna,' Crane said when he returned. 'I know it's hard to be without a ma. But don't you even think of going to that party.'

'I got a ma,' she whispered. 'Somewhere.'

Across the way, Joanna dropped her string of lights into the river, and Margo saw the end waggle and sparkle a few yards downstream. Despite the risk of electrical shock, Joanna was probably laughing as she fished the lights from the cold current. Margo could hear Joanna's voice in her head now, saying, *Quit brooding and sing with me, Sprite! Nobody likes a sullen girl.*

Joanna had been the one to pull the book *Little Sure Shot* off the hall shelf for Margo as soon as she'd taken an interest in shooting. The Murray boys had all refused to read about a girl. The cover drawing of Annie Oakley'd had a beard and mustache drawn on with a black crayon, but Margo had been able to scrub most of it off, leaving only a gray shadow over Annie's face. Margo was curious about the strange clothes that covered Annie head to toe, including high collars and leggings under her skirts. Margo loved to study the melancholy expression on Annie's face.

Margo knew Crane wanted her to make friends outside the family. And Margo was curious about other kids at school, but they took her quietness for snobbery, her slowness to respond in conversation as stupidity. Crane wanted her to speak more, but the calm and quiet of the last year had created in her a desire for more calm and quiet, and Margo wasn't sure there was going to be any end to it. Silence allowed her to ruminate not just about Cal and what had happened last year, but also about her grandfather, to know again the papery feeling of his skin and the sadness and fear he'd expressed on the sunporch when he was dying. Silence brought back the sound of her mother sighing when she felt too dreary to get out of bed on winter days. Margo wasn't sure she could move forward in time, when the past kept calling for her attention the way it did.

'You don't seem to understand what's been done to you by those people,' Crane said when he saw how intently Margo was watching Joanna. He grabbed her shoulders. 'If you would have spoken against Cal, we could have sent him to jail. Damn it, he *raped* you! That Slocum girl told me.' He let go of her and stomped off toward the house, shaking his head.

Rape sounded like a quick and violent act, like making a person empty her wallet at the point of a knife, like shooting someone or stealing a TV. What Cal had done was gentler, more personal, like passing a virus. She had not objected to

30

Cal's actions in the shed, had even been curious about what was happening. For the last year, however, it had been gnawing at her, and Margo had been forming her objection.

3

On Thanksgiving, Margo and her daddy had a meal of turkey breast, grocery-store stuffing, potatoes, and cranberry sauce shaped by the can. They played Michigan rummy until Crane fell asleep in his chair. On the following morning, Friday, Margo served him scrambled eggs and toast. The phone rang, and when Crane hung up, he said, 'Brian Ledoux's going to come get the venison. He'll give you some money for it.'

Margo nodded.

'You keep the money. You earned it. You probably need it for ammunition. But I can't have you killing any more deer, Margo. I'm taking the shotgun. I don't have to take the rifle, too, do I? Nobody else is going to kill a deer with a single-shot .22, but I'm afraid you might.'

She shook her head no.

'Promise. Say it, or I'll take the rifle.'

'I promise,' she whispered.

'I guess you need something to protect yourself if one of them Murrays comes over here,' he said. 'But don't you do anything unless you got no other choice. You think before you shoot. You consider the consequences.'

Margo nodded.

'And you know better than to go to that party. If you even set foot on that Murray property, I'll drive over and drag you home by your ear.'

She nodded again, didn't know how much

longer she could stand her imprisonment here. Next summer she would swim, no matter what he said.

'I'll be home at seven. We'll have dinner together, Margo. We've got the leftover turkey, and I'll try to get us an apple pie if they got one left in the grocery deli. That's the best I can do. You know you're the only reason I'm still alive on this earth. Don't you?' He looked at her until she nodded, and then he slid the twenty-gauge into its case and folded down the truck seat to place it back there. Margo was glad for his affection, but maybe it was too much to be the only reason another person was alive.

After Crane went to work, Margo took his rifle out and shot at the auto-reset target he had welded together for her at his old job. It had four hanging targets along the bottom that flipped up when struck, and when she shot the fifth target on top, it reset all five. She repeated that cycle twenty times without missing, reloading for each shot. She even wore the spongy yellow earplugs that Mr. Peake had insisted on; he'd given her a big plastic bag of them, along with a stack of paper targets. Then she got the little shaving mirror out of the bathroom and held it against the butt of the rifle and shot over her shoulder, copying one of Annie Oakley's tricks. After twenty-some rounds going awry into the side of the hill, she hit the paper bull's-eye affixed to a piece of plywood, and then she hit it ten times in a row. The shooting warmed her enough that she could unzip her Carhartt jacket — one of her daddy's that she had claimed.

33

At noon she sat on the riverbank and ate a fried egg sandwich on store-bought bread. Joanna would have baked at least a dozen loaves fresh for the party, plus a cinnamon loaf for breakfast tomorrow. Margo raised her rifle and aimed across the river at each person who showed up at the Murrays'. After a few hours, when the wind shifted, she smelled the meat roasting. She could hear the music coming out of the outdoor speakers. She aimed at Billy.

'You planning to take out some partygoers?'

The man's voice startled her. He was in the driver's seat of a pontoon boat, maybe sixteen feet long, that was drifting toward her. It said Playbuoy across the siderail. She had been focusing so intently that she hadn't heard the boat approach. She lowered her rifle and moved down to the water's edge and out onto the dock. When the boat drifted near enough, she reached out and grabbed the side. Two of the three men on board had beards and curly black hair; they were so similar that one might have been a copy of the other. The third man, thinner and blond, was sleeping across a bench seat on the port side. The black-haired man behind the wheel was Brian Ledoux, Grandpa's friend, though he was Crane's age. The man standing beside him had the same giant's body, but his skin was pale, and that made his dark hair seem more striking. There was something strange about his eyes.

'You got a buck for me?' Brian said.

She pointed to the deer, gutted and skinned, laid out on a blue tarp under the swing set.

'I talked to your papa last night. I hear you've

34

become quite the hunter, Maggie. A crack shot with that rifle, too.' He winked.

She didn't know why Brian called her Maggie, but she liked the way he grinned.

The two big men hoisted the carcass onto the boat and put their own tarp over it. She had been to Brian's cabin with her grandpa, usually when nobody else was there. The cabin was more than thirty miles upstream on a wild section of the river, with no road access or electricity. His cabin seemed to lean on its stilts as though wanting to be even closer to the water than it was. The trees there, Margo remembered, were tall and mossy, snaked with poison ivy vines. The time she remembered best was when somebody had caught a possum in a live trap. Grandpa had been ready to shoot it when Margo pointed out the babies stuck in the wiry fur, a dozen tiny pink clinging creatures with bulging eyes and translucent limbs and noses. He had seen how fascinated she was and let the clumsy mama amble off.

'I admired the old man, your grandpa, may he rest in peace,' Brian said, 'but I've got to tell you, girl, I'm not so fond of some of them other Murrays of Murrayville.'

'Brian knocked out a couple of Cal's teeth,' the other bearded man said, squinting one eye. His voice was thinner than Brian's and nervous sounding.

'Hey, the sonbitch fired me,' Brian said. 'Didn't have the nerve to do it himself, sent his secretary. So I went into his office and told him what I thought. Said he didn't like my attitude,

35

so I figured I'd better show him some attitude, just so's he'd know next time he saw it.'

Mumbled words came out of the man passed out on the bench seat of the boat. He shifted on the seat cushions, and Margo saw he had a mustache.

'Will somebody wake that asshole up? Or throw him overboard,' Brian said. Both men laughed.

'Darling, no,' the drunk man moaned.

'They seem to have put the teeth back into Cal's mouth,' Brian said. 'It makes me want to knock a few more out just to see how that works, putting them back in.'

Margo wondered if Brian knew Crane, too, had knocked out Cal's teeth. She wondered if they had knocked out the same ones.

'Meet my brother, Paul. Pauly, meet my dream girl. Prettiest thing on the river. If you'd put on your glasses, you'd probably faint dead away like Johnny here.' And then to Margo, 'I'm keeping my brother off the drugs. No need for speed out here on the river, unless it's in your boat motor.'

'Don't tell her that,' Paul said. 'For Christ's sake.'

'Don't worry, she won't say anything,' Brian said, and winked. 'I've about got him cured of all that junk, Maggie.'

'Will you shut the fuck up, Brian?' Paul turned so he was looking at Margo out of his left eye, and she wondered if he might be blind in the other.

Margo accepted two twenties from Brian — more than she had hoped for — and shoved

36

them into her jeans pocket. Her jeans were getting tight, but she didn't want to waste her ammunition money on new ones.

The man lying in the boat moaned again.

'Five bucks says Johnny falls onto that deer,' Paul said.

'He can rub up against it if he feels romantic,' Brian said. His big hand was resting on the boat's steering wheel again, and Margo saw the back of it was covered with scars, white lines, as though somebody had cut him and cut him, but was not able to hurt him. She would have liked to touch him, see what those scars felt like.

'You come upstream and see us sometime, Maggie,' Brian said. 'You know where the cabin is.'

The blond man rolled over, fell off the bench seat and onto the tarped deer, but didn't wake up. Brian and Paul roared with laughter. When the man's open hand moved across the buck's haunch, Margo had to smile, too.

'Let's get going,' Paul said finally, looking back and forth from Margo to Brian. 'If you and jailbait here can bear to separate.'

'I just can't get enough of a girl who don't talk,' Brian said to Paul and started the boat's motor with a roar. 'Goodbye, Maggie.'

The men headed upstream. Margo watched their boat get smaller until it disappeared around the curve. Directly across the river, Junior Murray arrived at the wooden steps leading to the kitchen door of the big house, maybe just home from the military academy. Joanna, who was outside, put down the pan she was carrying and took him in her arms, held him for a long time before ushering him up the stairs and inside.

When Margo could no longer sit still, at about five o'clock, she got into her boat. She laid the rifle across the back seat and floated a bit downstream, so no one across the way would see her coming. She then moved upstream and tied *The River Rose* at the willow near the whitewashed shed where all the trouble had started. She kicked at the frozen grass to warm herself. She aimed her rifle at patches of frosted ground a few times, pretending she saw rabbits. When she saw a squirrel pause on the ground near the shed, she closed her eyes, lifted the rifle to her shoulder and her cheek, aimed it blindly where she had been looking, and then opened her eyes. Her sighting was almost perfect. The squirrel scampered off. She listened to the clinks and shouts from the horseshoe pit, listened to Hank Williams Sr. wailing. The next song was Johnny Cash's 'Folsom Prison Blues.' She wondered what would happen if she walked up and took a can of pop off the table, served herself a slice of apple pie, and acted like everything was okay. Like she was part of the family again.

Back home, across the river, there was movement. Crane's blue Ford pulled into the driveway, hours before he was supposed to return home. He got out of his truck, went into the house, came right back out, and looked across the river. She realized Crane would notice her boat tied on the wrong side of the river, so she hurried down to the water to wave and let him know she was not at the party, but by the time she got to where he would have seen her, he was already back in his truck. Crane's tires spat mud from beneath the crust of frozen ground. Margo was grateful Cal was nowhere to be seen. But then, as if conjured by her thoughts, Cal appeared on the riverside path, walking in her direction, looking drunk. Maybe Crane had seen him, maybe that was why he was driving here instead of just yelling across the river. Margo silently backed away and then hoisted herself into the apple tree above her and up onto the wooden platform Grandpa and Junior had built a few years ago. She knelt and watched and listened as Cal approached. When he stopped beside the shed, he was only twenty feet away, close enough that she could see him blink, close enough to see that one of the buttons was missing from the plaid shirt he wore under his unzipped Carhartt vest. She wondered if there might be a girl in the shed, but through the dirty window glass she saw only a skinned deer carcass hanging from the ceiling. It was hard to tell, but it looked smaller than any of those she had killed this year.

Cal stood facing the river. He put his plastic cup of beer on the window ledge next to the door, so he was in profile between her and the white shed wall. Margo heard Crane's noisy exhaust on the road bridge downstream, but Cal lit a cigarette and did not pay any attention to the sound. She watched Cal inhale, saw his chest rise and then fall as he exhaled a blue cloud. The air was colder than it had been last Thanksgiving. The platform was just high enough off the ground that Margo could see the roof of her daddy's Ford when it pulled up to the rail fence a few hundred yards away. Cal fumbled with his fly. He didn't seem to hear the truck door creak open or slam shut. He drew on his cigarette and stared down at his pecker in his hand, waiting for something to come out. Margo shifted to sit cross-legged, nestled the butt of the rifle into her shoulder, and looked at her uncle Cal over the sights.

She slowed her breathing and heartbeat in order to focus more clearly. Her daddy had threatened to kill her uncle, and that was likely what he was coming to do. Margo thought Crane could not survive being locked up for the crime he was about to commit. She also knew Crane wouldn't shoot a man who was hurt or lying on the ground. She wondered if she should take Cal down herself before Crane got there, injure Cal rather than kill him. Margo took aim at one of Cal's insulated work boots. At this distance, her bullet would cut through the leather and insulation to strike his ankle bone.

Margo lined up the side of Cal's right knee, saw how she could shatter the kneecap.

She aimed at his thigh. For a split second Cal would not know what hit him. A stray horseshoe? A hornet's stinger? If the bullet grazed the front of his thigh, it could continue on through the wooden siding of the old shed, bury itself in the dirt floor.

Years ago, Billy and Junior had held Margo

40

down and put a night crawler in her mouth, and she, in turn, put dozens of night crawlers in the boys' beds. Junior had stopped picking on her after that. The time she had revenged Billy with the dead skunk he'd put in her boat, she had to endure Joanna's tomato juice bath — a consequence she had not considered, as her daddy pointed out — and she stank for a week anyway. But it had been worth it to rub that skunk in Billy's face and hair. Her cousins had teased her, enjoyed her shrieks when they could elicit them, but they were also scared of her because she always evened the score. Except that she had not done so with Cal.

As Crane reached the place where the path widened, Margo realized he had left his shotgun in his truck. Seeing him unarmed now was as shocking as first seeing him without his beard a year ago at the hospital — they'd shaved his face for the stitches on his cheek and along his jaw, and he'd never grown it back. The grocery store didn't allow employees to have beards. Under his Carhartt jacket he still wore his aqua smock. He hadn't left work for the day — he had only come home to check on her. And he had not come to get revenge — he was here to bring her home *by her ear* as he'd said he would. Her daddy, angry as he might be, was never going to shoot Cal, never in a million years. And it was better this way, better that she would do this thing herself.

Her father would beg her, *Think before you act*, but she had thought long enough, and now she had only a short time to do something.

Margo fed a cartridge into the breech silently

and the bolt made a gentle *tap* when she engaged it. Cal was still concentrating on peeing. He looked out over the river. She studied the side of his head and knew an apology was not what she was looking for. She lowered her sights to a patch of Cal's chest and then looked away again, at her father approaching, empty handed. It was amazing Crane had been able to hurt such a big man last year. If they fought again, Margo feared her father would get more than a broken jaw.

Margo had made a shot like this from ten paces a thousand times with these Winchester long-rifle cartridges. She had shot from this very tree stand in years past, had shot and missed running squirrels, but Cal was a nonmoving target. Margo aimed the muzzle of her rifle down at Cal's hand, still loosely clutching his pecker, from which a poky stream dribbled. She aimed just past the thumb of that hand. Cal had taught her to shoot tin cans, crab apples, and thread spools off fence posts, and she was steady enough to take off the tip of his pecker without hitting any other part of him. And then Cal let go with his hand, lifted his beer off the windowsill, and took a drink, leaving her a clear shot.

The shout of her rifle was followed by a silent splash of Murray blood on the shed's white wall. She kept her arm steady through the shot, did not blink, and heard one last horseshoe clink from the pit. Cal's mouth was open in a scream, but it must have been a pitch discernible only by hunting dogs. Margo grasped the branch above with her free hand to steady herself. She gripped the rifle firmly in the other. She closed her eyes to lengthen that perfect and terrible moment and hold off the next, when the air would fill with voices.

4

For several seconds the job seemed done. She and Cal were even, and they could all resume their lives as before the trouble. She saw her father arriving, but didn't notice Billy running toward them, gripping a shotgun in one hand. Crane reached up into the tree and grabbed Margo's hand. He pulled, and she fell onto him. He took the rifle into his own hands awkwardly as he tried to get her on her feet, despite her jacket being twisted around her. Billy saw Crane holding the rifle. He saw his father down and blood splashed on Cal's pants and the shed wall. Blood was smeared on Cal's face. Billy aimed his shotgun at Crane's chest.

'Put that down, Billy!' Crane yelled and moved toward him. 'You hyperactive punk!'

'You shot my dad, you bastard.'

Cal was trying to zip his pants.

'Put the gun down now,' Crane said.

'Billy, no,' Margo said, but her voice didn't carry. Maybe Crane didn't realize how he was pointing the Remington as he approached Billy. And Billy was focused only on Crane, so he did not see how Cal was getting to his feet and urgently gesturing to him.

'Put the damn gun down,' Crane said, 'before somebody gets hurt.'

Margo found her voice as Billy fired. It came out as a dog's howl. Crane staggered backward.

Billy grinned at her as if to say she was not the only one with dead aim, but the smile fell away instantly.

Crane landed hard on his back, and Margo crouched beside him. She smelled metal, as though the blood rolling out of his chest were liquid iron, as though he had worked for too many years at Murray Metal Fabricating to be regular flesh and blood anymore. Grandpa Murray had died slowly, gradually disappearing and giving Margo time to imagine life without him, but Crane, whose eyes had flown open at the blast, was dead in an instant. Cal fell to his knees. He spoke to Billy in a strained voice. 'You dumb little fuck! What did you do?'

Billy looked stunned. 'He shot your dick, Dad. He was going to shoot me.'

Margo saw pain in Cal's face, and fear, and then she saw calculation.

'Call an ambulance,' Cal said thinly. He lurched forward and grabbed the shotgun out of Billy's hands. 'Somebody run get Jo. Tell her a man's been shot. Jesus fucking Christ. Run!'

At Cal's command, two Murray kids and two Slocums who'd been lurking nearby took off running.

Crane's chest was torn open. The fabric of his aqua-colored work smock was soaked with blood. Joanna arrived at her husband's side and put an arm around him.

'You're covered with blood,' she said, breathless. She touched the crotch of his pants.

'I'm fine,' Cal whispered, 'but Billy just shot Crane. The dumb little fuck just shot a man in

45

the heart with a deer slug. Call an ambulance.'

'I did,' Joanna said. She gasped when she saw Crane.

One of Cal's cousins, a former military medic, got between Margo and her father and placed both hands on Crane's chest. He pushed rhythmically, causing more blood to pump out, but gave up on CPR in less than a minute. He moved away, and Margo moved to take his place.

'He shot Dad,' Billy said and began to whimper. 'Look at the blood on Dad. He had that rifle. I thought he was going to kill me. And kill Dad.'

Margo let her face fall to her daddy's chest, but she felt Cal's gaze on her. When she turned and met his eyes, she saw there a look she knew from her own father, a look that said, *Be careful, think about the consequences.* Cal's face was wet from tears, though he wasn't crying exactly.

'Cal?' Joanna said. 'Is that right?'

'That's right,' Cal said weakly. 'Crane shot me. I thought he might shoot again. Billy was protecting me.'

Joanna moved as though in slow motion. She took off her long plaid coat, lifted Margo up — she felt incapable of resisting — and draped the coat over Crane's head and chest. Margo pressed her face onto the plaid wool. Joanna moved to Billy, took him in her arms. He folded himself into his mother's embrace and sobbed. Junior appeared. He took the shotgun from Cal and leaned it against the shed. Margo had not seen Junior in five months. He knelt at her side and put an arm around her for a few moments, before Joanna asked him to go get the car.

The two county cops assigned to Murrayville arrived a few minutes later, as dusk gave way to darkness. They confiscated Crane's rifle and Billy's shotgun and wrapped them in plastic. They said an ambulance was on its way. The bigger cop said, 'Somebody bring a washrag to clean that poor girl's face,' and Margo let Aunt Carol Slocum wipe her with a warm, wet cloth. Margo listened to Cal lie to the officers in a pinched voice. He said between shaky breaths that Crane had been upon him with the rifle, that Crane had shot out his tires a few days ago. Cal had been afraid something like this would happen. Cal guided Margo through the lie that condemned Crane but saved Billy and her. He said the girl was welcome to stay with them until they could find her ma.

After that, the officers spoke softly to Margo. She nodded in agreement about her father shooting Cal and pointing the gun at Billy. She repeated in a whisper what Cal had said. She hated involving the cops, and even if she had been inclined to tell what had really happened, she didn't have the strength to disagree with Cal. And what would have been the point? Her father was dead, and nobody alive had any use for the truth. She did not want Billy imprisoned for murder. She wanted to deal with Billy herself, as she always had. An officer led him away. Junior and Joanna followed the police car out of the driveway in the family's white Suburban.

When the ambulance first arrived, the paramedics checked Crane for vital signs and shook their heads, and one of them made a phone call. They countered Cal's objections, convinced him to get into the ambulance, leaving Margo and a dozen others waiting in the cold for the medical examiner. Aunt Carol Slocum urged Margo to go inside the house and get warm, but she would not leave her father. The longer she clung to his body, the more the others seemed wary of her, as they had been wary when she sat with her grandpa during the weeks when he was dying. The rest of the family had avoided Grandpa at the end, and Margo had pitied them for not seeing the last part of his life, when pain made the big, opinionated man quiet and thoughtful.

They were all Murrays gathered around her now. For the first time in a year, she was, horribly, part of the family. When Julie Slocum came close to her, Margo reached out and grabbed her arm.

'Let go of me.' Julie pulled against Margo's grip.

Margo looked her in the eye.

'Ma, she's hurting my arm,' Julie yelled, and everyone looked over.

Margo whispered, 'Why'd you have to go and get my dad?'

'You're covered with blood,' Julie said. 'You're getting it on me.'

'Last year. That's why all this happened,' Margo said. She held Julie's arm like an oar handle. The girl was thicker now, with heavy breasts. She had a toughness in her face.

'Cal doesn't want you anymore,' Julie said and

pounded on Margo's wrist with her free hand.

When Margo let go of her, Julie scrambled to her feet and moved away.

The police seemed satisfied with Margo's minimal testimony. They also seemed to think Margo was with family, so she would be okay for the night. Why would a Murray kid need a social worker or a place to sleep in Murrayville? Carol Slocum grabbed Margo and wiped her face again with a warm rag. It was two hours before the medical examiner arrived in a white van. By then Margo's fingers felt brittle with cold. The examiner's assistant lifted her gently away from her father. They wrapped him in a plastic sheet and loaded him into the van. She watched the van depart. The river flowed in the direction of the funeral parlor, which was five miles downstream, beside the cemetery and across the river from the big Murray Metal shop building, which covered five acres of Murrayville under its metal roof.

Some of the women milled beside her. The men who remained were drunk or dumb with excitement. A few exhausted children stared with glittering eyes. Their ears were red, and their cheeks were flushed. Margo thought somebody should get them to bed.

'You'll stay here tonight?' a woman said.

Margo shook her head and spoke as clearly as she could. 'First I have to go home.'

'Do you know where Luanne is?' a woman asked eagerly from a few yards away. Margo was at first startled, thinking somebody knew and might tell her, but nobody knew. When her mother had first disappeared, Cal often asked Margo where she was. He said he'd like to set her straight about abandoning her child, he'd like to drag her back home.

When a woman Margo didn't know snaked an arm around her, she slipped away and headed down to the water and into *The River Rose*. She wished she could have carried her daddy's body with her across the river, as she had carried that buck's carcass. In what there was of the moonlight, she paused to study the Red Wing work boots Crane had bought her a few months ago when he figured her feet had stopped growing. Some drops of his blood pooled on the oiled leather. She pushed off with an oar.

Once she reached her own dock, she climbed out and tied up her boat. The water was inky black. At Grandpa's graveside ceremony last January, everyone had been lost in grief: Luanne wept nearby with Cal and his older sister, and Joanna tried to comfort her sons. Margo had felt the desire to step into the icy river and flow downstream. The only thing keeping her from doing it had been the solid body of her father beside her.

Margo took off her jacket and boots and put them at the base of the dock. She rolled off her socks and stuck them in her boots. Her feet were already numb from the cold. She eased into the water. She let her bare feet slide into the cold muck, stepped out farther from shore, sank deeper into the river's bottom, screamed without making a sound when the water rose to her thighs. She walked out until her water lily

— her mother's phrase — was electrified by the cold. People across the way were milling under the yard lights, and she kept quiet so no one would notice her and think she needed rescuing. Margo's hips pressed against the current, and her belly clenched when the cold reached it, and finally her heart rattled inside her chest. She shivered inside the electricity formed by her own body, felt carp and stinging catfish whipping by her. She imagined water snakes and black snakes coiling around her legs. Instead of feeling trapped by the river, which might freeze her or drown her, she felt terribly, painfully free. Without her father, she was bound to no one, and with the water flowing around her, she was absolutely alive.

She imagined the scent of cocoa butter in the cold air, that smell that had never quite left her mother's skin, not even in winter, when she smoothed on cocoa butter lotion after showers. Margo held on to the floating dock and was able to pull her right foot free of the muck. She pulled the other bare foot free with as much difficulty, almost forgetting about her father in her own struggle. She dragged herself to shore.

She carried her boots into the kitchen and found the room bitterly cold. Crane had disconnected the furnace to save money, figuring they'd be fine heating the place with wood. Margo had meant to split kindling today, but hadn't gotten to it, and now she didn't know if her frozen fingers worked well enough to grip a hatchet or even to ball up newspaper. She looked around the kitchen. There were three pine chairs.

And in the corner there was the wooden baby chair, made of maple. Margo retrieved the axe from the screen porch and struck the baby chair with the side of the blade, and then struck again. After the chair's old joints rattled loose, she continued busting the wood into kindling on the kitchen floor. With those dry pieces and sheets of newspaper, she was able to start a fire.

She warmed her hands in the flames, and then took the axe to the other chairs. As the fire crackled, she stripped off her wet clothes and wrapped herself in a blanket. The wood from the chairs created such heat that the creosote must have burned clean out of the chimney. Eventually she put on two split logs from the screen porch and climbed into her daddy's bed. As she went to sleep, she smelled cigarette smoke and sulfur from matches, spice shaving cream, and the mildew of their river house. She smelled the river in every corner of the house, in every molecule of the air, in every pore of her own body. Even the fire smelled of the river, even the flames.

5

The following day, Junior Murray came into the house without knocking, something that was normal within the Murray family, though it had driven Margo's daddy crazy.

'It's after noon. Everybody's worried about you,' he said, sitting on the edge of the bed where she was lying. 'I came over to tell you that the cops are on the way.'

'What?'

'Ricky's working in the township office, so he heard they were coming over. That's Ricky in the kitchen.'

'Why are they coming here?' Margo heard a vehicle pull into the driveway.

Junior said, 'That sounds like a cop car to me. They probably want to ask you a few more questions. They have to make sure you're okay. It's the law that cops have to hassle people who don't want them around.'

'Cops are here,' Ricky yelled from the other room. Ricky was their youngest uncle, Cal's littlest brother, twenty years old. He was studying to be a paralegal.

Margo wrapped the covers around herself, sat up, and leaned against her cousin. She was afraid that Junior would go away if she didn't say something. 'I've missed you,' she whispered.

'I've missed you, too, Margo,' Junior said and put an arm around her. 'I've missed everything and everybody. It makes me suicidal to even think about going back to that academy.' Someone knocked on the door, and when voices sounded in the next room, Junior stood up. 'You'd better cover up those tiny titties before you come out.'

Margo adjusted her blanket. When he left the room, she put on a pair of Crane's jeans, one of his turtlenecks, and a flannel shirt. She went into the kitchen, where two officers were talking to Junior, who was taller than either of them. The smaller cop, whom everyone at school knew as Officer Mike, said, 'We wanted to make sure you were okay, Margaret.'

'See, *everybody* was worried about you, Margaret,' Junior said. Margo had the feeling he was making fun of the cop, but she didn't understand exactly how.

'We need to look around, see if there's anything here to help us figure out why Mr. Crane would have been shooting at Cal and Billy Murray. Did he keep anything like a diary?'

Margo shook her head. The most they would find from Crane would be a grocery list jotted on an empty matchbook. His anger at Cal would not be written on anything they could find.

'Any other firearms here? Any unregistered pistols? Can we look around?'

She shrugged, and they took that as a yes.

'Cal Murray said if your daddy didn't have any money, he'd pay funeral expenses,' said the bigger cop, when the two had given up on finding anything of interest. 'Can we give you a ride to Cal's?'

She shook her head.

'Are you sure?'

'I want to row my boat over there,' she said. When they kept looking at her, she began to fear they wouldn't leave. 'My mom will come to get me. When she hears about my dad.'

'We'll get her over to our house, Officer Mike,' Junior said, adopting a trusty Boy Scout demeanor.

'Let us know as soon as your mother contacts you,' said Officer Mike. 'We may need to talk with her. And we'll contact you again in a few days if we need an additional statement.'

'And if there's anything for your ma in the estate, we'll have to track her down,' Ricky said.

Margo knew there'd be no estate. Crane still owed payments to a guy on his ten-year-old Ford, and he owed the dentist, too. He had sent Margo to get her teeth cleaned every six months — even when he had been drunk and unemployed, he'd sent her with a twenty-dollar bill against the account.

'There won't be a trial, will there?' Junior said.

'Nobody's denying what your brother did was self-defense, but he did kill a man. Someone's evaluating him now.'

'I'm sorry, Margaret,' Officer Mike said. He held up a business card and placed it on the counter. 'Call my number if you need a ride to Cal's. Or if you need anything.'

'We're sorry for your loss,' the bigger cop said.

When they closed the door, Ricky Murray spoke up. 'We ought to find your dad's papers, any official documents. If he's got a will, you'll

55

want to locate that.'

Margo's eyes were swollen from crying, and when she leaned down beside her father's bed, her head ached. From beneath it, she produced an army-green tin box. It felt like a violation putting it on the kitchen table and opening the lid in front of Ricky and Junior. The first thing she saw inside was her cut-off ponytail, wrapped in wax paper. In a bulging envelope, she found dozens of photos of her mother smiling ear-to-ear at the camera. While Luanne had rarely smiled enough to show teeth in real life, she had smiled that fake way for every camera snap. There were no photos of her parents together, not even a wedding photo. The only picture of Crane was a tiny dark image on his Murray Metal Fabricating employee ID card.

A business-sized envelope contained a piece of lined yellow paper on which was handwritten, *Last Will and Testament. Please cremate me and don't waste money on any service. Give everything I have to my wife and daughter. Sorry it's not much. Signed, in full faculties, Bernard Crane, October 14, 1971.* Margo would have been almost eight years old then. Nothing bad had happened yet.

'That's clear and simple,' Junior said. 'Are the cops all the way out the driveway?'

'*The Man* is gone,' Ricky said.

'Then it's time to light up.' Junior dug something out of the pocket of his jean jacket. It was a plastic baggie containing several joints. He sat on the kitchen table. 'What happened to your chairs?'

Margo shrugged and sat next to him.

'They shouldn't have let you come home last night.' Junior straightened out one joint carefully and lit it with a white lighter. He took a long toke and held it out to her.

'I don't know.' Margo let her legs dangle beside Junior's. She noticed how her cousin's hair had been cut short at the military school, so it no longer curled down his neck. She'd heard last night that he'd be going back to the academy again right after the holiday weekend, so this might be her only chance to see him.

While still holding his breath, he elbowed her and said in a squeaky voice, 'This will help you. I stayed high for three months when Grandpa died.'

Margo accepted the joint, took a long draw, and coughed. She passed it to Ricky, who inhaled as he studied the will, turning it over several times, though the back was blank.

'Too bad this will isn't notarized,' Ricky said.

The next time Junior passed her the joint, Margo inhaled deeply and held the smoke. She didn't like to feel disoriented, but she hoped the pot would dull her feelings. They passed the joint in silence until it was gone. Then Ricky began to rifle through the papers in a more serious way. 'Divorce papers,' he said. 'Finalized eight months ago.'

Margo wished she could puff on the joint once more. Crane had never mentioned anything about a divorce.

Junior was reading over the land contract with an absurd intensity. On the third page it was signed by both their fathers.

'Are you going to stay with Cal and Joanna?' Ricky asked.

'Ma said you'll have to stay with us,' Junior said. He was gazing intently at Crane's employee ID card now. 'You can't stay alone when you're fifteen. Where else are you going to stay?'

'I turned sixteen on the twentieth.'

'If you're staying with an aunt and uncle,' said Ricky, 'maybe the cops won't have to get social services involved.'

'Social services?' Margo took the ID card out of Junior's hand. She had heard that kids who got involved with social services ended up living in group homes and with strangers who did weird things to them. And she was sure it would mean living far from the river. 'I wish you were going to be home, Junior,' she said in a voice that felt slow. 'Then it would be easier to stay at your house.'

'Me, too. I'll be back at Christmas. Maybe then I can talk them into letting me stay home after that.'

Ricky and Junior seemed to move in slow motion as they pulled papers from the box — birth certificates, the title to the Ford. Margo noticed something else: a pink envelope with a handwritten address in the upper left corner, an address in Heart of Pines, Michigan. Her mother's name was not written above the address, but Margo recognized her loopy, back-slanted handwriting.

'Daddy kept some of his papers on the counter by the toaster,' she said, and when Junior's and Ricky's eyes went to Crane's pile of

58

bills, Margo slipped the envelope out of the box and into her back pocket. She took out her own birth certificate and Crane's and set them aside.

'Do you know about any other assets?' Ricky asked. 'We need to get information on what he owned.'

'You're not a lawyer, man,' Junior said.

'So? Somebody's going to have to figure this out. And Nympho here can't afford a lawyer.'

'He's got his truck and a chain saw and his tools,' Margo said. She wiped her eyes and nose on her sleeve. She didn't mention his rifle or shotgun.

'Savings account?' Ricky asked. He went into the bathroom and came out with a roll of toilet paper for Margo to use as a tissue. She unrolled a handful of it.

'He paid all his spare money against the land contract. Or to the dentist.'

'According to the land contract, it looks like the house goes back to my dad after two missed payments,' Junior said. 'That's bogus. I hope the dentist doesn't want your teeth back.'

'Life insurance?' Ricky asked.

She shook her head.

Junior picked up one of the many photos of Luanne and nodded his head. 'Do you know where your ma is? Dad always says we should drag her ass back to Murrayville. Maybe she'll come back on her own now.'

'Look at this,' Ricky said, holding out a full-body photo of Margo's ma smiling in a two-piece bathing suit. 'She looks like a movie star. I remember her lying in the sun with her top off.'

Margo blotted her tears with her shirt sleeve.

'Show a little class, man,' Junior said and kicked at Ricky.

'I'm sorry, Nympho. You know we all miss her.'

Margo wished she could find a photo of her mother looking the way she remembered her, smiling sadly or frowning, even. Luanne used to lie in bed sometimes through whole winter days. She had let Margo cuddle with her or read a book in the bed. Luanne had seemed to take comfort from Margo's presence.

Ricky Murray pulled from the tin box a new chocolate-colored leather wallet, identical to the one her father carried, and he handed it to her. Margo took from her pocket the wadded-up twenty-dollar bills she'd received from Brian Ledoux, straightened them, and put them into the wallet. She put in the Murray Metal ID card and the folded birth certificates, too.

'Did you know your dad wanted to be cremated?' Junior said.

She shook her head. 'There's no money for it.'

'You heard the cops. My dad will take care of it.'

She nodded. Though her sadness was powerful, the smoking had helped — Junior was right. Maybe she could survive her daddy's death if she stayed outside herself this way.

Junior lit a second joint, and after his first exhalation, he said, 'I won't get to smoke again until Christmas. It's hard as hell to smuggle anything into that prison. I'll promise Mom and Dad anything if they let me come home. Or I'll figure out a way to run off to Alaska and work on a fishing boat like Uncle Loring.'

'Do you think Billy will go to prison?' she asked.

'I don't know what'll happen to my hotheaded little brother. I know he'd end up in solitary if he went to my school.' Junior stood up. 'I've got to go home, Nympho — I mean, Margo — and Ricky's got to get back to work. He'll drop us off at the house. Come on.'

'I want to bring my boat.'

'Grandpa's boat? We can come back for it later.'

'I need to take a shower first. Please, just let me be alone for a little while.'

'All right. Don't wait too long,' he said. 'You'll want to get there in time for Ma to make you go to church with her tonight. She really wants everybody to go.'

'I promise I'll come along soon. Just go.'

He hugged her, gave her a joint in a baggie, and said, 'Just in case.' He put a wintergreen candy in his mouth, popped one into hers, and left with Ricky.

When Margo was alone, she took the envelope out of her back pocket, opened it, and smoothed out the letter, one small pink page that matched the envelope, featuring a cartoon flamingo:

Dear Bernard,
I'm sorry it had to be this way with the divorce. You know I never belonged there with you people. I don't think I can bear to see Margaret Louise right now. It would be too

painful. I'll contact you again, soon, when I'm in a better situation, and she and I can visit. Please don't use this address except for an emergency, and please don't share it with anyone else.

Love, Luanne

More important than what she said was the address on the envelope: 1121 Dog Leg Road, Heart of Pines, Michigan. Heart of Pines was the town thirty-five miles upstream, just beyond Brian Ledoux's place, a town with lots of rental cabins and restaurants and bars, a place where you could buy hunting and fishing supplies. It had been an all-day trip when she'd motored up there and back with Grandpa. Beyond Heart of Pines the river was too shallow to navigate.

She went through the tin box one more time, chose three photos of her mother and closed them in the pages of *Little Sure Shot*. She put the book in her daddy's old army backpack with CRANE stenciled on it. She loaded the pack with her favorite items of clothing, plus a few bandannas, a toothbrush, toothpaste, a bar of soap, a bottle of shampoo, some tools and paper targets, and what her daddy called *female first aid*. When she stepped outside, she could not take her eyes off the sparkling surface of the water; maybe it was the pot she'd smoked, but the river was shimmering in the late afternoon sun as though it were speaking to her with reflected light, inviting her to come out and row. She loaded up *The River Rose*, tossed in an army sleeping bag, two life vests, a vinyl tarp, a

62

gallon jug of water, and her daddy's best fishing pole. She climbed in, fixed her oars, and pushed off.

Margo headed across the river toward the Murray place, rowing at first in slow motion so she ended up downstream and had to struggle back up. As she tied off her boat, she felt her daddy's disapproval of the Murrays sift over her. Without him, she could cross the river and swim if she wanted, and she could pet the Murray dogs without getting yelled at. Crane could no longer get angry, and she would no longer be the reason for his or anyone's living. Maybe if she kept reminding herself of this, she could survive without him. The thought of surviving without him made her cry again.

Margo made her way to the whitewashed shed — someone had rinsed the blood off the wall and placed a blanket-sized piece of mill felt over the ground where her father had been lying. Margo picked up the trail that led to the road. When she saw the Ford truck still parked on the gravel driveway, the scene was so ordinary that she expected to see Crane sitting behind the wheel. After a few deep breaths, she opened the door of the truck and folded down the bench seat, but found no gun there. If the police had taken the shotgun, as well as the rifle, she knew she was out of luck. If Cal or someone from the family had taken it, she would find it in Cal's office off the living room with the rest of his guns. Margo wondered how she would be better off now, with the Murrays or without them.

Margo moved closer to the house and hid

behind some maples. The dog Moe pulled against his chain and whimpered. If Margo moved in with the Murrays, she would have to wait for her mother to come get her, and there was no telling how long that would take. It was hours later when Joanna walked outside and started the Suburban. Margo ducked down. She heard boys' voices arguing, maybe the twins. Junior came out of the house, held the door open for Cal, and walked slowly beside him down the stairs and to the driveway. Cal was taking small steps, as though just learning to walk. Junior opened the front passenger door and held out his arm as if to support his father.

'I don't need any damned help,' Cal said in a strained voice.

He got into the front passenger seat, and Junior got into the back seat. Finally, one of the twins climbed from the back to sit between his parents. None of them looked in Margo's direction. The Christmas lights on the oil-barrel float were still on, their colors muted in the early evening light. Saturday evening Mass would keep them away from home for at least an hour and a half. Usually Joanna went alone or with the littler kids — Cal had about as much interest in religion as Margo's father'd had — but today Joanna might have convinced them that they ought to pray for Billy and have their souls worked on. Maybe Joanna thought there was something to be gained by showing the family in public at this time. Maybe Cal wanted to show he had not been crippled.

Margo climbed the steps, found the door key

under the flowerpot where it had always been, used it in the lock, and replaced it. The kitchen was warm from the woodstove, which someone had damped down to last until they returned. The house smelled of cinnamon bread. Margo smelled turkey soup, too, which meant that Joanna, despite last night's events, had boiled turkey carcasses as she always had done the day after the party. Margo had last been in this big, bright room last Thanksgiving when she was helping Joanna with the dishes, before she'd gone out to join the party. Margo ventured into the living room, where she'd argued with Billy for years without feeling uneasy — it was only in the last year that Billy had become strange and scary to her. The Murray house never did feel empty, even when everybody was gone. Always the place was full of scents, warmth, and energy. This evening she could feel the Murray spirits hiding around corners, hanging from the ceiling and wall fixtures. Even when she'd been welcome in this house, she had preferred to stay in the kitchen. When she'd gone into the living room to watch TV, she sat on the floor beside Cal's chair, and he had sometimes patted her head and said, 'Good girl.' Billy had whispered, 'Good dog,' or 'Good Nympho,' whenever Cal did it, but she hadn't cared.

But she couldn't stay here now, after what had happened. Where would she sleep while she waited for her mother to come?

She found a sheet of paper and a pencil and wrote a note. *Dear Joanna and Cal: Thank you for your generous offer to let me stay with*

65

you. My mother wants me to come to her, but she asked me not to say where she is. Please don't tell anyone. Love, Margaret. She left it on the kitchen table.

Margo walked into Cal's office, a room she had never entered. Kids were not allowed, and it was a rule they all followed. The room smelled of Cal, of leather and gun oil and citrus shaving cream. It also smelled a little of sweat and whiskey.

The gun cabinet was closed but not locked. Maybe in his rattled condition, Cal had forgotten to lock it, or maybe he was so confident no one would mess with his guns that he never locked it. She opened both doors. Inside were a dozen rifles and six twelve-gauge shotguns, but not her daddy's twenty-gauge with his initials burned into the stock.

Margo's heart pounded as she extracted the Marlin, the gun Cal had let her use on special occasions, because it was like Annie Oakley's, he said. Margo ran her hands over the squirrel carved into the walnut stock, the chrome lever. Cal had kept the gun oiled and polished. An electrical charge passed through her as she touched the gold-colored trigger. When she had last shot with it, there had been a tooled leather strap attached, but it had been removed, leaving only the sling swivels. She lifted the rifle to her shoulder and pointed it out the window. She pressed her cheek against the stock and looked over the iron sights at a bit of orange plastic ribbon stapled to a fence post. If she was going to leave this place and all its familiar landmarks,

66

she would have to take this gun. She pocketed a box of .22 cartridges and gripped the Marlin in her left hand. She felt the ghosts of Murrays watching her as she returned to the kitchen. She grabbed the loaf of cinnamon bread off the counter and then headed out the same way she'd come in. The black Lab chained outside barked, and though she knew she should hurry away, she dropped to her knees on the ground beside him, held the bread away from his jaws. 'Oh, Moe, I've missed you terribly. I should have come over to see you, I know.'

She pulled herself away from the dog, and he barked behind her. The beagles barked in their kennel. When she reached her boat, she was shaking so badly that instead of dropping the rifle onto the back seat, she dropped it into the icy river. She pulled it out quickly, but not before it was entirely submerged.

She shook the gun and wiped it as best she could with a towel from her pack. Braced now by the cold and her fear of being seen, Margo laid the rifle on her tarp and swaddled it as she would a baby. She thought the sound of her getting into *The River Rose* echoed all across the river and through the woods. She took a few bites from the loaf of bread, the first thing she'd eaten all day. When she set out onto the water, she felt an urge to let herself go with the current, to slip effortlessly downstream. Her mother was upstream, though, so she began to row.

6

When Margo heard three shotgun blasts in succession, the sound rattled her, made her want to shoot in response. It would still be deer hunting season for a few more days. When she saw the Slocum camping trailers on the north bank, she rowed as hard as she could to pass quickly and avoid being seen. A few hundred yards beyond that, the river curved, and Margo heard voices and laughter coming from outside the abandoned cabin that Junior called the marijuana house. She ran her boat onto the sand-bar just below the place and decided to wait for full darkness, rather than risk being seen. She took off her leather work gloves and breathed onto her hands. The tiny cabin here was owned by the Murrays and until three years ago had been used by one of Grandpa's brothers for weekend fishing. Margo listened to the teenage voices. A girl's laughter exploded like automatic weapon fire and then was muffled by a closing door. When all was quiet for a while, Margo climbed up on the bank for a better look.

A white-tailed buck approached the river only twenty-five yards away, near the dock. Margo loaded six cartridges from her pocket into the magazine tube of the Marlin, chambered a round as quietly as she could, and cocked the hammer into the safety position. The loaded rifle felt good in her hands. When the buck stopped at the riverbank and turned to look in her direction, Margo slowed her breathing. With the rifle resting on one knee, she studied the creature, counted ten points, saw a raw V-shaped tear on his cheek, maybe a wound from fighting another male. Her hands stopped shaking. She could take it down with the .22 if she hit it in the eye or the temple. The deer lowered its head to drink from the river. The lever-action Marlin was slightly heavier than her daddy's bolt-action rifle, but while she aimed the gun, she felt weightless and free from her exhaustion.

'Don't shoot!' a female voice whispered loudly from behind her. The deer started at the sound, doubled up its legs, and bounded from the water's edge.

Margo jumped back down the bank, climbed into her boat, and pushed off.

'Hey, are you Junior's cousin? Come back and hang out with us!' the girl shouted. Margo kept rowing. The girl said to someone else, 'I think that was Junior's cousin.'

Margo recognized her voice. She was one of Junior's friends, a girl Ricky had once referred to as a slut. She cleared her throat and managed to say, 'I got no cousins. My name is Annie.'

Margo rowed upstream, warmed herself against the current. She was glad the girl had stopped her from shooting the buck. The meat would have gone to waste on the riverbank. Margo rowed harder when she realized she had left the Murray house unlocked in her hurry. She wondered if Joanna would make her family another loaf of swirled cinnamon bread to replace the one Margo had taken. After about two hours of hard pulling in the dark, she found a shallow stream, maneuvered herself a few yards up into it, out of view of river traffic, and tied her boat to the roots of a tree. She curled up in her sleeping bag on the back seat of her boat as she used to curl on the couch to wait for Crane to come home, and fell asleep. Rocked by the motion of the river, she slept hard and for a long time, until the sun was high the following day. She woke up cold, stiff, and confused about where she was, and also grateful no one had bothered her. She'd heard no one shouting her name, but she felt eyes on her. She moved her toes to warm them inside her boots and saw on shore a big buck. When she sat up and made a noise with the tarp, the buck turned to show a V-shaped gash and then walked a few yards deeper into the woods. She ate half the loaf of cinnamon bread and began rowing again.

In the middle of the afternoon, Margo sighted ahead a riverside gas station where boats refueled, and where a person who was not afraid of being seen could tie up and buy a sandwich and some chips without going more than a few yards from the water. Margo hid out in the channel of an island cottage just downstream of the place. Nobody was home. She wondered what it would be like to live on a little island like this, with water flowing around her on all sides. She was about twelve miles upstream of Murrayville, and she knew she could only cover about a mile an hour when rowing against the current.

At dusk she saw a ten-point buck approaching, so she set out rowing again. Behind her she felt the flapping of a big bird's wings, but turned and saw nothing. She passed the gas station unseen; and after that she mostly passed moonlit woods and fields, houses and cottages with floating docks and oil-barrel floats not yet taken out for the winter. In the dark, her rowing became as constant as her breathing. She saw the backs of car dealerships and machine shops. Some places were familiar: a cliff in which swallows dwelled in summer, a stone wall and tower that her grandpa had said were built by Indians, some ancient trees whose branches hung over the water in ways that seemed to Margo generous, the way Grandpa had been generous, or big and graceful the way Aunt Joanna always seemed big and graceful. The shimmer of security lights on the surface of the water reminded Margo that her mother was up ahead. She rowed much of the night, taking bites of bread until it was gone. When she was too tired to stay awake, she pulled over at a snag and slept again.

She awoke the next morning to a splash beside the boat, and when she looked into the dark water, she saw her father's angry face reflected there. But then it was her own weary face, framed by dark hair. Her cheeks and lips were chapped from the cold, and her muscles ached. She set out slowly, switching sides of the river whenever it curved, knowing how the water was shallow and slow-moving on the outside of curves, and fast and deep on the inside where it was in the process of wearing away the riverbank.

As she traveled around an oxbow, she remembered what Grandpa used to say, that such a bend in the river was a temporary shape, that eventually, over thousands of years, the river would reroute itself to the most direct path, never mind the houses folks had built in its way, never mind the retaining walls or the concrete chunks, the riprap they'd piled along the riverbank. The river persevered, Grandpa had said, and people would eventually give up. Margo remembered thinking she would not give up on making the river her own. It occurred to her now that Grandpa might have been speaking about his own house, the big Murray house, being eventually swept away. He might have been saying that the Murrays would not always be kings of the river. What had seemed permanent to Margo, the Murray river paradise, could have seemed fleeting to the man who'd created it.

By the afternoon of that second full day of rowing, she was tired and hungry beyond any exhaustion or hunger she had known. With each pull of her oars, she felt herself liquefying. A few times she paused and put her hands into the water to soothe them. When snow began to fall around her, she wondered if she might dissolve before she got where she was going, like the big flakes that fell on the water. When her legs cramped, she slipped backward with the current for a while, watched the same trees she had just struggled to pass fall behind her. She slipped easily by a whitewashed dock she had inched past with such effort a few minutes ago. She passed a great blue heron, four feet tall, standing in a few inches of freezing water, and the sight startled her awake. Before she let herself get carried away, she guided her boat to a sandbar. She turned to watch the heron, which should have flown off south months ago. The bird stiffened all the feathers on its head and neck and then stabbed at the water. It gulped down a finger-length fish and flew off upstream. Margo opened the plastic bag Junior had given her. She took the joint out and lit it with a safety match from her backpack. She smoked half of it, hoping to numb herself, and when it made her feel sick, she tossed the rest of it into the water. Within minutes, she was even hungrier.

She was light-headed at dusk. The marijuana's pleasant effects had worn off hours before, and she was left with an emptiness that began in her growling stomach and stretched all through her. The water jug, too, was empty. It was well into night when a familiar cabin on stilts rose before her like a miracle, with its windows of dim, wavering light. She rowed past it to give herself room to maneuver, but when she stopped rowing she slipped downstream too fast and had to approach again. She tried to flex her fingers on the oars, but they had frozen into a curled position inside her leather gloves. The times she had seen this place with Grandpa, it had been daylight. The flickering lantern light made the cabin look mysterious. Brian had invited her to come for a visit, but she'd imagined sneaking in while he was gone. From here it was only a few miles more to Heart of Pines.

She rowed past the cabin again, guided herself

toward the water's edge, and then grabbed the wooden dock as it came toward her, almost pinching her hand between the boat and the dock. She tied up beside the Playbuoy pontoon she'd seen a few days ago. Tied on the other side of the dock was an aluminum bass boat. The pontoon tapped against her boat a few times, but its prow was tucked close to shore. She approached the cabin on foot, carrying only the rifle and making as little noise as possible. She could hear men's voices as she climbed the wooden steps. The smoke churning from the cabin's chimney smelled of cherry wood. She noted a hip-high stack of split logs filling the space between two trees a few yards from the cabin. The primitive place seemed all set for winter, giving the impression that somebody was planning on living there rather than just visiting on the weekends. A clothesline was strung near the dock. There was a five-quart plastic bucket of clothespins just outside the porch door, under the overhang of the tin roof. Margo entered the screen porch silently and stood outside a glass-paneled door for a few minutes. She made out Brian and his brother Paul inside, with their black hair and beards. So much had happened since three days ago when she had seen them. Brian got up and opened the door, still holding a hand of cards. 'Who's out there?'

Margo inhaled.

'Sweet Mother of Jesus,' he said and folded his cards into a stack. 'Am I seeing a beautiful ghost, or has the maiden of the river come upstream to bless me? Come in out of the cold and shut the door.' He returned to the table, sat down, and leaned back in his chair to take a wider view of her. He seemed genuinely overwhelmed by Margo's presence. Paul was sitting with his back to the door, looking over his shoulder. He squinted one eye. 'Jesus, Brian. What's a woman doing here with a gun? Is she going to shoot us?'

'Put on your glasses, Pauly. It's Maggie Crane,' Brian said.

Margo might have cried in relief at being anywhere she could rest. She was grateful to be out of the elements, but the sheer size of the two men spooked her. Both of them were as tall as Cal and bigger around. She was at their mercy. If they didn't feed her, she would starve; if they sent her away, she would probably freeze; if they wanted to force her to do anything with them, they might well succeed.

'Put down your rifle, Maggie, and come sit.' Brian pulled a chair away from the table and patted the seat with his hand. She rested the butt plate of the Marlin on the pine floor and leaned the barrel in a corner, next to a broom. She sat in the chair beside Bryan.

'You came just in time for my winning hand,' Paul said.

Margo didn't know why she had earlier thought the two men seemed alike. They were the same size and their features were similar — black hair, beards, and blue eyes — but where Brian was broad-shouldered and solid in the middle, Paul was rounded in his shoulders and belly. Brian's hair was too short to go into a ponytail like the one Paul wore. Paul's face was thinner and paler and intensely focused on his cards, which he now put down reluctantly. He fished a pair of glasses from the pocket of his sheepskin-lined vest and put them on. One eye looked big through the glasses, and the other was half closed. Margo couldn't stop looking at him.

'One hand isn't going to drag you out of your five-year losing streak, you sorry bastard,' Brian said.

'I beat you last week.'

'Like hell you did.' Brian turned to Margo. 'We heard the news about your daddy. We're so sorry. I worked with him for a couple years in heat-treating. Old Man Murray said he was smart and very careful. That's what he always said about him. Loved him like a son. I mean, he was his son, I guess. I never knew the story there.'

'I'm sorry, too,' Paul said. 'I never met him, but that's a rough business.'

Brian said, 'Paul and I lost our daddy five years ago, and it wasn't easy, not even for us grown men. Even though the son of a bitch used to beat the hell out of us.'

'He sure did,' Paul said. 'That mean bastard beat us and made us tough.'

'Made us the mean bastards we are today,' Brian said.

Paul smiled and took off his glasses. One eye remained squinted.

'Why don't you leave them on so you can see?' Brian said.

'The damned things give me a headache. Worry about your own eyes, Brian.'

76

'When we were kids, I shot my brother in the eye with a BB, blinded him in his right eye, so I have to take care of him now,' Brian said.

'You don't take care of me, asshole.'

'Kept him out of Vietnam. Probably saved his goddamned life,' Brian said.

'Can we just finish the game?'

'The other eye went blind for the usual reason. Too much yanking his own chain.' Brian winked at Margo. 'The priest warned us.'

'Will you shut the fuck up, Brian?'

Margo took off her leather gloves and laid them on the table. They remained in the shape of her curled hands.

'Oh, poor Maggie. Paul, this child is freezing. Look at her fingers.' Brian took both her hands in his and exhaled hot breath on them. Earlier, when she had breathed on them herself, it had done little good, but Brian's big body — even his lungs must be big — created real heat. Even as she felt wary, she wanted to lean her head against him.

Paul said, 'I hope you don't mind me asking, Miss Maggie, but isn't your family wondering where you are right now?'

'Her family's the Murrays, Pauly. Would you want to be with them Murray bastards?'

'Still, her family's got to want her,' Paul said. 'What about her ma?'

'Her ma run off and left her a year and a half ago, run off with a man from Heart of Pines. Maggie, is that who you're trying to get to? Your ma?'

Margo inhaled sharply. She hadn't considered

77

Brian might know her mother.

'Give me two cards,' Paul said.

Brian let go of Margo's hands and gave Paul two cards, took two himself. Paul gripped his cards so tightly his fingertips whitened.

'We'll get you on your way tomorrow, wherever you want to go,' Brian said. 'Don't you worry. You're fine here tonight.'

'I understand a woman might leave her old man,' Paul said, anger coming quickly into his voice. 'But what kind of woman would leave her kid? Her daughter especially? My wife would die before she'd leave one of my kids behind.'

'Ours is not to judge,' Brian said and picked up Margo's hands again. After he rubbed them on and off for a few minutes, the pink began to return. Margo wanted to go stand by the woodstove, but she knew if she did she would never want to leave its intense warmth. As if reading her mind, Brian stood up, surprising her again with his great size, and fed the stove some split logs from a pile behind it.

Paul spoke up again. 'There's something else I heard rumor of. Brian heard it, too. Is it true, Maggie, that your papa shot Cal Murray's dick off?' Paul's voice was uneven. She was grateful to be sitting near Brian, who seemed steady and calm.

'No need to be crude, Pauly,' Brian said, grinning to show that he appreciated this particular sort of crudeness. Then he frowned. 'But maybe it's good you know the kind of rumors that are flying, Maggie.'

'Can I have some water?' Margo whispered.

'So she does talk!' Brian said. 'I never heard you talk before. Well, don't you say anything you don't want to say. We'll figure it all out tomorrow.'

'Brian don't believe your daddy did what they said,' Paul said.

'Never mind all that,' Brian said. 'You stay here tonight. We'll get you where you need to go. Or stay as long as you like. Will you have to get home for the funeral?'

Margo shook her head. There would be no funeral, no fuss.

Brian poured a glass of water from a kettle on the counter. 'We boil the well water here just to be safe,' he said.

Margo drank the glass down and accepted a refill.

'Let's get some food into you, Maggie,' Brian said. 'We've got some leftover trout and a piece of venison steak from that deer of yours. I took it to do your daddy a favor, but now I'm glad, because I haven't gotten a deer myself. Maybe beautiful girls are luring away all the bucks, leaving nothing for us big, ugly men.'

Though Paul complained about another delay in the game, Brian lit the propane stove, and within a few minutes he presented her with an orange plate containing meat, a section of fish with the bone in, a couple of chunks of potato, and some greasy green beans with bits of bacon on them. While Paul and Brian played, she ate. When Brian handed her a piece of store-bought white bread, she wiped the plate clean with it.

'You sure can eat,' Paul said, 'for a little gal.'

'She's a good eater, all right,' Brian said.

She stopped chewing the bread.

'Don't stop,' Brian said. 'It's good you have an appetite. You don't live if you don't eat. Some people give up and waste away in hard times.'

With the last bite of bread, she scraped a last bit of fish off the comb of its bones.

'Pauly, can you believe this vision of loveliness has come to us for help?'

'I got to say, Brian, I'm not feeling good about that. How old do you think she is?' Paul spoke as though she weren't sitting right there.

'Eighteen,' Margo said quietly.

'Are you coming to stay, then?' Brian asked and winked at her. 'To cook me pancakes every morning and tell me I'm a handsome man? Because I've been looking for a girl like that.'

'Oh, for Christ's sake,' Paul said. 'How much have you had to drink? If she's eighteen, she's half your age. And I'm not so sure she's eighteen. You got to watch out for my brother, Maggie. He finds trouble for himself.'

'Can we get you more food?' Brian asked. He took a slug of ginger brandy out of a pint bottle that was almost empty and held it toward her.

She shook her head no to the bottle and was less certain about saying no to more food.

'Poor lost lamb.' Brian screwed the cap back on the bottle.

'You should be with your mama right now,' Paul said, shaking his head, 'not out here.'

'You said you know where she is,' Margo whispered. She fumbled in her pocket, opened her wallet, and got out the envelope with the

80

address on the corner.

'More than a year ago she was around,' Brian said after studying the envelope. 'I saw her a dozen times in Heart of Pines with a man named Carpinski. That could be his address. I never said so to your papa, but she was a real looker. She left here after a few months, I think. Somebody said she went to Florida. You've got to stop crying, honey.'

'Of course she's crying,' Paul said. 'She's a little girl.'

Margo wiped at her eyes with the paper towel she'd been using as a napkin.

'We'll find your ma for you. I'll go talk to Carpinski. He's an okay guy, lives in a little A-frame on Dog Leg Lake. You can stay here until we find her.'

'Brian, are you crazy? You're going to get yourself arrested.'

'Eventually I'll get arrested for one thing or another, and if I get it for helping a girl, well, that's better than some other reason.'

Brian smelled like cigarette smoke and ginger brandy and the river, and his stoking the fire intensified the cabin's food smells. It warmed the room so much that Paul took off his sheepskin-lined vest.

'Cal Murray is a son of a bitch,' Brian said again, shaking his head, 'and his bad nature got bred right into the next generation in that boy Billy. Is he going to jail for what he did?'

'He'll pay,' Margo said quietly.

'Did you hear that, Pauly? This girl's going to get revenge. That's how you make it through this, Maggie. Your daddy was a good man, and Cal Murray and his kid, neither one was fit to lick his boots.'

Margo let herself focus on Paul's mismatched eyes one more time. When she sensed annoyance, she looked away and took comfort in Brian's shoulder like a sturdy wall beside her.

'You telling us nobody's looking for you right now?' Paul said.

She shook her head, though she couldn't be sure.

'How old are you, really?' Paul said.

'Eighteen.'

'Contrary to my brother's ideas, I haven't fooled around with an underage girl since I was fifteen,' Brian said.

'Shit,' Paul said and shook his head.

'Pauly, what's got into you? We were raised to take care of lost souls. Are you saying we can't help her because she's too pretty?'

'I'm just saying you ought to be careful in your situation.' Paul turned to look at Margo. 'And she ought to be careful of you.'

'As long as you aren't storing drugs here again, you've got nothing to worry about what I do, Pauly.' Brian put an arm around Margo and pulled her close for a moment.

'I'm telling you, Brian. She needs her ma or somebody like that,' Paul said.

'Don't worry, Maggie, we'll find your ma, wherever she went. It's rare for people to just disappear,' Brian said.

'Try as they might.' Paul shook his head.

Margo shivered. Her blood was racing to her

full belly. She flexed her fingers and wiggled her toes in her boots.

'Goddamn it, Brian. You're looking for trouble. They'll report her missing.'

'I'm not looking for trouble,' Brian said. He let loose of her to lay down his cards. 'But trouble does find me somehow or other, little brother, doesn't it?'

'You make your own trouble,' Paul said. 'Ask any of them guys you picked a fight with lately. If they're still breathing.'

Brian drew hard on his cigarette. Margo felt the air in the room change, fill with tension, until Brian shook his head. He laughed out a puff of smoke. 'Listen, Paul, I'm not kicking this little girl out into the cold, so get used to her sitting here at this table for as long as she wants to stay.'

'Well, some of us have to work tomorrow,' Paul said. Before he left to go home, he brought in Margo's backpack from *The River Rose*. Brian made up the couch with a slightly musty sheet and a heavy quilt he brought from the bedroom. As she got under the covers, he fed the fire again and put more wood on top of the stove to dry, and then he knelt on the floor beside her. He tucked the quilt around her to protect against drafts. When she finally closed her eyes from exhaustion, he kissed her mouth. She was too tired to be startled, and she let him kiss her.

'Don't worry about anything, Maggie,' he said after he pulled away.

She knew that until she found her mother, she had nowhere else to go, and she wondered if she could make herself welcome here. She reached up and took hold of his beard, which was soft, and gently tugged him to her. Though only her and Brian's mouths touched, she felt as though he were kissing her with his whole body, and it both frightened her and made her skin come alive. When his tongue slipped into her mouth, the hair on her arms and legs stood on end. He was still kissing her when she felt she was awakening from a long sleep, though surely only a minute or so had passed. The steady kissing quieted her sadness. She thought she could live and breathe inside this dampening kiss. When he finally pulled away, her lips felt swollen.

'Oh, Maggie,' he said, shaking his head. 'You'd better get some sleep.' He pushed her hair back from her face, kissed her forehead, and went into the bedroom. She was grateful he left the door open. It made her feel less alone.

When Margo awoke, it was still dark outside. The room was lit by the kerosene lamp turned down low. She listened for an owl, but heard nothing. She realized all over again what it meant that her mother had left Heart of Pines. Of course her mother would want to go to Florida, a place where she could be warm year-round. Winters had been hard on Luanne.

Margo had shot Cal, and so Billy had killed Crane. By this middle-of-the-night reckoning, Margo had as good as shot her own father in the chest. She sat up on the couch. She did not want to be in her own skin right now, and she did not want to be alone. Though it must have been hours ago that she had kissed Brian, she was still feeling the force of his mouth. His scent permeated the quilt and the air around her. She could still taste the smoke and ginger-candy flavor of the liquor he had been drinking. She could still feel his beard on her neck.

She tucked the quilt around herself, but the wind coming through the windows was too much for the woodstove when it was damped down for the night. She would help Brian put plastic on the windows if he would let her stay here for a while. She would feed his fire and keep it going when he was away. She stood up from the couch, fed a log into the stove, and put another on top. She turned up the wick on the lantern. She draped the quilt over her shoulders and moved to the doorway of the cabin's bedroom. She did not know if Brian would force a girl, but he couldn't force her if she went to him on her own. She stood beside the bed until she saw Brian's eyes glittering in the lamplight.

Brian pulled back the covers — a sleeping bag and a sheet — to open up a place in his double bed, and she moved across the floor of the little room. She let her jeans fall from her hips, and climbed into his bed in her underwear and T-shirt. She pulled the quilt over them both.

'Sweet Mother of Jesus,' Brian whispered. 'Look what you've brung me. Are you sure about this, Maggie?'

She nodded.

'Say it,' he breathed, 'and I won't send you away.'

'Yes, I'm sure,' she whispered. She was sure this was the best defense against the cold of winter, the best way to make sure she wouldn't get sent back to Cal and Joanna or to social services. The best thing for her right now when she could not endure lying alone. Her body was already warming to Brian's, flushing wherever he touched her.

'Have you been with a man before?'

She nodded and then whispered, 'Yes.'

He ran his hands up her arms and down her rump and her thighs, and she let herself be reshaped and warmed. She watched Brian, and he watched her. When she had been with Junior's friend, she'd felt clumsy, but Brian was easy to follow. When her muscles stiffened, Brian's hands continued to move over her, and a memory of Cal fell away. When Brian's hands moved underneath her T-shirt, the cotton fabric seemed to dissolve, and when he pushed her underwear down by her knees, it seemed she had willed them away. His hand was between her legs, his mouth was on her mouth and then on her belly, and then his body was on top of hers. Despite his size, he was not heavy on her. Margo gripped his arms, and she saw how he formed a house around her, how his big body became a dwelling in which she could live and be safe. His eyes were open, still watching her, reflecting orange from the light of the kerosene lantern in the other room. She noted the way he studied each part of her, and this made her admire each part of herself. While she was touching him, her arms seemed as powerful as his arms, her small, blistered hands as capable as his big hands.

Her body tensed as he entered her, but then she relaxed and moved with him. She ran her swollen hands up and down his arms. She touched the spaghetti-ridged scars on the back of his hand with her fingertips. She wanted to feel the scars against her face. When the pleasure got to be too much, she closed her eyes.

7

In the morning, Margo faked sleep while Brian got up and fussed around in the main room of the cabin. A while later, he brought a bucket of warm water into the bedroom and placed it on the floor beside the little table with the mirror. He also brought in her army backpack and leaned it against the wall. Once he left the room and closed the door, she sat up and looked through the window at the milky light on the water. The cabin was on the south side of the river, as was her father's house in Murrayville. She moved to sit before the dim mirror. Her face seemed old, not as though she herself had aged, but as though she were a person from another time in history. Even after she had washed her face, her reflection reminded her of the sepia-toned photographs of Annie Oakley.

Margo didn't regret what she had done with Brian. Her body felt different, as though she had been taken apart, piece by piece, and put back together in a new way. She washed her arms, which were swollen, and between her legs. Her shoulders hurt when she lifted her arms and hurt again when she released them. Her hands curled as though still gripping the oar handles. Just a few days ago she had been eating breakfast in her kitchen with her father, surrounded by familiar dishes and furniture, and now she was in a stranger's house, and her future was uncertain.

She brushed her dark hair and let it fall loose over her back, and then she took aim at herself in the mirror with her own double-barreled gaze.

She used to like being naked or mostly naked around the river, at least when the weather was warm, but now she wanted to cover every part of herself as Annie Oakley had. Margo had the feeling that her newly shaped body had a power that she needed to keep secret. She put on clean underwear, a turtleneck shirt, and her fresh pair of jeans.

With the door closed, the bedroom grew gradually cooler, until finally Margo was starved for the stove's warmth.

'Good morning, beautiful,' Brian said when she stepped into the main room.

When she saw her rifle in the corner, her heart pounded. 'I dropped my rifle in the mud. I have to clean it.'

'We'll eat first,' Brian said, 'and then we'll clean and oil your rifle. Everything will be okay.' He held out his arms until she sat on his lap and let herself be kissed. Despite all she had eaten the night before, she was ravenous.

She followed Brian outside to a hand pump, where he began to refill the galvanized bucket. The iron pipe was wrapped in insulation to keep it from freezing. He pointed the way to an outhouse a few yards farther on.

When she returned to the kitchen, she watched how Brian battered and fried the fish fillets he took from a cooler, so that she could cook them next time. The smell of frying fish and bacon was so powerful that she felt light-headed.

For as long as she needed to stay, she would make herself handy, helpful to Brian, and not take anything for granted. Brian placed the plate of fish, bacon, potatoes, and toast in front of her. He sat beside her rather than across from her, as though they were sitting at the drugstore lunch counter in Murrayville, and he ran his scarred hand along her arm. Her muscles were loosening up, but she couldn't eat with him touching her, so she reluctantly put down her fork.

'I'm sorry,' he said and let go of her. 'Eat!'

While they drank their second cups of instant coffee, he kept reaching out and touching her shoulder or her face or petting her hair. He told her again how he'd been fired from Murray Metal Fabricating in the last round of layoffs, how he'd fought with Cal and knocked out his teeth. She didn't mind hearing the story again, because it meant that, already, something was familiar between them.

They washed the dishes in a big aluminum roasting pan full of water they heated on both burners of the propane stove, and finally Margo and Brian sat down with her rifle. Margo showed him how removing one screw revealed all the moving parts of the Marlin, as Cal had shown her.

Upon studying the chrome and the carving of the squirrel on the stock, Brian said, 'I think this is a limited edition. It's probably worth something. Was it your papa's?'

'Cal's.'

'Good girl.' He laughed.

She let Brian separate the stock from the

barrel. They spent the morning disassembling the Marlin and reassembling it, drenching the air in the room with the heavy scent of solvent and then gun oil. When Brian wasn't explaining something or telling stories, he often was humming popular songs from the last decades, Beatles songs especially. For a long time, he was humming 'Norwegian Wood.' They found a few drops of water in the barrel, but no harm had been done. They put the rifle back together, well oiled. Then she and Brian went out in the pontoon boat, parked at a snag, and caught bluegills for dinner.

'So why would your papa have shot Cal's dick? Did Cal Murray mess with you?' Brian asked, while Margo was cleaning the fish in the sink.

Margo said nothing, even when Brian turned and looked right at her.

'He did, didn't he? Cal raped you.' It wasn't a question by the time he finished asking. 'Holy shit. That's why you took the man's gun.'

She grimaced. She still didn't think that word made sense in relation to what had happened.

'Your papa was revenging you. Well, it's not enough. If I see Cal, I'll knock another tooth out of the son of a bitch's head. I'll knock them all out.'

While Brian was frying the fish, Margo stood at the window and searched the river until she saw a shadow fly across — a red-tailed hawk, maybe, or at least a crow — and she was able to imagine following its flight path with the barrel of the Marlin. She figured that whatever Brian wanted to do to Cal, it had only a little to do

91

with herself. She might be the spark that got Brian riled up, but any fire would be all about Brian and Cal and whatever was already between them.

———

'All right, Maggie, let's test your rifle, make sure it still works,' Brian said after breakfast the following morning. Margo carried the Marlin, wishing again it had a sling, and Brian carried a bigger rifle, an M1, something from World War II. While they were cleaning the Marlin, he had mentioned that he'd been in Vietnam, but volunteered only that his 'damn M16 jammed about every fucking day.' Knowing how Crane had not wanted to talk about his Vietnam experience, Margo didn't consider asking Brian about his. Brian set up a couple dozen empty beer cans and plastic bottles on a railroad tie twenty-five paces farther down the river and handed Margo the pair of ear protectors he had on his arm. He loaded the big rifle and fired eight rounds. He went through two more clips, and when he was done, after twenty-four shots, he'd hit about half of the targets. He replaced the cans and bottles he'd destroyed with new ones, including two sardine cans he propped up. 'I think I'm out of practice,' he said. 'Maybe my sights need adjusting.'

Margo lifted her .22 with some difficulty. Her arm muscles were still strained from rowing. She experienced some kind of electrical shock when she first pulled the trigger, and she missed the first can. She focused and dinged it on the second shot, and then caught the top on the third, sent it flying. She inhaled the faint smell of gunpowder. She reloaded the Marlin with fifteen of the long-rifle cartridges she'd carried from Cal's gun cupboard and listened for a moment to the river. Holding the rifle steady would have been easier with a sling, but she held her arm up until her body remembered it as a natural position. She hit the next can and each can after that, and she reloaded and knocked all the bottles from their perches. And in that several minutes of intense focusing, she felt peaceful. Margo lowered the gun, pressed the barrel against her face to feel its heat.

'Holy shit,' Brian said. 'A guy has got to respect that.'

Afterward, he exchanged his M1 for a shotgun, an old Winchester 97 twelve-gauge pump-action with a full choke. He shot at some frozen hunks of driftwood he'd dragged over from the edge of the river, and she saw that the buckshot created a tight pattern of holes only a few inches wide at thirty feet. With her first shot, the kick of the thing knocked her back. After that, she jammed it tightly into her shoulder and absorbed the recoil with her whole body. She loaded and shot until she knew she would be bruised. Though the sound was muted by the ear protectors, each blast moved through her and settled and soothed her.

Brian offered to stay at the cabin with her the following day, but said there was two hundred bucks cash if he cleaned the roof and gutters at an apartment complex. There was no road leading to the cabin, meaning a boat was the only way in or out, and this made Margo feel easier about being alone there. If anyone came for her, she would see him coming on the water. Brian said that if the river froze over this winter, they'd be stuck, so they needed to keep their supplies of food, bait, and ammo laid in, and the prospect of winter preparation seemed to please him. After he disappeared upstream, Margo found a piece of a rope that was too short to use for much of anything, so she unraveled it and then set about braiding the sections to create a rifle sling.

That evening, Brian visited Carpinski and got a report on Margo's mother. After a few months of living with Carpinski, Luanne had apparently gone off with a truck driver. Carpinski provided an address in Florida, but the first letter Margo wrote came back the next week to Brian's post office box with a note handwritten across it, *No longer at this address*. Brian said he would keep asking around, would talk to Carpinski again to see if he remembered anything else. According to Brian, the man was still pretty broken up about Luanne more than a year after she had left.

Brian was a storyteller, recounting his own tales and others he had collected, and in the evenings he often told about growing up in the Upper Peninsula of Michigan in logging camps, about damming creeks to catch fish, about dipping smelt, about men who were killed by walking too close to the edge of the road when a wagon full of logs was passing. There was a long, complicated story about killing and eating rattlesnake in Idaho. He told her about two men who went out in a boat with one of their wives and came back without her, neither of them realizing she was missing, so relieved had they been by the quiet. She'd shown up hours later, having walked from the other side of the lake, mad as hell. He told a story about a Michigan Department of Natural Resources official going out with his friend fishing in the middle of a big lake. The DNR man watched his friend light a quarter stick of dynamite and toss it into the water. After the blast, twenty fish floated up dead, and the man collected them. When he lit another stick of dynamite, the DNR man said, 'You know I'm going to have to arrest you for this.' So the guy handed the DNR man the lit dynamite and said, 'Well, are you going to talk or fish?'

The nearest neighbor downstream on Brian's side of the river was a half mile through wild woods. And it was a lonesome sort of relief not seeing the Murray farm across the way as she had her whole life. Upstream on the other side was a plain white clapboard house, apparently unoccupied during the winter months. A few hundred yards downstream, separated from the white house by an empty lot tangled with small trees and brambles, was a tidy yellow house, in which there lived a man who drove a green Jeep, a woman who wore a slim-fitting white winter jacket, and a big loopy dog, maybe a yellow Lab-Irish setter mix. The house was built way back from the river, but the dog hung around at the river's edge and gazed into the water. Margo had never had her own dog — the no-pets policy had been a rare point of agreement between her parents — but she had spent so much of her youth with the Murray dogs that she had come to see dogs as her natural companions.

It was after the new year when Margo came up with the idea to write to the occupant of her mother's old address in Florida, asking him or her for information about Luanne. Brian said she should offer a fifty-dollar reward — he would pay for it, he said. The reply came to Brian's PO box. The address the man provided was not in Florida, but in Michigan, Lake Lynne, a town west of Murrayville and north of Kalamazoo. Margo worked for days to write the simplest note she could, giving no details about her life, telling her mother that she was doing fine and would like to visit her. Brian mailed it to the new address.

Over the course of the next few months, Margo was grateful that nobody came around looking for her. If the police or the Murrays were searching at all, they weren't looking very hard. She'd seen a sheriff's boat traveling upstream a few times, but the craft had always sped toward Heart of Pines and then back downstream a while later. Nobody ever came to the cabin to inquire about a missing girl. Sixteen was the legal age for dropping out of school in Michigan — maybe sixteen was also the age when folks stopped worrying about you. Margo had a feeling that Cal and Joanna didn't really want to find her.

During those cold months, Margo worked on *leading*, shooting just in front of running rabbits and squirrels. She also shot, plucked, and cooked the occasional nonmigrating duck, from among the half-domestic oddities that appeared on the river. Brian worked odd jobs in town for cash, especially snowplowing, for which he used a four-wheel-drive truck he kept somewhere in town. He and Paul owned a stand of woods south of Heart of Pines, and so he cut trees, split logs with a hydraulic splitter, and delivered cords of firewood around the county. He also was able to fix cars, but he hated to do it in winter unless he could use somebody's heated garage. Once a week or so, he visited his kids in town, one of whom was just three years younger than Margo, he said, which meant the boy was only one year younger, really. He invited Margo along on some trips, but she did not want to risk encountering the police or the Murrays. At first Brian had seemed uneasy about leaving her alone, but he soon took for granted that when he returned, she would be there. He said he felt like a better man knowing she was waiting for him at the end of a day of digging trenches or cutting down trees. She was his *salvation*, he said, his reason to settle down and mend his ways. Sometimes, when he said this sort of thing, his grin took on a ferocity that scared Margo.

The letter that came in March was in a yellow envelope. The paper folded inside featured cartoon bumblebees. After reading it a few times, Margo noticed it smelled like flowers and honey. There was no return address on the envelope.

Folded inside the paper was a postal money order for two hundred dollars. The letter read:

Dear Margaret Louise,
Thank you for writing to me, Sweetheart. I'm glad to hear you are fine and still living on the river. I know you always loved the river. I could not endure that mildew and smell. Though it breaks my heart, I cannot encourage you to visit me at this time. My situation is delicate. I will write to you soon and arrange to meet with you.

Love, Your Mama
p.s. Don't tell your daddy
or Cal you heard from me.

Margo couldn't speak at all that evening, but she nodded in agreement with Brian when it made sense to do so, and she fell asleep early. The following day, when Brian went to work, Margo loaded up his twelve-gauge and went into the woods dragging the heavy-duty sled Brian used for firewood. Though it was not deer hunting season, she tromped downstream through the snow until she found a deer trail cutting to the river. She sat against the trunk of an oak tree and waited. A few hours later, the first deer to follow the path down to the water was a doe, and a second doe followed, her belly swollen. Margo watched them drink at the river and then jump back up the bank and nuzzle the snow for buried acorns before continuing on. She watched them chew disinterestedly on saplings, and finally they wandered away, still unaware of her presence. A little after noon, a bigger deer, surely a buck that had dropped its antlers, went down to the water to drink. Margo focused on the muscle movement in the deer's shoulders and neck, the twitching of the ears and the tail. She pushed thoughts of her mother into the quietest place within herself, until she was inside the sound of leaves rustling and the wind-sound of the moving surface of the river. The deer jumped back up onto the bank, and Margo calmly followed its motion. When it stopped and nuzzled the ground, she aimed into the heart and lungs and pressed the trigger.

The deer fell hard. When Margo went to the animal, she found that she had shot the slug into a doe. From its musculature, she had been certain it was a buck, but now she could see its sex and its slightly swollen belly. Though her aim had been perfect, the doe was not dead. It attempted to lift its head, watched Margo, terrified, through a big, clear eye. The creature kicked with its back legs as though trying to run. Margo took the army knife out of her pocket, unfolded the biggest blade, and sliced through the deer's jugular, an act that took some strength. She folded up her knife with the blood still on it, wiped her hands on her jeans, and only then did her hands start shaking.

Margo sat down cross-legged beside the doe's warm body, sick about what she'd done. She stroked the rough fur stretched across the cage of ribs as the body grew cool. After a while, she heard the approach of another deer. She remained still while it passed close to her and went down to the water. She watched it drink its fill, lift its head, and look around. She wondered how the deer could be completely unaware of the dead doe and of Margo when both were so near, not twelve yards away. The deer climbed the bank, and Margo was once again almost sure it was a buck. It paused and sniffed the bark of a wild apple tree and took interest in something. It pawed at the ground. It reared up and put its front hooves on the tree, so it was standing on its back legs, exposing its chest and balls. Then the buck nosed upward and bit at something in the crook of the tree. Margo fired her second slug into its heart. As the deer hit the ground, it seemed to sigh. From its mouth tumbled a gray bird, a mourning dove, with its dark eyes bulging and darting and then closing.

She suppressed a cry of surprise. She'd never seen or heard of a deer eating a bird. There was still more to learn about life along the river. She moved in and nudged the deer's chest with her foot to make sure it was dead, and a flurry erupted beside her as the dove woke up and launched itself into the air.

Margo had to sit still for a while and survey the mess she'd made. After killing the doe, she should have unloaded the shotgun. She was hunting out of season, so killing either deer was already a crime. She promised herself if she ever killed a doe in the future, she would gut it and skin it, same as a buck. She ate female rabbits and squirrels all the time. But not this time, not this doe. She covered its body with leafless branches, frozen leaves, and snow and hoped no one would come upon it. She rolled the buck over onto the big sled and pulled it slowly upstream, over the snow.

By the time Brian got home, after he'd had a few beers at The Pub in Heart of Pines, Margo had dressed out the deer on a vinyl tarp and deposited the guts in the river, hoping they would float away.

At first Brian seemed shocked to find her with a deer out of season, but he produced a hacksaw and helped her take off the legs. They tied a rope around its neck and strung it up in a tree behind the house, out of sight of passing boats. He offered to help her skin the thing and seemed glad when she declined his offer. He sat on a stump, sipping from a half-pint bottle, while she worked. He told her a story about his buddy skinning a deer by tying up a golf ball inside the deer's skin between the shoulders and making a knob out of it. Then his buddy tied a rope around the knob, tied it to a four-wheel-drive truck, and drove slowly.

'Hide peels right off in a minute,' Brian said. 'You wouldn't believe it. Wish I could show you.'

'Did you ever hear about a deer eating a bird?' she asked.

'I've seen a deer eat a fish. Paul said I was crazy, but I know what I saw.'

She nodded.

'It was when we was kids, and I'd caught some carp nobody wanted to eat, and I dumped them in my ma's garden. I'll be damned if I didn't look out my window that night and see a deer eating them.'

'Why would it eat fish?'

'I don't know. Protein? Calcium? Because it tastes good? Same reason we eat fish.'

'How about a bird?'

'I haven't heard of that.'

Margo liked having something new to wonder about, how or why one deer might need something different than what the others needed. More happened in this world than a person would come up with on her own. When she was finished skinning and the deer's hide lay crumpled like a towel on the ground, Brian drank the last of his whiskey and let the bottle drop.

'Maggie, you're the kind of girl I want to spend my old age with,' he said and pulled her onto his lap. He put his arms around her, not seeming to notice or care that she was gripping the burned handle of his butcher knife with the ten-inch blade. 'If I am so fortunate as to have an old age, that is. What should we do with the head?'

'Sink it in a gunnysack full of stones,' she suggested. Brian's talk about their growing old together made her feel queasy. She liked living with Brian, loved feeling protected in the cage of his embrace, but she didn't mean to stay forever. Her mother would contact her soon and tell her to come. From her mother's place, she would be able to figure out what to do next. 'Have you got a gunnysack?' she asked.

'That's it, Maggie. I'm giving you that twelve-gauge. That's your shotgun now. You're a better shot than I am. Anyway, I got a new shot-gun in my truck in Heart of Pines. So that one's yours.' He was slurring his words a little.

'Thank you,' Margo said and sighed. 'I wonder why my ma doesn't want me to come see her.'

'People have all kinds of complications, Maggie. I bet she writes to you again soon.'

Margo nodded.

'You don't think that son of a bitch Cal raped her, too, do you?' Brian asked.

'No.' She answered before she could let herself think about it.

'All right. I'm hungry. Let's get this deer under cover on the screen porch.'

Margo slept twelve hours that night, soundly, the way her mother used to.

8

From Brian, Margo learned to thin-slice half-frozen venison across the grain and dry it on the woodstove to make jerky. He explained to her the qualities of different types of firewood: hickory burned the hottest and smelled the best, but was hardest to split. He taught her about keeping under the radar of the authorities, insisting that she park her boat behind his and cover it with a green canvas tarp whenever she wasn't using it. Margo was grateful for all she was learning and for a place to stay where she could be herself. She loved to have someone to cook for; Brian appreciated all the foods her daddy had liked. Margo was getting an idea that maybe she loved Brian, that love was different than she'd expected, that it was something ordinary. If you knew every detail of a person, if you studied his pink-skinned, black-bearded face every day for hours, if you knew the feel of his soft hair and knew how he felt in his skin when you touched him, if you listened to every word a man spoke, his truth and his lies, then you couldn't help but love him. And loving a new person might even eventually dull the pain of having lost the people you had loved before, even if it didn't happen as quickly as you wanted it to.

On most days, she spent hours shooting with the Marlin, going through the stack of paper targets Mr. Peake had given her. She'd sighted in her Marlin for the Winchester long-rifle cartridges at thirty to fifty feet for hunting small game, and she was learning to adjust her sight picture to other distances and ammo. Brian brought her mostly longs and long-rifles, but occasionally shorts or something like low-velocity CB cartridges, which fired quietly and didn't penetrate the target as deeply. She shot enough with her left hand that she became fairly accurate — Annie Oakley had been able to shoot expertly with both hands, according to *Little Sure Shot*. For plinking, Brian had gotten hold of a four-tang auto-reset target similar to the one she'd had in Murrayville. Once in a while she took out the shotgun Brian had given her and blew apart plastic bottles and pieces of trash she'd found floating in the current. This variety of targets helped her resist shooting another buck out of season, though she saw them often enough drinking at the river.

When Brian forgot to get her ammunition, Margo didn't want to bother him about it. A couple of times she put his outboard motor on *The River Rose* and went upstream to Heart of Pines to the grocery store to get a brick of ammo and some food. Before going inside, she pulled a stocking cap over her long hair, and no one at the store paid her any special attention. She loved the freedom of traveling alone. She spent the forty dollars she had and wanted to cash the money order from her mother, but she feared for her name coming up at the post office. As far away as she felt from home, Heart of Pines was only thirty-five miles upstream from Murrayville. The DNR official who she feared would find her dead doe was the same guy who could have nailed her for killing more than her fair share back home. She had visited the doe's body all spring, kept her covered with branches, and noted, day by day, how much of her the coyotes, raccoons, and crows had eaten, how her skeleton collapsed with the cartilage fetus inside, how her bones disappeared from the heap one after another. Last week, she had been able to pluck her deer slug from the flattened remains.

As the weather warmed and the ground thawed, Brian picked up jobs removing trees, landscaping, and digging, either using machines he rented or a shovel when it was a tight space or when folks were worried about the ornamental bushes over their septic tanks. Margo didn't miss her father any less as the weather warmed, but by then her body had absorbed the habit of sadness, so that sadness flowed all through her and became a natural part of her movements. Missing her mother was different; her mother was an agitation and a puzzle. She tried to imagine situations her mother might be in that were so *delicate* that they couldn't meet, not even for a visit. Was her mother being held prisoner? Was she taking care of some man's children, a dozen of them, so that she couldn't take care of one more person? Luanne should have known that Margo didn't need much taking care of.

The most satisfying part of Margo's days was watching the yellow dog downstream on the opposite bank. The creature hardly ever barked, and it remained still for as much as an hour, its nose just above the water. Whenever the man or the woman returned home and let the dog out, whenever it bounded to the water's edge, Margo shared its pleasure at being released. In the early spring, the woman seemed to be gone more often, and then the woman and her car stopped appearing at the house at all. After that, in early May, she watched the man spend hours alone in the evening, repairing the oil-barrel float before launching it and setting out the gangplank, trimming the hedges around the house, and painting the little shed. She watched the man sweep debris off the roof of the house and then watched him clean the gutters, even wiping them with a towel. Brian's cabin didn't have gutters.

The first night Margo saw Brian drunk as a skunk, she was sitting up late, cleaning the shotgun, when she heard the sound of his boat pulling up to the dock. Paul and another man wrestled Brian up the stairs and onto the screen porch.

'Here's your man,' Paul said. 'Do what you want with him. He was too drunk to drive himself. We passed a sheriff's boat on the way down, so we're all going to stay the night here.'

She determined from the slowness of Paul's gaze, as it moved from her throat to her face, that Paul, too, was drunk.

'Paul dropped his glasses in the drink.' Brian got up from the couch on the porch where they had placed him and stumbled to the doorway and stood there.

'You knocked my goddamned glasses in the drink,' Paul said. 'I didn't drop them.'

'Sorry about that, bro. Listen,' he said, but then seemed to forget what he was going to say.

Margo knew it would take forty-five minutes to get the place warm again after the men had left the door wide open for this long.

'What's your point, Brian?' Paul said.

'Well, I know I love my brother. I love you, man. And I'm sorry I shot you in the eye.' He supported himself on the doorframe, and then suddenly lurched toward the table, knocking dishes to the floor. A plate and a glass broke. Margo's gun-cleaning supplies scattered. She righted her bottle of solvent before much leaked out, but the oily smell filled the room.

She picked up the pieces of the orange plate. Brian grabbed her shoulder and pulled her onto his lap so suddenly that she cut herself on a shard. Blood dripped onto the Annie Oakley book on the table, onto a depiction of a frowning Sitting Bull, who had given Annie the name Little Sure Shot. Margo felt embarrassed for these men to see she was reading a children's book. It was meant for the nine-year-old she had been when Joanna had given it to her.

'Oh, damn,' he said when he saw the blood on her forearm. He bent his head and closed his mouth around the wound. And as he did, she noticed that the knuckles were bleeding on his scarred right hand. 'I didn't mean to hurt you, Maggie. Your blood tastes sweet like wine.'

'What happened to your hand?' She settled into his lap. There was no rag on the table, so she used her sleeve to dab the blood off the book.

'You know, Pauly tells me he's still off the

108

drugs. I'm so fucking proud of my little brother. Brother,' he slurred, 'I'm fucking proud, and I'm not going to deny it.'

'Oh, shut up, Brian,' Paul said.

Margo didn't realize she was staring at Paul, but he turned sideways to see her through his better eye and said quietly, 'Stop always staring at me that way. It drives me crazy. I don't know what you're looking for.'

Margo thought he would not have spoken to her so harshly if Brian were sober. When Paul entered the cabin, the other man appeared in the doorway behind him and raised his hand in greeting.

'Maggie, this is Johnny. A half-wit from Kalamazoo,' Paul said. The blond man with gray eyes followed Paul into the room, wavering, as drunk as Brian but lighter-bodied. 'He'll sleep on the couch, and I'll sleep on the screen porch,' Paul said. 'That way I won't have to listen to any of these assholes snore.'

Brian stood and slurred, 'I'm going to pass out.' He stumbled into the bedroom and fell onto the bed with his clothes on, including his big insulated canvas jacket. Margo wondered how on earth she would get into the bed and under the covers with him lying there like that.

Johnny winked at Margo as she unrolled her old army sleeping bag for him. 'Paul says I'm a fool, but I know what I see.' Johnny laughed and plopped onto the couch.

'Yeah, you're a fool,' Paul said. 'You signed away your birthright for whiskey money.'

'I'm not a farmer,' Johnny said. 'I never

wanted to be a farmer.'

Paul shook his head and returned to the porch. Johnny did not seem inclined to do anything with the sleeping bag other than pet it with his hand. He looked at Margo and slurred the word 'beautiful' a few times, and Margo found she didn't mind the attention. She realized that Johnny was the blond guy who had been passed out on the Playbuoy, the man who fondled the deer carcass she had sold to Brian in Murrayville. That moment had been funny enough that she laughed a little remembering it. Of course, Johnny had not even seen her that day. And as drunk as he was now, he probably wouldn't recognize her next time he saw her.

When Johnny fell over sideways, he finally pulled his legs up and shifted into a lying position. Margo leaned over and covered him as Brian had once covered her. When she adjusted the sleeping bag, he grabbed her arm and pulled her down close to him. To avoid having her face so close to his, she turned away and ended up sitting on the edge of the couch, her backside against his chest. He snaked both arms around her waist and then tickled her ribs until she giggled. He whispered, 'You need to get out of this place and have a little fun, girl.'

He gradually loosened his grip until his arms were draped lightly around her. Margo had seen female dogs and pigs stand still for males when it was clear they meant to run away. She didn't mind this weightless feeling of indecision.

'I wish it was summer,' he whispered. The kerosene lamp turned down low made Johnny's

110

skin look smooth, made his eyes glitter. He smelled good, she thought, less musky and less smoky than Brian. 'We could go skinny-dipping.'

Margo didn't intend for anything to happen with her and Johnny, but she wanted to remain in this strange moment for a while, to figure out what this feeling was. The moment did not seem to have anything to do with Brian. Instead, she was thinking about her mother, wondering if her mother might have left her father just to have a lighthearted moment with another man. Her father had not taken her mother out on a date since they'd been married, Luanne used to complain.

When Margo sensed somebody watching her, she looked up to see Paul in the doorway holding boat cushions.

'What the hell is this?' he said. He shook his head as though confirming something he'd known all along. Margo stood up, let Johnny's hands drop, and moved to the bedroom. She felt Paul's gaze on her until she went inside and closed the door.

'Do you want to get yourself killed, asshole?' Paul said behind her. 'Just fuck with my brother's precious river princess while he's in the next room.'

Meanwhile, Brian had gotten himself out of his jacket and under the covers. As Margo climbed in, he made space for her. He laid a heavy arm over her.

A month later when Brian arrived home drunk again, this time alone, he crashed his boat into the dock with enough force that he cracked some boards. He cursed as he entered the cabin. Margo saw the neck of a pint bottle sticking out of his jacket pocket. Usually she'd seen him with half-pint bottles.

'Who's been here with you? I smell a man.' His voice was blunt.

'No one's been here.' Margo moved around so she was closer to the door, just in case she had to run outside to get away from him. There was something different in him tonight. She'd seen this in Crane the one time he'd struck her — it was about a month after the trouble with Cal, and Crane had demanded she speak to him. When she remained silent, he slapped her face, only his hand was half curled into a fist. Afterward, he went out and sat in his truck and didn't come back in until Margo was asleep. In the morning she discovered she had a broken blood vessel in the corner of that eye, a blood mark spreading over the cornea, and a bruise had formed under her eye. Crane had never taken a drink of alcohol again.

'Are you two-timing me, Maggie?' He stepped into the center of the room.

'No.' She studied the door. She would not hesitate to run.

'Are you a two-timing slut?' Brian slurred. He sounded a little tentative, as though he were less certain about his words than usual.

'No,' she said. That word had hit her hard coming out of Cal's mouth — it had hurt her feelings — but now it made her angry. She said, 'Why do guys want to call girls sluts?'

Brian sat at the table, and she sat across from him. He lit a cigarette and studied her. While she sat quietly mending the collar of her jacket, he tapped his fingers. Finally he crushed out the cigarette and said, 'Okay, Maggie, I won't call you that again. I was just worried. You know I love you.'

She reached across the table and touched the scars on his hand. 'Why are you getting mean?'

'I worried that maybe you weren't alone. Something Pauly said. I couldn't stand for anybody else to slip in and have you.'

'If you're not here, I'm alone, Brian. I got nobody else. I don't even have a dog. I need to find my mom, but she doesn't want me. Why hasn't she written back telling me to come, even just for a visit?'

'Did you tell her your daddy got shot?'

'No.'

'Maybe you ought to tell her. Maybe she doesn't know.'

Margo shrugged. She had tried, but couldn't bring herself to write the words.

'Don't worry, Maggie. You got me. I'll always take care of you,' he said. 'Maggie, how much would you do for me? Would you kill for me?'

'I killed that rabbit for you. It's overcooked now.' She had thought of Brian the whole time she'd skinned and cleaned it at the edge of the river, thought of how he'd enjoy eating it. She had started making a blanket of rabbit skins, cured with salt, something to put over their bed.

It was the softest thing to touch on the fur side. Everything she did now was tangled up with Brian, for better or for worse.

'Would you kill a man for me?' He held her wrist while he waited for her answer.

'If a man was going to kill you, I'd kill him.'

'I've never known a woman who'd kill for me. I'd kill a man for you,' he said loudly, as though showing off for someone who wasn't there. 'I'd kill my own brother if he messed with you, Maggie. If I ever see Cal Murray again, I'll kill him.'

'Nobody has to kill anybody,' she said. 'You're hurting my wrist.'

'Oh.' Brian pulled away with exaggerated care. 'I don't want to hurt you.' He reached out clumsily to touch her hair at the side of her face, and the motion, performed in drunken slowness, spooked her. 'I promised myself when you came to me that I'd never hurt you, that I'd always be gentle. I told God, I said to God in my head, *If she'll stay with me, I'll treat her good*. Please don't leave me, Maggie. Promise you won't leave me.'

Margo would have liked to ask him not to drink whiskey, but she knew he wouldn't listen when he was this drunk. The best thing now would be to get him to bed.

'Where else would I go, Brian? I got nobody else.'

'I never knew I'd be so lucky, to have a girl like you in my life, a beautiful girl who cooks me dinner and makes love with me and doesn't ask me for anything.' He pulled her around the table to sit on his lap, and he wrapped both arms around her. Margo usually liked the feeling of being contained by and connected to Brian — it was like being attached to a powerful weapon.

When Brian went outside to relieve himself, Margo sat at the table listening to the croaking snore of leopard frogs through the walls. She wondered how much longer she could stay here.

'I'm doing my best, Daddy,' she whispered, in case Crane was aware of what was going on. 'Don't worry about me.' This was the first time she had spoken aloud to him. If there was a heaven or hell, Margo worried about how Crane was getting along in either place without her.

━━━━━━▬

The river never flooded that year. The late spring rains were steady and mild. It wasn't until June that the first pair of seventy-degree days came up with a wind out of the south. Brian came home from the bar on the second of those warm days with his knuckles cut up again. A man had taken his jacket, he said.

'You let somebody take your jacket, he thinks he owns you. You don't know what he'll do after that. Next thing you know, he'll be screwing your woman.'

Margo looked at him, startled.

'You know about evening the score, girl. I know you understand that. I know you'll get even with your cousin someday.'

She nodded. She knew better than to want revenge, but she couldn't let go of her desire for

115

it. She did not tell Brian what else she knew and knew too well: you couldn't always keep things even, that in trying to keep things even, you could lose everything.

9

One day in August, Brian went to town and did not return by nightfall or by the next morning. Several days later, he had still not come home. Each morning when Margo woke up alone she listened for a long time to a phoebe calling its own name from a branch outside the window, until she could copy it perfectly. Each night he was gone, she listened to the orchestra of crickets, cicadas, and tree frogs and wrote letters to her mother. Sometimes she tried to sound lighthearted, and other times she demanded Luanne explain about her *delicate situation*. Whenever she finished a letter, she tore the paper into pieces and sprinkled them on the water from Brian's dock.

For the last few months she had feared Brian coming home drunk, but now she worried he might not come back at all. At first she found sleeping difficult without his big body beside her, but she soon was stretching out and using the extra space.

At dusk on the eighth night, Margo saw the Playbuoy coming downstream. She stood on the dock and waved. The black-haired, bearded driver turned out to be Paul. At the noise of the boat's big outboard motor, the yellow dog across the river moved up the lawn toward its house, and a great blue heron that must have been fishing below the cabin launched itself into flight. Margo watched it ascend. Another guy was with Paul, not Johnny, but a smaller man. She hoped they had brought some meat or store-bought food. She was tired of eating fish. She had run out of rifle cartridges and shotgun shells and had no money left to buy more until she got up her nerve to cash her money order. She grabbed the siderail of the boat as Paul idled alongside the dock. The boat was riding heavy in the water.

'You got Brian's boat,' Margo shouted. Paul cut the engine just as she asked, 'Where is he?'

Margo was shocked to hear her own voice over the river sounds. She had not spoken aloud in a while, and she didn't usually talk to Paul at all. There was something in the center of the boat, covered by a blue tarp. By its shape, she figured it was a fifty-five-gallon plastic drum. That explained why the boat was sunk up over its pontoons. Water sloshed over the Astroturf carpeting.

'Brian's in jail.'

'For what?'

'For beating on Cal Murray.'

'What? He didn't hurt him?'

'The hell he didn't. He hurt him bad. Did it for you.'

'I never asked him to do anything to Cal.' Margo felt spooked by the intensity of Paul's voice.

Paul got out of the boat and tied it off. 'Brian should have known better, but he couldn't stand it when Cal Murray walked in the bar like he owned it. Cal thinks he owns Murrayville.'

Cal did own Murrayville, thought Margo, didn't he? 'What happened?'

'It ain't good,' Paul said. He turned his head to favor his bad eye. 'Stop staring at me, damn it.'

Margo had not meant to stare. She looked back at the cabin. The green building, tippy on its stilts, blurred as her eyes filled with tears. Margo wiped her face and pointed at the fish pail that Paul was lifting off the boat. 'Give me that,' she said.

'Maggie, honey, crying about it ain't going to do him any good. There's nothing that's going to do him any good except a better lawyer than he can afford.' Paul's voice turned softer. He rested the bucket on the dock and put his arms around her. Paul was a little fatter than his brother. She thought he smelled odd, of ammonia. She thought of pushing him away and running, but it would be crazy to run into the woods, which were full of stinging nettles and poison ivy.

She pulled away from the embrace and grabbed the bucket, sloshing water on herself and Paul. Two of the three bullhead catfish inside were the length of her forearms, with long barbels. Those seaweedy whiskers brushed the sides of the bucket as the fish slid over one another. 'These are big catfish,' she said.

'They come from around Willow Island upstream,' Paul said.

'Who you got with you?' she asked. The other man had made no motions to disembark, as though waiting for the signal from Paul.

'That's just Charlie. He works at the plant

119

with me.' Paul had long held a job at a pharmaceutical plant that made generic drugs. Paul was a *factory rat*, Brian said, though Paul didn't like the phrase. Charlie was skinny, and one cheek was sunken where he was missing some teeth.

Paul took the fish from the bucket one by one, used his knife to slit the skin all the way around their necks, and nailed each head to the nearest oak; the three tails strained and curled against the bark. The men stood by while Margo stunned one with a hammer and began tearing off its skin with pliers.

'Tell me what happened.' Though she knew better, Margo brushed against the catfish dorsal fin, and her middle finger burned.

'Well, we left The Pub and was at The Tap Room in Murrayville having a few beers, and Brian and this guy he's playing pool with get to arguing, and then Cal Murray comes in. It's like my brother has been waiting for Cal Murray but Cal's been keeping a low profile. So Brian says to him, 'I heard a guy shot your dick off. Heard all you got now is a nasty little stub,' which is funny, but everybody's scared to laugh. Cal Murray asks Brian does he want to suck it, and Brian tells him there ain't no forgiving what you done to that girl. Brian hits him a couple times, and Cal don't hardly even defend himself, which seems odd. I don't know if he was drunk or what. Brian pushes him down some stairs, don't seem to notice Cal isn't fighting back, so he stomps the shit out of him on the steps. He broke both Cal's legs.'

'What?' The fish skin split.

'Broke bones in his legs. You heard me.'

Margo took a deep breath and regripped the skin with her pliers. 'Why'd you guys go to Murrayville?'

'It's a free country, that's what Brian said. We can drink anywhere we want. But you know it's been eating away at Brian what you said Cal done to you. He didn't have any choice but to fight him.'

Margo had never seen Brian hit anybody, but she could imagine him, drunk beyond talking to, slugging and kicking Cal. Margo's finger trailed the pectoral fin of the catfish. The pain was so sharp this time she was surprised not to see blood on her knuckle. Brian was a weapon, all right, but more like a land mine or a grenade than a gun or a knife.

'Next thing you know, the ambulance and the cops are there, and Brian's going to jail. And now that they got him locked up, they're getting him for killing that man.'

'Cal's not dead, is he?'

'No. It's the manslaughter charge.'

'What manslaughter charge?'

'Well, whatever the hell they're calling it. Up in Rapid River, in the UP last summer. Brian must've told you. Why do you think he's been out here in the woods laying low?'

The trees became thicker and taller around her. She tugged on the second catfish skin, trying not to let it split, but she stung her wrist on the spine of a dorsal fin and jerked away, making a mess of it. As she worked, the half-skinned

121

catfish woke up. It curled its tail out away from the tree, still trying to swim.

'Hey, Charlie, toss me a beer,' Paul said. Margo looked up to see the can fly through the air with surprising speed and accuracy. Paul caught it with a smack, and when he opened it, foam poured onto his hand. 'I thought you knew, Maggie.'

She worked slowly with the pliers on the last catfish, tugging around the sides evenly, removing the skin in one piece down to the tail and slicing it free. If what Brian had done in the UP was an accident, why hadn't he mentioned it?

'All the police had on that trouble up north was a description, but it included them knife scars on the back of his hand. It was the same deal, Brian drunk and not knowing when to quit.'

'Can I see him?'

'It'd be better if you didn't, honey. His wife isn't going to like you.'

'His ex-wife.'

'He's got an ex-wife, his first wife. He was planning on getting a divorce from his second wife soon, but the dumb son of a bitch hadn't told her about it yet. He was hoping she'd take up with another guy, make it easier, get him better terms for the divorce. I'm not saying they were together exactly, but now she's rallying 'round him. And she can do him more good now than you can.'

Inside the cabin, Margo moved numbly. She filleted and fried the catfish the way she would have for Brian, with cornmeal and flour, in the last of the bacon grease, which was on the verge of going rancid. When they finished eating, Paul turned on a brand-new battery-powered lantern with a humming fluorescent bulb. Margo was distressed at how bug-stained the walls were, how ratty the rug looked in the cold bluish light, and how grimy she had let herself become. She pulled her braid over her shoulder and looked at how frayed it was. Paul and Charlie took the lantern outside and started digging a hole with round-end shovels, and Margo was grateful to be out of the harsh light. She undid her braid and brushed her hair. When Paul came inside to get another beer, she asked him to tell her more.

'There ain't nothing more to it.'

'Does Brian own this cabin?' she asked.

'Me and Brian own it together. You can stay here as long as you want, Maggie. Don't you worry your pretty head about that. But I'm going to be storing a few things here, and I got to warn you, don't touch any of them. You'd better take me seriously when I say that.'

'What's in that barrel?' Margo noticed that Paul's hiking boots looked brand-new, as did his watch.

'Don't you worry about what it is, Maggie. I've got a drum full of a very valuable substance, and you're just going to have to leave it alone.'

She nodded. 'Do you know if Brian checked his PO box?'

'I wouldn't know,' Paul said.

'Maybe my ma wrote a letter saying she wants me to come.'

'He didn't say nothing about a letter. I can ask him next time I visit him.'

When Paul went back out to dig more, Margo washed the dishes with water she'd lugged in and heated on the propane stove.

Margo didn't usually drink, but she needed to do something different as a kind of protest against this new situation. She opened a beer and, though the first few sips sickened her, she drank it down. She folded up the letter she'd been writing to her mother — in it she'd asked what Luanne thought about being loyal to a man, what it was worth. All these questions she was asking her ma added up to one question: how should Margo live? She had chosen this life for now, and she had chosen Brian to be her anchor, keeping her steady and in place. Now she was adrift. She opened a second beer and found she didn't mind the taste so much. After finishing the dishes, while the men were still working outside, she reread her mother's old letter on the yellow stationery with the bumblebees — the flower scent had faded — and she drank a third beer. Afterward, she stumbled to the bedroom and passed out.

Just before sunrise, she awoke with a parched mouth and a headache, and with a man's heavy arm over her in the bed. She gasped when she realized it was Paul beside her. She extricated herself with difficulty. After more than a week without Brian, Margo had almost forgotten how a big man generated heat around him. The bedroom was stifling. She was grateful he was dead asleep, more grateful to find herself still fully clothed. She heated water for instant coffee. There wasn't much propane left; Brian had intended to get some in town the day he disappeared. Charlie was curled in a strange position, half on, half off the narrow couch.

She carried her coffee outside, and from the dock she watched the Jeep pull away from the yellow house downstream. She admired the straight diagonal lines the man had mowed into his lawn, all the way down to the river, where he trimmed with a weed whip he swung like a golf club. In contrast to the rangy wild bushes on her side, the hedges around his house were trimmed flat as tabletops. She looked forward to this evening, after Paul and Charlie were gone, when the man would come home and let his dog out to hunker at the river's edge. The dog was able to catch fish in its jaws; she'd seen it do so a half dozen times.

Margo found her siphon hose and sucked gas out of the Playbuoy's tank into a milk jug, enough to mix with two-stroke oil for a trip up to Heart of Pines with the small outboard motor, or two trips maybe, if she rowed back down without power. Or maybe she would take a fishing trip to Willow Island, where one time she had seen a heron carry a snake up to its chicks in the trees.

Margo had never given Brian any details about her and Cal, had never suggested he should punish Cal.

She rinsed the fuel taste from her mouth with

coffee, spat it into the river. She thought she might be okay living alone here, having the bed to herself, making the breakfast she wanted at the time she wanted, not worrying about what state Brian would be in when he got home from work or the bar. She would have to cash the money order and lay in supplies for the winter, including bacon, flour, and powdered milk. Maybe she would make bread, something she hadn't gotten around to doing. She would miss Brian, but if she could stay here, she could survive on her own. She would get ammo and sleep with her rifle beside her.

Charlie was stirring on the couch. Margo sifted meal-moth larvae out of the last of the flour for pancakes. Paul and Charlie would appreciate a cooked breakfast. She opened a beer, poured half of it into her dry ingredients, and then handed the open can to Charlie, who sat up to accept it. He tipped it up and drank the remainder in one long slug.

'Are you hungry, Charlie?' she asked. 'Did you sleep good?'

'You's got a toilet around here?' he asked. She led him outside and directed him along the path that led to the outhouse.

Paul called her name from the bedroom. She pushed open the door and stepped inside, where she smelled smoke that wasn't from cigarettes. She saw a glass pipe on the windowsill by the bed, alongside a pack of matches. He turned to favor his bad eye.

'I'm mixing pancakes,' she said. 'Charlie went to the outhouse.'

'Come here, river princess.' He grabbed her before she'd even realized she was within reach of him. He pulled her down onto the bed.

'Paul, what?'

'Kiss me,' he said.

'No, Paul. What if Brian . . . ?'

'Brian's not here. He's not going to be here.'

'No. Don't,' she said, but he pulled her against him.

He seemed not to notice her complaints. He pulled down her loose jeans without unzipping them — she had grown thinner in these last months — and pushed her T-shirt up around her shoulders. She bent her knees and tried to sit up, but he held her down with one hand and ran the other along her stomach and over her right breast. In school she had wrenched away from boys who had grabbed her in the stair-well, but she had never fought a big man. She tried to push Paul away, tried to get her feet up to kick. As her leg came up, he pushed her knee out to the side and heaved himself onto her. When she continued to push at him, he flipped her over with an ease that shocked her. His fingers held her down like straps. She had always thought of herself as strong, but compared to Paul she was nothing. She yelled and tried to push him off.

While her arms were trapped beneath her, he forced her onto her stomach and worked his way into her. She cried out loudly enough that Charlie would have heard her if he'd returned from the outhouse, but there was no sound from the next room. She couldn't take in a full breath, crushed as she was against the mattress, and she

127

feared she was suffocating. The time she had crawled beneath the buck's carcass back in Murrayville, she had been able to calm herself, but there was no way to be calm with Paul on her. She tried to lift herself to throw Paul off, but he was heavier than the buck. She smelled Brian's musk in the sheets and Paul's sweat and rotten breath. She wished for him to be as dead as that buck. When she croaked his name and begged him to stop again, he responded, 'Oh, Maggie,' as though she had said something sweet. She struggled to free her arms until she felt too weak to struggle anymore. Paul was on her for a long time.

After he rolled away to the other side of the bed, he looked at her and smiled. She wanted to punch him and kick him, but she feared he would grab her fist or foot if she did, and more than anything she wanted to get away from him. She picked her clothes up off the floor and carried them into the other room. She dressed with shaking hands and wished she had more clothes to put on. Her rifle and shotgun were in the rack beside her, useless without ammunition, though the shotgun might work as a club until Paul could wrestle it out of her hands. She had wasted her cartridges on target practice, expecting Brian to bring her more. From now on, she knew better. She would count on no one to help or protect her.

She tied her boots, buttoned her shirt. She thought about running into the woods in order not to face Paul, but she did not want to leave her boat behind. She could get in her boat and row away from the cabin, but in the pontoon boat he could chase her down if he wanted. And there was no point of leaving now that he had already done what he had wanted to do with her. Once she was dressed, she picked up the butcher knife and moved to the bedroom doorway. While she stood there, she tested the sharpness by puncturing her skin near her wrist. A drop of blood formed there. If he came after her again, she would protect herself with it.

'I ain't used an outhouse in years,' said Charlie, as he entered the cabin from the screen porch. 'It's mighty relaxing.'

Margo returned to her pancake batter and put down the knife.

'You making us breakfast?' Charlie asked. 'You're a nice girl.'

'Charlie, do you do drugs?'

'Nosirree,' he said. 'But Paul says that shit out there's going to make us some serious money.'

'How about Paul? Brian said he was off the drugs.'

Charlie shrugged. When he looked away, Margo spat into the pancake batter. She saw the dozen meal-moth larvae were still in the sifter, so she dumped those in and stirred.

———

As Paul and Charlie powered upstream, Margo traced their progress with the barrel of her unloaded rifle, sized Paul up as a target, and dry-fired at him. Before pulling away, Paul had given her food from his cooler — a hunk of cheese with a hardened edge, summer sausage, and a couple sleeves of saltines — and though she thought of knocking it all off the table where he'd placed it, she was too hungry to waste it. When Paul had tried to kiss her mouth before boarding the Playbuoy, she moved away and spit on the ground. He laughed as though she'd been making a joke. Later Margo discovered two twenty-dollar bills on her pillow.

She went back outside, took off her jeans, squatted beside the pump, and scrubbed between her legs with the cold water until she felt raw.

She slung her empty rifle over her shoulder to feel its weight, and the rope dug into her shoulder. It had been hurting her for a while. She found two leather belts on a wall hook in the bedroom and cut both buckles off. She punched holes in them with a hammer and a Phillips screwdriver, sewed them together with fish line, and threaded the leather through the sling swivels. She practiced to get the length right, flipping the rifle from her left side quickly up to aim and press the trigger with her right index finger. When she finished, she thought her homemade hasty sling felt as fine and solid as the one on her daddy's old Remington, the rifle with which she'd performed that miracle of winning the 4-H competition.

Margo made herself a supper of cheese, crackers, summer sausage, and wild blackberries and was grateful not to be eating fish.

Though she knew revenge was as likely to hurt as it was to heal, she hoped she would make Paul regret what he had done.

Hours later, after the Jeep returned to the house across the river, the fishing dog appeared in its usual place on the water's edge. To lighten the boat, Margo lifted off Brian's outboard and placed it carefully on blocks so as not to bend the propeller, and then she rowed across. She had never touched the fishing dog or even seen it up close, but when she called, the dog walked out onto the oil-barrel float and stepped down into her boat without hesitation. Margo petted the yellow head. 'I'll call you King,' she whispered, thinking of the big-headed kingfisher bird who had always fished just upstream from her house in Murrayville.

Then she noticed that this was absolutely a female fishing dog, a female kingfisher, a female king.

She didn't consider it stealing when she rowed the dog back to her side of the river and let her out to sniff the water's edge. She always used to row the Murrays' dog Moe across the river to her side for a visit. If this dog wanted to stay and chase raccoons up trees, that was her choice. Margo followed the dog on foot along the river and into the woods. With a companion like a fishing dog, Margo wouldn't mind staying here alone. She could train the dog to bark when an intruder came. But it wasn't long before Margo heard a man's voice shouting, 'Cleo! Where are you? Come, Cleo!' The dog jumped off the river-bank, plunged into the water, and swam downstream and to the other side. She shook herself and ran up the lawn to greet the man.

Margo looked around where the dog had been sniffing, and she found some ragged shelf fungus, yellow as an egg yolk, growing on the base of a tree: a chicken-of-the-woods mushroom. Clearly this dog was good luck. She snapped off a hunk of mushroom and brushed away a few ants. She would cook it for dinner tomorrow with her last two chicken bouillon cubes.

A week of heavy rain made Margo a prisoner in the cabin. When Brian was there she hadn't minded being without a phone or a radio, but now she longed to hear a voice. The rain banged on the tin roof, reminding her of the sound of rain on the roof of the big Murray barn. The water rose until it was level with the dock. Most kids her age would have been getting ready to go back to school in a few weeks; Margo hadn't looked forward to school in past years, but at least school would have put her with other people. She wished Brian had more books at the cabin, something besides the guidebooks for tying knots and identifying animal tracks, both of which she'd read and reread.

The first day the rains let up, Margo crossed the river. She called the dog out to the float, and the dog jumped in her boat. But before Margo could push off, the man appeared from behind the shed and stepped knee-deep into the water in his swim trunks and tennis shoes. He grabbed the back end of her boat. He was thin and at least a few inches taller than Margo. 'Evening,' he said calmly. 'Where are you taking my dog?'

'A-cr-cr-cross the river. I live over there.' She glanced behind her at the dog sitting on the prow seat. The dog's mouth was open in what looked like a smile. She barked happily.

'I know where you live, but why are you taking my dog?' His biceps strained against his bones. Tendons stood out on one side of his neck, and he was losing his balance as Margo continued rowing in place. 'You're just plain not going to answer me.'

Mosquitoes landed on Margo's legs and arms, and they bothered the man, too. When he let go of her boat with one hand to swat at them, Margo broke free. The man folded his arms and stood in the water watching her, looking more perplexed than angry as she rowed away.

'Cleo, you and I probably need to have a talk,' the man said in a loud but conversational voice. To Margo's relief, he did not call the dog right away. His figure grew smaller as she rowed upstream and approached the cabin. She parked at the dock, and King jumped over the side of the boat and swam to shallower water to sniff along the muskrat holes and twisted roots. The man across the river disappeared and returned with binoculars. A while later he called, 'Cleo!' and the dog dove into the water and headed home.

A few days later, Margo motored to the gas station at Heart of Pines to buy food, ammo, toilet paper, and bottled gas with the money Paul had left. She had not dared bring her rifle. She couldn't carry it into the store for fear someone might recognize it as Cal's, but she didn't want to leave it in the boat and risk it being stolen. She tied her boat a ways from the other boats and draped her tarp over it. Inside the store, she added up prices, calculated tax in her head, and managed to put together a purchase totaling $33.82. She had planned to buy gasoline, but there was a line at the single pump and she didn't want to wait around with the dozen men who were hanging out there. She figured she would get gas next time.

Halfway back, just above Willow Island, she cut the engine and floated downstream with the current to save gas, rowing only to fix her direction, keeping an eye out for dogs, birds, and kids — any sign of life — along the water's edge. The miles of dark, empty river belonged to her. She drifted near the riverbank and imagined some people inviting her to a meal or just to sit and listen to stories. Instead, as she rounded the last bend above her cabin, she saw Brian's boat parked at the dock. A bright, cold light shone from inside the cabin — Paul's fluorescent lantern. She steered herself toward the opposite bank and hoped Paul would not be watching the river as she floated past. She pulled over at a snag just below the yellow house and watched the cabin until she saw Paul and Johnny go outside. A few minutes later, they returned to the cabin, carrying a jug of something. She wished she had taken her chances with her rifle and hadn't left it under the bed with her backpack. The night grew darker, and she waited for the men to leave, but they did not. A half-moon appeared and disappeared behind the trees. The night grew cool. When their light went out, she unfolded her canvas tarp and curled atop it on the boat's back seat. She pulled the rest of the tarp over her like a blanket and used her orange life vest as a pillow.

Margo awoke shivering to the sound of barking. The light of the rising sun was diffuse behind a haze of clouds. She was no longer in the boat, but was wrapped in her tarp in the sand. And then King was beside her, licking her face. Margo studied the beautiful eyes and perfect dark nose. She pushed her fingers into the dog's fur, but when she saw a man standing over her, she stood up, stepped into her boat, and fumbled with her oars. 'I'm sorry,' Margo said.

'Sorry for what?'

'For taking your dog.'

He shrugged. 'Dogs are loyal. You feed them, and they come back to you.' He nodded upstream toward her cabin. 'If you're hiding from this guy, you can come to my house. Once the sun rises, he might see you if you stay out here.'

With the sun rising behind him, the man's face was in shadow, but he seemed harmless. He hadn't bothered her about his dog, even. Unsure what else to do, but sure she did not want to be seen by Paul, she decided to trust him. She checked the rope and knot she'd tied around a fallen maple, a clove hitch, according to Brian's book. She had also learned the name of the knot on the ring at her boat's prow: round turn and two half hitches. The spray of leaves along the branch would camouflage the boat so long as no one was looking right at it. So long as Paul hadn't replaced his glasses, there was nothing to worry about. She carried her oars and the bag from the store and followed the man along the river path. The dew that coated the weeds and grass soaked the bottom of her pant legs. Where the poison ivy had climbed to the tops of trees for sunlight, she saw those triple leaves had already turned blood-red. Autumn was coming.

Margo put down her oars, food, and ammunition before they entered the yellow house by the side door. She found herself in a kitchen with white walls, yellow countertops flecked with black and white, and a glossy wooden floor. But the baseboards were missing, revealing an uneven gap at the bottom of the wall around the room. Though the kitchen counters were clean and orderly and the floor was swept, the table was comfortably messy with newspapers and books. 'Bathroom's through there if you need it. Do you drink coffee?' the man asked.

She nodded and ventured through the kitchen, into what should have been a living room but contained a big bed with an unwrinkled bedspread. She walked around it and looked through the sliding glass door. Upstream, parked at the dilapidated green cabin on stilts, was the Playbuoy. She unlocked the glass door and tugged it open a few inches, to assure herself she could leave that way if she needed to.

The top drawer of a dresser at the foot of the bed was open a few inches, exposing a cache of white bras and underwear. She traced her finger along the scalloped lace edge of a bra. These were the kinds of fancy underthings her mother used to like to wear, and now probably wore all the time in Lake Lynne. Luanne had complained about how the iron in the water stained her white clothes, just as she had complained about the green mold that crept over her leather shoes in the closet.

When the man appeared in the doorway, Margo hurriedly shut the drawer.

'Oh, don't worry. She's long gone. I guess she left those for my next girlfriend.'

'I'm sorry.'

The man handed Margo a mug of coffee, light with cream. She and Brian drank their coffee strong and black, and what they had at the cabin was instant. She inhaled the aroma from the cup so deeply that she had to touch the dresser to steady herself. She had eaten potato chips from the gas station in Heart of Pines yesterday, but nothing else.

'Do you want to take a shower?' he asked.

'No, thank you.'

'You can't wear those wet clothes. Take something of Danielle's.'

Margo looked at the dresser and back at him.

He laughed. 'I was going to throw all her

clothes in the river, anyway, let them float downstream. Go ahead and take anything you want out of there.'

Margo kept her eyes on the fishing dog lying on a rug at the foot of the bed, and after a minute the man went back into the kitchen. She took a long draw of the coffee, which tasted so good she didn't want to swallow.

She looked for a place to rest her cup, but she didn't want to leave a ring on the dresser top. In fact, she didn't want to leave any trace of herself. Finally, she set the cup on the unfinished plywood floor. In the middle dresser drawer she found neatly folded blouses in pink, white, and mint green. The other dresser contained the man's blue jeans. She put on a faded pair and cinched the waist with the most worn of his belts and cuffed the legs. In the same drawer, she found a T-shirt and a dark blue sweatshirt. She draped her muddy clothes over the side of the tub in the adjoining bathroom.

She retrieved her coffee from the plywood floor. Another room opened off this one and was probably supposed to be the bedroom, when it wasn't torn down to wall studs. In the middle of the room, balanced on sawhorses, was the curved wooden skeleton of a rowboat, bigger and deeper than her flat-bottomed boat. Back in the kitchen, she found the man cooking, and she might have felt at ease if only her gun and her backpack were leaning in the corner by that corn broom rather than lying under the bed wrapped in rabbit skins at the cabin with Paul. The man apologized for what he called 'this mess' and placed items on the round table one at a time. Each thing glowed as it passed through a shaft of sunlight: plates, forks, two glistening jars of preserves, and a stick of yellow-white butter in a glass dish. She wondered if she was losing her grip; otherwise why did butter and jelly seem like otherworldly miracles?

'Sorry this place is such a construction zone,' he said. 'I'm determined to do all the work myself, save money. I want to learn how to fix and build everything. That's one of my goals in life.'

She nodded.

'You've got to be hungry.' He held out his hand, and she shook it. 'I'm Michael. Mike Appel.' The stress was on the second syllable, like the word *repel*. 'I've lived here all alone for four months, and you're the first person from the neighborhood who's been in my house. You'd think on a river people would always be socializing.' He gestured with the spatula. 'You haven't told me your name.'

She almost said *Maggie*. 'I'm Margaret,' she said, and when he didn't seem entirely satisfied, she added, 'Louise.'

'That's a pretty name.' He repeated it wistfully. 'Margaret Louise.'

That was what her mother had called her, as if one name weren't enough.

'People don't use two names so much these days.' He laughed.

'Or just Margo,' she offered.

'What's your last name?'

'Crane.'

139

'Margaret Louise Crane. Very nice.' He pushed aside several books that lay open on the table and set a glass of orange juice and half an omelet in front of her. One book with a library sticker was called *Building Bookshelves*.

'Thank you,' Margo said.

'I shouldn't let this table get so cluttered,' Michael said. 'So what do you do over there at that little house?'

'I fish.' The omelet was buttery and cheesy.

'I've never fished,' he said. 'Don't even know how to fish, but I'm building a boat. I'd like to be more self-sufficient, like you.'

'Fishing is easy,' Margo said. She lifted the edge of the omelet and admired the tiny, uniform cubes of green pepper, onion, and mushroom inside. 'Mostly you just have to sit there and wait.'

'Maybe you can give me a lesson, tell me what tastes good out of this river. Hell, I don't even know what to put on a hook.'

'I use worms and minnows. Sometimes crayfish.' She moved her feet so the dog could lie under the table, next to a neat stack of newspapers.

He said, 'I work for the power company, so I know you've got no power over there. Have you got a generator? A two-way radio of some kind?'

She shook her head. Margo worked her bare feet beneath the heavy body of the fishing dog. Her boots and socks sat beside her chair.

'It's incredible you live like that. And you don't have a job or go to school?'

'I'm nineteen,' Margo said, as if that would

140

explain it. She looked across the river at the cabin. She was eager to open the brick of ammo and load her Marlin. She hoped Paul would have no reason to look under the bed.

'Your place looks like a hideout, you know, like a place in a movie where criminals get away from the cops. Would you be the gangster's daughter?' He lifted his eyebrows. 'Or his girlfriend, maybe?'

A knot began to form in Margo's stomach. He probably meant to be playful, but she feared answering his questions could get her into trouble somehow.

'You don't talk much. Now, Danielle, she could talk.' He pointed a fork at Margo. 'And yet she never thought to mention she was sleeping with a very good friend of mine. Funny. Of course, he didn't mention it, either. But they're in love now, so everything's swell.'

Margo clung to her silence. She looked into his face, into his clear eyes, for as long as she dared. He was lonely, she saw, maybe as lonely as she was. She pulled her feet out from under the fishing dog and put on her damp socks and then her boots. She tucked Michael's jeans into the boots before tying them, in case she had to sit outside and fend off mosquitoes. She glanced around for her gun again, though of course it was back at the cabin.

'I moved up here from Indiana three years ago for my job,' he said. 'With Danielle. That was before I realized how materialistic she was. Where are you from?'

She saw he was going to wait for an answer.

141

'Murrayville,' she said.

'That's thirty-some miles down the river, halfway to the dam.'

She nodded and watched out the window. Paul was messing around on the dock.

'When Danielle was here, I hardly noticed the river as a backdrop. Now it's all I think about. I watch it going by for hours.'

By the time Margo finished her omelet, Paul had gotten into his boat and pulled away, heading upstream. When he was out of sight, she let her fork drop onto her plate, and the sound startled her. 'I've got to go,' she said.

'Can't you stay a few minutes longer? I promise to stop complaining about women. Here, I'll make you another piece of toast.'

She sat back down, but kept her weight on the balls of her feet.

'You seem like a girl who was raised by wolves or something.' He dropped two slices of bread into the shiny toaster.

She squinted at him.

'I guess I didn't say that right. I don't mean you seem like an animal.' He pushed down the knob, and right away she smelled toast. It made her miss the way Joanna's kitchen smelled in the mornings, like fried ham slices and toasted cinnamon bread. Michael went on, 'There've been lost kids who were taken in by wolves. Even after the kids were rescued, they never could stand being in enclosed spaces. They wanted to spend all their time outdoors. That's what I meant.'

Margo didn't have to pay attention. She'd only come here to be safe from Paul.

'Thank you for the food.' She stood and hurried out the kitchen door, leaving the toast to pop up behind her. She picked up her things and made her way downstream to her boat. Out in the middle of the river she felt a momentary sense of freedom, but upon reaching her dock the first thing she noticed were the rotting catfish heads still nailed to the big oak. She unlocked the padlock with her key, squatted beside the bed, and retrieved her rifle and pack. Both were undisturbed. Then she realized she had forgotten to buy matches — she had only two left in the box.

She balled up the last few letters she had written to her mother on the backs of used targets and put them in the woodstove. On top of those she assembled a pile of chipped kindling. She started a fire in order to drive the dampness from the cabin and dozed off. When she woke up, the fire was out, and she didn't want to use her last match to try again. The sky was fully lit, so she moved to the dock for the sun's warmth. She looked down and was surprised to be wearing Michael's clothes. After his Jeep rolled away across the river, she pressed her face into the clean sweatshirt.

10

When night muscled in, Margo used her last match to light the lamp. There wasn't much kerosene left, and the flicker of light only seemed to intensify the darkness. She heard rain on the roof, and it occurred to her, as if for the first time, that Brian really would not be coming back and that Paul surely would. She thought of the Murray farm, of the shoulder-high stacks of wood Uncle Cal and the boys must have already cut, split, and stacked for the winter. Her own supply was a sled full of split oak and two armloads of broken branches. Last winter, Brian had kept the cabin well stocked with food and fuel, but Margo didn't have the resources. She didn't even have a chainsaw, since Brian had taken it to town the day he was arrested. Maybe she ought to get out while she could, row across and hide her boat somewhere, and then hitchhike to Lake Lynne. If only her mother wanted her to come.

All evening Margo sat on Brian's bed with blankets around her and watched the lights in Michael's house. She imagined she could make out his silhouette hunched over the table, where he was probably reading. She wondered if he had to clean house every night in order to keep things as tidy as they were, and she wondered if there were really girls who had been raised by wolves.

She had no matches left; if the woodstove and lantern went out during the night, she wouldn't be able to relight them or the propane cooking stove. And Paul could show up at any minute. Though it was late, she had to get out of the cabin, at least until she was certain Paul wouldn't come that night. The gas station was open until ten o'clock. She pulled one of Brian's wool sweaters over Michael's clean sweatshirt and carried the sleeping bag to the boat in case she had to sleep outside. She wrapped her Marlin in the sleeping bag and put it on the rear seat beside her. She couldn't put anything under the seat because she hadn't bailed the water after the recent rains. Past Willow Island, her engine sputtered out of gas and died. She took up her oars and rowed for a few hundred yards, before she paused. She patted her front pants pocket where she'd put her bills and change yesterday, and she found it empty. The pants were Michael's. She had her wallet, but it contained no money. She had left her bills and change in her own jeans on the edge of Michael's bathtub. She lifted her oars out of the water and let herself be pulled back down the river. No stars shone tonight, and cold rain began to pour down.

Rainwater pooled around her feet. Instead of going to her own side of the river when she rounded the last bend, she pulled up at Michael's oil-barrel float. She could get her money back, and surely he had some matches she could borrow. He probably even had lawn mower gas she could use in her motor to get

145

back upstream. She tied up her boat, checked the shed door, and found it padlocked. With her rifle in one hand, the sleeping bag held around her with the other, she approached the house and looked in through the sliding glass door. At first she could see only the glowing numbers on a digital clock. As her eyes adjusted, she saw King rise from the floor at the foot of the bed.

As quickly as King began to bark, Michael was standing on the other side of the glass, wearing boxer shorts and no shirt.

He switched on an outside light and slid the door open. 'Margaret Louise? Don't you ever sleep in a bed?'

'I'm sorry.'

'Well, come on in. Be sorry inside. Sorry for the way I'm dressed. I wasn't expecting a visitor.'

When she stepped in, Michael looked down at the puddles forming on the plywood.

'Damn, I've really got to finish this floor,' he said. 'That's my next project.' He took the wet sleeping bag from her shoulders, pointed at where she should leave her shoes, and retrieved a towel from the bathroom to clean up the mess.

Margo had not realized how chilly she was until she stepped into the warm house.

'So you've come to me armed and dangerous this time,' he said. 'If you leave your rifle here in the corner with your shoes, I promise nobody will touch it.'

'Do you shoot?'

'I'm the only guy in my family who doesn't. My dad thinks I'm an aberration.'

'What's that?'

'What?'

'An *aberration*.'

'An oddity, I guess. A freak.'

'Like a girl raised by wolves?'

He smiled. 'Your blanket's soaked — I'll put it in the dryer. I'll put your other clothes in there from this morning, too. I already washed them. Hey, talk to me, Margaret Louise.'

She stammered and said, 'Thank you for the omelet.'

Michael laughed. 'Take a shower, and you can thank me for the hot water tomorrow.'

Margo rested her gun in the corner just inside the door. For the first time in a long time, she had wanted to get the thing off her shoulder. She followed Michael into the bathroom. He was explaining how the hot water took a while to heat up and was showing her how to switch the flow from bath to shower. She peeled off her three shirts before considering she shouldn't undress in front of a stranger. Michael looked away and abruptly left the room. Margo hardly recognized the thin, dirty creature in the mirror. She didn't think her body looked strong enough to accomplish anything. Her shoulders were hunched from the cold. Her mud-colored curls were matted, and her face was a mess of scratches, insect bites, and poison ivy blisters. Her small breasts seemed shriveled. Her mother might've said she looked like a Slocum. Three times she shampooed her hair before the water rinsed clean.

Though she was in a stranger's shower, she felt safe. With the water running, she could let herself cry, and when the hot water finally began to peter out, she composed herself by recalling the serene photos of Annie Oakley aiming her rifle, preparing to shoot, knowing she would hit her target every time. There was one photo Margo liked of a young Annie Oakley standing with her new husband, Frank Butler, and their big white dog, George.

Margo put on the dark terry-cloth robe that hung on the back of the door and padded across the hall into the room with the boat skeleton. It looked too big to fit through the doorway. The room did not even have a view of the water, so it was no wonder he didn't sleep in there. A half dozen tools were lined up neatly on a wooden chair. She returned to the room with the sliding glass door and curled with King on the floor. Michael came in and sat on the foot of the bed, looking amused. 'Are you a wolf girl? Or maybe a dog girl?'

'I watch King fish from my house.'

'Why do you call her King?'

'For the kingfisher bird. It has a big head like hers.'

'I didn't have a dog before I bought this place,' Michael said. He squatted down and stroked the dog's head. 'It was the craziest thing. When I closed on this house, the old owner asked if I'd keep her, because she loved the river and wouldn't be happy anywhere else. But he called her Renegade. Cleopatra fits her better. Cleopatra, Queen of the Nile, a river dog. Cleo for short.' He tugged gently on the dog's ear and her mouth opened in a smile. 'You sleep in my bed,

148

and I'll sleep on the floor. You might have noticed I don't have a couch.'

'We can both sleep on the bed,' Margo said. 'It's huge.' Still wearing the bathrobe, she climbed in on the river side. Michael sat on the end of the bed for a while before shrugging his shoulders and joining her.

'What's that mysterious light at your house?' he asked.

'A kerosene lamp.' She had left it burning, figuring it would burn itself out, but it hadn't.

'Are you going to teach me how to fish?'

'I need some matches. And I ran out of gas. If you let me borrow some, I can pay you back.'

'Did you see my boat in there?' Michael waited for her to nod. 'After Danielle left I thought I should redo that room, but then I figured I'd rather have a boat. As soon as I finish it, I'm rowing up to that island with the black willows.'

'My grandpa gave me my boat.'

Michael nodded. 'I built this bed out of red oak. I slept on a mattress on the floor for two months after Danielle left, until I finished it. Odysseus built his own bed, you know. I want to build everything that matters myself.'

'What about a car?'

'Cars don't matter,' he said. 'So what kind of wood is your boat made of?'

'Teak. The only teak boat on the river, my grandpa said.' Margo didn't have the energy to ask who Odysseus was. She ran her hand over the headboard above her. It was made of solid planks, nothing fancy. It was the kind of bed

149

Margo would like to have, though she wouldn't need one that took up most of the room the way this one did.

'It must be heavy,' Michael said. 'I have a teak cutting board. It's like a brick.'

'It's fine in the water. But I can't go farther downstream than Confluence, because it's too heavy to carry around the dam. My grandpa used to say he was *stuck on the Stark*.'

'Maybe you can take me for a row one of these days.' Michael was propped on one elbow. '*The River Rose*. I like how your boat's name is a complete sentence.'

Margo had never rowed her boat with a man in it, and it struck her as a fine idea that she would take this handsome Michael with his hair parted in the middle up to Willow Island. She looked at Michael, fixed him in her sights. She moved closer and kissed him. The kiss she got in return was so mild that she wasn't sure it'd happened. When Brian kissed you, you knew you'd been kissed.

'Talk to me,' he said and laughed. 'I don't kiss just any girl who wanders in here.'

She kissed him again, and this time he pulled away more slowly. She was surprised at how much she wanted to keep kissing him, though he was practically a stranger. She was feeling the same urgency she felt when she had a buck in her sights. Only she didn't want to shoot Michael.

'Why were you out in the rain?' he whispered. The way he asked questions suggested to Margo that problems could be discussed and solved,

150

that nothing was as dire as it seemed. She wasn't able to answer him yet, but she considered telling him something else, something interesting — maybe that she'd once seen a heron carry a little snake up to its nest — but then he would want her to talk more, and she wanted to be silent with him. She wanted to know his smooth chest, his ribs, his solid shoulders, his delicate throat. His arm lay above the blankets, thin compared to Brian's or Paul's. This arm couldn't hold her down, couldn't put her anyplace she didn't want to be. A girl could stand and fight a man like Michael, instead of running away. She would do with him only what she wanted to do. The kerosene lamp across the river dimmed, and a few minutes later it flickered and went out.

'What are you afraid of out there?' Michael asked.

'I'm not afraid of anything,' she whispered. Even if it was a lie, she liked saying it. She wrapped a hand around the back of Michael's neck and kissed him hard, as though pulling the trigger of a rifle and holding it steady all through the shot. She pushed her fingers through his hair and felt along his shoulder, wanting to touch as much of his skin as possible all at once, to have his whole body of skin beneath her hands. She leaned across him, felt the curve of his back and his buttock, and continued down his leg until she felt him shudder and move toward her. Fresh air trickled through a window not quite closed. The dog sighed on the floor. From the end of the hall she heard the clothes and sleeping bag in the dryer. Michael worked his hand between her legs and her breathing collapsed into laughter — something that had never happened before. He rolled onto her easily, like waves onto sand.

Later, when she closed her eyes, she felt his affectionate gaze on her. As she drifted off, she thought maybe she had drowned with Paul and was now revived.

She awoke alone to light pouring through the thin curtains covering the sliding glass door; the sun was warm on her clean skin. Brian's cabin had no southern exposure, and she usually slept with her clothes on. Margo sat up and saw her sleeping bag folded on the far corner of the bed. On top of it were her jeans, her dark blue turtleneck, flannel shirt, and sweater. Paper money was folded on top. Her heart thudded before she realized that it must be the bills and change that she had left in her pants pocket. Her Marlin was still sitting in the corner where she'd put it last night. She dressed and found Michael in the kitchen wearing a button-up shirt and sport jacket. She put her rifle next to the broom in the corner and sat at the table.

'I'm going to church,' Michael said. 'I'm meeting with a study group afterwards. We're going to explore how various skills can help those who are less fortunate. I'm going to talk about home improvement skills. Would you like to come? You could talk about fishing.' He leaned back against the sink with his arms crossed, a cup of coffee in one hand. She tried to remember being wrapped in his arms, held tight against his chest, but this morning his body seemed stiff beneath his shirt and jacket, and she

152

couldn't imagine him without clothes. 'I wish you would. It's a very relaxed church. Some people around here call it the hippie church.'

'I'm going home,' she said automatically.

He handed her a cup of coffee with milk already in it. 'How old are you, Margaret Louise? I'm twenty-eight.'

'I'll be nineteen in November.' She then remembered she'd told him she was already nineteen. In fact, she'd be seventeen in two months.

'You know, I had no intention of doing that last night. I don't really even know you.' He stared at Margo in a way that seemed rude, so she sipped her coffee without looking up at him and stroked King's head. The silence in the room grew large, and Margo let herself settle into it. Silence was a game she could play.

'And I didn't use protection. Don't worry about pregnancy — I've been snipped — but still we shouldn't have. Is there anything you want to tell me?'

She looked into his face. His eyes looked a little frantic, but they were kind.

'I'm sorry,' Michael finally said, sitting across from her and relaxing. 'I just don't know anything about you. For all I know you're some lost heiress or a girl who just killed her whole family and buried them in a garden.'

'Or a girl raised by wolves?' Margo said.

'Or maybe I'm dreaming you.' His voice grew quieter. 'Because, believe me, if I dreamed a girl, she'd be just like you. She'd have beautiful arms like you. She'd be smart, and she'd even smell like you. She'd teach me to live off the land.' He stood up, picked up a dishcloth, and wiped the clean counter with it.

What could she smell like? Margo wondered. She'd just had a shower.

'Except this girl would talk.' He folded the cloth and put it down. 'She'd argue with me. And if I was lucky, she really would be an heiress with an island in the river.'

Margo kept his words on the surface. She wasn't a wolf girl or a murderer or an heiress. Or a dream. She was a girl who needed some matches and gas for the outboard motor. King pushed her head beneath Margo's hand until Margo resumed petting her.

'But maybe that big guy you live with will come back and use me for bait.'

Margo thought it was the first sensible thing he'd said. She smiled.

'You've lived with him since last December, but now you're afraid of him.'

Margo looked at her cabin. She was grateful no boat was parked there. After last night, she realized she no longer wanted to see either Paul or Brian. Margo had appreciated the home Brian had given her, but she didn't want to be with him again, not even if he were set free. She had learned a lot from Brian, but last night it had been so nice to be the equal of a man, and to feel safe and comfortable.

Michael took a drink of coffee. 'Are you going to live in that cabin all winter? Keep warm with a woodstove? Or do you have a propane or kerosene heater?'

'I might go stay with my ma,' she said. She wanted to hear how it sounded.

'Oh, of course you have a mother! Where does she live?'

'Lake Lynne.'

'Will you come back tonight?' Michael's eyes were as brown and hopeful as King's. 'We can eat dinner. I could come get you in the Jeep.'

'The closest road is a half mile from the cabin,' she said, slinging her Marlin over her shoulder. 'Then it's just a walking path.'

'And I don't have a boat yet, so I guess it's up to you, Margaret Louise.' He watched her stand, drain her coffee, and walk toward the door, just as he had watched her row away with his dog on the day they'd met.

A half hour later, Margo was back at the cabin, sitting cross-legged on the dock, enjoying a warm breeze off the river, watching Michael's Jeep pull out of the driveway again. She wished she'd told him she would come to dinner. If he asked her again, she would accept his invitation on the spot and offer to bring something — fish fillets, maybe. She watched the Jeep pull onto the river road that led upstream to Heart of Pines and past hundreds of regular houses like his. She should write to her mother and ask if Luanne was living a regular life in Lake Lynne or if she was an aberration in her new town. A heron dropped from the sky and settled out of sight downstream. Two mallards drifted near shore, and from their slightly rusty chest feathers Margo figured they were first-year males. She wondered if they were all that survived of a

155

dozen chicks that a mama had hatched in the spring. Margo quacked, and they made a gentle noise in response, but kept moving.

That evening, while Michael was still away, a silver car pulled into his driveway. Though Margo didn't recognize the car, the driver was clearly Danielle, the woman who had left Michael. She disappeared on the road side of the house, and shortly afterward King appeared and bounded down to the water. It occurred to Margo that the woman might have come to take Michael's dog. Margo reeled in her line and dragged the outboard motor off the boat without taking care to protect the propeller. She pushed off from shore and in a few minutes was downstream and on the other side of the river. King ran out onto the float to greet her, bowed playfully, and tossed her head instead of climbing into the boat. 'King! Come!' Margo barked. 'King! Come!' As the dog finally jumped in, the woman appeared from inside the house. She wore a white blouse under a thin white vest. She was holding a glass of something clear with ice in it and carrying a lawn chair. She rested her drink in the grass, unfolded the chair, and then sat and stretched her legs out.

'Hey, what are you doing with Cleo?' she yelled when she saw Margo and Cleo in the boat. The woman's hair was the color of caramel.

'She's not yours!' Margo yelled, but she was starting to realize the woman probably wasn't there to take the dog at all. Instead, the woman was making herself at home, no doubt planning to step back into the life she had left. Michael must have known she would come back, and that was why he hadn't gotten rid of her things.

'I'll call the police, you little freak,' Danielle said mildly and took a long drink from her glass. She crossed her ankles.

Margo's hair was clean, and she had braided it neatly. Was it her worn jeans that made the woman call her *freak*? Her old Carhartt jacket? Was it her dark, heavy rowboat with its splintery oars? Or her gun visible on the back seat? Or was she a freak, plain and simple, a wolf girl, an aberration? Would her mother see her that way when they finally met again? Was that why Margo had never been able to make new friends in Murrayville?

'You left the dog and went away,' Margo said, too quietly for Danielle to hear. *And you left Michael*, she thought, *and you left the river*. Whatever Margo might be, this woman had been a fool. Margo supposed the woman knew better now, and that was why she was back.

As Margo rowed upstream toward the cabin, Michael's Jeep appeared and parked next to the silver car. The woman stood and met him half-way to the driveway. When Margo saw the two of them standing side by side, she felt a little sick. They seemed to belong together.

'Cleo! Come back!' shouted Michael. At the call, King moved around Margo to get to the back seat. She jumped out of the boat, causing it to tip. It happened so quickly that Margo could not compensate for the dog's weight, and a blast of water splashed into the boat.

Michael shouted, 'Margaret Louise! Come

back!' And then he began to engage in intense conversation with Danielle.

And upstream and coming toward the cabin was the Playbuoy.

Margo's boat began to turn in the current, and soon her prow was headed downstream. She maneuvered herself toward the edge of the river with one oar so she would be less visible to Paul.

She glided slowly out of sight of the cabin and Michael's house, past a solitary black fisherman holding a bottle twisted in a brown bag. The green heads of willows wept nearby. Painted turtles and blue racers sunning themselves on fallen trees slid into the water at her approach. A great blue heron fished silently from its perch on a root, one bulging banded eye on her as she passed, wary but not alarmed so long as Margo was moving with the current. She was tempted to take up the oars and row toward the bird, but decided to leave it in peace. She felt the exhaustion of her journey of the last ten months, the whole foolish, failed journey upstream to find her mother. She needed to just sit and let things run through her head as if her life were just a story that she could read or hear about.

A man steered his aluminum motorboat around her. She tossed side to side in his wake, and then she twirled. She had not swum since long before she'd left home, and she had forgotten the freedom she'd once known in letting the river take her where it would. She passed a half dozen sandpipers on a sandbar, and then watched a green heron slinking through poison ivy vines along the water's edge. She knew she should pull over to the side of the river and take charge of her situation, but then she saw a tree that resembled Paul with his arms upraised. Another tree had her father's brooding face. Her mother's willowy, suntanned arms momentarily appeared as reflections of branches, but the water was swift there, providing no place to rest. She did not want to go back to Murrayville, but she could not go back to her cabin. She climbed onto the boat's back seat beside her rifle and curled there and thought about how nice it was to float, to let the river guide her, and how nice it had been to lie with Michael last night in his big bed.

The next she was aware, she was no longer moving. The air had grown cooler, and she seemed to be tilted to the starboard side on the back seat of the boat. Above her was a rickety dock with one pole missing, but it was not the marijuana house in Murrayville as she had thought for one confused moment. Her prow was stuck in a sandbar beside a burned-out cabin she'd seen on trips downstream with Brian. The sun was sinking, but not more than half an hour had passed since she'd closed her eyes. At first she thought she was hallucinating when she saw a great blue heron standing before her, not four feet away, on the middle seat of the boat. Margo moved not a muscle, tried not to blink. She studied the clear, savage banded eye, the dagger of a beak, and wondered if this animal was going to attack her. Drops of water beaded on the bird's spiky crest. She remained perfectly still as the heron stepped off the seat onto the wet floor of the boat, coming even closer, as though Margo might be prey. She had watched herons spear fish in tangled underwater roots and feed their chicks in the tops of trees, but she had never dared hope she would be close enough to touch one. Margo followed the bird's gaze and realized it wasn't really looking at her; it was stalking something in the shallow water in the bottom of the boat, a gold shimmer, a little fish, perhaps. Suddenly the dagger beak dipped and snatched the bright object. It was a gold-colored .22-caliber long-rifle cartridge. The bird looked into Margo's eyes and began to take flight. As it spread its wings, its feathers brushed Margo's knees, and, as if realizing its folly, it dropped the cartridge onto Margo's hip. Margo held her breath as the bird rose and flew upstream. She studied the cartridge and wondered if it was some kind of message.

She sat up and let herself imagine the flush of wings again, the swoosh of air; she thought about Michael in his bed, the night wind through the window, his warm skin brushing hers. She would follow the heron back upstream. She wasn't certain how far down she had floated, but if it was three miles, it would take that many hours to return to where she'd started. To lessen the effect of the current, she hugged the edge of the river as closely as she could without scraping bottom with her oars. She faced backward, toward a fiery orange sunset, and as the color faded, her eyes adjusted to the darkness. She rowed steadily past the unlit wooden cottages and shacks, alongside the ancient trees. A whip-poor-will's haunting cry raised the hair on her arms. A nighthawk made a crazy flutter and followed her for a while. A big hoot owl appeared silhouetted in a tree. Muskrats and other night hunters slid into the water, rose alongside her boat, and then slipped below the surface again as she made her way upstream. When a quarter moon appeared, Margo pulled herself into a snag to rest. Her arm muscles burned, and her hands were roughed up from the oar handles. She felt the night pulling at her boat, luring her into the dark, easy current. She pushed off again.

The river curved and narrowed slightly, and she recognized a familiar irrigation pump and boat-houses on the north bank. She held the brightest stars in her sights until they disappeared behind trees.

But once she neared the cabin, she saw the Playbuoy was still there. When she reached Michael's oil-barrel float, she misjudged the distance from shore and stepped out into thigh-deep water. She tied the boat under the gangplank, between the float and shore, where it would be less noticeable. The noise must have woken Michael or King. A light came on in the bedroom, and King soon jogged out into the yard, over the planks, and onto the float. Margo petted her and held the Marlin out of the water.

She saw the kitchen light go on, and she dragged herself to shore.

Michael opened the kitchen door before she knocked. 'Margaret!' he said.

'Can I have some matches?' It was all she could bring herself to say, not knowing if

161

Michael's dinner invitation was still open. Margo should have checked for Danielle's car in the driveway before coming to the door.

'Margaret, come in,' Michael said. She saw the clock behind him. It was ten-thirty. 'It's cold out there. Feels like fall.'

'Is Danielle here?' Margo clenched her teeth. King stood beside her.

'Nope. I'm all by myself.'

'I brought King back. She came out to find me.'

Michael looked at Margo. 'Do you want to talk about whatever's going on?'

Margo hunched her shoulders to stop her shivering. 'That island with the willows upstream,' she said. 'I'll row you up there if you want. Tomorrow.'

'Come in, and let's talk about it,' Michael said. He leaned against the doorframe. 'Tell me about that man at the cabin.'

'Do you like great blue herons?' Margo asked. She felt drunk, dizzy.

'Who doesn't like them?' Michael said.

'There's herons on Willow Island. A campment of herons, living in the trees.' She put one hand against the doorframe. 'Dozens of them. One came so close that it brushed my leg with its wing.'

'I don't suppose you know the story about Leda and the swan?'

Margo thought of the word. '*Heronry*,' she said. 'The herons are in a heronry.'

'I like cranes, too. Not as common in these parts, of course. The females are reclusive. Now

162

it's time to come inside and dry off.' He tugged at her wrist, but stopped when she resisted. He took her hand. 'If you seriously don't want to come in, I'll just give you some gas for your boat, okay? And I've got a box of matches you can have.'

'Thank you,' she said. 'You know, I miss my dad. And my ma. She doesn't want me to visit her.'

'Come inside, Margaret. We can talk about it.'

'I mean . . . I miss them so much.' She couldn't imagine Michael or anyone understanding how even losing Brian had been difficult.

Michael nodded. He held both of her hands gently. 'Cleo's going to get cold out there waiting for you. We'll let her have two names, like you. She can be *King Cleo*. Come in, and I'll make you an omelet. By tomorrow afternoon you'll be thanking me for it.'

Before she stepped through the doorway, Margo looked behind her, across the river, toward the dark little cabin. She would row across tomorrow, after Paul was gone, to get her belongings — hopefully her pack would still be under the bed. King followed her inside, where it was warm and safe.

PART
II

11

Margo brought in the mail from the box. It was April, and she had been staying with Michael since late September. The danger of freezing and flooding had passed, and yesterday they had launched the oil-barrel float. Margo had walked the gangplank onto it no fewer than twenty times today, enjoying the way it tipped beneath her weight. The arrival of a letter addressed to *Margaret Louise Crane* made her hopeful it would be from her mother, to whom she had written and sent Michael's address. She had received a Christmas card from Luanne saying once again that now would not be a good time to visit, but that she would write again soon. It contained a twenty-dollar bill. This envelope, however, was from the Secretary of State and contained the Michigan ID card she'd applied for three weeks earlier. She would use the card to get her hunting and fishing licenses.

When Michael got home that evening, he went into the house as usual. Then he came out the back door and approached Margo, who was skinning a bullhead catfish near the upstream edge of his property. Out of squeamishness and a dislike of mess, he usually avoided watching her prepare the fish and game she caught.

'Your ID says you were born in 1963.' He seemed to choke on his words. 'I saw it sitting on the table.'

'So?'

'You just turned seventeen in November, after you moved in with me. Jesus, Margaret.'

The tail of the bullhead curled away from the tree. The fish arched its half-skinned body, kept pushing against the nail that held its head to the tree. On this pleasant afternoon, Margo had forgotten about how her age could matter.

'For Christ's sake, Margaret, can't you hit it on the head or something?'

'What?'

'Do you really want to skin something alive?' Michael said. 'The damned fish. It's in pain. Can't you kill it first?'

'My grandpa taught me — '

'He taught you to skin a creature alive?'

'Told me, I mean . . . fish don't feel pain.'

'Jesus, Margo, look at that thing writhe — if that's not pain, I don't know what is.'

Margo picked up her knife and slashed through the bullhead's spinal cord. Its body fell to the ground.

'I'm sorry I said it like that,' Michael said. 'I've just never seen one struggle that way. Really, it's okay.'

'I do hit them on the head, but sometimes they wake up.'

He was holding her ID between his thumb and finger. 'You even take a beautiful driver's license photo. God, Margaret.'

She stood quietly, headless fish in one hand, knife in the other. Silence had so far been her best response when Michael was upset.

'You told me you were turning nineteen when we met. You were sixteen. I slept with a sixteen-year-old girl. And now I'm with a seventeen-year-old girl. Stop looking at me that way. It's maddening when you stare.'

Margo looked beyond him, at the river.

'What is the age of consent in this state? I didn't think I would ever need to know.'

Margo watched him cross the lawn and disappear into the house. When Michael was upset, he didn't usually stay that way for long. She didn't know if this time would be different or what that might mean. She finished skinning the fish, stinging her hand only once.

The winter had dragged on too long, and now that spring was here, hundreds of daffodils bloomed alongside Michael's house. Thirty-some miles downstream, Joanna had planted hundreds of daffodils around the Murray house and yard, ones she called jonquils and narcissus and paper flowers, some etched with orange, so that every April the Murray place looked like a fairyland. Occasionally Margo thought of shooting their blossom heads off with .22 shotshells, but it was only to see the petals spray like fireworks, to create a different kind of beauty. Shotshell was what Annie Oakley used to explode glass balls in the air at exhibitions.

Margo was enjoying living with Michael, but after all these months she still had not dared unpack. She washed her clothes in his machine and stuffed them back into her army bag. She felt restless whenever she spent too much time indoors, but knew she would have a hard time living without Michael's household comforts again, without furnace heat, hot water, and store-bought food. She had reshaped her life around Michael's routines and his sensible habits so thoroughly that she could go for hours without thinking about her daddy or her old life, or even about Brian or Paul, despite the cabin being right across the way. Michael worked patiently on his projects in the evenings with her assistance, finishing the floors and installing the baseboards in room after room, striving to master the skills he needed to make his house perfect. The thought that he might finish the remodeling made her uneasy — she feared that when the house was to his liking he might turn his attention to improving her. Fortunately, he was nowhere near finishing the boat, so that could occupy him awhile.

Margo had been learning more about Annie Oakley ever since Michael brought her a copy of *Annie Oakley: Life and Legend*. It said that Annie had been born Phoebe Ann Mosey and changed her name as an adult. After her father's death, the girl's mother sent thirteen-year-old Phoebe away to live with a couple who had no children. They worked her hard, beat her, and didn't feed her enough. She called them the Wolves. As soon as she could escape from the attic where they locked her, she ran home to her mother's. Only then did she take the old family rifle off the mantel and start hunting, as a way to earn her keep.

Twenty minutes later when Michael returned, he was still agitated. Margo wiped her hands on her jeans.

'The age of consent is seventeen in this state,' Michael said. 'But seventeen. It's so young. Should

170

we go talk to your relations in Murrayville? Maybe it's time we track down your mother. What the hell is the matter with her, anyhow?'

Margo shook her head. She wasn't desperate enough to go where she wasn't wanted.

'Will you swim with me when it gets warmer?' she asked in a quiet voice. She wanted to change the subject.

'I'm not much of a swimmer. Maybe we should get married,' he said. He looked into her face.

'Why?' she asked.

'*Why?* For all the normal reasons. Love. I love you, Margaret Louise,' Michael said, 'and maybe I'm a little afraid that if I don't marry you, what we're doing is wrong.'

'Would I have to go to church?' she asked. 'Or school?'

Every Sunday Michael tried to get her to come with him to his hippie church. She had gone once, had listened to the minister. The man meant well, she could tell, but he was as dull as a schoolteacher. She had enjoyed the guitar music, but she didn't like the way people wanted to shake her hand and talk afterward. She didn't dislike people, she told Michael, but at church there were too many all at once. He said it was okay that she didn't go, but he was disappointed she didn't want to be part of his community. He was also disappointed that she didn't show any interest in school. He thought Margo needed to set personal goals, that it was not enough to live a beautiful life on the river, fishing, shooting, and collecting berries, nuts, and mushrooms.

'You wouldn't have to do anything you didn't want to do. Okay, forget I asked.' He moved away from her. Then he said, 'This wasn't the right way to ask you. Or the right time, when I'm all riled up.'

Margo looked off downstream. People said Joanna and Cal had a solid marriage, and Margo was sure Joanna would say she was glad she had married Cal. Her own ma and pa were a different story.

'But if I did ask you, what would you say?' Michael knelt in the grass and took her hand, which was still sticky with fish guts. 'This is a little better. Will you marry me?'

She looked down at him. He was still wearing his creased work pants. He had taken off his tie in the house, but his white shirt was still buttoned up to the neck.

Since she had been living with Michael, she talked more, said things even when she wasn't certain she should, about her father and mother and some of the Murrays, but she hadn't told him about Cal or Paul or Brian.

Usually Michael seemed happy to listen to her. Their life together was easy. They made love most nights, with no worry about getting pregnant. Despite the way she knew and loved Michael, marriage had never occurred to her.

'Why are you looking at me so strangely?' Michael asked. 'Don't people get married where you come from?'

'Okay,' she said.

'Okay what?'

'I'll marry you.'

'The answer is *yes* or *no*,' Michael said and grinned. '*Okay* is a little less enthusiastic than I was hoping for.'

'Okay, *yes*.'

'Are you sure? I shouldn't have asked this way. And I don't even have a ring, Margaret. A man can't propose without a ring.'

'Annie Oakley married Frank Butler when she was seventeen,' Margo said. 'He was twenty-eight. Same as us. They spent the rest of their lives together. With dogs.'

'No kids?'

'Nope.'

'All right, then, if it's good enough for Annie Oakley, it's good enough for us. Now, what can we use for a ring around here?'

From what she had read, Margo knew there was some uncertainty about Annie Oakley's real age. The Wild West Show had an interest in making her seem as young as possible. She also knew that Annie longed to have children, but was unable to.

Michael said, 'God, a few minutes ago I was miserable with guilt, and now I'm the happiest person I know.'

He plucked a single dandelion, one of a few that had bloomed so far, and he asked to borrow her fish knife. He cut a slit in the dandelion stem near the flower's head, looped the bottom of the stem through it, and pulled it tight around her finger, so her hand had a big yellow flower on top.

'We used to make these!' Margo said, delighted. 'My aunt Joanna showed me how.'

'Do you want a church wedding?' He clasped her hand. 'I guess I know the answer to that. We'll have riverside wedding.'

She was feeling overwhelmed. She kept looking at the dandelion on her hand.

'We'll keep it small, just us and a few friends and family. Maybe your mom will show her face.'

They kissed at the river's edge with the quaking aspen fluttering its new silvery leaves above them. The breeze picked up coolness from the thawed ground and blew it past them into the warm air.

'Should we wait until you're eighteen? Until the end of November? That's seven months from now.'

She nodded. Michael sat down cross-legged in the grass and tugged her down beside him. 'I'm sorry about the way I yelled at you earlier,' he said, and took both her hands in his. 'I freak out sometimes.'

12

Margo sat across the table from Michael, eating lunch distractedly, keeping an eye on the activity upstream and across the river. Paul had been at the cabin since midmorning with Charlie and Johnny, and Margo planned to stay inside until they pulled away in the pontoon boat. Usually they were at the cabin just long enough to fill glass jugs from the blue drum buried behind the house, but Charlie was sweeping the cabin's screen porch, and that made Margo worry that one of them might be planning on staying. She took some comfort in the fact that Paul's eyesight was poor and that Michael's house was set back from the river's edge.

'It's a hot one,' Michael said and took a bite of his grilled ham-and-cheese sandwich.

'Maybe King and I will fish downstream today,' Margo said, bringing her attention back to Michael and their lunch. Wednesdays were his late day, when he went in to work at noon and got home by eight-thirty or nine at night. 'Do you want to have brown trout tonight? Maybe I can get a couple with night crawlers in the evening.'

'Don't you ever want to do anything more than fish and shoot?' Michael said hesitantly.

'You know, Grandpa taught me to skin rabbits and muskrats. He said it was a skill that would benefit a girl. And you know I can cook.'

Michael laughed. 'Your grandpa probably imagined you would have other skills as well, like math and history, on top of skinning animals.'

'He only went to school through the eighth grade. Annie Oakley only went through the fourth grade.'

'It was a different time. Now you need education to get anywhere.'

'I could be a trick shooter,' Margo said.

'Says here in the newspaper Murray Metal Fabricating is laying off another eighteen people. Tough times for manufacturing. Are you sure you don't want to go visit the Murrays? I'll go with you. It says here, Cal Murray has been in a wheelchair since he was attacked in that bar last year.'

'I told you, we don't get along,' she said. 'Not since my grandpa died.'

'Well, I wish I had met your grandpa. I mean, he was a man of the wild, but a businessman, too.'

'His father started the company. Grandpa never really wanted to be president, he said. But he made the company grow.'

'Sometimes people have to do things they don't want in life.'

'Do you want me to make money?' Margo asked. According to the book Michael had gotten her, Annie Oakley supported her family through hunting and trapping. She killed animals and birds to eat and sell in town. Only later did she make her shooting a show.

'That's not it. I want you to have the joy of learning new things. And sometimes it's even worth it to tolerate what you don't like in order to achieve your goals. You don't have to graduate high school. I think you can get a GED and go to community college. You could get a two-year degree in biology or something like that. Maybe you could get a job working outside.'

'You said I didn't have to go to school to learn. I could read books.'

'You don't like any of the books I've gotten you other than the Annie Oakley book. Tell me what else you want to read.'

'I like the Indian hunter book, about the guy who lived in the cave up north,' Margo said. 'And I'd like to read more about shooting, I guess. Trick shooting.' She glanced across the river. Paul seemed to be wiping down the seats of Brian's boat with a bucket and a rag, and though it was hot, he was still wearing jeans and boots. While she watched, Johnny slipped out of his cutoffs and tennis shoes and posed naked at the end of the dock. His arms were tan from his biceps down, but his torso below the neckline was pale, and the sight made Margo smile. He dove off the dock with a pretty splash. Why hadn't she swum this year? Margo wondered. It was already July. Why hadn't she swum at all since she left Murrayville? Johnny emerged from beneath the surface.

'What about a vacation?' Michael said. 'Do you want to go somewhere?'

'We could go up the river and camp overnight on Willow Island.'

'We should go see something new,' Michael said. She shrugged. Johnny dragged his body out of the water and climbed onto the dock. He was grinning, no doubt, shouting something to Paul. His bottom was moon-white against the lush foliage around the cabin.

'Maybe I'll swim today,' Margo said.

'After the wedding we'll have to go on a honeymoon.'

'You mean like to the cabins in Heart of Pines?'

'The herons go to Florida in the winter,' Michael said. 'I've heard you can see hundreds of water birds in some places down there. Maybe cranes, too. Wouldn't you like to see sandhill cranes, Miss Crane? To work on your crane calls.'

Margo thought it was incredible that Michael didn't seem to notice anyone was at the cabin across the way.

After Michael went off to work a few minutes before noon, Margo went into the bedroom and looked out the sliding glass door. She didn't worry the first time she saw Paul looking across the river, but then he kept looking, and she saw he held binoculars. She slipped away from the glass door and regretted having stood there like a target as long as she had.

The house might be the safest place to stay, but if Paul and the other two showed up, then she'd be trapped inside. Despite the heat, she left the doors open while she did dishes and cleaned the kitchen, wiped the counters even though they were already clean, the way Michael would have done. Her anxiety remained even after the three men closed up the cabin and headed upstream and out of sight. She thought she would do something nice for Michael, and she mowed part of the lawn with the old reel push mower, but her lines weren't as straight as she'd hoped they'd be. The wind that afternoon brought a tar smell that she had never noticed before. Mallard ducks and a few black ducks landed on the river between her and the cabin, but they did not respond to her quacking, and they let the current tug them downstream. Normally she felt fine spending a few hours staring into the water alongside the fishing dog, but she now wondered if she ought to be doing something more productive. A few days ago she'd retrieved some overgrown zucchini that had been floating down the river. They were bigger around and longer than any fish she'd ever caught, and it had been fun chasing them down and dragging them out of the current. This afternoon she carried them into the woods and set them up as targets. It had been months since she'd fired the shotgun Brian had given her. She carried the twelve-gauge out and put on the ear protectors that Michael had given her for Christmas. She had several dozen small-game shells in her pocket, along with a half dozen of the large-sized buckshot. She didn't like to lock up Cleo when she shot, but she had promised Michael she would after the time he saw her studying the photo of Annie Oakley and her dog, Dave; in that photo Annie was preparing to shoot an apple off Dave's head.

Margo then moved through the woods, imagining the zucchinis were Paul and Billy or some unknown rapists and killers, and blasted them to pulp, one after another. If Michael would only shoot with her, the two of them together could rig up a launch for clay pigeons, but when she had mentioned it recently, he suggested she join the gun club. The notion surprised her. Cal and his sons belonged to the Rod and Gun Club between Murrayville and Confluence, but Margo didn't know of any women members.

Margo shot at hunks of squash until the light became gold-tinged. She took off her ear coverings and sat cross-legged against a tree and waited for the birds to return. The sound of the cicadas rose to a screechy roar and then gradually subsided. Margo imitated the nasal *yank-yank* of a white-breasted nuthatch and then the meow of a catbird perched between her and the water. When she heard Michael's car pulling in the driveway, she smiled and meowed in his direction, though he couldn't see or hear her. A few minutes later, as she was heading back toward the house with her shotgun, she saw a pontoon boat pull up and tie off at the oil-barrel float. Margo ducked down and watched Michael make his way across the gangplank and onto the float to talk to the visitor. As she crept nearer, she confirmed what she'd feared: Michael was talking to Paul. Margo stayed hidden and moved closer so she could hear their voices.

'Well, where is she, then?' Paul said. His face was haggard. 'I'd like to talk to her.'

'She seems to want to avoid you.'

'She doesn't belong to you. Tell her I want to talk to her.'

Margo crouched so quietly that a coot continued moving downstream past her.

'Of course she doesn't belong to me,' Michael

180

said. 'She belongs to herself.'

'Is that her in the house?' Paul said. Margo saw that Cleo was standing up almost as tall as a small person with her paws against the screen door. Margo hid herself behind the trunk of a willow. The cicadas grew louder again.

'That's my dog,' Michael said.

'I saw her earlier, from across the river. I know she's here.'

As if on command, the fishing dog barked.

'Did you do something to her?' Michael said.

'She doesn't mind what a man does. She's a game girl.' Paul stepped off the front of the boat and onto the oil-barrel float. It tipped under his weight. He stepped to the center and stood a few feet from Michael. No one else was on the boat. Margo glanced across the river at the dark, empty cabin. When Paul had gone up the river some hours ago, he must have ferried Charlie and Johnny back to Heart of Pines.

'What do you want with her?' Michael asked.

'I want to tell her that my brother Brian will be away for eight years on an assault charge, plus six more for manslaughter. Damned lawyer convinced him to plead guilty. He said he'd get a few years off for good behavior. Problem is, my brother forgets what good behavior is when he's got to show off for a bunch of guys.'

'Who's Brian to her?' Michael asked.

'She doesn't tell you anything, does she? My brother is in prison because of doing a little dirty work for her.'

'She's just a kid. She's not responsible for what men do.'

'And she's got some things she took from me and Brian. A shotgun, for one.'

Margo wanted to scream over the cicadas that Brian gave her that shotgun, but she stayed put.

'Maybe I'll take her boat instead. As an exchange.'

'Why don't you leave now?' Michael said. 'Get off my property.'

'It's funny for a little feller like you to threaten me.' Paul stepped backward, causing the float to tip, and then rocked it a few times by shifting his weight. The current held the Playbuoy tight against the float, and its side knocked against the planks.

'I'll call the police if you don't leave,' Michael said. He fought to keep his balance. Margo wanted to tell Michael that threatening Paul with the law wasn't going to calm him down.

'Do you really think the police would get here in time if I wanted to hurt you?' Paul grabbed the front of Michael's shirt and pulled him forward. Margo remembered Paul's strength when he had grabbed her in Brian's bedroom. Michael stiffened, pushed against Paul, and almost fell backward into the water. Then he straightened up and stood his ground again.

'Just bring her out here,' Paul said.

Margo moved closer. Paul's face was almost as familiar to her as Michael's. At this distance, she saw how even his good eye looked strange, red-rimmed and oily.

'And I hope you don't think you've got some innocent flower,' Paul said to Michael. 'I've had a piece of her myself.'

Margo's heart raced. Her daddy had begged her, *Think before you act*, and so she was thinking, but then Paul stabbed Michael's chest with his finger. 'Next time you're in the sack with her, ask if she remembers — '

'Leave him alone!' Margo shouted. Her voice echoed down the river. She crouched again behind some red osier dogwood.

'Is that you, Maggie? Why don't you come over and talk to me, sweetheart?' Paul said. His voice sounded strangely intense. He was high.

Margo didn't move.

'No, Margaret Louise,' Michael yelled. 'Don't do anything.'

'Oh, it's *Margaret* now? *Margaret Louise.* Very nice. Why don't you come on out and talk with us. I'll tell you how you ruined my brother's life.'

She could run to the house, grab her backpack, and head out, leaving Michael and Paul to work this out themselves. But she could too easily imagine Paul knocking Michael out and throwing him into the water.

As if reading her thoughts, Paul grabbed Michael's collar and pulled him closer. Then he pushed him away, and this time Michael fell backward onto the float. His head clunked the wood and made a hollow sound.

'What do you want with that little slut, anyhow?' Paul asked Michael and put his boot on Michael's chest. 'You seem like a respectable guy here. Nice house. You wear a goddamned tie to work.' The toe of Paul's work boot pressed Michael's tie now, and Michael was no longer fighting.

Michael coughed.

'Let him go,' Margo shouted and approached until she was only about twenty feet away.

Michael shouted, 'No, Margaret! Go into the house, call the cops.'

'You know you'll talk to me eventually, Maggie. And your boyfriend's got to go to work sometime and leave you alone.'

'Please leave now.' Margo raised the barrel of the shotgun to point at Paul's knees, his groin, his stomach, his heart and lungs like a buck's.

'Give that shotgun to me, Princess. You're not going to shoot anybody.'

Paul pushed his toe into Michael's neck. Margo knew its delicate bones and sharp Adam's apple. With those heavy work boots, Paul could crush his throat.

'Let me go, man,' Michael spat.

'You're really not in a position to tell me what to do.' He moved his foot and Michael gagged. Margo remembered that feeling of being crushed, unable to breathe, with the heat of Paul's breath on her. She adjusted the butt of the shotgun in her shoulder, got her sight bead on Paul's good eye.

'You're hurting me!' yelled Michael.

'I'm going to hurt you more,' Paul said. 'And her, too.'

Margo pulled the trigger.

At twenty feet, the twelve-gauge sprayed a tight pattern of buckshot into Paul's face, hitting him seemingly even before she had finished pulling the trigger. Margo was so solidly planted, she hardly even felt the shotgun's recoil. Paul flew backward, slammed into the side of his boat, which bobbed wildly under the impact, as did the oil-barrel float once his weight had left it. Paul's feet were barely touching the float, while his shoulders and arms leaned backward over the siderail of the Playbuoy. His back was bent the wrong way. The blood from his face poured down his body, onto the portside pontoon and became a red river flowing into the Stark. Margo wondered how so much blood could be in him. Michael had not managed to stand, though he was apparently unharmed. He gripped the planks beneath him.

Margo pointed the shotgun barrel down and walked toward Michael. She studied Paul's body, frozen in a position with his head thrown back, his chest tipped upward. Paul's body looked as unnatural as her body had felt beneath his. She heard a jet overhead, slowly crossing the sky.

'Margaret, what's happened?' Michael asked. He attempted to stand again, but sat back down. 'Call an ambulance. He's bleeding bad.'

A seagull screeched somewhere; a second gull answered. Margo tried to get her bearings.

'I'll call. I'll tell them to hurry.' Michael stood up at last. He looked at the body. His hand reached toward Margo and retracted. 'He's not dead, is he?' Michael said.

'I had to protect you,' Margo said.

'What the hell? Oh, my God. He's dead?'

'He was going to kill you,' she said. 'He had his foot on your throat. You have a mark there from his boot.'

'Margaret, please put the gun down.' Michael

sounded scared. 'I wish you'd gone into the house and called the police.'

'I couldn't leave you alone with him. He was stoned. Did you see his eyes?'

'Let's call the police right now. We'll go together.'

'He raped me,' she blurted.

'Oh, God. I should have known. I wish you'd've told me. We could have gotten a restraining order. Or something.'

'That wouldn't have stopped him.' She couldn't bear the way Michael's face was falling apart.

He reached out and grabbed at her shotgun. She jumped away from him and dropped the gun on the planks between them.

'It all happened so fast,' she said. 'But you don't realize. He was really going to hurt you.'

'We were the happiest people on earth. That's what we were at noon, the happiest people in the world. Do you remember?' His voice increased in pitch until it was shrill like the sound of the cicadas.

Margo kept her eye on the shotgun. Yes, she remembered. She remembered eating lunch today. The sunlight on the table, the yellow-and-white-patterned plates speckled with crumbs.

'There's no blood on the float. Nobody saw,' Margo said. Though blood continued to run in red ribbons down the side of the boat, there was not even a drop visible on the planks. She glanced up and down the river and saw no one approaching or departing, no one milling about near the water. The next-door neighbor's

186

driveway was empty. If she did this right, she thought, then tomorrow they could have breakfast as usual, eggs and toast, butter and jelly. The river's surface glimmered gold with the setting sun. Her first thought was to push Paul the rest of the way into the boat and launch it from the float, send it down the river, but it might not drift far enough away before it was discovered adrift or pushed onto shore by the current, as her rowboat had been when she'd fallen asleep in it.

'We have to call the police.'

'Nobody saw, Michael. Let's get him onto the boat.' Her voice sounded weak. She wished she hadn't spoken aloud. This was not the time for talking.

'This is a crime scene. We can't move the body.' Michael continued to shake his head. 'I need to think, Margaret. Let me think a minute.'

Margo recalled the buck she had shot across the river in Murrayville. She had struggled with the big body before figuring out the trick of negotiating herself beneath the corpse and lifting it using the strength of her legs. She should have been able to do that when Paul was on her in Brian's bed, should have been able to lift him with her shoulder and topple him. Should have then put a knife to his throat and prevented him from going any further. Then she wouldn't have had to shoot him in front of Michael. While Michael stepped away slowly, Margo got herself beneath Paul's legs and shoved. The body slid sideways, rolled up over the siderail, over the bench seat, and onto the Astroturf floor, where

187

Johnny had once fallen onto her tarped deer. Paul's work shirt rode up and revealed his pale stomach. Margo splashed water over the side of the boat and kept rinsing until the blood disappeared from the fiberglass. The current carried the residue downstream. Her own T-shirt was plain black, so blood would not show on it. She bent down and rinsed her hands in the water and smoothed her hair. Then she picked up the shotgun.

'This is a crime scene, Margaret. Disturbing it is a whole new crime. You don't understand. You need to stop now and do the right thing. You need to realize the gravity of what's just happened.' He backed up farther, until his heel hit the end of the gangplank, and he tripped and almost fell.

Margo tugged a folded blue tarp from a compartment beneath the bench seat at the back of the boat. She unfolded it over Paul's body, covered the pool of blood forming around him, soaking through the Astroturf that carpeted the boat's floor.

'Talk to me,' Michael said. 'Tell me you realize what you've just done to another human being.'

The only regret she felt at that moment was what was happening to Michael, the way he was moving away from her when she needed him.

'Nobody will know.'

'Margaret. You're not thinking clearly. We have to report this. The authorities will understand you were protecting me.'

Margo turned the key in the boat's ignition, and it fired right up. She checked the gas tank and the gauge registered more than half full. She turned off the engine and looked around, grateful to see nobody else, no lights coming on in the nearby houses. She dug in the boat's toolbox for work gloves and put on a brown cotton pair. She rubbed the shotgun all over to get rid of the fingerprints. She re-covered the body and the shotgun with the tarp.

'Margaret, honey, we'll tell them he raped you. We'll tell them he threatened to kill me. You said I've got a mark on my throat.' He reached up and felt his neck. 'Let's call them right now.'

'I'll go to jail, won't I?'

'I don't know,' Michael said. 'God, you're so young, too young for this. Too young to know a man like that. When I learned your real age, I should have sent you home.'

Margo thought of Billy, how the police took him, and he was a Murray. Murrays could do about anything without paying a price.

'They'll want to question you,' Michael said. 'And me. Both of us. Let's get in the Jeep right now and drive to the police station. Tell them the whole story.'

Margo squinted downstream into the setting sun. Darkness often crept in without her noticing, until suddenly the riverbanks were black. Now she was grateful to sense night coming on.

'Say something, Margaret. You're scaring me.'

'You don't have to worry,' she said.

'You've never done anything like this before. They won't be hard on you. Though I hate to guess what they'll think of me when they find out I'm with a seventeen-year-old girl.'

Margo resisted the urge to go into the house to retrieve her rifle for fear she might change her mind or lose confidence in her plan. Really she didn't want to go upstream with Paul; she wanted to stay with Michael and soothe him, try to make him understand how dangerous Paul had been, how he wasn't like other people. She had saved Michael's life, but so far he wasn't listening to her.

She took a few breaths, absorbed the river's movement through her feet and legs. Fish and turtles and water birds were her family, she supposed, not humans, despite the comfort she might get from food and beds, from hot showers and lovemaking. Even when she had lived in her father's house, every morning in summer and winter the river had spoken to her more clearly than he had.

She sat in the driver's seat, started up the boat's engine, and studied the dashboard. Gasoline fanned out on the water behind the boat, glistened in colors that became psychedelic in the fading light.

As she moved upstream in the growing darkness, she heard a *crunch* behind her. Cleo tore through the screen of the aluminum storm door. She jumped out through the hole she had made and ran to the edge of the river, out to the float. The last time Margo turned around, she saw Michael sitting cross-legged, hugging the fishing dog.

When she returned on foot just before five a.m., Michael was in the shower. She dug a T-shirt out of her backpack, put it on, and checked to make sure her jeans were dry before sitting on the edge of the bed. She ran her hands over King Cleo's head and waited. When Michael entered the bedroom and saw her, he dropped the towel he'd been adjusting around his waist.

'I should go to the police,' he said. He picked up his towel and covered himself. 'I've thought about it all night.'

'The boat is in Heart of Pines,' she whispered. 'It's tied up in his regular spot, upstream of the Gas and Grocery. They might not find him under the tarp for days. Maybe weeks.' She reached her hand out to Michael, and he automatically accepted it.

'Don't tell me any more,' Michael said and let her hand go.

'I didn't leave any fingerprints. I hid out until dark and then parked the boat. Nobody saw me.' Then she had walked back along the river road. She'd tied her bloody T-shirt around a rock. She'd filled her work gloves with muck and sunk them.

'You can't kill a person and not pay the consequences.'

She pulled her hand back into her lap. She didn't know if that was true, or whether any of Michael's rules would hold up over the long haul. After all, Brian had gotten away with killing a man up north, until he'd stupidly attacked Cal. Maybe she would pay different consequences than the ones Michael expected.

She knew Michael hated it when she clammed up. She had hoped he would've changed his mind during the night, but if anything, now he was more certain they should call the police.

'Over this last year, I thought you'd changed,' he said and closed his eyes.

'Changed how? I thought you liked me how I was.'

'But you haven't learned anything.'

'What do you want me to learn?'

'That you can't live like a wolf girl. That there are laws for a reason, that laws allow us to live together. Even finishing school — there's a reason for it, so you can be a better citizen. Now I see that. If you turn yourself in this morning, I'll do anything for you. I'll hire you the best lawyer I can afford. I'll spend every penny I have to get you free. Maybe you won't even go to jail. I could tell them he was crushing my throat, like you said.'

She studied his face, tried to figure out whether he would really turn her in, whether he would be able to lie for her. He was an honest person, and she didn't want him to have to lie.

'Stop it,' Michael said. 'Stop sitting there looking like a kidnapped Indian maiden. I didn't steal you, Margaret Louise. You came to me. Remember. You came to me.' He shook his head. 'You came to me with no home, and I took you in.'

She went back to petting the fishing dog. Maybe Michael had seen her the way he saw Cleo, as a pleasant creature for whom he could provide a home.

'I'm trying, Margaret, but I'm scared,' he said. 'Tell me you've never done anything like this before. Tell me you've never shot anybody.' He let his face fall into his hands. 'Oh, God, you have killed someone before.'

'No. I just shot him. I didn't kill him. He did something. I was just getting even so I didn't have to send *him* to jail. Jail is worse than being shot for some people.' Margo looked out through the sliding door, settled her gaze on the reflection of Michael's security light on the surface of the dark river.

Michael sat at the end of the bed beside her. 'Why did this have to happen?' he said. 'Tell me what you're feeling, Margaret.'

'He could have killed you,' she said. She didn't know how she felt except that she was scared.

'You're probably right he could have hurt me,' Michael said. 'Was that his shotgun?'

'His brother gave me that shotgun. I didn't steal it.'

'Maybe it would be just a little while in jail. A juvenile home, maybe, with other kids.'

'I don't think I could stand one day,' she said. 'Would you turn me in?'

'I'd have to. Or I'll go to jail, too, for being an accessory. But you'll turn yourself in, won't you?'

'Why don't we just wait and see what happens?'

'I can't live that way, dreading what might happen. Knowing I'm guilty of a crime. Thinking any day the hammer could fall.'

Margo herself had lived with dread, like every

other creature in the wild. Dread about what she might lose or who she might encounter that day, maybe someone who wished her harm.

'You can't stay here if you don't turn yourself in,' Michael said.

She was startled to hear the words spoken so bluntly, but it all made sense. She'd known this orderly, comfortable place wasn't her home. Michael had given her clothes and books, but he hadn't changed who she was.

'I can't have anything to do with you ever again if you don't turn yourself in,' he said.

The dog raised her head from Margo's thigh and looked at her.

Margo stood up and dragged her backpack from the closet. If she turned herself in, not only would she be locked away, but Michael might spend all his money and destroy his own life in the process of defending her. She had no choice. She would give up the comforts here and return to her real life on the river.

'Oh, Margaret. This is all a mess,' he said.

Margo took her hairbrush off the dresser. She moved as deliberately as she could, putting her few stray things into her bag, which was already packed, as it had been the whole time she'd been there. She pulled her rifle from the wooden rack Michael had built. She slung it over her left shoulder, dropped the four boxes of .22 cartridges into her bag, and looked around for any other evidence she had been there. She hadn't brought much into the house other than what they'd eaten. She took the new Annie Oakley book from the bedside stand. She wanted

194

to take the Indian hunter book, but Michael had not given that to her. She said goodbye to the fishing dog and to Michael without looking at either of them and headed toward the river.

13

When Margo arrived at the marijuana house, the midnight crickets were screaming. On her twelve-hour, thirty-some-mile trip downstream she had passed swampy places croaking with bullfrogs, but here the tree frogs chirped like insects. Margo pulled her boat onto the sand and climbed up the bank. The place was overgrown, spooky in its neglect. The dock was pulled out of the water, and grass and weeds poked up through the slats. Plywood was nailed over several of the windows, and glass shards in the dirt reflected moonlight. Both doors had padlocks on them. She lit the kerosene lantern she'd swiped from Brian's cabin before heading down the river. She held the lantern up and read the signs posted on both doors: KEEP OUT NO TRESPASSING, with THIS MEANS YOU spray-painted beneath. Junior's pot leaf had been painted over. When neither of the uncovered windows would budge, she began to pry at one of the pieces of plywood.

Before coming down the river, she had hung around downstream from Michael's house for a few days, but did not see any police. She knew they would eventually find Paul, and they'd almost certainly investigate the cabin on stilts. She'd slipped inside the cabin to procure a few items for her journey: the lantern, a small folding military shovel that she was now using to pry at the plywood, a fishing pole, a bottle of bug dope, and a jug of water. She had wiped clean all the surfaces that might contain fingerprints, but if the police brought drug-sniffing dogs, they would smell her. She hoped that Michael had not contacted the authorities. She was sorry to have hurt him.

She worked at the quarter-inch plywood for a long time, pulling out one nail after another, until eventually it was loosened enough that she could slip beneath it and through the empty window frame. She carried the lantern inside with her. The kitchen area was the same as before, with candles melted onto the Formica tabletop. The mattress on which Junior and his friends used to sit to smoke pot in the main room had been replaced by a plaid fold-out couch. She peeked in the bedroom and found it a mess, with bits of mattress stuffing spread across the floor along with wood scraps. Only splintered pieces remained of the wooden bed frame on which Margo had first fooled around with a boy. She closed the door.

She searched the empty cupboards. Inside a bread box she found a boxed brownie mix, and in the drawer beneath the oven, a tin pie pan. She collected paper and wood in a bag to use for starting a fire and carried them outside through the window. She ventured a little downstream until she found the Slocums' garden. Margo knew that if she took vegetables, it was stealing, but she remembered how her father had done favors for the Slocums, once fixing a space heater that had gone out on a cold night, and she picked four tomatoes and a big handful of beans.

She built a fire just upstream from where her boat was hidden. She stirred water into the brownie mix and balanced the pie tin of batter above the fire on three rocks, and while it cooked, she munched the raw vegetables. The brownies burned on the bottom, but still tasted sweet and good.

When her belly was full for the first time in days, she noticed the moon was full, too. Being back in Murrayville gave her a way of thinking about the last year and a half, her journey up the river and back. Traveling upstream had taken her no closer to her mother, but she had gotten Luanne's address and a response. Margo was not yet ready to think about Paul, and she pushed those thoughts away. She would focus for now on surviving each day, figuring out where to hide if the police came and where to go so her mother could contact her. Also, she wanted to find Junior. Maybe with him she could talk through everything that had happened. Junior would have graduated from high school last month, and so she figured she'd see him hanging around.

Margo wiped on more bug dope. She lay on her back on her father's old army sleeping bag, listening to crickets and looking at the stars. Three in a row would make up a man's belt, according to her grandfather, but she couldn't find them. He had said she could navigate by the stars, but who needed that? The river had just two directions, upstream and down. A screech owl whinnied, and Margo whinnied back with a sound so mournful she spooked herself.

Junior didn't come around the next day, and a

week passed and he still didn't come. Once she thought she saw him driving down the road toward her, but Joanna was in the passenger seat, so Margo stayed hidden in the ditch behind the black-eyed Susans. If Junior or his friends showed up at the marijuana house, she'd offer to cook fish for them or catch a snapping turtle and fry up the meat. How nice it would be to feed somebody, to have some company. After the second week, she decided that if Junior didn't show up soon, she would go to the Murray house and throw rocks at his bedroom window.

Margo stole enough food to feed herself, never too much from any one garden, and drank water from the spring. She saw a few of the Slocum kids, including Julie, come to the spring to fill their jugs and buckets. Margo would have liked to talk to Julie, but if she was still the tattler she always had been, she would tell everyone Margo was there. She wished she had made the effort to talk to Julie during the last year in Murrayville, but back then she'd been unable to shake her anger at her cousin for telling Crane what she'd seen in the shed.

As July melted into August, Margo listened to gangs of newly fledged robins picking at the underbrush in such numbers that the woods floor seemed alive. She watched nuthatches spiral down trees headfirst to the ground and back up again. She watched turkey vultures spiral high above, searching by scent for those creatures that had not survived the summer. And Margo still did not see police boats searching the river for her.

She rediscovered her favorite old mossy places in the Murray woods, where there grew lichens, fiddlehead ferns, and toadstools — some of them brightly colored. She searched for giant puffball mushrooms and chicken-of-the-woods, and each evening at dusk she watched thousands of fireflies charge and discharge. She kept herself hidden as best she could, and was happily surprised that nobody came around to investigate the modest fire she burned each evening and put out each morning. She kept her belongings in the boat, which she covered with her old green tarp and branches. Unless it was raining, she stayed outside. She collected pine needles to create a soft bed beside her campfire, and she gathered mattress stuffing into a plastic bag to make a soft pillow. She found that on the nights when she felt safe and comfortable under the stars, on the nights when she had fed herself well, that was when she felt particularly lonely. Loving a person the way she had loved Michael was something she couldn't shake off or be done with when it was over. Even having lost Brian saddened her; she had come to know him so well and had learned so much from him, and now the part of her that had been Brian's companion was of no use.

Michael had given her a regional map with Lake Lynne on it, and they'd discovered that her mother's road ran alongside the big lake, which was almost a mile across and five miles long. Maybe there was a way to get there by water, if only Margo could get her heavy boat around the dam at Confluence. If only she weren't, in her grandfather's words, *stuck on the Stark*. Margo usually kept the map in her Annie Oakley book, but one night, while sitting at her fire, she tore out the portion of the map surrounding her mother's place and put it in her wallet so she'd always have it close at hand.

After dark, as the weather was mild, Margo rowed the several miles downstream into town, stood on the unlit iron walking bridge over the waterfall in the park, where a dammed pond flowed into a little stream that led to the river. She walked past the small brick high school she had been so eager to leave every day, and she wondered if she should have tried harder to be more like other kids. She couldn't see herself ever being very much different than she was, but maybe when she had a chance to make friends in the future she would try harder.

Margo sometimes ate leftover pizza slices from the dumpster behind the Murrayville pizza shop. One night she was sitting on the high curb there reading discarded newspapers by the streetlight, and she came across a news story from Heart of Pines. It detailed how gunshot victim Paul Daniel Ledoux was discovered in a pontoon boat that was found parked in Heart of Pines two weeks after he was shot. A shotgun was found beside the body, under a tarp. The only fingerprints on the gun were the victim's, but officials did not think the death was a suicide. The boat was found to contain a gallon jug of some raw material for making an amphetamine that was capturing the attention of law enforcement. The killing was assumed to be drug related. There was no mention of the cabin or the drum of liquid or a riverside informant. The victim left behind a wife and three children, ages five, seven, and nine. Margo put her mushroom-and-sausage slice back in the pizza box. She read the last paragraph again. She had not thought of Paul's wife when she pulled the trigger, or of their three children, who would now grow up without a father.

From the dark river, she sometimes watched her daddy's house and the stranger living there, a tall, stoop-shouldered, gray-haired woman Margo had seen at a Thanksgiving party a few years before. The woman smoked a pipe the way a man would. Margo saw her toss things into a big hole someone had dug behind the house. Margo didn't dare approach because the woman kept a white pit bull chained to the swing set frame Margo had used for stringing up her bucks. It occurred to Margo that two years ago she had been gutting and skinning her deer in the most obvious place, so that all the Murrays must have known about her kills. Her daddy had been right that she was reckless. She felt sorry for the white dog for being chained up, but the one time she approached, it barked a high-pitched, manic rhythm and strained against its tether as though wanting to attack her. The old woman came out with a pistol in her hand and shouted into the darkness, 'Who's out there?' but Margo was already on the water, rowing away.

The following midday, Margo was poking around in the woods upstream when she saw a white Murray Metal Fabricating truck pull into the driveway of the marijuana house. Out of it toppled a tall man, who leaned against the truck's door pillar until he could get hold of forearm crutches. Margo was too far away to make out features, but she knew who he was. He unlocked the door and entered the little building. Margo hoped she'd left the plywood flush against the window so he wouldn't notice it had been messed with. A few minutes later a dark-haired girl came running to the door, and she looked both ways before entering. Julie Slocum. Margo did not approach the house, but headed upstream to her camp. She had been foolish and unkind to ever be angry with poor Julie.

Margo returned to the Murray place that night and climbed the riverbank to investigate the barn beside which she had shot clay disks with Billy and Junior. A lone pig snorted under a corrugated metal hut. Grandpa had always kept the barn painted, but now the red was peeling all along the side by the river. The whitewashed shed was padlocked from the outside. The golden light of incandescent bulbs showed in the windows of the big house, giving the impression of safety and warmth. Margo was wary of setting off the beagles, but when she got up her nerve to come close to the house, she heard no barking. The kennel was empty. Moe was nowhere to be seen, either. Margo stood beneath Junior's bedroom window, listening to the squeaks of flying squirrels. She was readying to toss a rock when she saw the figure of a younger kid, Toby or Tommy, looking out. She considered knocking on the kitchen door, but chickened out and instead went behind the house and stole pole beans and Brandywine tomatoes from the garden. More beans were toughening on the vines than usual, and more tomatoes had been left to rot, suggesting Joanna was behind on her canning.

Margo returned the following night and circled the house, trying to get a glimpse inside. The house was built on concrete block footings that raised it above the hundred-year flood level, so in order to see into the living room at close range, she pulled herself up into an old apple tree. She saw Joanna sitting in her chair sewing only a few feet away. She was wearing a blue print dress, and as always her hair was pulled back in a knot. Her shoulders looked a little more stooped, her face slightly more lined, her hands a bit more arthritic than a year and a half ago, but Cal, sitting beyond her, looked very different. He was gray-haired now, though he couldn't have been much more than forty years old, and his face looked pinched and stern. His arms and shoulders were bigger than before, maybe from working wheelchair wheels and those crutches that lay on the floor beside him. His legs were straight out in front of him on a footstool, covered with a blanket. His gaze was trained on the TV. A sleeping figure that Margo took to be Junior lay on his back on the floor, his body impossibly long, his arms folded under his head, on which he wore headphones. Robert Murray, who must have been eleven years old by now, sat cross-legged on the couch and was watching TV intently. Toby and Tommy, aged seven, sat with their backs to her. What shocked Margo was the stillness of the room, apart from the movements of Joanna's hands working needle and thread. So different from the lively old river paradise they had once all been a part of.

She leaned out of the tree, closer to the window, figuring she was well hidden by the foliage and darkness. She wished she could somehow get Junior's attention. Then Joanna looked out the window. Her face was so sad that Margo had to swallow hard. She'd been naive to imagine that, after all they'd been through, the Murrays would have been the same family she'd known, full of fun, stories of their escapades, and plans for hunting trips. Margo wondered if Joanna ever worried about her. Joanna had plenty of other things to worry about, Billy, of course, and Cal especially. Margo understood the sadness and exhaustion in Joanna's face. Margo had to shake that same sadness out of her joints in order to get up every morning and work up the energy to hunt for food to eat that day.

A white-bellied flying squirrel flashed above her — her grandpa had referred to them as sprites when he glimpsed them at night, the same as he'd sometimes called her. Margo was shifting her weight, and she slipped a little. She caught herself by grabbing a branch, and when she looked back into the room, Joanna was looking out at her. Margo slowly raised her hand to wave, but instead made a gesture of peace the Indian hunter from Michael's book might have made when he was trying to hide his wolverine heart. Joanna glanced toward Cal and her sons. She laid aside her mending — it was Junior's jacket with the pot leaf stitched on the back. Margo slid down the tree, followed Joanna from outside the house, climbed the wooden steps, and waited among the mosquitoes at the riverside kitchen door. She slid the Marlin off her shoulder and leaned it against the house where Joanna wouldn't see it. Joanna opened the door and then took hold of the knob to steady herself.

'Margaret?' Joanna whispered. 'Is that you?'

Margo nodded.

'What are you doing here?'

Margo took a breath, tried to speak, but nothing came out. Maybe Joanna was reading the pain in her face, because her tone softened.

'You look thin. And your hair. Your pretty hair. It's . . . '

Margo reached up and touched her hair, brushed away some pine needles. She had not washed her hair since she'd left Michael's three weeks ago.

'I need a shower,' she said.

'Oh, Sprite, it is you, isn't it?' Joanna leaned toward Margo as though she wanted to hug her or inspect her, but then pulled back and glanced behind her at the door leading to the living room. 'Oh, dear. Are you all right?'

'I'm okay. I was just in the woods. Looking for

mushrooms.' Margo whispered because Joanna was whispering. She could smell the cinnamon bread Joanna must have made for the next day's breakfast, and also some greasy meat.

'I thought you were with your mama, Sprite. You left us that note. Your uncle Cal was angry at you. He still is.'

'I know.' Hearing Joanna use her old nickname made her feel acutely all she'd lost.

'You stole his most valuable rifle.'

Margo nodded and glanced at the Marlin leaning against the wall. She would have liked to ask if she could come inside, clean up, sit quietly in the kitchen for a few minutes, but she only choked out, 'Could I . . . ?' and stopped.

'What do you want from us?' Joanna was crying, and Margo found she was, too.

'To come back for a while,' she said, 'until I can go to my mom's.' Annie Oakley had begged her mother to let her return.

'Oh, Margaret. God knows I could use your helpful hands in this house.' Joanna glanced again at the door to the living room. She said, 'I don't want anyone to hear us. You knew that man who broke your uncle Cal's legs? He told everyone in the courtroom he was doing it for what Cal did to 'a certain young girl.' That was a hard time for Cal, with everyone thinking the worst of him.'

'I didn't want him to hurt Uncle Cal,' Margo said. She looked down at Joanna's bare shins and at her feet, clad in the worn leather shoes Margo remembered. Joanna was blessedly the same. Margo felt mosquitoes bothering her face, but

207

she didn't move to slap them. One landed on Joanna's cheek, and Margo hoped Joanna wouldn't shut the door yet.

'Cal's started walking with the crutches. We're very hopeful.'

'I saw him,' Margo said. 'With Julie.'

Joanna squeezed her eyes shut.

Margo recognized Joanna's homemade dress. The blue-flowered fabric was more faded than when Margo had last seen it. Margo had never loved a dress more than she loved Joanna's dress now. Joanna opened her eyes and shook her head. 'You know, a strong marriage is a strange thing. It makes you have faith in your husband regardless of how things appear.'

Margo kept looking at Joanna's exhausted face. Joanna, in return, seemed to be studying Margo for a clue to what had happened to all of them. Joanna had always been the opposite of Margo's mother, strict where Luanne was permissive, plain while her mother was pretty, hardworking while her mother was bone-lazy, modest and religious while her mother was egotistical and dramatic. They were as different as Brian and Michael.

'I blame your mama,' Joanna said. 'She should have taken you with her. I'm sorry if I had something to do with her going away.'

Margo didn't know what she meant.

'Where are you staying? With friends?'

Margo hesitated, but because of the concerned look on Joanna's face, she nodded and said, 'With a friend.'

'Cal had someone on the school board look

for you at all the schools in the county, and you're not enrolled. This is no way to grow up, with no schooling, sneaking around at night. Let me think about this. Let me try to figure out whether there's any way for you to live here until we find your mama.'

Margo did not want to disagree with anything Joanna might say, not about her mother, not about where she would be staying, not about going to school. She wondered if it would be easier to go to school now that she'd missed two years. She'd be with all new kids, younger kids. She'd heard of kids going to school part-time.

'I've got her address,' Margo said. 'She wrote to me. Said she wasn't ready for me to come yet.'

'I don't know how much you know, but things aren't going well for your uncle Cal and the company.' Joanna glanced behind her.

Margo nodded.

'If anybody comes in the kitchen, don't let them see you. Billy will make a big fuss if he sees you. He's still mad about his grandfather's boat, you know.'

'Billy's not locked up?' Margo felt her heart sink.

'Of course not. I mean, he had a little trouble, but he's out now. Did you hear about that?'

'The police took him after he shot my dad.'

'Yes, for questioning and evaluation.' Joanna was looking at her strangely. 'That was all. It was self-defense, defense of his papa. You and Billy both told the police that. So did your uncle Cal.'

'Oh.' Margo felt confused. 'I wish I could say hi to Junior.'

'Junior's in Alaska.'

'Alaska? With Loring?'

'He graduated from the military school. He was living back at home, and he and Cal were fighting all the time, so he went up there with a school friend. Now he's working on a fishing boat. He says he loves it.' Joanna smiled.

'But I just saw him in the living room. You were sewing on his jacket.'

'You saw Billy. He's gotten taller than Junior or his papa. The doctors put him on medication that helps him with his moods and his temper. Junior asked me to mail him his jacket, and I'm trying to put a flannel lining in it to surprise him. Now wait here a minute.' When Joanna returned less than a minute later, she stuffed a paper grocery bag into Margo's arms. 'Here's some slices of my bread that you always loved and a little jar of your favorite peach jam. You can share it with your friend.'

'Thank you,' Margo said. The bag was warm and smelled of cinnamon. She glanced inside to see that Joanna had given her about a third of the cinnamon swirl breakfast loaf. Some of the boys would have to eat plain bread tomorrow.

'Are you sure you have a place to stay?' Joanna asked. 'You could sleep in the barn if you needed to. Some of the kids had a sleepover out there last week. There's probably still blankets out there.'

Margo would not take a chance on staying in the barn, so far away from where she could hide her boat. And so long as it wasn't raining, she preferred to sleep outside, where she'd hear someone coming and be able to run.

From inside, upstairs, Margo heard a wail.

'Randy's crying,' Joanna said.

Margo must have looked confused.

'You don't know?' Joanna said, and her eyes spilled over. 'Of course. How could you know? I had a baby.'

'A baby? Congratulations.' Margo hoped it was the right thing to say. What Margo had done to Cal, then, had not stopped him from making another baby. It had been exactly what she had intended to do — not damage him permanently, but only make him hurt. Her revenge had been just right, and yet it had all gone so wrong.

'A boy?'

'A boy. Yes.' Joanna's voice cracked. 'I was so sure it would be a girl this time. I was going to name her Rachel, after my sister.'

'What's he like? I wish I could see him.'

'Your new cousin has Down syndrome,' Joanna said and swallowed as though she dreaded explaining. 'That's why we had to get rid of the dogs. The barking made him scream and cry. *Down syndrome* is what they say now, not *Mongoloid*.'

'Down syndrome,' Margo said and nodded.

Joanna shook her head. 'I love him, but I'm so tired. I paid Julie to help me for a while, but . . . Oh, Nymph, you were the only one of the kids who was ever really helpful.'

'I always loved helping,' she whispered.

'You know, Cal was furious when you disappeared and left that note. Why didn't you stay for the burial?'

211

'What burial? Daddy was cremated.'

'But we interred his box of ashes in the cemetery, on the north edge. Cal made all the boys go along.'

'I didn't know they put ashes in a cemetery.' Margo had thought that when a person was cremated, he was simply gone. 'Did Billy go?'

Joanna nodded. 'For three months, your uncle Cal wouldn't tell the police you were gone. Not until they needed your signature. Then he told them you'd gone to your mother's, out of the state.'

Margo shook her head. She had been living with Brian at that time.

'They looked for your mother,' Joanna said, 'but said they couldn't find her. How did you find her?'

'I asked around and sent letters,' Margo said. She wished she could have been at her father's funeral, despite Billy's being there. Margo's heart started to feel squeezed when she thought about Billy living comfortably with his family, as though he'd done nothing wrong.

'I hear somebody coming. Come back and talk to me tomorrow morning if you can. The boys'll be at day camp, and Billy's in summer school. I'll make you something nice to eat.' Joanna closed the door.

14

Back at the Marijuana house, Margo devoured Joanna's bread with jam and wiped the jam jar clean. As kids, Margo and Junior used to pile the chunky peach preserves on their toast as thick as pie filling. The food fired something up in her, and it took her a long time to fall asleep. The following morning was hazy, and Margo slept late. She wanted more bread and jam so powerfully that she couldn't bring herself to eat the vegetables she'd collected and so went hungry. While she packed up all her things, she was feeling dopey, and because of the hazy sky she couldn't get a sense of what time it was. She parked her boat downstream from the Murray house, by the shed, and snuck up close enough to lie on her belly and spy. She saw Joanna at the window over the kitchen sink. After about twenty minutes, Joanna stepped outside, wiped her hands on her apron, and searched the horizon. Margo was happy to know that Joanna was looking for her. Soon she would stand up, walk to the house, and rest the Annie Oakley Marlin in the rack on the porch, but for just a little longer she needed to observe this place, to let it sink in that she was returning home, at least for a visit. Joanna tilted her head as though hearing something, the baby crying perhaps, and she hurried back inside. Margo knew how badly Joanna needed her help, so maybe she would find a way to bring Margo back to the family. After school, Margo would come home to babysit and care for the Down's baby. Margo would help cook bread and pies for the Murray men and boys, and Joanna could teach her to cook soups and stews this winter, ones Margo hadn't yet attempted. Joanna knew how to cook everything. Maybe Margo could learn from Uncle Hank how to smoke pork and make bacon.

She lay for a long time in the cool, damp grass, waiting for another glimpse of Joanna. If Joanna went out to the overgrown garden to pick tomatoes, Margo would join her there and pick beside her. After a while Margo noticed the front of her shirt was soaked from the grass. She sat up and aimed her rifle at the kitchen door. She thought she smelled cinnamon across the distance, maybe from a pie or tomorrow's cinnamon bread. She let her rifle lie in her lap. This was the time of year Joanna might be making more peach jam. Apples would be ripe soon, the golden delicious for eating and the tart Jonathans for making pies. Some years Joanna made apple butter, cooking the fruits down until they had a smoky, caramel flavor and then adding spices. Margo had never tired of peeling apples in the Murray kitchen.

Margo would always have enough to eat if she could return to the Murrays', and she would not be lonely for people. Too bad there would be no Junior to crack jokes and commiserate with, no dogs to pet. Probably she would not have a rifle of her own. Still Margo's mouth watered for

214

all the delicious foods she would cook and eat, and she would have Joanna's companionship in the kitchen. Margo looked forward to the rowdy dinner conversation she had always loved listening to.

'Nympho!' shouted a voice from the river, a man's voice.

Margo stayed low as she moved toward the shed and her boat. There, standing at the prow of *The River Rose*, gripping some kind of long gun in one hand, was Billy. Joanna was right that he'd grown taller than Junior. He froze as he listened for a response, but didn't see Margo twenty-some yards away. She flattened herself on the ground the way the Indian hunter did when stalking. As she took aim at Billy, her breathing slowed. She could shoot Billy through the back of his neck, sever his spine without his ever seeing her. She knew it must be river fog or her hunger for bread and jam making her hallucinate, but she thought she saw several other Murrays standing alongside Billy. Real Murrays were never truly alone, she thought.

'Bang,' she whispered to herself, to release a little of what was pent up inside her. She had been so distracted and in such a hurry to see Joanna this morning that she had left the oars in the oarlocks, left the oar blades resting on the back seat, flanking her backpack, which sat so that the stenciled name CRANE faced up. She hadn't even placed a branch over the boat to camouflage it.

Billy squatted at the river's edge. He touched the prow, pressed his hand where *The River*

Rose was burned into the wood. People considered .22 rifles to be squirrel guns, but a .22 bullet in the temple at this range would penetrate Billy's skull, bounce around and scramble his brain, and he wouldn't make any more trouble for anyone. Something scratched her throat. She had to resist coughing with such effort that her eyes watered.

Billy looked on the other side of the prow and probably saw the discoloration where the registration numbers were before she pried them off — a boat with no motor did not need to be registered, and since she'd left Brian's, she'd had no motor.

'Nympho!' he shouted. He stood and looked around. 'Where are you?'

Margo hated the way the nickname echoed over the river. He might disturb Joanna and the baby. Didn't he know how hard it was to get a baby to sleep sometimes? When he turned more or less in her direction, she saw that he was wearing, under his jean jacket, a black T-shirt with a rock-and-roll decal resembling a bull's-eye, directing her to shoot just above his solar plexus. The sun was at the top of the sky behind the haze, so this was as bright as the day was going to get. He shouted again, not quite as loudly or with such confidence, 'Nympho?'

'Get away from my boat,' she said and stood up. From this angle, she noted that the gun in his hand was his old pellet rifle, the one he'd gotten for his fourteenth birthday. He could take out an eye with a lucky shot, but he wasn't going to kill anything more than a bird or a squirrel.

'You're supposed to be in summer school,' Margo said. Every muscle in her body was tensed to slide the Marlin up to her shoulder and press the trigger. If only her eyes would stop watering. She swallowed again to get rid of whatever was in her throat.

'This morning Ma asked me what if you wanted to stay with us for a while, how would I feel about that? I said *no way*. I figured that meant you were hanging around. That's why I skipped school today.'

Margo wished she had anticipated this situation and thought it through so her brain wouldn't feel so muddled now.

'This is a Murray boat,' Billy said. 'You know it was never meant for you. And because of you, Dad's crippled. Everybody knows you told that guy to beat Dad up.'

She wanted to protest, to say she was a Murray, too, and she had not wanted Cal beaten up. Instead she said, 'I could shoot you easy.'

'Go ahead and kill me. You'll rot in prison. I've been in the juvey. I know what it's like.'

'Your ma said you didn't go to jail.'

'I went to the juvey this year, for two months.'

'For what?'

'A little problem with a fire getting out of hand.' He smiled, but it seemed forced. 'We were just trying to keep warm, but nobody would believe us.'

'Why'd you have to shoot my dad?'

'You know why, Nympho. That ain't no kind of thing for a man to do, shooting my dad that way. That ain't something you do, shooting a

217

man's dick.' He spat into the river.

Margo wondered again if there was anything to be gained by telling the truth.

'And I don't care if you shoot me. Go ahead. Life around here sucks, anyway. We're poor now. Junior went away to Alaska, and the new baby's a retard.'

Margo aimed and fired, right at the butt of his pellet rifle, knocking it out of his hands. He yelped, and the rifle hit the prow of the boat and fell onto the sandy muck. She expected him to run or at least beg her not to shoot him, but he stood his ground. When he reached down and picked up the gun, she shot the stock again, knocking it into the boat this time. Billy pulled his hand away as though he'd been stung by a wasp. Margo could feel his fear, but he did not outwardly express any. He let the gun lie on the prow seat and stood up and crossed his arms. 'You been off with your ma? You two should stick together, seeing how you're both whores.'

'You don't know anything about my ma.'

'Junior saw her with Dad once. In the barn. He said not to tell you, but I don't care.'

'Shut up.'

'I know she ran off with a man and didn't care nothing about you. That's what Ma said.'

Margo fired once more past him, so he would hear the bullet whiz two feet from his ear before it went into the water. She hoped he would shut up and run away, but he hardly flinched.

'Aren't you even sorry you killed my dad?' Margo was surprised to find herself asking this question, so similar to the one Michael had asked her about Paul. She felt the muscles twitch in her arm.

'I didn't have no choice. He was going to kill Dad.'

When her arm twitched again, she lowered the gun.

'You were there,' he said. 'He already shot Dad once, and he was pointing it at me, pointing it at Dad. You saw him, Nympho. You told the police the same thing.'

'He wasn't going to kill your dad. There wasn't even a bullet in that rifle. He was just trying to save me. I'm the one who shot your dad.' Margo heard some blue jays fussing, and one made a sound like a crow. She smelled wood smoke from the Murray house. She wondered if Joanna were calming the baby. She reminded herself to stay focused on Billy.

'You're lying, Nympho. Your dad came over and shot my dad's tires out. He was crazy. We all saw him do that from upstairs. All of us were too scared to come down 'cause he might kill us.'

'He only shot the tires, though. Not any people.' Margo wanted to convince Billy how wrong he was, how they all were wrong about her dad, but the energy was going out of her. It occurred to her that she might have been wrong, too, about what Paul had been doing to Michael.

'He shot dad's dick,' Billy said, and his voice took on an angry urgency. 'What kind of man does that, Nympho? A crazy man, that's who. I didn't want to kill anybody. I had to.'

Margo began to feel tired, too tired to lift her rifle. Billy was a jerk, had always been a jerk, and

219

was no doubt a criminal, but he was not a cold-blooded killer. She thought back to the day her father was shot. Crane had been holding the rifle as he'd helped her to her feet, and then he'd lunged toward Billy. Billy should have known Crane wasn't trying to shoot anybody, that the gun wasn't even loaded, but everything had happened so fast. Billy had fired, thinking he was saving himself and his dad, just as Margo had been thinking she was saving Michael from Paul. Billy was a lousy punk, but he didn't deserve to die for doing what he thought he had to do. And Margo did not want to kill her cousin. When she had shot Cal beside the shed, she had felt calm and confident in every cell of her body that she was doing what was right and necessary. Before she had fired at Paul, she had felt that certainty again. She did not feel any such calm or certainty now.

'You can go ahead and shoot me if you want. I'll stand right here. In the juvey, I bet guys money to burn my skin with cigarettes, and I never moved. The smell of it made them gag before I'd make a sound.'

She held down the hammer and slowly pressed the trigger to put the Marlin into safety position, and then she let the rifle hang half cocked at her side. She thought of Cal and Joanna, how sad they would have been if she had killed Billy, how miserable Toby or Tommy would have been if either had come upon their brother's body while digging night crawlers or fishing in a snag. She felt plain relief at Billy's not being dead. The whole world would have changed, as profoundly as it had changed when her own father died or when she shot Paul. And if she had shot Billy for what he had done, then maybe somebody would have had to shoot her for what she'd done to Billy. She took another deep breath and let it out.

'I'm taking this boat,' Billy said. He had always wanted *The River Rose*. Not long after Grandpa Murray died, Billy had taken the boat from her, and Cal had made him return it.

'Grandpa gave it to me,' Margo said.

'Grandpa was out of his mind and you tricked him. If you want to stop me, you'll have to kill me, and if you kill me, you'll go to prison because you're seventeen now. Ma probably already heard you shooting. She'd be out here except for the retard is probably crying.' Margo thought she saw those Murray ghosts again, standing beside Billy, supporting him, whatever he decided to do.

'Please don't take it, Billy.'

'Too late, Nympho. It's mine now.' He pushed off from shore and jumped into the boat as it was moving away. Margo laid her rifle in the grass and ran down the bank and into the water. She grabbed hold of the back of the boat and got dragged into deeper water by the force of Billy's rowing. She was slowing him down, almost stopping him, but then, with both feet, Billy kicked her pack off the back seat and onto her, and she had to let go to catch it. He rowed hard toward the center of the river.

'I'll get it back,' she said, standing hip-deep in water, trying to hold her pack and sleeping bag out of the current. 'There's nowhere you can hide that boat, Billy. I know every hiding place on this river. If you lock it to a tree, I'll chop the tree down.'

'You'll never touch this boat again,' he shouted. 'How dare you shoot at me with Dad's rifle.'

'Uncle Cal will make you give that boat back, and you know it.' She didn't feel as confident as she was trying to sound — Cal might not side with her against his own son this time. The other time, when Cal had made Billy return the boat, Billy had given it back with four snakes in it, including one orange-and-white milk snake that was halfway through devouring one of the three smaller garter snakes. At the time, Margo had simply lifted the mess of snake flesh out with an oar and flipped it into the shallow water, but that memory sickened her now.

Margo climbed onto the riverbank and threw down her damp pack with the folded tarp, sleeping bag, and little shovel attached. She picked up her rifle, cocked the hammer, and got Billy in her sights again. As she watched him, her rage doubled, tripled, and she had to shoot at something. She aimed and shot at the prow of her boat, between the words *River* and *Rose*.

'All I care is that you don't have it, Nympho,' he shouted. 'And if you shoot me, you won't have your precious boat in prison, either.'

She had to admire Billy's coolness. She could never have let herself be burned with cigarettes to prove a point. He slipped downstream, along with her fishing gear, the kerosene lantern, and her water jug.

'There's nowhere you can hide *The River Rose* that I won't find it!' Margo shouted, though Billy was too far away to hear. She wiped tears from her eyes and looked toward the big Murray house. If she walked up to that door, Joanna would greet her and cook something delicious for her, might even ask her to move in. Margo imagined Joanna welcoming her, embracing her, the way she'd always embraced her sons after their troubles. But Joanna was not her mother. In that house Margo could only be a ghost of herself, an overaged tenth-grader with no rifle, at the mercy of Billy's temper, following the rules Cal and Joanna would set for her. Trying to make her life with the Murrays would be like trying to back up the current of the river, like gathering up the water that had already flowed over the dam, into the Kalamazoo, and out into Lake Michigan and bringing it back to the Stark. Margo couldn't bear to see Joanna again, not even to say goodbye. She would never again help Joanna in the kitchen. Instead, she had helped Joanna one last time in a way Joanna would never know about. She had not shot Billy as a gift to Joanna and the family who had once cared for her.

Margo wanted to walk along the riverbank after Billy, but she reconsidered. If Margo didn't show up at the house, Joanna might be worried enough to contact the police or to send somebody out looking for her. Margo dug a pen out of her pack and wrote on the back of her last paper target. *Dear Joanna. You're right. I need to go to my ma's house. My friend will take me.*

Thank you for the bread and jam. Love, MLC. Margo pinned the note to the clothesline beside a row of little T-shirts.

With her wet pack and sleeping bag, her progress over land was slow. Billy had rowed out of sight, but she figured she would see the boat wherever he might park it or when he headed back upstream to the Murray house. Nobody was going to try to wrestle that heavy boat onto a trailer, so it had to pass her on the water.

In the nearly four years since Old Man Murray had gotten sick and given her the boat, Margo had not gone a day without seeing it. When the river had threatened to freeze, she and her father had winched the boat out of the water and chained it to a tree to await spring outside her bedroom window. The new oars Michael had bought her were covered with a shiny preservative that made them move through the water smooth as glass without ever giving her splinters. She had rowed silently in the water with those oars, the way the Indian hunter with the heart of a wolverine stalked silently through the woods.

It took Margo until early evening to hike to the Murrayville cemetery, though it was only a few miles downstream. She had searched both sides of the river along the way and was certain Billy had not brought the boat upstream past her.

The cemetery was located right across the river from the Murray Metal Fabricating plant, and the biggest thing in the cemetery was Grandpa Murray's memorial, a six-foot-high stone, which he had commissioned himself, with

224

two leaping trout and a buck's head sculpted in relief on the front and a bear and a wolverine carved on the back. She had seen a bear her grandpa had brought home from up north — it had nearly filled the back of his pickup truck. She had helped him skin it, and she had felt spooked and thrilled when the skin was off, when the body looked like a man's.

Margo put her hands on the carved wolverine, which was baring its pointed teeth. 'Grandpa, you would not believe how much has happened since you've been gone,' she said. What a pleasure it would be to hear the old man's voice again. 'I've learned so many things. Seriously.'

She wished she'd spoken up more before he'd died, to ask him questions about hunting, about wolves, about the wolverine he'd told her about that had gotten into his camp up north and torn it apart. A glutton, as he'd called it, was an animal a man couldn't hope to see, let alone catch. She wanted to ask her grandfather, would a deer eat a bird? Why would a heron stalk a .22 cartridge?

She hung the wet sleeping bag on the Old Man's marker to dry in what was left of the day's hazy light and then searched until she found a small engraved stone, flat against the ground. She traced the letters and repeated his name, *Bernard Crane, Bernard Crane, Bernard Crane*, like one of Joanna's bead prayers. He was the only Crane in the cemetery. His mother, Dorothy Crane, had gone off to Florida to live with a cousin and died of what her father called *female cancer* and was buried there without

Margo ever having met her.

'I'm okay, Daddy. Don't worry about me. But I just can't go back and live with the Murrays,' she whispered. 'But don't worry. I'm never going to kill anybody else ever again.'

Margo studied the grass around the marker and considered where the box of ashes might be. She saw that a rectangle of grass four feet in front of the carved stone was slightly sunken. She untied Brian's little military shovel from her pack, unfolded it, and dug down more than a foot, until she met resistance. She continued to dig and clear away dirt. Finally she saw dull metal. She continued until she uncovered the edges of the box, similar in size to the one she'd pulled out from under Crane's bed. She dug around the outside of the box until it came loose, cleared the dirt off the attached bronze-colored plaque that read BERNARD CRANE, 1947–1979, same as the stone.

The box was heavier than she'd expected it would be, maybe eight or ten pounds, and she was pretty sure it had been made at Murray Metal, maybe by someone who cared about her father. The welded joints had been ground smooth, with great care. It was coated with a dark gray baked-on enamel. Cal had done right by Crane's wishes. She brushed the rest of the dirt off and pressed her cheek against the cool metal. Having held the box, she could not put it back into the ground. She filled the hole with the dirt she'd removed and some silt from the river, combed the remaining dirt out of the grass, and replaced the sod as best she could.

226

She slept in the cemetery that night, next to the river. Not long after she drifted off to sleep, she awoke to screams, and it took her a while to realize they weren't people or ghosts, but raccoons. The following morning, she awakened dew-soaked, to the vision of the big blue fabricating plant churning orange smoke across the river. A flatbed semi truck was backing into an open loading bay. The parking lot was half full, mostly with pickup trucks. She hung her tarp, sleeping bag, and wet clothes over gravestones to dry and kept watch on the river, something she never tired of doing.

When she finally set off walking, she tucked the ashes under her arm. The box was going to slow her down even more, but she knew she could not leave her father behind this time. She trudged downstream a few miles before resting in a windbreak beside a farmer's field. She was beginning to fear she might have missed Billy rowing back upstream while she slept more heavily than she'd meant to. Or maybe he'd hidden the boat somewhere on the opposite side of the river, though she knew there weren't any creeks over there. Maybe it was behind someone's oil-barrel float, though she'd looked pretty carefully. She hiked farther until she heard the diesel thrum and whir of a big haybine. Somebody was mowing an alfalfa field. She camped at the river's edge.

The following two days she continued downstream, covering only a mile or so between rest stops, and finally found herself in the state park, the Pokagon Mound Picnic Area. She realized it was night when she arrived only because of how brightly a campfire ahead of her burned against the darkness. She was about twenty-four miles downstream from the Murrays', but she felt as though she had traveled farther, to another land.

She snuck as close as she could without letting the teenagers around the fire see her. Two of them were smoking cigarettes, a couple were making out, and one of the remaining two seemed focused on creating a line drawing with a pencil. She recognized some of them from her class at school; though their names didn't come to her, she was sure they were Billy's friends. Seemingly an eternity had passed in the last twenty-one months, when she would have passed these people in the hallway at school. Though she had never sought out their company before, she now wanted to be near their wood smoke and cigarettes, their mint gum, and even the perfume that used to irritate her in the classroom. She wanted to sit with them and let their voices roll over her, but she didn't want them to tell Billy she had been there so she moved on. Margo unrolled her sleeping bag and tarp on the other side of the Pokagon Mound, a hillock maybe six feet high, twenty feet in diameter, that was full of Indian bones, if the stories about it were true.

The following morning Margo awoke dreaming of cinnamon bread and apple butter so vividly she could taste it. She investigated the fire pit where the kids had been sitting. There she found a stack of dark wood that somebody had cut with a chain saw. Beyond this pile was another pile.

'Oh, God. Oh, God.' It took her a while to realize that the moaning she was hearing was her own. She bent down and picked up an eighteen-inch-square chunk of wood that resembled a slightly curved cutting board. The wood was heavy, dense as stone. Teak. She hugged the piece to her chest and wondered how her boat had ever floated. Her ability to maneuver that boat had been magic, her grandpa's magic passed down to her. She fished through the pieces until she found one that said *River Rose* with only a tiny bit of the first *R* cut off. She ran her finger across the embedded bullet, flush with the wood. She put the piece of scarred teak with her daddy's ashes and her pack. She and Billy had come from the same place, had learned the same skills, and they had both killed someone. But Billy's meanness and his desire for revenge had grown so strong inside him that he was willing to destroy even what he, himself, loved.

The following night, the teenagers returned, again without Billy. They reduced the pile of slow-burning teak one piece at a time. From the shadows Margo listened to their chatter. One girl was going to the community college in the fall, and she sounded excited. Another boy was leaving town to go to a state university. A third was starting a job with an insurance agent. Margo admired how carefree they sounded, despite some of them not knowing where they'd live or how they'd get enough to eat. They grabbed and kissed one another, passed a joint around, talked and laughed.

Margo kept her own camp as small as

possible, and when the teenagers stopped coming after a few nights, she was able to burn her own fire. She packed up her things every morning and hid them in a tree behind the Indian mound, along with a juice bottle she filled with water. The picnic area turned out to be a convenient place to be stuck while she figured out what to do next. Not only did it have running water in the public bathrooms, but it was within a half mile of a couple of big gardens where she could find vegetables, especially tomatoes. Rather than stealing, she wished she could trade with the gardeners, wished she had her fishing gear so she could provide fish-guts fertilizer or some bluegills for the gardener to fry up, but she figured she would cause more trouble if she tried to arrange a deal — it was better to lie low. Some domestic ducks wandered over every morning from a nearby farm; when Margo discovered the place where they occasionally laid eggs near the river, she built up the nest, lined it with corn-husks, soft grasses, and rabbit fur to encourage them to use it more often. In the field across the street there were plenty of rabbits. Margo found and ate some of the wild edible plants she'd read about in the Indian hunter book: ground-cherries, wood sorrel, and sunchoke (which Joanna called Jerusalem artichoke and grew on her property as a flower). The Indian book mentioned sweet acorns, but she had found only astringent ones. The black walnuts, hickory nuts, and apples were ripening, and when they were ready, she would find a way to store some for winter, wherever she ended up.

Margo washed at the river's edge the way she had done as a little kid, but stopped shy of stripping and swimming, which would have made her vulnerable if someone came along. Sometimes she thought she saw Crane's ghost hanging at the water's edge or near his box of ashes, a brooding look about him. She wanted to tell him not to be angry with her or to feel sorry for her. She was doing okay. Loneliness was a small price to pay for not being locked in prison and not being at the mercy of the Murrays. Each night she spread her vinyl tarp out on the moist ground and unrolled the sleeping bag. She put the box of ashes between herself and the fire. Luckily, she did not encounter much rough weather; during a few rainstorms, she hung out in the bathroom beside the parking lot.

In the second week of September, the nights became cool. The disappearance of the hummingbirds and the arrival of a dozen white-throated sparrows, as well as the red tinge on the snakes of poison ivy spiraling the oldest trees, told her autumn was coming, soon to be followed by winter. She would have to figure out how to survive the season. The previous year, Michael had taken her in. Oh, what a heavenly thing it would be, she thought, to be invited into his house again, to be fed and given coffee, to climb into his big bed and make love and sleep and then get up and eat breakfast, day after day. How impossible and far away from where she was now — she had traveled on past Michael, and there was no reversing the current of her life. She wondered if Luanne might have written to Michael's address in the last month, during the time Margo had been gone. *The time is right, Margaret*, she might have written. *Come live with me in my house on the water.*

One night she heard a young raccoon in the distance, crying like an abandoned baby. She studied the sky into the early hours of the morning, until the constellation of the man with his belt finally appeared on the southern horizon. She thought about the Indian hunter. He was living on his own, but his family was all the while hoping for him to return. No one was waiting for Margo. Margo had let herself become a person who was no longer connected to other people. She comforted herself with knowing that she did not carry with her a rage like Billy's, or anger like her father's. Either would have weighed her down more than her loaded pack.

15

Early one evening in September, Margo heard a car pull into the Pokagon Mound parking lot. She went ahead and sawed the front feet off the good-sized cottontail she had shot. She continued on with the back feet and then paused, listening to the ratcheting sound the car door made. After two months of living alone on the river, Margo was dismayed to find that her army knife had been rendered dull. She had tried sharpening it on some stones by the river, but that had made it worse. A dull knife made the work bloodier and more difficult than it would otherwise have been. She knew it was easier to cut herself with a dull knife, so she used great care.

At this time of the year, the local gardens were brimming with peppers, tomatoes, and eggplants. A few days ago, she had even snagged a small cabbage and managed to steam a few leaves in her pie tin. She gleaned some starchy sweet corn left in a farmer's field across the road. She had pilfered three big Brandywine tomatoes, so ripe their skins were bursting. She would eat some alongside the rabbit, which she'd killed with one shot to its eye on a hillside upstream.

She was running low on ammunition, and would have to save her nine remaining cartridges for critical shots. Since she'd been here, she hadn't had any paper targets, so she'd been practicing by hitting acorns and hickory nuts off the top of a fence post. Today she'd found the season's first Osage orange, and she put it on the post and dry-fired at it whenever she felt the need to shoot, though she wasn't sure if that was good for her Marlin's firing pin. She was surviving fine as autumn approached, but she was in a holding pattern, waiting for a sign that would point her where to go next.

Margo slit the rabbit's fur, groin to chest, and then did the same to the membrane below the skin and emptied the guts onto a paper bag. She scraped out the cavity with her fingers, finally tugging free the lungs. Suddenly a man was standing beside her. She slipped and almost jabbed her own wrist. She stood up, knife in one hand, eviscerated rabbit in the other, and took a look at the stranger who was standing way too close. He was probably Michael's age, but he looked softer and slower.

'Good evening, miss,' he said, stepping back. 'Don't let me interrupt you.' He had a short, thick frame and black hair and was wearing a sweatshirt with a university crest on it. After he took another step back, she squatted down again and returned her attention to her carcass, cut around the tail and made a slit across the middle of the back left to right. This was not how her grandfather had taught her to skin a rabbit, but was Brian's much faster method for retrieving the meat if you didn't want to save the skin. She held the rabbit's head in one hand and reached the fingers of the other into the slit she'd made and dragged the back half of the skin all the way off the back legs so only the tail area still had fur on it. She did the same with the front end, working her fingers underneath the skin, and then tugging the skin off the shoulders and front legs, up to the neck. She sawed off the rabbit's head and twisted to finish disconnecting the spine. She kept an eye on the man's loafers. She'd read in the Indian hunter book about slashing an enemy's Achilles tendon so he couldn't give chase.

'Are you poaching?' the man asked.

Margo removed the tail and laid that beside the head on the bag with the guts. The man didn't look dangerous, and if he grabbed her, she figured she would stab him or clunk him with the butt of the Marlin.

'That's impressive, what you're doing,' he said and pushed coarse black hair out of his eyes. 'I'd like to know how to skin a rabbit.'

'I'd show you for five bucks,' she said. Five dollars would get her enough ammo to keep her going for a while. She fished through the intestines for the liver, ran her finger over it to assure herself it had no spots that could signal rabbit fever. The man followed her to the river's edge, where she tossed the guts to the fish and turtles. She put the rabbit in a potato chip bag, mushed it around in the salt, tied it up with a string, and submerged all but the top of the bag in the water. She held it down with a rock.

'What if I asked to see your hunting license?' he asked. He was standing behind her, smiling. One front tooth lapped over the other.

She ignored him.

'My people used to live in this place, I'm pretty sure.' He clasped his soft, puffy hands in front of his chest. 'Would you share your food with me?'

'You just go around asking people for food?' Margo watched four blue jays swoop in and screech in unison.

'When you're in a strange land, you have to depend on the generosity of the local inhabitants.'

Margo thought about the rabbit and decided there was plenty for two people.

'I've been trying to eat Indian food while I'm out here,' he said.

'Why?'

'I'm an Indian, for starters. That's what I mean that my people came from around here.'

Margo studied him more carefully. Ever since reading Michael's book, she had been hoping to meet an Indian hunter. She had imagined he would be a strong, wolverine-hearted Indian with a bow and arrow, not some soft-looking guy with a weird way of talking and no weapons.

'That rabbit and those vegetables over there look good.'

'You don't seem like an Indian,' Margo said, although when she studied him more closely, she saw that he did resemble the guy in the Indian hunter book, though he wore jeans and a sweatshirt instead of buckskin.

He squatted down so close to her she could feel his breath on her neck. 'Why on earth is a young woman skinning a rabbit in a picnic park? I've seen some weird things since I've been in this state.'

'I shot a man's pecker once,' she said. 'Just so you know not to bother me.'

He stood up and moved to look at her from another angle. 'Don't worry about me. I'm a happily married man. Listen, if that meat's safe, I will give you five dollars and some delicious dried papaya and pineapple in exchange for dinner,' the man said.

She held out her hand. She had never heard of papaya, wondered if it was Indian food.

'How old are you?' He dug in his wallet for a five-dollar bill and handed it to her.

'Twenty-one.'

The setting sun put a gold sheen in the man's hair. His skin was golden, too, the same color Brian's had been in summer after he'd worked outside. This Indian was pretty, she thought, much prettier than Sitting Bull, who looked in his photos like a man carved out of stone and not happy about it. And unless this man really intended to report her to the DNR, he posed no danger. When the potato chip bag in the water beside her floated up, she put another rock on it to keep it under. She knew if she left it even for a few minutes, one of the park's fat, bold raccoons would grab it.

'Why do you chill the meat like that?'

She wished she had asked her grandpa or Brian the same question. Maybe it had something to do with parasites or bacteria. The Indian hunter had also cooled his game before eating it. 'Seems like an Indian would know,' she said.

'I grew up in Lincoln, Nebraska. We didn't

cook rabbits. Closest I came was watching Elmer Fudd.' The man squatted again beside her at the water's edge. 'You aren't twenty-one. You look seventeen, nineteen tops.'

'So why'd you ask me, if you think you know?'

'It's hard to see you underneath all that dirt. Shouldn't your parents be calling you home soon? Or are you out here waiting for some man your parents disapprove of?'

'I don't like men,' she said.

He laughed and gave up on his squatting, let one knee fall to the ground. Margo didn't shift her weight, though her legs were growing stiff. The man studied the river, but Margo knew she could study it longer.

'This place used to be called River of Three Herons, from what I can deduce. This part of it anyway,' he said.

'It's the Stark River,' Margo said. 'Named after the explorer Frederick Stark.'

'Well, there were folks here long before Mr. Stark wandered by with his cap and fife and tweed vest,' he said and eyed her. 'I'm following the Potawatomi migration route. The whole tribe walked down from the Upper Peninsula, all the way to the Kalamazoo River, four or five hundred miles.'

'Why?'

'Why did they walk down? Or why am I following their route?'

'You're not walking.'

'What's your name?'

'Margaret,' she said. 'Margo.'

'Names matter a lot. Do you want to know my

name?' He asked this in what seemed to Margo an arrogant way, as if he imagined his name had some special importance.

'No. I don't care about your name.'

'Then I won't tell you. You'll have to guess. It'll be like Rumpelstiltskin.'

'You're not from around here, are you?' Margo meant it as an insult, but the Indian just shook his head.

'I spent the summer teaching some kids math at a reservation in the Upper Peninsula. Now I'm on my way home. Unless eating that rabbit kills me.'

A while later, she skewered the rabbit on a sharpened hickory stick and cooked it over the fire. She tried to pay attention to the birds and water creatures near her camp, but the Indian was a distraction, and it took all her energy to remain quiet. When the rabbit was close to being done, she propped the ears of corn up at the edges of the fire and steamed them in their husks. Then they sat cross-legged on opposite sides of the fire, eating from paper plates the Indian had brought from his car.

'I like eating the food of my ancestors,' he said.

Margo thought it was an especially good rabbit, probably fattened on beans and cabbage from somebody's garden.

By the time they finished, the sun was setting. They burned the plates in the fire, and the Indian went and got a pint of Wild Turkey from his car. He sat back down and held the bottle out to her. 'Do you want a sip?'

'No. Is that what your ancestors drank?'

'Oh, I guess the Europeans brought us a few valuable things.' He cracked open the bottle and inhaled deeply. He seemed to relax even before he took a drink. He said, 'I do have a bottle of whiskey from the reservation, but I'm saving it until I get to the Kalamazoo River.'

'There's a dam between here and there.'

'In a car, that's not a problem.' As he drank, he watched the darkening river. 'The problem is that the Kalamazoo River is polluted all to heck, polluted beyond any possibility of rejuvenation. It's the same all across the country. Everything's poisoned,' he said. After only a few sips, his voice was different, deeper.

Margo took her gun-cleaning kit from where she kept it tied on her pack. Without breaking her rifle down, she cleaned the barrel, stinking up the air with her Hoppe's #9 solvent. Then she disassembled her cleaning rod, wrapped it in an old T-shirt of Michael's, and put it away. The air chilled and the sky went mad with stars. Margo wrapped herself more tightly in her father's Carhartt jacket and watched the Indian get drunk. By the firelight, she saw his eyes grow red and his lids droop. She watched his shoulders relax until he was slumping. Finally he tipped over, still clutching the empty pint bottle in his right hand. With his left arm, he held his knees to his chest.

At this time of night, usually Margo would have raided a garden for more vegetables, but instead she stayed put. Letting herself look, really look, hard and long at somebody was a pleasure, almost as soothing to her as aiming and shooting. Margo had needed food and shelter from other people, but this was the first time somebody needed her; this guy had come to her, and she had fed him. She liked the idea of him paying her for the food. She was still too close to Murrayville to cash her mother's money order. There was no expiration date on it, but the edges of the paper were starting to fray.

She folded the tarp over the Marlin to keep the dew off, thought of it as tucking the rifle in to sleep. Later in the night, the Indian stumbled to his car, peed in the dirt behind it, and went to sleep inside. Margo put the metal box of ashes between herself and the fire and listened for a barred owl that she'd heard a few nights ago. She softly called into the silence, *'Who-who, who cooks for you?'* again and again, but got no response.

The Indian paid her four one-dollar bills the following morning for a breakfast of tomatoes, tiny river clams she steamed in a frying pan the Indian had, and two eggs from the domestic ducks she'd been luring over. After they burned their paper plates, he announced he was heading south to the Kalamazoo River to have a look before returning to California.

She heard some goose honks and looked up to see a V of geese crossing the river high above. The thought of creatures migrating, moving effortlessly through the sky, made her miss her boat. Margo looked around her campsite, at her bag, which was all packed. Her sleeping bag was rolled up and attached to it.

'Can I go with you?' Margo asked. She tucked her jeans into her boots and retied them; she did this out of habit, though the mosquitoes weren't bad today with the breeze blowing. 'My ma lives near Kalamazoo.'

'I'm not taking a girl with me.' He stood and looked down at her. 'I'm a married man.'

'My dad is dead, and I need to find my ma.'

'I'm sorry about your dad. But I'm not in the business of helping lost girls find their mothers.'

'I can show you some plants Indians ate. Watercress, wild onion, ramps, hickory nuts.' Of course, the ramps and onions were out of season already. Maybe she could get him some rose hips — that was something the Indian hunter ate — or crab apples or sweet, custardy pawpaws, which must be about ripe now if she could find a tree. Black walnuts were starting to fall. She stood up to look into his face. 'As soon as there's a rain we'll have giant puffball mushrooms.'

'Let me think about this.' He squatted, and after a few minutes he gave up on squatting and sat down cross-legged. 'Stop staring at me. A person can't think with another person staring at him.'

'I'll cook you a duck when we get there. Your ancestors probably ate duck.'

'I do love duck.'

'There's tons of mallards.' She walked to the river and washed her hands and face, rubbed her skin with a little sand, and rinsed. Then she looked back at him across the distance.

'If you get there and change your mind, I can't bring you back,' he shouted. 'And if I take you,

you're not taking any guns. And don't try to feed me any weird mushrooms.'

'I only got a rifle,' she shouted back.

'I'm against guns. And anyhow there's laws about transporting guns.'

'You can carry a rifle in a car so long as it's in the back, unloaded.' She walked over to him, took her rifle off her shoulder, and showed him the stock. 'See, it's got a squirrel carved in it. Annie Oakley had one like this, for trick shooting. This metal is chrome.'

'I don't care if a gun is pretty. And you're not a trick shooter.'

Margo wondered if practicing trick shots had made her into a trick shooter yet. 'If I can shoot that fruit off that fence post from here, will you take me to the Kalamazoo?'

'What is that thing anyway?' He walked over with Margo and picked up the Osage orange she had put there. He put it back and wiped his hands on his jeans. 'It looks like a green brain. Did my ancestors eat these?'

'No, but they keep bugs and spiders away. As kids we called them brain fruit.'

He picked it up again, this time with two fingers, sniffed it, and put it back. 'It's sticky.'

'If I can knock that off the post from twelve paces with one shot, can I come with you?' The sun was shining on the Osage orange, lighting it up.

'Even I could probably hit that,' the Indian said. He picked up a nut from the ground and held it out to her. 'What's this? It looks like a miniature one of those things.'

243

'It's an acorn from a burr oak.'

He put it on top of the Osage orange. 'How about this? If you can hit this acorn without hitting the ugly fruit here, you and your gun can come along for the ride, so long as you're both unloaded.'

'That's pretty small.' It was big for an acorn, really, an inch and a half in diameter. Before she'd run low on ammo, she'd been consistently hitting crab apples smaller than that off this same fence post eight out of ten times.

'So's my car when it comes to girls and guns.' They counted out the paces, and he stood beside her. She rested the butt of the rifle on her bent knee, removed the magazine tube, dropped in one of her nine remaining cartridges, and secured it. She worked the lever to chamber the round. She never tired of that motion.

She lifted the rifle to her shoulder, pressed it into her cheek, took a breath, and exhaled. She fired. She knew she had released her trigger finger too soon. Maybe the tip of her barrel went slightly up as the bullet left the chamber.

'No cigar,' he said.

She had feared that not having paper targets to give her feedback these last months was going to result in her losing her edge. On the other hand, she had been shooting grazing rabbits with great accuracy. Mr. Peake had always said every shot was a matter of probability, and Margo knew an occasional miss was part of that.

'Wait,' she said. 'I said one shot for the Osage orange. I get two shots for the acorn.'

'Okay, one more, but that's it.'

She put one more cartridge into the Marlin while the Indian watched. In her pocket she had her remaining seven.

'You're standing too close to me,' she said and flapped her left arm.

He took one exaggerated step back away from her. She lifted the rifle to her shoulder and felt it shaking slightly. Mr. Peake had always said she should wait to pull the trigger until she could make a good shot. She dropped her arms, held the rifle loosely in her right hand, studied the river beside her. She had never wanted to leave the Stark when she was young, but now, without her father and her boat, she thought she could not bear to stay here one more day. If she couldn't go with the Indian, she'd walk.

She held the gun in her left hand, while she shook out the right. There was no reason that having somebody there with her should screw up her shooting. She'd won the 4-H competition with plenty of onlookers. And even though it had been two months since she'd shot paper targets at Michael's, she had been shooting well then, better than ever in her life. She took a deep breath, relaxed her shoulders, and slowed her heartbeat.

She studied the railroad-tie fence post from its base to its top, as it rose to about her own height. She studied the green fruit with the burr acorn on top. Beyond it was the smooth expanse of river. She wrapped the sling around her left hand and elbow and pushed against it. When she nestled the stock in her shoulder and pressed her cheek against it, her stance and grip were solid.

The Indian disappeared, and she was alone with her gun and her target. She looked through her sights. Her instructor had talked about the 'wobble' in a person's hold, had said a person could never be absolutely solid, but for Margo there usually came an instant like now when she felt solidly rooted to the planet. Without a conscious decision to do so, she smoothly pressed the trigger straight back and held it there as the rifle sent the bullet down the barrel on its way to the acorn. She knew it was a good shot. She held steady even after she heard a sound like the final hard tap of a woodpecker's beak against an oak branch.

They walked to the tree and found the acorn gone and the big fruit untouched.

'Dang,' he said. 'Was that a lucky shot?'

She shook her head. Unless you considered skill and probability luck. When she caught her breath she noticed him looking at her in a very intense way.

'That ability of yours is something special,' he said. He retrieved the Osage orange and sniffed it again. 'That's as good as proving a mathematical theorem. I guess I'll put this thing in my car to keep the spiders out. There's too dang many spiders in this state.'

She put the Marlin over her shoulder and returned to where her pack was sitting.

The man kicked the ground, looked back at Margo, and then burst out laughing. 'I've got to be out of my mind. You know, if the police pull me over I'll say heck yes, we've got a gun.'

Margo found herself smiling, as she hadn't in

246

a while, at her own excellent shooting, at the warmth of the sun, at the Indian's surprise, and at the prospect of finding a new river. The Indian opened the car's rear hatch, and she laid the gun on a sleeping bag. He covered it with loose clothes. She put her pack in beside it.

Once he got into the driver's seat and shut the door, she rolled down the window and took a last look at the Stark, a river she had never expected to leave.

'Are you sure you're not running away from home?' the Indian said as they pulled away.

She nodded and watched the river disappear behind them.

'I talked to an anthropologist up north to figure the most likely places the Potawatomi might have lived around Kalamazoo,' he said, once they'd negotiated themselves onto a highway. 'There's a farmer there who's given me permission to camp on his land for a night.'

'You don't act like an Indian, going to anthropologists. Shouldn't an Indian follow animal trails?'

'You know, you ought to be grateful. I'm only taking you to save you from whoever else might give you a ride if you go out hitchhiking. There's a lot of bad men out there.'

'I'm not afraid of men.'

'Right, by golly, you shot a man's pecker.' He slapped his leg for emphasis, and the car jerked to the left. 'For crying out loud, I am crazy for bringing you along.'

'That's what I mean when I say you don't sound like an Indian.' Margo had never liked being on the highway, and this was as bad as driving with Junior when he'd first gotten his license. Maybe the sick feeling in her gut was sadness about leaving the Stark, but his driving wasn't helping.

'What do you think an Indian sounds like? You don't know anything about Indians.'

'Sitting Bull wouldn't say *for crying out loud* and *heck* and *dang* and *by golly*.' Arguing this way helped settle Margo's stomach, so long as the Indian kept his hands on the wheel. She sat rigid while they moved into the left lane to pass a semi truck that seemed a mile long. The forty-five minutes on the highway felt like an eternity, and she was relieved when they finally slowed on the exit ramp.

'I don't suppose I can ask you to navigate,' he said, as they continued on a two-lane road. He looked at the horizon and then at her again. 'You're looking rather pale, girl.'

She opened her mouth, wanting to make a comment about being a paleface, but changed her mind. She rolled down the passenger window as they turned onto a smaller road. She reached behind her and felt around. She put her hand on the box of ashes, steadied herself. Then she smelled the river, and her muscles relaxed.

16

The Indian turned into a driveway marked by a wooden post, and they parked in front of a gate beside an unpainted barn. Once out of the car, Margo saw a whale-sized tangle of rusting scrap metal, the largest chunks of which seemed to be old broken farm implements. They stepped around the gate to see, at the back of the barn, a pile of tree stumps, twisted branches, and uprooted bushes. On the opposite side of the driveway was the foundation of what must have once been a house. She couldn't see the river, but she was soothed by the smell of it in the distance and by the way the land sloped toward it. She returned to the car, uncovered her rifle, and slung it over her shoulder.

A line of trees served as a windbreak between a field of corn and a field of soybeans and led from the road to the river. As Margo and the Indian walked along it, the windbreak widened, and they discovered a trickle of water running beside them. Margo picked a bean pod, cracked it open, and nibbled the soybeans raw as they walked. They were hard and chewy, ready to harvest, she guessed. Eventually the trees became a patch of woods, mostly maples and walnuts. The land sloped gently for about a third of a mile, until it dropped off near the river. When they stood on the riverbank, Margo guessed the Kalamazoo here was almost twice as wide as the Stark was in Murrayville, maybe fifty yards across. On the other side of the river, the land rose abruptly. Margo scanned the far steep bank and saw no path leading to the river, only an orange-and-black sign reading NO HUNTING NO TRESPASSING. Downstream there was another such sign.

'We can camp right here tonight,' Margo said.

'I suppose we'll have to leave the car up by the road,' the Indian said. 'We'll carry down what we need.'

Margo wondered how long it would take the water that had flowed by them on the Stark earlier today to flow over the dam and reach this part of the Kalamazoo. The river's chemical smells were different from the chemical smells on the Stark. There was a tinge of mold in the air. The river water was brown, and the edge of the river looked mucky. The only sandy area was where the spring they'd walked beside emptied into the river. Margo noted a disturbance in the water and wondered if Crane's ghost would accompany her this far downstream. A muskrat surfaced, saw her, and plunged back under.

'Oh, Lordy,' the Indian said. He looked around. 'My cousin said he'd heard stories about this river valley. There were so many trees you never ran out of firewood. The sugar maples filled every barrel and bucket with their sweet sap. Too bad it's all cleared for farmland.'

'With woods by the river like this, there's probably lots of creatures we're not seeing now. They'll come out at night to eat the corn and beans.'

'My cousin heard stories that deer in

250

Michigan would pose in front of your arrows,' the Indian said, 'and ask to be rendered into food and skins. They were tired of their rich earthly lives and wished to be released to the spirit realm, or something like that. He said ducks used to shed their feathers upon dying to make themselves easier to prepare. Fish leapt from the water so you needed only to reach out and grab those you had a taste for. The women used to grow vegetables, what they called the three sisters: corn, beans, and squash. The soil was black and fertile, and they used the gardens of the ancient ones, whatever that means.'

'Did they swim in the river?'

'Probably. It wasn't polluted back then.'

'Look. There's your Indian dinner. I'll only charge you five dollars.' Margo pointed at a male mallard alone by the river's edge about fifteen yards away. She pulled the Marlin off her shoulder, rested the butt on her knee, and loaded two cartridges into it.

'You can barely reach the end of that gun barrel to load it.'

'Shhh.' Margo chambered a round, moved closer, and aimed at the duck's head. The duck drifted a few inches and then was treading water at the river's edge. She lifted the butt to her shoulder, pressed her left arm against the sling for stability, and aimed, and the duck moved again, away from shore. She dropped to one knee and raised her gun barrel. She sighted the duck's eye and shot it dead.

'Ouch,' said the Indian.

Margo retrieved the duck with a stick and held

251

it by the foot to drain the blood.

The Indian set off for town, and Margo tugged at the duck's feathers for a few minutes, until she realized she didn't want to wash and soak the duck in the river if it was polluted. The trickling stream was too shallow. She needed a bucket to fill with clean water, and she had not noticed one up at the barn. She looked downstream and upstream; she decided that when in doubt a person should go upstream because if she found a boat, then she could float back down. She had her gun over one shoulder, and she held her duck over the other by one foot.

An animal path followed the riverbank. She encountered an electric livestock fence running across the path and almost all the way to the water. She jumped down to the water's edge and scrambled up the bank on the other side of the fence to find herself in a pasture full of plump beef cattle. One by one the cows looked up at her with white, red, or black faces, and one by one they returned to grazing. When a red-and-white Hereford stared and tossed its head, she imagined shooting it at close range; she wondered if she could take down a bony-headed cow with a shot through the eye. She knew how killing and eating somebody's cattle would create a whole new host of problems, and that was why she was thinking rather than acting. She wove through the pasture, avoiding cow pies.

At the far boundary, she ducked through strands of nonelectrified barbed wire to get out. Here the river curved. There were a dozen oaks towering over tall grasses near another sandbar, where Margo saw the footprints of water birds, and she noticed a cluster of houses up ahead. She walked along until the overgrown path led away from the river up to a paved road. The road dead-ended at a rundown white house and then curved to follow the river above a row of houses. Below the first house, at the water's edge, was a homemade camping trailer the size of the smaller of the Slocum trailers. It was surrounded by a low metal fence, and she saw there inside the fence two five-gallon plastic buckets. The overgrown yard contained a half a dozen concrete lawn ornaments. There was a twelve-foot length of wooden dock that ran parallel to shore and extended five feet over the water. Tied to it was an aluminum row-boat with an outboard motor on the back, sheathed in plastic. Margo felt comforted by the modesty of the house and the rustic surroundings.

An empty wheelchair sat on the flagstone patio in back of the house. The property was separated from the one beyond it by a wooden privacy fence, and over it Margo could see the top of a newer cedar-shingled house. There was a kind of freedom in knowing nobody would recognize her here. She was only about forty-five miles downstream of Murrayville, but she'd never known the Murrays to come beyond the dam or to travel to Kalamazoo for any reason. She didn't see anyone around and so walked onto the backyard patio and followed the steep steps down to the river. From here, she could see the back of the camper, where PRIDE & JOY was written in stylized block letters. The camper, it turned out, was not sitting on the riverbank, but was affixed to a sort of platform on pontoons in the water. The camper was the cabin of a boat that had been dragged up against the retaining wall. A big black dog lay beside the camper. The dog's ears lifted as she approached. She stepped off the retaining wall and onto the boat through an opening in the galvanized metal fence. It barely moved under her weight. The buckets were on the other side of the dog.

'Hey, dog,' she said and barked. The dog nodded his head. 'You must weigh at least a hundred pounds.'

'Is somebody out there?' a weak voice called.

Margo peered inside the camper through a curtained window. Inside was a miniature sink, a set of small cupboards, a tiny woodstove. And then a ghostly pale face, half covered by sunglasses, appeared before her. She yelped, and the dog yelped, too.

'Pull open the door. I'm stuck in here.'

Margo twisted the aluminum door handle until it came unstuck and found an old man with a thick hank of silver hair leaning against the doorframe. 'I was just petting your dog,' she said.

'Long as he's not drinking out of the river.'

'Why do you care if he drinks out of the river?'

'It's polluted.'

'Do you live in this trailer?' Margo looked out at the houses upstream and across the river, all three of them tidy, two with small boats up on sawhorses. At the nearest house, an upside-down canoe was chained to an oak. The chain holding the canoe appeared to have grown into the tree's bark.

'Help me up to the patio,' the old man said. Margo switched her rifle to her right side and let him drape his bony arm over her shoulder. He was only a couple of inches taller than she was, and thin, but he grew heavy as they traveled up the concrete-block steps, the dog at their heels. Margo helped him into his wheelchair. An air tank was hooked to the back, and the old man affixed plastic tubes to his face. He adjusted his black glasses. He took a few breaths, and then color came into his cheeks.

'Are you okay?' she asked.

'Okay?' He took another labored breath. 'You mean, except that I'm dying? Hell, no, I'm not okay. Can't even get up the damned steps.'

'Never seen a boat like that,' Margo said, 'with a camper on it.'

'Life is a lousy goddamned business at this end. You take note, kid.'

'Is your wife here?' Margo asked. 'Should I get her?'

'Got no wife. Dog's better company than any wife.'

From where she stood, Margo thought she could see a raccoon skin drying over the back of a lawn chair outside the garage. Behind it a deerskin was stretched on a pallet on the ground.

'That's Fishbone's deer hide.'

'But it's out of season.'

'He's got the crop-damage permit from the farmer.'

'A permit that lets you hunt out of season?' Margo asked.

'Lucky son of a bitch got himself a deer.

255

Nowadays Fishbone usually can't hit the broad side of a barn. He won't admit he's getting old.'

'Who's Fishbone?' she asked.

'Fishbone is the man who needs to get here with my smokes.' He nodded at the little aluminum boat tied to the dock.

Margo squatted beside the hundred-pound black dog. She stroked him with both hands.

'Do you sell those skins? I mean, does your friend sell them?'

'Sells them to a guy on the north side.' The old man wore a dark blue uniform-style shirt. The name tag said *Smoke*. He readjusted his oxygen tubes on his bristly cheeks.

'How much money does he get?'

'Not enough to pay back what he owes me.' He looked around, as though hoping the man in question would come out of the garage or rise up out of the river to argue with him. The orange sticker on the window of the garage said CONDEMNED.

'Could I borrow a bucket?' Margo asked. 'Oh, crap. I left my duck on the boat.'

'Wait,' he said. 'Nightmare, go get the duck, boy.'

The big dog barreled down the concrete steps, onto the boat. He picked up the mallard by the shiny green head and brought it to the old man, laid it at his feet without a tooth mark on it.

'That's a good dog you got, Mr. Smoke.' Margo noticed that the porch door was missing, and just inside, plain as day, was an enameled canning kettle being used as a garbage pail. If she had that pot, she could not only wash the

256

duck, but could make duck soup afterward. 'Can I borrow that kettle?' Margo pointed.

'Hell, no.'

'Can I buy it?' She was surprised at his harshness. 'I've got some money.'

'What do I need with money? Here in paradise.' He laughed and disconnected his oxygen tubes. Then he lit a cigarette.

'Everybody needs money.'

'What about that fancy rifle? Is it just for poaching ducks?'

'I can't give you my Marlin.' After a moment she added. 'I'm a trick shooter.'

'You're no goddamned trick shooter,' he said and then grew thoughtful. 'Unless you can shoot an apple off my head.'

'I could.'

'I haven't got an apple. How about a peanut? Can you shoot a peanut off my head?'

Margo paused to study the old man. 'I could shoot the ash off that cigarette in your hand.' The cigarette's burning end was about as big a target as a duck's eye. Hitting the cigarette in someone's hand was a shot that Annie Oakley had done again and again. From ten paces, Margo estimated she had about a fifty percent chance of making such a shot, if everything went perfectly.

'How about out of my mouth? Can you do that?'

'Same thing,' she said. 'But a .22 bullet can travel a mile and a half. Might go through that fence.'

'Shoot it into the garage.'

'It could hit something, a can of paint or acid on a shelf.' She thought of Crane's old shed, stuffed with paint and lighter fluid, carburetor cleaner, and six kinds of lubricant. But the wall of the garage would give her the best sight picture.

'Nothing to hit that I care about.' He coughed into his fist.

'You really want me to shoot a cigarette so close to your face?'

'You want my canning kettle?'

'Does it have a lid?'

'You'll have to dig in the cupboard for it. But I'm not giving it to you for doing nothing.'

'What about the dog? Won't the shooting bother him?' The Murrays' black Lab went crazy when guns went off. He was a great swimming dog, but no good for hunting.

'Nightmare doesn't mind gunshots. He just doesn't like strange men. Dog doesn't believe me that women are just as dangerous.'

The old man dropped his unfiltered cigarette butt, still burning, and lit another. He turned away from her so he was looking out over the river. She was now facing the right side of his body in profile. Margo's head cleared as she began to imagine her shot, the beginning, middle, and end of it.

'What do you do with that camper?' Margo watched the man to see whether he tended to make sudden movements that could screw up the shot.

'Built it myself to be lightweight. Used to stay in there when the house got too hot. Took it up and down the river. Lived in there for three years once when my sister and her brats were staying here.'

'It's got an inboard motor?' She asked. If the man suddenly lurched forward at the wrong time, she'd take off his jaw or knock out a few of his lower teeth, but she saw his motions were slow, measured, even when he coughed. She loaded another cartridge into the magazine tube — the probability was good she could hit it within two shots — and then she changed her mind and put in three more, saving just one in her pocket. If she missed the first, she would keep aiming, sighting, and shooting, so long as he remained still. She opened and shut the lever, and the hammer cocked. The man's spine straightened at the sound.

'Rigged up for an outboard, but I didn't go anywhere in a hurry,' the man said. He dropped the lighter into a pocket on the side of the wheelchair and put the cigarette between his lips. 'So what are you waiting for? High command?'

She knew she ought to do this while the cigarette was still long, so she would be shooting as far from his face as possible. She noted the man's whole body was shaking very slightly, but not enough to screw up the shot. She nestled the rifle butt into her shoulder, pressed her cheek into the stock, stretched her hasty sling tight, and sighted, but didn't feel stable enough. She squatted down, with one knee on the ground, and finally sat cross-legged on the flagstones and rested her elbows just below her knees.

Before lifting the muzzle, she took a breath

259

and considered everything around her: the wheelchair, the black dog, the soft autumn sun lighting up the green-and-gold-tinged leaves of the sugar maples, the red ribbons of poison ivy climbing a swamp oak at the river's edge, water flowing under the houseboat, geese clacking, the smell of wood burning somewhere nearby. She had only just arrived on the Kalamazoo, but this world was one she understood. She studied the old man's feet and legs in the chair. His hands were in his lap, long-fingered, stained yellow from smoking. She considered the top of his head, where the thick, shiny hair belied the rest of his physical condition, and then the rectangle of his black glasses. She was startled when he took off the glasses and looked at her through wide-open, red-tinged eyes. For a moment he reminded her of her grandpa, though of course he looked nothing like him — Grandpa had been a tall man with a crooked nose and a gray beard, while this guy was compact with a round, shaved face. But there was something about him that struck her: he was dying, as surely as her grandpa had been dying.

'Shoot, goddamn it,' he grumbled.

She was as much aware of the man's jaw as she was of her own breath and heartbeat. The man growled to the dog, 'It's okay, boy.'

Margo knew she had to make a good shot of this for the old man and for herself. She looped her hand through her sling and tightened it against her left arm. She knew the glowing tip of that unfiltered cigarette as well now as she knew her own finger on the trigger. There was nothing

260

in the world but herself, her rifle, and her target. She exhaled and pressed the trigger. She held steady as the bullet left the chamber and then the barrel. She heard it hit the side of the garage and then there was silence. She closed her eyes, and when she opened them, the old man was slumped forward in his chair. She got up and ran across the patio to him. She lifted his shoulders to look into his face. Tears were rolling from his naked eyes. His lips still pinched a cigarette end. When she let go of him, he laughed a low rumble, and the dog nuzzled his empty hand.

'You weren't shitting me you can shoot,' he said between breaths. He put his glasses back on. 'Of course, I was hoping you'd miss and shoot me in the goddamned head.'

Margo got the canning kettle from the porch, removed the paper bag of trash that was in it, and stuck the bag in a ceramic crock, the kind Joanna used for making bread-and-butter pickles.

'The lid is in the lower cupboard to the left of the stove, and you'd better wash the pan out if you're going to cook with it. And you are filthy, kid. Don't you ever take a bath?'

'I'm staying with a friend.'

'A man?'

She nodded.

'Thought so. Then you're making your own bed, I guess.' He turned away and spoke to the river. 'Girl your age ought not to be out fooling around. You ought to go home to your ma.'

'My ma doesn't want me.' Saying it aloud hurt.

261

The man's hand moved to his glasses as though to take them off again, but he only touched them and let the hand fall back into his lap. 'If you want a shower, you'd better ask for it.'

'Could I take a shower in your house, sir?' Margo said.

'You can take a shower. But don't bring your boyfriend around. My dog will bite him.' He fiddled in the pocket of his wheelchair for a cigarette and the lighter and lit up. After a drag from the cigarette, his voice was calmer. 'My last cigarette. Unless you got some more.'

She shook her head. 'It's been two months since I had a shower with hot water. We're camping out, on the riverbank on a farmer's land.'

'Young girl ought to be wary of men,' the old man said and smiled a little. His open mouth showed he had no upper teeth, and this made him look like a little kid. 'Even I might not be as harmless as I seem.'

'Are you blind?' she asked.

'Not yet.' The man rested his cigarette on the patio, inhaled through his nasal tubes a few times. Then he disconnected the oxygen and picked up his cigarette again. 'Don't worry, there's nobody else here to bother you.'

The kitchen, the first room beyond the porch, was cluttered with dishes, books, papers, and tools, as was the hallway. The windows were all closed. She meant to hurry through her shower, but she couldn't make herself turn off the water until the hot ran cold. She inspected the towels

262

hanging on the towel bars and across the chair beside the tub. She reached all the way to the back of the closet shelf for the one folded towel. It smelled a little of mildew, but it looked clean. She put her clothes back on and opened the bathroom door to find the dog right outside. He followed her out onto the patio, where she found the old man slumped, asleep in his chair with his oxygen hooked up.

She could go back to her camp, or she could dress out the duck right here where there was running water. She sat on a milk crate and worked silently, plucking the duck's chest feathers, then its wings, and finally its back, using the dragging motions of her fingers. She enjoyed being in the presence of the dog and the old man, whose slumped body emanated a sweetness in sleep. She dumped the guts into the river and washed the pan out at the spigot at the side of the house. The big dog watched. After checking to be sure the man was still asleep, she tossed his dog the raw, rinsed heart. He caught it in his jaws and swallowed.

17

Margo hiked back downstream. She lugged big rocks from the woods and the river to encircle her fire pit. A carp jumped out of the middle of the river and splashed down. People called carp trash fish, but Margo thought they tasted fine if you could work around all the bones. Sometimes she even thought they were beautiful in their iridescence. She sat by the water's edge and cooled her duck in a plastic bag. Brian had always soaked a duck in salt water overnight, but Margo didn't have that much time, and for salt she had only the little packets she got from the Indian. She watched the birds drink at the sandy place where the spring trickled in, blue jays first, then a red-bellied woodpecker, followed by a few tree swallows that glided over from across the river. Three crows landed in a tree and looked down at her. One by one they rose from their perches and resettled in an adjacent tree. Watching the crows move their wings made Margo's desire to row a boat so powerful that she let her head fall back and closed her eyes. She relived shooting the cigarette out of the old man's mouth. When she opened her eyes, she admired her new canning kettle, big enough that she could heat water in it for a sponge bath, big enough to boil a few gallons of maple sap down to a cup of syrup, as she and her cousins had done in one of the Murray sheds, rendering everything sticky. The canning kettle was something she had earned by her own skill. This was how Annie Oakley must have felt when she discovered her shooting was not just fine, but profitable.

She figured she wouldn't start cooking the bird until the Indian returned — nobody liked overcooked duck — but she got the fire started. By singeing the plucked bird in the flame, she removed the last hair-like feathers and made a stink that took a while to dissipate. Margo thought she did not need a big kitchen to eat well, just a few more things that she could buy, trade for, or shoot for, maybe a heavy kitchen knife like the one she'd secretly borrowed from the old man, as well as a big metal stirring spoon. If only there were a river's-edge cave around here, she might even be able to survive the winter.

As the air was beginning to cool, Margo spotted something white in the windbreak: a giant puffball mushroom twice the size of a human skull, something she could eat for a week. She felt she had been looking for such a puffball for years. She'd last gotten one this size on the day her mother left Murrayville. Normally it would've had to rain for a puffball to grow this big, and that suggested to her that the dew along the river would be heavy.

When the Indian finally returned, the sun was setting. He said he'd spent the afternoon at the township library, talking to the librarian about local history and looking at old documents. Margo found a decent-sized hickory stick and whittled off the bark in order to use it as a spit. She skewered the duck and got it balanced over the fire. When a bit of duck fat began to drip onto the coals, Margo caught it in the Indian's frying pan so she could use it for cooking a slice of mushroom. She considered herself lucky — mallards usually had no fat. Maybe this duck had been living well on the farmer's corn.

Margo instructed the Indian not to leave the duck unattended, and she hiked up to the car to get her pack. As she was closing the trunk of the station wagon, she saw a woman the size and shape of her aunt Joanna come out of the house right across the road to fill a bird feeder and spread seed over a patch of her lawn. Before she even stepped away, a half dozen cardinals fell upon the seed, four blood-red and two military-green. The woman, maybe ten years older than Joanna, wore her gray-streaked hair long on her shoulders, and she had on an old denim barn coat. When the woman looked up and saw she was being watched, she regarded Margo in a good-humored way, as though she were accustomed to seeing all sorts of people, but had not yet seen one quite like her. Beside the house was a big garden, and Margo could see rows of eggplants and tomatoes. The woman waved at Margo, and Margo automatically waved back.

Only then did Margo see the teenage girl in the yard, lying barefoot in a lawn chair. She was wearing frayed cutoffs and a purple sweatshirt and looked to be about Julie Slocum's age. The girl was reading a book, and it took Margo a few

266

seconds to make out what it was she had on her stomach: a giant rabbit, weighing maybe twenty pounds. She was using that rabbit to hold her book up. The rabbit's ears were longer than the girl's hands, and they twitched, but otherwise the rabbit just sat there. Margo laughed out loud. She put on her pack and picked up her box of ashes and her piece of *The River Rose* and headed toward the river.

When the sun was setting orange downstream, Margo and the Indian were sitting beside the fire eating the duck and some salted tomatoes the Indian had bought at a farm stand. In the frying pan was a thick slice of puffball mushroom Margo had browned in the bit of duck fat, along with some butter from foil-wrapped packets the Indian gave her.

'You know I'm not touching that mushroom,' the Indian said.

'I don't care. I'll eat it all. You still owe me five dollars for the duck.'

'I don't want to be hallucinating. And I'd rather you didn't, either, not with that rifle.'

'It's not that kind of mushroom,' Margo said. The rifle was wrapped in its tarp near the fire. 'Your cousin said the duck would release its feathers, but it was dang hard to pluck.' She had never really been good at swearing, so she was trying out the Indian's words, *heck* and *dang*.

'Oh, that's just a story.' He handed her a ten. 'Keep the change.'

'I'll make you breakfast,' she said and put the bill in her front pocket.

'How'd you get so clean?' the Indian said.

'Took a shower at an old man's house.'

'You make friends fast. I think your hair changed color. It matches the river now.'

She pulled some of her hair out in front of her and studied it. It seemed to have grown longer, too, since she took the shower. She smelled the old man's Breck shampoo.

'You're way too pretty a girl to stay out here alone,' he said. 'You're too vulnerable.'

Margo ate some more puffball.

'But don't worry, beauty fades eventually.'

'I shot a cigarette out of the old man's mouth. That's why he let me have a shower.'

'You what?'

'He was in a wheelchair, and he said if I shot the end off his cigarette, I could have this big pan.' Margo regretted that she hadn't nabbed one of his buckets, too, while he was sleeping. 'I'm going to make soup with our leftovers.'

The Indian let himself roll backward, and he lay there on the ground, hugging his knees, laughing. 'You could have killed him. I mean, it's not funny, but . . . oh, Lordy.'

'I wish you'd stay here for a little longer. One more day.' She regretted the words as soon as they came out of her mouth, for the way they made her sound like a beggar. She knew the Indian wasn't going to stick around, whatever she might say.

'In one week I'll be teaching, and in two weeks I'm cohosting a math conference. I'm leaving tomorrow. And why aren't you enrolled in college?'

'I didn't finish high school.'

'You can't get ahead in this life if you don't finish school.'

'I don't want to get ahead. What's so great about getting ahead?'

'I loved school,' he said. 'I was bored out of my skull at home. I was an only child, and my adoptive parents were old and boring.'

'I liked school when I was little. But later I couldn't figure out what the teachers wanted. They said I was too quiet.'

'You don't seem all that quiet to me.' He took another bite of meat and said, 'I've always thought of duck as tender.'

'Not old wild duck.' Margo made herself keep on chewing through the tough, slightly gamey meat. He was right — she wasn't quiet. The realization made her laugh.

After they finished eating, Margo put into the kettle the rest of the meat, the bones, and the wing parts she'd managed to pluck. She added fresh water from the Indian's jugs and put the pan on the fire to simmer. Margo then carried heaps of pine needles from beneath the evergreens in the windbreak and piled them around the fire to make soft places to sleep. They unrolled their sleeping bags on opposite sides of the fire. The Indian produced a quart juice bottle with masking tape around the lid. The contents were the color of apple juice. He unscrewed the cap and sipped from the wide mouth. His whole body shivered visibly as he swallowed. He said,

269

'It's bitter. Raw. Must have something in it besides mash.'

'You don't have to drink it,' she said. 'Do you? If you don't like it?'

'I didn't say I didn't like it. Here, taste it.'

She shook her head, but he held it out and kept holding it there until she accepted the bottle. He watched until she pressed it to her closed lips. It burned worse than siphoning gasoline. She handed it back.

'I should only drink about half of this,' he said. 'I'll tell you a story if you promise to stop me at half the bottle.'

She nodded. By the firelight, she could see all the details of his face. His cheekbones were wide and his features, like his hands, seemed soft.

'My cousin told me this story his great-uncle told him. It probably happened on this very river. There was a girl who was marrying age, maybe your age. She loved growing corn and beans and squash. So there was a boy from another tribe a week's walk away, and he wanted to marry the girl, but there were no gardens where he was taking her, because the land was wooded and the soil was rocky. He told her she would gather food in the woods and she would make him clothes and raise children and preserve meat for winter.' The Indian looked at Margo as if to make sure she was listening. He reached out and touched her hair, smoothed it over her shoulder.

'The thought of giving up gardening broke this girl's heart. She said she had to wait to marry him until the corn was harvested.' He

270

took another drink of whiskey and shivered.

'Was it Indian corn?' Margo asked. 'My aunt grew Indian corn for decoration.'

'Yup. It was a big harvest, and the corn kept coming. Nobody understood how, but new ears sprouted on stalks that were already finished, and the new ears became ripe in weeks instead of months. But the girl knew that bits of her broken heart were generating the ears of corn, and the corn silk was made from the strands of her hair. She knew that soon her heart would be gone, and she would have to marry the man and leave her home.'

'And she'd be bald-headed,' Margo said.

'Yup,' said the Indian, apparently not registering what she'd said. He took another drink. 'When her heart was finally gone, she threw herself into the river and drowned. An opossum dragged her body back up onto land, and her family buried her in her garden. And they say that corn continued to grow above her body, and even when the white people marched the Indians away to Kansas, the corn grew. Though the farmers tried to plant wheat for their cereal and oats for their horses, only corn would grow.'

'How did a possum drag her body onto the riverbank?' Margo stretched her legs in front of her, alongside the fire, and moved Crane's ashes farther away. The sky was dark and starry.

'I'm not sure,' he said. 'It just did.'

'I mean, a possum weighs like eight pounds,' Margo said. 'And its hands are tiny. Like doll hands. I'll shoot one and you can look at it.'

'Maybe he had help from his possum friends.

271

Or maybe he was a really big possum. I don't think you're getting what's important out of the story, focusing on the possum.' The Indian stretched his own legs out and nudged the toe of her boot with his loafer.

'Possums wouldn't help anybody.' She felt strangely cheerful to be arguing with this drunken man in a way she never would have argued with her father or Brian. Even Michael had seemed distressed when she had disagreed with him. She said, 'Possums have their own plans. They don't even walk. They waddle. And they have three rows of sharp teeth.'

'Maybe I don't have the story right, but you're missing the point. The girl wanted to have her garden and not have any man. If she moved up north to marry, she'd have to give up gardening.'

'I'd rather hunt.' For the first time in her life, she was getting the idea that talking was as pleasurable as shooting. She thought of things she might like to tell the Indian if she got the chance, that a deer can eat a fish or a bird, that a heron can swallow a snake and the snake can still slither free. It warmed her to know she had things to say that he would argue with.

'If you were an Indian woman, you'd know it's a heartbreaking story. That's what a young woman can do in a community. That's one of her powers, to break hearts.'

'Is your wife an Indian?'

'She's a quarter Sioux. But let's not talk about her now.'

'Sitting Bull used to tell Annie Oakley stories in the Wild West Show.'

'Sitting Bull was a great man. The Wild West Show was an insult to his sensibilities.' The Indian was slurring his words. He held up the bottle, which was two-thirds full. 'I think there's something funny in this whiskey. Jimson weed, maybe. I'm seeing things that aren't there.'

'I wish I could live right on the river, like the old-time Indians did,' Margo said.

'Indians never lived on the river,' he said. 'The river was their highway. They got up above it so they could keep an eye on who was coming and going. We had a lot of enemies in those days. The men were always fighting some other tribe.'

'I don't have any enemies on this river.'

'Your hair looks just like my wife's hair. Let me comb it for you,' the Indian said. He took another big drink and produced a comb from a small zippered bag. 'I always brush my wife's hair.'

Margo hadn't had anyone comb her hair since she was little. The Indian worked gently, starting from the tangled ends, and he didn't lose patience and pull as her mother and Joanna used to. And every time one of his hands brushed against her, her skin flushed and her body seemed to swell. When he declared his work finished, he put his arms around her and pulled her back against his chest. She let herself relax there, as though she had dived into the river and was letting herself go with the current. He kissed her neck, and she twisted around and pressed her mouth to his. She had not meant for this to happen, but she wanted it now.

They made love for a long time, rolling over

onto soft pine needles. She felt the minutes stretch into hours, as if the normal rules of time had been suspended. She had never made love with a man outdoors. The wind gave them something, as did the water flowing past. Every creature that scurried on the ground, or flew in the air nearby or swam or splashed in the river passed some energy to them. After a while, the river itself seemed to creep up over its banks to flow around them and the current pushed them closer to each other. When he finished, he said, 'You know, there's an idea that when a woman makes love to a man, she gives over the strength and power of the other men she's been with.' When he realized her breathing was strained, he rolled off and propped himself on his elbow. He lay naked in the cool air. 'Tell me what I get from you.'

She shrugged. 'You look like an animal.'

'What animal?'

'I don't know.' She brushed pine needles off his hip, studied his resting cock.

'A fox?' he suggested. 'I always think if I could be an animal I'd be a fox.'

'Why a fox?'

'Because the fox is clever. What about you?'

She glanced around at the ancient landscape of trees and river. She didn't want to choose any single animal.

'I need another drink.' He glanced around for the bottle, which Margo saw was leaning against one of the stones by the fire, half full.

'You said you didn't want to drink more than half the bottle.' Margo got up and retrieved a few small chunks of wood she had split earlier with the Indian's hatchet. She moved her soup aside and tossed them on the fire.

'That wasn't the real me. This is the real me. Naked me.'

She handed him the bottle, and he took a long drink and replaced the cap. Margo sat at the foot of her sleeping bag near him. Though it was cool, she liked being naked under the stars. She thought maybe if the Indian was hungover he wouldn't leave in the morning. He'd have to wait another day to drive, and she could put off being alone.

'You have to take a drink of this,' he said.

'I don't like it. I already tasted it.'

'You can't know this whiskey from a taste. You didn't even open your mouth before. You have to take a swallow.' He sidled up close to her, so his naked shoulder was pressed against hers. She had hoped that his effect on her would have quieted, but she felt the electricity, stronger than before, and pressed back against him in an effort to subdue it. She listened for a clue from the river, but it had gone silent. 'I don't like to drink alcohol,' she said.

'Whiskey is a religion, a spirit in a bottle. Take a swallow, feel it move through your whole body. You know, Margo, I've never betrayed my wife up to now.' He leaned into her neck. 'My wife uses that same shampoo. I know the smell. Your hair looks black like hers in the dark.'

'I'll take a drink if you take a bite of puffball mushroom.'

'I don't know.' He rested the bottle on her knee.

'You saw me eat it, and I'm not poisoned.'

'Okay, I'll eat it for breakfast. If you're still alive then,' the Indian said. 'I promise.'

Margo took a deep breath, tipped the bottle up, and swallowed. Her mouth and throat burned. 'God,' she said, when she could speak.

'That's the first time I've heard you say *God*. Now what do you see? An animal?'

'I don't know,' she said, choking. Her brain was short-circuiting as the whiskey moved through her. When the burning in her mouth subsided, she tasted more clearly the bitterness.

'Close your eyes,' the Indian said. 'What do you see when you close your eyes?'

She did not close her eyes. 'God, how can you drink that?'

'You have to tell what you see.'

'Just the river,' Margo said, though the animal was as real as life before her. She wanted to keep the vision of the wolverine to herself — it was just like the one in the Indian hunter book, just like the one her grandpa described, the glutton. For the Indian hunter, a wolverine hissing in his cave meant he should return to his tribe. But this animal was not threatening Margo. It regarded her calmly, seemed to accept her, and then it disappeared. Margo couldn't shake how clearly she'd seen it standing before her, dog-sized, with skunk colors and long claws. She wished it had made a sound she could make in turn, but it had been silent.

The Indian put his face in her hair and said, 'I think you're a river spirit.'

'I'm not a river spirit. Why do guys always

want to make a girl into something other than what she is?' Margo asked. She was not a wolf child, as Michael had called her. Even her grandpa's naming her Sprite and River Nymph seemed odd now, as though he wanted her not to be a person, exactly.

'It makes a better story,' he said. 'But there's no story better than how you look naked, my dear, in this ancient place.' He lifted the hair off her neck and caressed her shoulders. When he finished the bottle, he kissed her. Once again, Margo could imagine no reason on this earth not to trust her body.

But this time, he was different. This time he rolled over her like floodwaters surging downstream. He sucked at her breasts as though he were feeding from her.

'What's your name?' she whispered. She wanted this whole experience, whatever it was, but the change in the Indian scared her. 'Who are you?' she asked.

'I don't know my name. I swear I don't know,' he whispered into her chest, and she felt his jaw grind against her breastbone. He took a deep breath and exhaled heat over her. 'But we'll never be here again in the land of my ancestors.'

'Now you sound like an Indian,' she said.

He climbed on top of her, and she rose to meet him. They moved their bodies on the sleeping bags and pine needles with such force that Margo felt her insides shaking. Her teeth rattled. She was too warm with his body on hers, and even when she straddled him, the night air couldn't cool her. When the Indian pulled her down hard onto him, together they were a flood that rolled through the river valley, cleared the land, and swept away everything not tied down. The river noises and the slap of carp bodies on the surface filled the air around them, and above them the flying squirrels chittered and squeaked. Beneath them, the ground, which had been cool, now radiated heat.

By the time he rolled off her, they were slick with sweat. Margo could hardly breathe. She lay still, expecting to see steam rising off their bodies into the cool air. Even after a few minutes, she could not catch her breath. When he passed out, she curled beside him and calmed herself by listening to the gurgling sounds of the river.

She fell into a state that was not quite sleep, her body awake and wrestling with itself. Margo reached out to touch her daddy's ashes, but found the box too hot. After a time she did sleep, and she dreamed of the wolverine, big as the black dog and with a weasel face, and then the wolverine became a fish coming up the river, big as Paul, and then, in the dream, she shot Paul and felt how it was a terrible thing to take a man's life.

She awoke with the Indian pulling her close to him. She felt the cold zipper of his unzipped sleeping bag touch her naked belly. When she opened her eyes, she met his black eyes staring into hers. She told him she'd dreamed of a big fish, and he whispered, 'I dreamed it, too. A sturgeon. They used to be in the river, big as cows.'

It wasn't until later that Margo realized how

crazy that sounded, that they'd both dreamed the same giant fish. In the morning she lay still, too exhausted to move or speak, while the Indian pulled away from her and stumbled up the path toward his car. He left behind his sleeping bag and camping pad, his frying pan and his hatchet. She didn't try to stop him.

When she opened her eyes again, it was full daylight, and she was still exhausted. Her body ached. Everywhere she touched herself she found stones and pine needles and plants stuck to her skin. Tucked beneath her sleeping bag was a small cowskin bag with a drawstring and a simple bead design, and inside was a folded note and a roll of twenty-dollar bills.

Goodbye, Margo, the note began. *I've never been unfaithful to my wife in the three years we've been married. I'm going to forget what happened between us. I hope you will do the same. Remember you have options in this life. Go back to school.* The note was dated *September 14, 1981*, but signed only *XXX*.

'Jerk,' she said. A big carp surfaced and a smaller carp did the same, and then both returned to the depths. She sat as still as a bird on a nest of eggs for hours that afternoon, clutching her rifle, but with no inclination to shoot anything, not even a squirrel when it scampered over her sleeping bag. She was drunk with the Indian's scent, hungover with him, was half in love with him after just two days, but she thought she would be okay once she worked him

279

out of her system. He had come to her for help, and she had helped him. She had fed him, and he had paid her for the food. Sex with him had been like nothing she had known, but if he had stayed any longer, they might have hurt each other. She needed to get some rest and think about how she would survive until her mother wrote to her. The Indian had left enough money for her to buy a boat. That evening she ate the soup she'd made from their leftovers.

PART
III

18

Two weeks after the Indian left, Margo didn't start flowing as she should have, and one afternoon she realized what that meant, that she was with the Indian's child. She had been foolish to trust her instincts when she was feeling lonesome. She had been foolish to follow her body's desire and inclination in this strange new place. She did not stop crying for a long time, until she looked up on the ridge and saw a tall, thin man looking down at her.

The farmer owned the land where she had camped alone for two weeks. During this time, he and the men working for him were harvesting the nearby fields of soybeans. Upon spotting him, she stopped crying instantly, the way a baby bird stopped piping for food when a predator was near. Though her hands itched to lift her rifle, she sighted him only with her gaze. After a good long look, she turned away and set about combing out her loose hair with her fingers. She wound it up and twisted it against the back of her head and fixed it with her barrette. Her sleeping bags and camping pad were already rolled together into a thick bundle. She folded her tarp and collected her other things. The small amount of food at her campsite was piled into the big pot she'd gotten from the old man, and that was already hidden away in the windbreak, with the lid tied down against animal invasion. Her father's ashes were in their metal box beside it. She was bothered that she could no longer pick up and carry everything she owned. Having the extra gear made her more self-sufficient, but less able or willing to run away from trouble, should there be any.

Though her fire was more or less extinguished, she filled a gallon jug in the river and doused the ashes to show the farmer her presence was not a fire hazard. She tied her oversized bedroll and tarp onto her pack and walked a little upstream. After she entered the cover of trees, she turned to see, through the branches, the figure still silhouetted there, although now he appeared to be looking off over the field.

Margo would return to the campsite this evening. She liked the privacy this place afforded and hoped to stay until she had a boat or another plan. Sometimes the sound of the river moving past her made her feel free in a way that the Stark River had not for a long time. She occasionally heard shots in the distance, but she was down to one cartridge and needed to brave going into town to buy more. Between the fish, game, black walnuts, and garden pilfering, she was doing fine foodwise, and she got her clean water at the hand pump in the barn.

Margo hid her pack away in the branches of a tree in the wind-break and continued upstream with only her rifle, swinging around and through the fence to get into and then out of the cow pasture, landing once again beside the house of the old man in the wheelchair. She had spied on him most days. He often sat alone on the flagstone patio in that wheelchair, staring down at the water through his black glasses. His hair shone bright silver whenever the sun was on him.

The old man was not out today. Margo ventured through the patio, kicking at the pretty orange and yellow maple leaves scattered there. She moved down the steep steps and out onto the boat with the little camper on it. Again, it moved only slightly under her weight. The padlock was hanging loose, and when she turned the handle on the aluminum door of the cabin, it opened, and she was greeted by a mildew smell. Inside she found a narrow upper bunk bed and a bigger lower bunk that could be transformed into a table and seats, a propane stovetop with two burners like the one Brian had, an oven big enough for a cake pan, and the smallest wood-burning stove she had ever seen. She opened the door to the firebox, saw it was maybe twelve inches high by fifteen deep by eight wide. A person would have to cut her own firewood extra-small for this. A six-inch pipe exhausted through the wall behind it.

She heard barking, and when she came out onto the deck, she found the black dog wagging his tail. The old man was sitting on the patio behind the house, dappled sunlight glinting off his wheelchair and his silver hair. He motioned with his hand for her to come to the patio, and she obliged. 'What do you want, kid?' he asked.

Margo had some difficulty making out his words through his wheezing, but she remembered what he'd said last time, that if she'd wanted a shower, she should ask for it.

'Can I sleep in your camper for a while?'

The man cleared his throat in a way that sounded painful. His skin was pale and slightly damp, and his hair was sticking to his face.

'You look sicker than you did,' she said. When the dog settled beside the wheelchair, Margo knelt and petted him with both hands.

'There's good days and bad days. I have emphysema, but the doctors tell me it's the tumors that're going to kill me.' He cleared his throat again. 'Unless you're going to save everybody a lot of trouble and shoot me.'

'Do you want me to shoot another cigarette out of your mouth?'

'Yeah, stand right in front of me this time.' He tapped his forehead as if directing a bullet there. 'I was too exhausted to come outside, but then I saw you, and I told myself, I'd better kick that kid's ass.'

'I'm not a kid.'

'Everybody's a kid compared to me.' He stifled a cough. 'Even people my age seem like kids.'

'What can I give you for your boat? I got some money.'

'You've got no goddamned money. You've got a rifle and a soup pot. And a big kitchen knife that belongs to me, if I figure it right.'

'I'll give you the knife back. I was just borrowing it. I can't give you my rifle.'

'I've already got two rifles and a shotgun that I can't aim anymore. And you can keep the damn knife. It's not my best one.' He held out his pale, shaking hand as a sort of exhibit. 'I made my living setting type, and now I can't tighten a screw or chop stew meat.'

'Can I look inside the houseboat some more?'

'You've seen enough. I don't need a kid sleeping on my boat. Don't need the neighbors seeing anything.'

'I could help you out in exchange, maybe,' Margo suggested. 'I could sweep this patio. I can cook and chop up stew meat for you.'

'My friend Fishbone said he saw you with a Mexican man over on the farm two weeks ago, the night you came here.'

'He's an Indian. Anyway, he's gone.' Margo was surprised she'd been spied on.

'Did the son of a bitch break your heart?'

'I'm relieved he's gone. I don't need a man.'

'Well, what do you think I am?'

'Sir, your boat is the only way I can live on the river.' As Margo spoke to the old man, she felt strangely aware of something being in her belly, and she worried that he might be aware of it, too.

'Go away,' he said. A coughing fit overtook him, and when he finally straightened up, there was blood on the corners of his mouth. He motioned to her to leave.

'Can I stay here and pet your dog?'

He shook his head. 'Come back in the morning.'

━━━━◆

Margo spent the night in her sleeping bag by her campfire, with the Indian's pad and sleeping bag under her for comfort, the tarp over her to protect against the heavy dew. She dreamed she

287

was lying with the Indian, and several times she awoke with a start, feeling as though her body were being pitched from rough waters onto land.

In the morning she made her way upstream, and as she reached the white house, she heard sounds that could have been crows. The sounds became voices, and she noticed two cars in the driveway where she'd seen none on her earlier visits. A little farther down the road was parked a two-toned Chevy pickup truck she had seen a few times. She crept closer. The old man was on the patio with two women. Both were about Margo's height. One had long, dark hair, straighter than Margo's; the other had shorter, lighter hair and looked younger, but otherwise they resembled each other.

'You're supposed to use your oxygen all the time, but whenever we come over, you don't have it hooked up,' the dark-haired woman said.

'I use it when I need it, Shelly. Don't bother about it.'

'It's getting cold, and the doctor said the cold can cause your lungs to seize. Let us help you back into the house.'

The old man wore nothing over his work shirt. Margo wished one of them would get a jacket from the house. Or maybe they hoped his being cold would make him go inside.

'What do you know about anything? You or your sister?'

'Well, I know we love you, Uncle Smoke, and we promised Mom we'd take care of you,' said the blonde niece. She knelt beside the chair to look him in the face, and he turned away from her. She said, 'But you can't stay here. You don't weigh half what you used to.'

'I don't try to run your goddamned lives.' His dark glasses made it hard to tell what direction he was actually looking, but Margo thought his attention was on something by the garage.

'It's all about smoking, isn't it?' said Shelly. 'That's why you don't want to go, because they won't let you smoke. You think you can't give up smoking, but you can if you want to. They have ways to help you quit.'

'The Nazis had ways, too. I want to be right where I am.'

The blonde niece said, 'If there was one thing in this world I could get rid of, it would be cigarettes. They hurt so many people.'

The man put his hands on his wheelchair wheels and moved them a few inches. The blonde stood up. The dog sat smiling on the patio beside the man, seeming to enjoy the company of the women.

'Will you drink a breakfast shake at least, so we know you're getting some vitamins and protein?' Shelly said.

'Have you tasted that shit? And have you tasted any of that other so-called food they gave your mother in the All Saints home? Turkey bacon, margarine, sugar-free cookies, Sanka? And I won't have a tube put in me.' He was becoming breathless. 'I signed a paper with my doctor saying so. He sent a form to both hospitals.'

'I drink the Carnation breakfast, Uncle Smoke. I like it,' Shelly said.

'Well, you can have the damn stuff.'

'Can't you let us talk to your doctor?' she asked. 'Just tell us his name.'

'No.'

'You make me want to cry. I worry about you all the time,' said the blonde niece.

Tears were indeed running down her face, Margo noted.

'You're acting plain crazy, Uncle Smoke.'

'Is that what you two wrote to the judge?' the old man asked.

'Why do you have to be so mean?'

'Mean? You want to lock me up at the All Saints home, and I'm mean?'

'It's *Alsand's Comfort Care*, not *All Saints*.' The younger woman sounded defeated. 'Why do you keep saying *All Saints*? And Mom said they treated her good there. And if you would come live with me, then we would take care of you, and you wouldn't have to go there.'

'In your apartment with your boyfriend and three cats? I've got my own house right here.'

'The township said they sent you a letter about that garage,' said Shelly, nodding toward the sagging building. 'They're going to take it down. You should tell that friend of yours to take out anything he wants to keep. Township says it's going to collapse, and there's probably rats in there.'

The old man held back a cough with what looked to Margo like a great effort. She saw the deer hide was still stretched on a pallet beside the garage, not visible from where the women were standing.

'And I know it's him buying you cigarettes,' Shelly said.

The blonde said, 'You would live longer if you got the right treatment. Don't you want to live?'

The dog's ears perked up. Margo heard rustling from near the fence beside the garage. She moved the barrel of her rifle toward the sound as if tracking a squirrel, all the way to a burning bush that was beginning to turn red. Behind the foliage, she made out a dark-skinned arm, leading to a short-sleeved blue shirt, and then a face half obscured by a fedora. Bluish smoke rose from under the hat's brim. He was watching, same as she was, only more conspicuously if you considered he was smoking a little cigar. When she met his eyes, she registered an angry look and quickly dropped her muzzle.

'Well, I've got to go to work. Goodbye,' Shelly said and shuffled off the patio. The blonde kissed the old man's head and followed her sister around the side of the house. The man in the fedora stood and moved to the patio, and Margo hesitantly did the same.

'Don't you ever point a gun at a person, young lady!' the man said and shook his head in disapproval.

'I'm sorry. I didn't even know you were there. I thought it was a squirrel making that sound in the bushes.'

The man was thin and wore a button-up shirt with a short collar, creased jeans, and polished black leather shoes. He could have been in his early sixties, but his figure was that of a younger man.

'Smoky, do you know anything about this girl here who's sneaking around trying to kill a man?' he said calmly. 'Is this another niece you haven't told me about?'

'That's nothing new to you, is it? A woman trying to kill you? Your wife's been trying to kill you for — ' The old man couldn't finish his sentence before his words degenerated into a coughing fit. Both Margo and the man in the fedora moved a few steps closer and stood waiting for the coughing to subside.

Margo thought it was an interesting situation here, that two different people had been hiding behind this old man's house.

'It's been a while since a woman wanted to kill me,' the man said to Margo. His voice was reassuring. 'Since my wife got her blood pressure, she tries to stay calm.'

'Fishbone, you got to — ' The old man had momentarily seemed to recover, but now he coughed some more and pulled a bottle of medicine out of a pocket in his wheelchair. After he fumbled with it awhile, Fishbone took it, pushed down and unscrewed the cap, and handed it back. Smoke drank from the bottle.

'That dog sees me five days of the week. Why's he going to growl at me?' Fishbone asked after Smoke recapped the bottle.

'But you still got to take care of him after I'm dead. You promised me that.'

'You're not dying anytime soon, you spooky old man,' Fishbone said.

Smoke took off his glasses and wiped his eyes. 'What are you two staring at?'

'We're staring at you, you crazy coughing fool. You think that codeine is going to save you? That codeine's going to shut you down one of these days. That's why the doctor won't let you have more than a bottle a week.'

'It's part of my plan.' He put the glasses back on. They covered half his face.

'Your nieces are busybodies. Why do they want the township to tear down my lovely cottage?' Fishbone noticed a tiny burr stuck on the bottom of his trousers, and he lifted his foot and brushed it off. 'You ought to ask those girls to clean your house, Smoky. Get some good out of them.'

'You live in that garage?' Margo asked.

'I live in Kalamazoo. That there's my *river cottage*, where I skin deer and tan hides. There's more rats in Smoke's house than in that garage.' Fishbone wore a thick gold band etched with a cross on his ring finger. 'By the way, here's your death sticks, Smoky.'

Smoke accepted the carton of cigarettes from Fishbone. He turned to Margo. 'Why are you so late?'

'You didn't tell me to be here at a certain time,' she said.

'Old folks get up early. Isn't that right, Fishbone?' His breathing sounded better.

'What would I know about *old*? I ain't old like you,' he said.

'At the print shop I had to open the doors at seven in the morning or the Dutch folks would take their business elsewhere. It used to kill me to get up so early. Now that I got nothing to do,

I can't sleep past sunrise,' Smoke said. 'Fishbone here, my setup man, felt all right wandering in with half a doughnut at ten o'clock.'

'I prefer a more relaxed lifestyle.'

'Why were you hiding, sir?' Margo asked.

'Didn't want those harsh ladies seeing me. I try to keep clear of that kind of woman.'

'You've got to meet this girl, Fishbone. She can shoot that cigar out of your mouth.' Smoke brushed an unfiltered cigarette butt, half burned, from the seat of his chair onto the stone patio. It must have been hidden there while his nieces visited.

'So I hear,' Fishbone said. He took the burning cigar out of his mouth, studied the plastic filter, and then stuck it back between his teeth.

'I saw your skins, Mr. Fishbone. I can skin animals, too.'

'Not many girls know about skinning nowadays.' He regarded her, head to toe.

'I do. Rabbits, squirrels, deer. I helped my grandpa skin a bear once. And I know how to cook wild meat, too.'

'My wife'll cook me a squirrel, but I got to bring it to her skinned and gutted with the tail cut off. So she can pretend it's a chicken.' He regarded her again, this time more suspiciously. 'What are you coming around here for, anyway? Smoky's got no money.'

'He said for me to come today.'

'I've got plenty of money,' Smoke said. 'I'm a desirable man in every way, in case you haven't noticed.'

'Aren't you supposed to be in school?' Fishbone said.

'I'm finished with school. I'm eighteen.' She was less than two months away from being eighteen.

'Thought all you people went to college nowadays.' As they'd been talking, Fishbone had relaxed his posture. 'Smoky, will you tell that dog to stop growling at me? I do believe he's showing off for the young lady.'

Smoke yanked the dog's collar and the big dog flattened himself against the ground.

Fishbone stood about six feet tall, and his neat appearance contrasted with what Margo imagined to be her own. She wished she had taken the time to wash her face and hands and to brush her hair before dragging it up on her head.

'Two of my boys dropped out, said they don't need school, said the teachers are racist, and they don't got a chance.'

'Don't look at me,' Smoke said. Margo flinched, thinking she was in trouble for staring again, but he was speaking figuratively, to Fishbone. 'I'm not disagreeing with you.'

'They're right about the racists,' Fishbone said, 'but they still need to go to school.'

'Is your name really Smoke?' Margo asked.

'Terry here doesn't know any better than Smoke's a black man's name. So he's got it all wrong on two counts.' Fishbone winked.

'Go to hell,' Smoke said. 'And this fellow in the stylish clothes is Leon Barber, the Fishbone.'

'He wishes he was black,' Fishbone said, 'so he'd have something more to complain about.'

Fishbone's thin face was clean-shaven. His eyes bulged, giving him a slight look of panic, though his calm demeanor countered that impression. Margo had hardly ever looked at a black man, and now she couldn't stop looking. 'That's a funny name, *Fishbone*,' Margo said.

'Because of the way he smells,' Smoke said. 'Believe me, I worked with him on a daily basis.'

'I'm Margo Crane.'

'You come close to me, Margo Crane, and you'll know I smell like a flower,' Fishbone said. He reached out and took her hand. His long fingers were callused, warm, and dry.

'You smell okay,' she said. He smelled a little like flowery aftershave, but mostly he smelled like his cigar.

'Them cigarettes tell you why this white man's called Smoke.' He gently released her hand.

'Could I sell you animal skins?' Margo asked. 'If I had them?'

'You got to be licensed with the state of Michigan before you start dealing in skins. I won't even talk to anybody who hasn't got a license from the DNR.'

'I can get one.'

'You get one, and I can get you a few bucks for a muskrat skin. Russians want them, but they don't hardly want to pay for them. And raccoons are worth something for the skin and the meat. But you have to leave a coon paw on the pelt in order to assure folks you didn't skin a cat.'

She nodded. Until now she had not known *why* Grandpa had left a paw on a coon's hide. It was one of the many questions she'd wished she'd asked the old man.

'Pelts have to be perfect, no bullet holes. Shooting cuts them up.'

'What if I shoot them through the eye with my .22?'

'Lord, Smoky. Where'd you find this girl?' Fishbone pulled the butt of the little cigar out of the plastic holder, let it drop to the patio, and crushed it with his shoe. He put a new, unlit cigar in it, stuck it in the side of his mouth, maybe to cover a smile. 'Thinks she's going to shoot critters in the eye.'

Margo knew she'd have to solve the problem of the bullet continuing out the other side of the head.

'See, you old stink,' Smoke said, 'girls are capable of anything these days. If you want her to shoot that cigar out of your mouth, you just say the word.'

'You get yourself a license, and then come talk to me. Do you live around here?'

'I want to live on that houseboat down there.'

'Is this child living on her own?' Fishbone asked.

'The Mexican left town,' Smoke said.

'Young ladies living on their own get taken advantage of. Girls aren't as smart as they think they are.'

'He was an Indian,' she said.

'Yeah,' Smoke said. 'Girls are almost as dumb as boys. Almost as dumb as grown men.'

'I can take care of myself,' Margo said.

'Maybe not if the farmer's brother's around,' Fishbone said. 'The fellow is reputed to pluck

297

the fresh fruits wherever he can find them.'

'Your daughter thought he was a charming fellow,' Smoke said.

'Back in the day, I wouldn't let my younger daughter near that boy,' Fishbone said. 'Now I'll have to worry about my granddaughters. And the man's only, what, thirty-five?'

'Thirty-three, I think. Just a pup.' Smoke tore the foil off a fresh pack of cigarettes and held the pack out toward Margo. 'You'll have to worry about your great-granddaughters.'

'Don't offer her a cigarette,' Fishbone said. 'Just because you want to kill yourself by smoking don't mean you've got to drag this young lady into it.'

'Can I please sleep in your houseboat, Mr. Smoke?' Margo said. 'I'm sleeping outside on the ground right now.'

'Neighbors'll tell my nieces there's a girl hanging around. That, along with a black man gutting out raccoons in my yard, and they'll say I can't look after myself. They'll lock me up in the All Saints home on principle.'

Margo looked around and saw that if she stayed in the camper, people might see her from the windows of several houses. She would not want to become a curiosity for the neighbors.

'Better somebody uses it,' Fishbone said. 'You're not using it.'

'I had a serious plan for that boat. Now my big outboard won't run. Try moving that thing upstream with the five horsepower.'

'You got plans, all right,' Fishbone said. 'Especially that plan to smoke yourself to death.

298

That's working out fine.'

'That boat saved my sanity,' Smoke said to Margo. 'It's my *Pride & Joy*. It's got everything a man needs. If I could drag the hose down, I'd fill up the tank and have running water again.'

'Your pride and joy is that set of lungs you turned black and crusted up with tumors by smoking all them cigarettes,' Fishbone said. He took a seat on an upside-down milk crate at the edge of the patio, pulled his unlit cigar out of his mouth, and looked at the plastic filter again, this time more critically.

Smoke turned to Margo. 'I lived in that trailer every time my damned sister and her daughters had to move in with me. I couldn't stand to be around that cackling bunch of females.' His choked laughter caused him to drop his burning cigarette onto his lap. Margo plucked it up and handed it back to him. Smoke took one more long drag and then dropped the cigarette onto the patio. He rigged up his oxygen tubes to run below his nose.

'Don't you got nobody?' Fishbone asked Margo. 'No place?'

'I'm waiting to hear from my ma. She lives in Lake Lynne.'

Smoke looked at Margo intently.

'How is she going to get ahold of you?' Fishbone asked.

'I need to write her a letter.'

'Don't give her my address,' Smoke said. 'I don't need another woman poking around.'

'I'm getting a post office box. If they've got them in that town of Greenland.'

'Smoky, maybe you ought to let this young lady stay in the boat until she finds her ma. I don't like to see a girl out alone with nobody looking after her.'

'Take her to your house.'

'I got fifteen people living in my place this week. The folks I'm related to seem to think I'm a free hotel. There's nobody on your boat but a few mice.'

'Well, she's going to have to give me something for it,' Smoke said. He turned toward Fishbone and then back to Margo. 'You can buy that boat from me on one condition. That you shoot me in the head before they take me to a nursing home.'

Margo wished she could read his expression through the glasses.

'What you saying that for?' Fishbone said. 'I'm not going to help you, and she isn't, either. You'd take killing more seriously if you'd been in the war, Smoky.'

'It ain't my fault I couldn't go in the army,' he said.

'Well, if you had, you'd've seen how killing anyone, yourself included, is nothing to joke about.'

'You spend too much time at church,' Smoke said. 'You're becoming a regular church lady.'

Fishbone shook his head. 'Smoky, you ought to be careful what you say to people.'

'You heard my nieces. They have it all figured.' The old man paused to catch his breath. 'They're having me declared unfit in court. I'm going to lose my freedom.'

300

'Don't ask other people to do your dirty work, Smoky. I could probably shoot and bury all the black men I wanted, but I'll go to the electric chair if I start killing white people, even useless old ones like you.'

'A hundred bucks for my boat,' Smoke said to Margo and took a breath. 'But you're going to help me when the time comes. And I reserve the right to buy my boat back if you don't hold up your part of the bargain.'

'Do it yourself if you've got to do it. Don't go dragging anybody else into it,' Fishbone said, leaning down and brushing a bit of cigar ash off his black leather shoe.

'I'm going to try,' Smoke said to Margo in a quieter voice. 'But if you want my boat, my *Pride & Joy*, you're going to owe me.'

'You people always surprise me,' Fishbone said. 'Talking that way is unnatural. Life and death is God's business, not yours.'

'I went to that goddamned nursing home every day for lunch when my sister was in there. I saw people turning into ghosts made out of those mashed potatoes they got, taste like plaster of Paris. I'm not going to die in that prison.'

Margo nodded at the word *prison*.

'I need somebody to shoot me before they come get me. I need a beautiful kid like you to finish me off. You'll kiss me on the cheek and then blow my head off.'

'You want to get her in trouble with the law?'

'Nobody's going to care about a sick old man dying,' Smoke said.

'If this young lady shoots you with that

301

Marlin,' Fishbone said, 'they'll trace the bullet to her microgroove barrel. And if she shoots you with a shotgun, everybody is going to hear the blast. You're not thinking about what happens to anybody else after you're gone.'

'So drown me in the river.'

Fishbone shook his head, as though giving up on serious talk for the day.

'Maybe I'll die in my sleep and you'll both be off the hook. Kid, you give me a hundred dollars and I'll sign over my *Pride & Joy*, and you can go register it in your own name. You'll have to take her a little ways downstream. But don't go far.'

'Don't take the girl's money. What do you need a hundred bucks for? Just let her use the old thing.'

'To prove I sold it and didn't give it away. If I start giving things away, the judge will say I'm losing my faculties. I'll write her a receipt saying she paid for it and keep a carbon copy.' His color looked healthier the longer he argued with Fishbone.

'Probably your nieces won't even notice if it's gone.' Fishbone bit the plastic cigar filter and spoke through his teeth. 'They are not your most observant ladies.'

'A hundred dollars.' Margo pulled from her wallet five twenty-dollar bills. She would have paid a lot more.

'And a promise you'll help me at the end,' Smoke said. He took off his glasses again and let them lie in his lap while he looked at her.

Margo was afraid to look back at him to see how serious he was. Instead she watched

Fishbone's wiry figure descend the concrete-block steps. Still shaking his head, he untied the aluminum boat, stepped in, took the cover off the outboard, and started it up. The boat moved upstream. He took the boat out for a run most days, Margo would learn, weather allowing.

19

Margo followed Smoke's directions for registering the boat. She filled out the form Fishbone got for her and mailed it in, listing her new Greenland PO box as her address. The transferred boat title was in her pocket twelve days later, and Smoke handed her the key to the padlock on the door. He talked her through filling up the water tanks, and while she had the hose down there, she washed the cabin's outside walls and scrubbed the deck with a brush. Margo carried Smoke's only working outboard — an old Johnson two-horsepower trolling motor — down from the back porch and fixed it in place, fed some unleaded gasoline mixed with two-stroke oil into the tank, but found herself unable to start it. Smoke tried to give instructions from the patio, but finally she had to help him down the stairs to the boat, where he leaned against the cabin. When he couldn't catch his breath after five minutes, Margo ran up to the patio and got his oxygen tank. Together they got the outboard going, though the action exhausted Smoke. Downstream with the current would be no problem for the trolling motor, but Smoke was right that she couldn't go upstream even at full throttle. She would have to find a bigger outboard.

'I'm going to miss this boat,' he said when he was back in his wheelchair on the patio, reconnected to his oxygen. 'My *Pride & Joy*. I designed and built every damned inch of that cabin myself, even welded up that little wood stove. Couldn't find one small enough.'

'Do you want me to keep it here?'

He shook his head. 'Go down to Harland's.'

'Who's Harland?'

'The farmer who owns that land you're camped out on. You're legally registered now, so just keep your flotation devices visible, and don't screw around with the DNR. Same thing for that trapping license. I don't know why a kid like you wants to kill muskrats,' he said and stopped to catch his breath.

'It really is mine, isn't it?'

'You've got the title. I think I'm out of my mind selling it to you, but there's nobody else who would go along with me.'

The title was in the camper, closed in *Annie Oakley: Life and Legend*. Before she headed downriver, she would go inside and look at it again.

'I wish I didn't have to be on any person's land.'

The farmer hadn't come around since the day she had seen him on the ridge, though occasionally she spied on him near his house and in his barnyard.

'And I'm sure he'd rather you wasn't on his place, but you can't motor around all the time. It's not that kind of boat.'

'I'll look out for someplace that doesn't belong to anybody.'

'Good goddamned luck with that.'

'I've been trying to figure out how to live,'

Margo said, but didn't know how to go on and so crossed her arms over her chest.

'Me, too. Haven't figured it out yet,' Smoke said and held out his hand. Margo uncrossed her arms and took the hand in hers so it stopped shaking. She wished she could see his eyes. He said, 'You've got every right to try to live any goddamned idiotic way you want to.'

Margo waved at his slumped, silver-haired figure as the boat sputtered downstream. She pulled the crumbling old rudder out of the water and steered the boat using the outboard, keeping close to the north bank of the river. The boat was heavy and hard to maneuver, and she had to lean down over the back to work the motor and use the mirrors to see what was in front of her. Finally she cut against the current and steered up onto the sandbar above where the spring-water trickled into the river. She lifted the motor out of the water as the propeller scraped bottom. By the time she could get off the boat to secure it with a rope, it had drifted, so she had to drag it back upstream, a few inches at a time. Finally she moored it above where the springwater trickled in, just upstream of her campsite, where the water was deep enough that the boat sat level. She tied it to a tree so it couldn't slip any farther downstream. She anchored the boat near shore using the five-gallon buckets half filled with concrete that she'd pulled up out of the water at Smoke's. At first she thought she would not need to be tied to shore, but the boat kept edging out into the river. There were two coils of rough manila rope on the boat, along with two five-foot-long stakes she pounded into the ground; she tied up to those to keep herself from drifting.

When she had filled out the form to register the boat, she had considered naming it *The River Rose II*. She considered *The Indian*, but decided he didn't deserve the honor. She painted over the words *Pride & Joy* with some white enamel she'd taken from Smoke's back porch and let it dry for a few days before painting in plain block letters GLUTTON, her grandpa's name for the wolverine, the animal she had seen right here when the Indian told her to close her eyes and she did not.

Smoke had given her a chain saw and a splitting maul along with the boat — said he couldn't use them anymore and neither could Fishbone, who lived in Kalamazoo. Margo set to work right away sawing fallen trees from the windbreak and splitting the logs into small chunks for the woodstove. The first day, she sawed and split until her back ached. She was grateful to have work to do.

She quickly adjusted to her new home, discovered all the storage spaces, found the odd bits of equipment Smoke had stashed on the boat, including fishing gear and kitchen utensils. The design of the cabin was clever, to make the most space for cooking, and plenty of room for sitting and sleeping. This was how she wanted to live. Because the whole big river was her home, her shelter against the elements could be small and efficient, inexpensive to maintain. Her gratitude toward Smoke nearly overwhelmed her when she thought about it.

Margo wrote her mother a letter saying she was settled outside Kalamazoo and she'd like to come visit. After that, Margo checked her PO box six days a week. Most mornings she stopped at Smoke's on the way, to visit him and to use his bathroom and hot water. There was a shower on her boat, with a hot water tank heated by propane, but using it splashed water around, and she would have to refill both the water and the propane when they emptied. The shower in Smoke's house was much improved after she scrubbed the mildew out of it. Even after cleaning, though, the yellow walls and white ceiling were coated with a rust-colored film, the same stuff that was on her houseboat camper ceiling. The same color stained Smoke's fingertips and, no doubt, the inside of his lungs.

Smoke liked having her wander in and out of his house, and every day he wanted to hear what she'd done, whether it was shooting a critter, cutting firewood, or repainting the inside of the houseboat with white paint to make it feel brighter — afterward, it stank so much of latex that for three nights she had to sleep outside by her campfire. Margo had never known anybody who took such an interest in her life as Smoke did. He gave her books from his shelf, including three volumes of *Foxfire*, which had stories about hunting wild turkey, boar, and bear. One of them told how to cure pork for bacon. Some days Smoke hardly said anything because of his breathing, but otherwise he told her about how dirty the river had been when he bought this property decades ago and how much cleaner it was now that the factories and the cities upstream couldn't dump their waste and sewage into the water. Margo thought of the Murray Metal elimination pipe, near which nobody fished. As far as she knew, it still spewed junk. He showed her a leather bag of lead type, opened it up on the kitchen table, said it was all that remained of his print shop. The notion that Smoke might really expect her to end his life seemed more remote with every passing day.

Margo thought there would come a day when she knew exactly what to do about the baby growing inside her. Almost every morning through October and November, before venturing out, she threw up into the river.

———————

The day before Thanksgiving, Smoke told Margo his nieces would be taking him to one of their apartments for a midday dinner. The following afternoon, Margo walked the half mile upstream and hid outside, watching the house and waiting for him to come home. The thought of those nieces having Smoke's company made her jealous, and she didn't trust the women to take care of him.

Margo stood out in the cold, leaning her back against his house. She stared at the deteriorating old garage with the CONDEMNED sticker on the window and willed it to collapse before her eyes with a *whoosh*. She listened to the birds on the neighbor's feeder, watched them rise and fall in the air above the privacy fence. After a while she sensed Nightmare inside the house sensing her outside. Always she sensed the tiny, ferocious thing inside herself, only two and a half months along. She felt it stealing her nourishment, her energy, and even her balance when she walked.

When Smoke's nieces arrived, there was some confusion in helping him out of the car and into his wheelchair so that he almost fell, but Margo stayed out of sight. While they were all in the house, she continued watching three chickadees descend in a rotation onto the bird feeder and up to a branch to eat the seed. She loved how these little black-and-blue birds showed up everywhere: in the woods, at the water's edge, outside houses, calling *chicka-dee-dee-dee*. When she had been in middle school, she had sometimes looked out through the window of a classroom and seen chickadees on the little trees. There had been moments like that when she had thought school could be a natural part of life.

A year ago, Margo and Michael had spent all day cooking two pies and a turkey breast and stuffing, and they had eaten dinner, just the two of them. She wondered where Michael was eating today. Brian was still in prison, probably telling his stories and jokes and learning new ones. Luanne was twenty-some miles away according to the map in Margo's wallet, in her *delicate situation*, whatever that was. The Indian was with his wife, no doubt. And the Murrays would be getting ready for a big party, though she had a hard time picturing such a thing, given the state in which she had last seen them. Smoke said she could decide how she wanted to live, but it was hard to figure out what she wanted for the future when there was so much from the past that she had not yet puzzled through.

As soon as Smoke was alone, Margo slipped inside. At his invitation, she opened the plastic containers his nieces had put in the refrigerator and ate everything in them, including turkey, stuffing, and buttered slices of bakery bread.

As Margo was finishing a second piece of pumpkin pie, Smoke said, 'To help my sister out, I paid those girls' college tuition, and now they think I should ease their minds by going into a nursing home. If my sister were alive, I'd tell her she raised those girls wrong.'

Margo nodded. There was a knock, and the riverside door opened before they could respond. When a blond man entered the kitchen, Smoke grinned.

'Grab Nightmare,' Smoke said. Margo got hold of the big dog's collar just as he lunged at the man's leg. 'Put him in my bedroom.'

'Why doesn't that dog love me the way every other dog in the neighborhood does?'

The man's voice was familiar to Margo.

'Dog can read your mind, that's why,' Smoke said. 'He knows another dog on the prowl when he sees one.'

'Who's this?' the man said as Margo was dragging the complaining dog from the room.

'Keep your paws off her. Or I'll let my dog bite you.'

'Pleased to meet you. I'm Johnny,' he said when Margo returned. 'You look very familiar. Are you some kind of movie star?'

At the full-on sight of him, Margo's stomach seized so hard she thought she might throw up the Thanksgiving meal. It was Paul's friend, Johnny. Her cheeks burned. Nightmare growled from the other room.

'She's nobody you need to know, Johnny,' Smoke said, still grinning. Whatever harsh things Smoke might say, Margo could see he liked this man and was made lively by his presence.

'I was just up at the big farmhouse eating a fine, sober meal with my upstanding, sober brother George and his attractive, angry wife.' Johnny took a can of beer out of one pocket of his jacket and another can out of the other pocket and set them on the table in front of him.

'Your brother George is a fine fellow, and you know it. Salt of the fucking earth.'

'Are you still refusing to go to the doctor, Smoke?' Johnny asked.

'I'm going to a doctor,' Smoke said. 'Just not the asshole in Greenland. He'll tell everybody in this town all about the pimple on my ass the next morning at the café.'

'You just don't want him getting into your lady parts, do you?' Johnny took a long slug of beer and seemed to relish his own outrageous question.

'You wish I had lady parts,' Smoke said, his cheeks coloring, 'but you're going to have to find your fun somewhere else.'

'I don't want this lovely creature to think I'm crude, now, Smoke.'

'Well, that doctor is the reason everybody knows when you get the clap, Johnny. That's how

312

the girls know when to avoid you.'

'Don't listen to him, sweetheart,' Johnny said, addressing Margo. 'I'm clean as a whistle.' His laugh was the same bright sound Margo had heard in Brian's cabin so long ago. She glanced at the door, beside which her rifle leaned, and took a good look at Johnny. She remembered his arms clamped around her middle on the couch. He'd been drunk, and she had stayed still for him like a cow in heat, curious to learn what a new bull might do. Margo began to feel desire now as she had not expected to feel it again anytime soon. She thought the smartest thing to do would be to get up and walk out.

Smoke grumbled a few harsh words that his smile belied, and Johnny laughed again.

'I guess I don't have time to mess around, anyhow,' Johnny said. 'I'm meeting somebody up the road in forty minutes. Just wanted to come by and see how you're doing. See if you'd taken up with a woman yet.'

'Well, if I could find one around here who didn't have your fingerprints all over her, I might consider it.'

'I'm on my way down south tonight, to Florida, and we'll make a little delivery back here in a few weeks. Or a few months, depending.'

'Florida, eh?' Smoke said. 'Be nice to be somewhere warm.'

'When I come back, I'll bring you two a little Florida sunshine.' He winked.

Johnny could not have known that Margo had spied on him swimming naked. He didn't know that back in Murrayville she had watched him

313

fall onto the carcass of the deer she had sold to Brian.

'Are you going to visit your old man?' Smoke asked. 'Be sure to tell that bastard I still want my money back for those tires.'

'More likely you'll get blood out of a stone,' Johnny said. 'I might stop and see old Jim and Doris in trailer land. Dad ought to be happy to see me, his prodigal son, but he isn't always.' Johnny smiled at Margo and said, 'I'm already looking forward to coming back to Michigan.'

'Well, you'd better leave this child alone, you lousy son of a bitch.' Smoke shook his head in mock despair. 'They ought to send you off to the vet, get you fixed.'

'You sure do look familiar.' The way Johnny grinned assured Margo he still didn't recognize her. He must have been truly drunk that night at Brian's cabin. Drunkenness Margo could understand, of course; what she didn't understand was why she couldn't stop grinning back at him, why she imagined herself stripping naked to dive into the river beside him. It was something basic about the man, his smell, maybe. She knew to resist him, and so long as she wasn't alone with him, she would be fine.

Margo saw Smoke shaking his head. She finally looked away from Johnny's gray eyes.

He stayed long enough to drink the two cans of beer he'd brought with him. He had offered the second one to Smoke and to Margo, but both refused. Margo couldn't stop looking at him. The whole thing was crazy, but she couldn't snap out of it. This was exactly how women got sunk, she knew. A woman would be doing okay, finding adequate shelter and feeding herself, and then a guy would start touching her and combing her hair. Electricity would start moving through her, and she would think she had found some great new fishing spot nobody knew about. A girl went off with a guy like this, and the next thing, she wouldn't care about finding her ma, or about making any sense of her life.

'Yep, going down to the Keys to see some Cubans I know down there,' Johnny said. 'I'm looking forward especially to one certain lovely Cuban lady.' As he was leaving, he reached out and tugged Margo's braid.

'That man is something,' Smoke said after Johnny left. Smoke's cheeks were still flushed. 'If he could package it and sell it, he'd be rich.'

Margo let Nightmare out of the bedroom. He sniffed where Johnny had been sitting and growled.

The first time Margo got a muskrat without putting a bullet hole in it she brought it to Smoke's as per Fishbone's request, with the fur brushed and cleaned, and she was glad to find Fishbone there, getting out of his boat. He accepted the long, limp creature she held out to him, took hold of it by the tail.

'What kind of trap did you use?' he asked.

'I didn't use a trap. I shot it through the eye.'

'Are you really that good of a shot?' Fishbone squinted and smiled enough to show teeth, and Margo saw that he was missing a canine. 'Smoky,

315

I believe our Margo is blushing. Young lady, I think you should ask the farmer to let you use his crop-damage permits. Tell him I'm tired of shooting his deer.'

'Tired of aiming at them and missing, you mean?' Smoke said.

'I got me two deer this year. That's more than you got the last ten years.'

'Can we keep the venison?' Margo asked.

'You can eat it or give it away, or donate it to the gospel mission. But you've got to talk to Mr. Harland.'

Though the farmer must have seen where the boat was parked, he hadn't approached her. She'd taken to sneaking around close to the farmhouse to spy on him, and once she'd seen him arguing with his wife, standing still and silent while his wife stomped around and yelled passionately. Margo also liked to watch the woman across the road from the hay barn. She spent a lot of time outdoors, feeding the birds and working in her garden. Margo watched through the slats of the barn, and tried to imagine starting a conversation, but hadn't yet figured out what she'd say.

'Do you have a shotgun?' Fishbone said.

Margo shook her head.

'Do you know how to use one?'

'Of course.' She nodded.

'I would've married a girl like you, if I'd known there was one out there,' Fishbone said and laughed.

Smoke shook his head. 'You need another wife, all right.'

'Smoky, you're going to have to give her your shotgun for deer hunting. She's got to do this right. I don't want her out there trying to shoot deer in the eye with a .22.'

'Give her your own damned shotgun. I might need mine.'

'Ignore that complaining old woman, Margo. You go get me a kitchen chair, a grocery bag, and some newspaper and bring it out here to the patio,' he said. 'Oh, and a big soup spoon.'

'Who's an old woman?' Smoke said. 'Speak for yourself, you old church lady.'

Once Fishbone was sitting on the chair, he flattened the brown bag on the ground, piled some newspapers there. 'Yeah, Smoky, you need that shotgun, all right. Like you need a hole in the head.'

'Aren't you going to mess up those fine leather shoes?' Smoke said.

'I'm not going to. And this is going to take me two minutes to show this girl how to skin a muskrat. You watch this, too, Smoky. You might still learn something in your old age.' He produced a heavy hunting knife. With one hand on the back of the blade and the other on the handle, he cut off the muskrat's back feet using the stack of newspapers as a cutting board. Then he put his foot on the muskrat's tail, stuck his knife into the back of one of the legs, and sliced up to the side of the tail. He made the same cut on the other side and then cut all the way around the tail. Drops of blood fell onto the paper between his shoes.

'What the hell are you going to teach me after

all these years?' Smoke muttered.

Fishbone laid his knife on the milk crate beside him and pushed his fingers under the skin, used his fingers to peel the hide from around the tail and back legs, toward the front of the animal. Margo noticed his fingers were long and straight, not crooked with arthritis like Smoke's, not even scarred. He rolled the hide off the backside of the animal. 'See? I'm careful with the belly, saving it till the end, trying to keep the guts from popping out.'

Margo nodded. She watched Fishbone work his fingers around each hind leg and break the hide loose and work over the back toward the front legs, leaving the belly skin attached. Fishbone's creased jeans remained clean. Smoke was watching intently. So was Nightmare.

'Now you hook your thumbs into the loose hide, with the rat's back facing up,' he said. Margo noted the muskrat's head was pointed away from him. She would copy his position and his grip. He continued, 'Use your fingers on both hands to push the rat's head into the hide as you turn the whole thing inside out. Now, work each front leg loose and pull the hide loose from each front foot. See how it snaps off at the feet? You don't even have to cut those off.'

Smoke lit another cigarette and leaned back to take a draw. Fishbone worked his fingers under the hide around the neck. From inside the skin, he cut the ear openings close to the skull and then pulled the hide toward the nose.

'See the white parts above the eye here?' Fishbone said. 'Cut in here above both eyes and keep squeezing until the hide comes loose. Of course, you messed up the one eye here by shooting it. How come you don't have an exit hole?'

'I used a low-velocity ammo.' She didn't mention she'd screwed up three hides before getting it right. 'The bullet is still in the brain.'

'That's all fine and good,' he said and smiled, 'but you really want to get a perfect eye hole with the lid and eyelash still on. For that you're going to have to use traps. I'll show you how to run a drowner line. You got hip waders?'

'There's some on the boat,' Margo said.

'How old are they? If they're Smoky's, they probably leak.'

'The goddamned things are only five years old,' Smoke said. 'I forgot I left them on there. Cost me seventy-five dollars.'

'And you're going to need some stretching boards.'

Margo nodded.

'Smoky's got traps he ain't using. Maybe a couple of them wire stretchers.'

'Stop giving all my things away before I'm dead.'

Margo felt better about talking to Fishbone when he was occupied, so she finally asked what she'd been wanting to ask for more than a week.

'Smoke told me to ask you, Fishbone, where a girl goes to get rid of a baby.'

'What do you mean?' He stopped cutting.

'The girl's pregnant,' Smoke said. 'She doesn't want to have a goddamned baby.'

'I don't like that kind of business.' Fishbone

319

went back to working the hide off the head of the carcass. 'And you should know it, Smoky.'

Margo said, 'I can't have a baby. I can't take care of it.' She noticed he left the muskrat's nose on the skin.

Smoke sipped from the bottle of over-the-counter medicine, which did not work as well as the codeine prescription stuff, but he'd already gone through all that.

'If she wants help, I would ask you to please help her as a favor to me,' Smoke said.

Fishbone removed the skin the rest of the way off the head. Margo stepped closer to see the naked skull. Without warning, Fishbone pulled the skin off the muskrat's belly, and the guts slipped out onto the brown paper bag on the patio floor.

Margo looked down to see splashes of fluid beading on her boots and soaking into her pant leg. Fishbone's shoes were still clean.

Fishbone looked up at her. 'Now get rid of these guts, young lady. You got a hole to bury them in?'

'The ground's frozen,' Smoke said. 'Nobody's digging a hole.'

Margo couldn't tell if this was real discord or their usual banter.

'I'll pay you for gas to take me,' Margo said. 'I've got enough money.'

'How far along are you?'

'Since the middle of September, not three months.'

'I figured that Mexican was going to be trouble,' Smoke said.

320

'I'll see about it. I'll tell you, though, there's too much freedom in this country when you got freedom to do that. Get rid of these,' Fishbone said and nodded at the entrails.

'What are you going to do with the meat?' she asked.

'You want to cook it? Tastes like rabbit, only fishy. You got to cut out these glands on the belly here, or you're going to get a nasty smell.' He pointed at the thumb-knuckle-sized sacs with his knife. He hacked off the muskrat's tail, laid it on top of the guts, and then wrapped the little carcass in newspaper. 'You mess up those glands, even Nightmare won't touch the meat.'

Margo knelt down and tugged the brown bag away from Fishbone's feet, and Fishbone pulled the hide gently down onto one of the stretching boards, inside out, and showed Margo how to remove the fat and membrane from the skin with the edge of the spoon. Then he took a bandanna from his pocket and wiped his hands with it. Fishbone's disapproval was making Margo feel uncertain, but she took some strength from Smoke's crossed arms.

Margo carried the guts down to the river and dumped them in. The snapping turtles would be deep in the muck hibernating, but there was always something hungry in the river.

A week later, Fishbone didn't speak as he drove her toward Kalamazoo in his old two-toned Chevy pickup, and his body seemed stiffer and more angular than usual. He hardly looked in her direction except to shake his head. He had insisted she leave her rifle in Smoke's kitchen, and she felt uneasy without it. The scenery as they approached the city seemed homely; the yards were small, and some contained decorations put up for Christmas, less than two weeks away — hard plastic Santas, snowmen, holy men, reindeer, and human-sized candy canes. Margo imagined that at night when the lights were lit, the decorations would seem cheerful. In Smoke's riverside neighborhood of one-story houses with big yards, people had hung lights on their front windows and over trees near the road, but nobody decorated near the river, which was where holiday lights looked prettiest, reflecting off the water.

Though the air inside the truck was smoky from Fishbone's cigar and sickly from the pine air freshener hanging from the mirror, Margo did not dare open the window for fear of irritating him. After fifteen minutes on the road, Fishbone pulled into the driveway beside a brick building and parked at the far end of the adjoining lot. He slipped an eight-track tape into the player — B. B. King — and as a guitar solo lurched forward, he crossed his arms.

She took a deep breath and looked toward the solid double doors beneath the sign reading CLINIC ENTRANCE. Four people stood alongside the building holding their own signs: STOP KILLING BABIES and MURDER SANCTIONED WITHIN.

She shut the truck door and walked across

what seemed a long stretch of asphalt. She felt small and unsteady when she reached the sidewalk.

'Baby killer!' shouted the tallest of the three women protesters.

Margo noticed there was a bit of water flowing in the ditch behind the building, and she figured that every stream, no matter how small or dirty, eventually made its way to the river. If Fishbone was gone when she came out, she could follow the flow through ditches to successively bigger streams to the Kalamazoo. She would be able to follow the river upstream to her boat.

Margo tugged open one of the painted steel doors, like the doors of her high school back in Murrayville. Her footfalls were silent on the greenish carpet of the lobby.

She approached the counter beneath the words CHECK IN. The receptionist seated there in a red-and-green sweater gave her a quiet smile.

'Good afternoon. Are you here for counseling?' She reminded Margo of her fifth-grade teacher, who'd had the same chubby figure and curly hair and had dressed up special for every holiday, even the Day of the Dead, the day after Halloween, when she drew skeleton bones on her face and arms. The lobby was decorated for Christmas, with gold-and-green garlands behind the desk and a Santa-with-elves statue on the counter. 'Is this your first visit?'

Margo nodded. The receptionist jotted down her name and handed her a clipboard with a stapled form attached. 'You can sit over there

323

and get started on this. Just give us a shout if you need anything. The nurse will call your name in a few minutes.'

As Margo crossed the lobby to the waiting area, the perfume smell reminded her of Fishbone's air freshener, only worse, and she feared she might sneeze. The fluorescent lights hurt her eyes, and maybe they were the source of the dull hum that was making her ears feel clogged. At Smoke's house, he and Margo usually sat in the sunlight coming through the window, and sometimes they even sat in the dark, because Smoke found it restful on his eyes. When Margo was on the *Glutton*, she cleaned her rifle, oiled her boots, read books, and repaired her clothes by the light of an oil lamp — Smoke had given her a bottle of clean-burning lamp oil and convinced her not to use kerosene. Now she longed for the muted movement of the river beneath her feet.

Two other women sat in the waiting area, one Margo's age, one older. Both held magazines in their laps. Margo took a seat and started filling out the form. For the address (where it said a PO box was not acceptable), she wrote Smoke's address, and then crossed it out for fear that Smoke would somehow get in trouble with his nieces.

When the door opened, a nurse called in the younger of the two other women. That woman closed her magazine and placed it carefully on the table so that its edges lined up with the magazine beneath it. The older woman glanced after her.

324

The form asked when Margo's last period had been, and she tried to calculate, but the calendar on the wall did not have the phases of the moon. The last several months had been a relief from that concern, from those five days of washing and drying the cloths she used. The form asked whether any relative of hers had high blood pressure or high cholesterol. She got up and walked to the window and looked out. She saw dirty snow and high curbs painted safety-yellow and a dozen cars, each parked far away from the others, and finally Fishbone's truck. The people with signs were chanting at a girl walking past them, and the girl was hiding her face. Margo grabbed at her shoulder for her rifle sling. As the girl entered the lobby from outside, Margo returned to her chair. A painting on the wall featured a white farmhouse, similar to the Murray house, with a big red barn beside it. She figured where the river should be in relation to the house — just below the bottom of the painting — and where she had long ago shot targets beside the barn. The hum of the lights or the machines behind the closed doors got louder. Margo took a deep breath and focused on the pages before her. They asked for her insurance information. On the last page, she read the question: 'Do you understand the following procedures?' and it listed three options that were written in what seemed like a foreign language.

Margo returned to the section on 'personal medical history.' Had she ever had seizures? Back pain? She checked the box *yes* and wrote *Chopping wood* in the space provided, and then she wished she could erase it, because she suddenly did not want to share anything more about herself with strangers. When a woman in a lab coat called her name, Margo stood and followed her through the doorway, down a hall, and into a small room.

'Are you okay, honey?' the woman asked. Her cheeks were powdery and her lipstick was pearly like the inside of a clamshell. When Margo realized the woman seemed concerned and was waiting for a response, she nodded and raised her eyebrows.

'Keep working on the questionnaire. The doctor will be right with you,' she said. 'Don't be nervous. He's very nice. He'll examine you and then talk to you about your options. There's nothing to be afraid of. Undress and put on this gown.' She patted the gown that lay folded on the examining table. Then she held up a paper sheet and said, 'You can cover your legs with this. It'll just be a couple of minutes.'

The perfume smell overwhelmed the room, which was about the size of the room in which she'd had her teeth cleaned as a girl. She took off her daddy's Carhartt jacket, rested it on the back of the chair, and folded its worn arms over the seat. She smoothed its frayed collar and then put it back on. The small window was too high to look out of, but she imagined it looked onto the flowing ditch. She studied a poster that featured a girl Margo's age with long blonde hair; her button-up striped shirt had wide lapels. She was smiling and holding hands with a boy who was all in shadow. PROTECT YOURSELF, it said in big yellow letters. Below that it said, in small type, AGAINST UNWANTED PREGNANCY AND VENEREAL DISEASE. Other posters depicted birth control pills in beige packets, one that had the twenty-eight green, white, and pink pills arranged like tick marks on a clock face. (Margo counted the marks while she waited.) The plastic thing the size of a loaf of bread beside the sink appeared to be a three-dimensional female body part, and in another situation, Margo would have liked to take a good look at it, but now she was too distracted. She put down the clipboard and tried to catch her breath. She had learned all she knew about birth control in a two-hour sex-education assembly in seventh grade, but it hadn't stuck with her how careful a person should be.

She imagined the doctor telling her where to sit. When to lie down. She'd never undressed for a doctor before. She ran her hand across the clean paper on the examining table. She picked up the gown and then put it down.

She wanted the thing inside her to slip out and disappear into the air. She wanted it to have never been there at all. But beyond that, she didn't know what she wanted to do about it. She only knew she couldn't stay here any longer. She wasn't ready to open herself up and put herself into the hands of the strangers here. No more than she could go back to tenth grade and sit in the stifling classroom and answer a question posed to her, no more than she could turn herself in to the police as Michael had wanted her to do. No more than she could let someone

327

burn her with cigarettes. Now that she'd come here, now that she'd seen what was here, she needed to go home and think about it.

She walked out the door, down the hall, and turned left. Her heart pounded in fear that someone would stop her and want her to explain. She pushed on the door that led to the lobby. She pushed again, but it did not move. A pretty, freckled woman in a white lab coat walked over to her, patted her shoulder, and pulled the door toward her. It opened. Margo walked through the lobby, through the steel doors, back out onto the sidewalk. When she got a few steps from the building and away from the protesters, she inhaled deeply, as though she had gone the whole time inside without breathing. She trudged through the slush of the parking lot and climbed into Fishbone's truck, onto the seat that had been repaired with duct tape.

'I didn't think you'd do it,' Fishbone said, putting out his little cigar in the truck's ashtray.

Margo knew there was no sense trying to explain why she'd left, since she wasn't sure herself. She crossed her arms.

'You need to go see your mother, young lady.'

Margo uncrossed her arms, opened her wallet, and took out the address and the section of map that showed the way to her mother's house.

20

'Your Ma a rich lady?' Fishbone asked as they pulled up in front of the house that matched the address Margo had been carrying around with her for a year and a half. A month ago, she'd finally cashed her mother's money order.

Fishbone said, 'I wouldn't guess it by you.'

'I wish I had my rifle,' Margo said.

'Not in this neighborhood, young lady. Rich folks get uneasy about poor folks carrying firearms.'

He waited alongside the road in the truck while Margo walked up the shoveled concrete path and rang the doorbell. In the driveway was a shiny white car. When someone opened the front door a few inches, Fishbone pulled away. Margo felt a cold panic rush through her.

'Who is it?' said a woman's voice, through the opening.

'Is that you, Ma?' Margo took off her stocking cap so that her mother would recognize her.

'Margaret Louise?'

Margo stepped back as her mother closed, unchained, and then opened the door.

'I wrote to you, Margaret,' she said, looking beyond Margo, searching the driveway and the road, 'and told you it wasn't a good idea to come yet.'

'Daddy's dead,' Margo said. Her own words struck her with the force and urgency of a revelation. She had never mentioned her father in the letters she'd sent to Luanne, nor had Luanne mentioned him in the notes she'd sent in return. Luanne's face lost all expression, and Margo wished she could take back the words. 'I'm sorry, Ma,' she said. 'I didn't mean to say it that way.'

Her mother remained motionless, didn't even blink. Margo thought she might crack like a dish.

'I'm okay, Mom. Really.' Margo had never called her mother 'Mom' before. It had always been 'Mama' or 'Ma,' but she wanted to sound like a normal kid.

Luanne glanced behind her, into the house, and said with a sigh, 'I heard about the accident six months after the fact. I should have come to you, but it seemed too late.'

'It's okay.' Margo smoothed her own hair, all the way down her braid. She tried to soothe her mother with her voice. 'I'm all right.'

'I figured Cal and Joanna would take care of you.' Luanne cleared her throat, and her voice grew in strength. 'You practically lived at their house, anyway.'

'Yes,' Margo said. She forced herself to smile.

'Come in,' Luanne said, just when Margo thought she couldn't hold her face that way any longer. 'It's been a long time without seeing my girl. You took me by surprise.' Luanne began to smile.

Margo would have liked a couple of days to sit quietly, study the new surroundings. Before talking, she would have liked to walk away from the flat-roofed house and then turn around and look at it from a distance, study its big windows, its sand-colored wooden siding, the evergreen bushes trimmed flat along the front of the house, and the two cone-shaped pines nearer the curb, dark against the snow-covered lawn. She would have liked to walk around the house and down to the water, so she could squat and study the surface of the lake for the rest of the day. She would have liked to observe her mother from a distance, to catch glimpses of her through the windows and get used to her movements before facing her this way.

Instead, Margo followed Luanne through a big kitchen with a shining white floor and into a carpeted living room with floor-to-ceiling windows providing a panoramic view of the lake. In the far corner of the living room was a Christmas tree evenly decorated with silver garlands, red bulbs, white blinking lights, and some painted wooden ornaments. Margo walked to the window. The expanse of the lake, a mile across, according to the map, made her mind go blank. She had a lot of questions to ask her mother, but couldn't think of any of them.

'I missed you, Mom,' she said, looking out at the lake. 'I'm so glad to see you.'

'You know I wanted to see you, Margaret. You know I would have given anything to see you, but it wasn't the right time.'

'Why not?'

'When I met Roger, I told him I didn't have any children. Now, if I change my story, he'll think I'm a liar. Roger's my new husband.' Her voice cracked. 'He's a lot of fun, a great guy, just

331

a little opinionated.'

The lake was the color of a heron's blue-gray wing. There was an island way out there in the middle of the water. Margo wished she were rowing her mother out to it in a boat.

'Oh, Margaret. I really am glad to see you.' Luanne walked over and wrapped her arms around Margo, hugged her long and hard. Margo remembered the way her ma had wrapped the jungle towel around her on the dock, but in her mother's embrace, Margo now stiffened. She searched for the smell of cocoa butter beneath the scent of her mother's herbal perfume. When Luanne pulled away, tears were streaming down her cheeks. 'I didn't want to leave you, Margaret Louise. Sit down with me.'

Margo followed her mother to the couch, took off her jacket, and folded it over her knees.

'I haven't cried in a while,' Luanne said, dabbing her eyes with a tissue. 'Roger's away until Friday. He's working in New Jersey, just coming home on the weekends. That means I can run around as much as I like, so long as I keep a low profile.'

'You have a nice Christmas tree,' Margo said. She wondered if Smoke would like a tree in his house.

'It's a fake one. Remember how your daddy always cut a tree that was too big for the living room so it was bent over? What did you used to put on the top of it, that cross of sticks wrapped with yarn?'

'A God's eye,' Margo said. Joanna had told her that a homemade God's eye allowed God to watch over the family. Luanne's tree had a silver-and-glass star on the top with a light inside. Margo leaned back on the couch and was amazed at how soft it was, how the cushions embraced and supported her. She wanted to pet the velvety fabric like a dog's fur. A tear dripped from her cheek onto the fabric of the couch before she even realized she was crying. She wiped her face. Luanne pushed a box of tissues toward her.

'What do you think of the lake?' Luanne asked.

'It's big,' Margo said. 'It's nice.'

'I knew you'd love it. Can you believe this house?' Luanne gestured around the big room, at the tall windows, white-painted walls hung with black-and-white photographs of what at first appeared to be beach landscapes, but were actually close-ups of women's bodies. The big fireplace with the marble mantel was swept clean, as though it had never contained a fire, and sitting on the mantel were a few abstract sculptures in sandy colors. The thick off-white carpeting had not a stain on it. Luanne nodded toward the lake. 'See how beautiful the view is? Roger fusses about goose poop on the lawn, but it doesn't bother me. He runs out and chases them away when they show up.'

'I'm pregnant,' Margo blurted out. That word felt ugly and dishonest in her mouth.

'What? No. Oh, no. Sweetie. How far along are you?'

'Three months.'

'You're not even showing. Don't worry, I'll

333

take care of you. I know I didn't take care of you when I should have, but I will now. Are you feeling sick in the mornings?'

'Not anymore.'

'Whose is it?' Luanne asked. 'Is the guy in the picture?'

'He's gone.'

'I guess we women have to take care of ourselves.' Luanne studied Margo beside her. 'God, you're beautiful, Margaret. I was so depressed back in Murrayville, I don't think I even looked at you the last few years I was there.'

'Joanna always said being beautiful was a curse.'

'She would say that,' Luanne said. 'Being beautiful should be fun.'

'I'm hungry, Ma,' Margo said.

'Of course you're hungry. You're eighteen. And you're pregnant. I was pregnant when I was eighteen.' Luanne stood and Margo followed her into the kitchen.

'I haven't eaten yet today.'

'Roger eats at work, and I try not to keep much food in the house when he's gone, so I'm not tempted by it. Here's something.' She pulled a metal can of cheese spread out of the refrigerator and put out some crackers. When Margo picked up the can and looked at it, Luanne took it from her, removed the lid, and sprayed orange cheese onto one of the crackers. Margo carried the plate and the can into the living room, and they sat on the luxurious couch. Margo ate one cheese cracker after another, enjoying the surging water sound of the spray.

She offered the plate to her ma. Luanne shook her head.

'I talked to Aunt Joanna a few months ago,' Margo said. 'She thought maybe I could stay with her at the house and finish school.'

'Poor Joanna. What a life she's got. Do you want to finish school?'

Margo shook her head.

'I didn't, either. You know I was only seventeen when I married your father.'

'Joanna had another baby. Another boy.'

'Christ. She's got to be forty. How'd Cal talk her into that? Six kids. Six boys.' She laughed.

Margo startled at the sound of the name *Cal* spoken so casually. Brian had said it with such venom, Joanna with such reverence. This way of saying his name made more sense with the weakened version of Cal she had seen. 'It's a Down's baby,' Margo said.

'Down's baby?'

'They had to get rid of all the dogs, even Moe, because they made the baby cry. Billy said the baby's a retard.'

'Oh, *Down's syndrome*. Like a Mongoloid. Joanna has her work cut out for her. Good thing she's such a hard worker.'

'If I stayed, I could have helped with the baby.'

'Good thing you got out of there. She'd have worked you to death, sweetie.'

'I don't mind working hard.'

'What about fun? What about pleasure? I think those things are the purpose of life. Women like Joanna find that view distasteful.'

Margo shrugged.

'But I do work hard, in a way. Nowadays I have to work hard to look young. Even a fifty-year-old man like Roger, who can't tolerate children, expects me to look like a teenager.' Luanne laughed. She took hold of Margo's hand and held it for a moment. 'I forgot how quiet and serious you are. You look so pretty that people probably don't mind you don't have anything to say.'

Margo watched gulls skim the water outside and land near shore. She wondered if they could stay on the lake all winter.

Annie Oakley's mother had not wanted her to come home at first; she had wanted to send her daughter back to the wolves. Annie won her way into her mother's home through the hard work of hunting and trapping, by being able to support the whole family, including her mother's new husband. There was no wood to chop here, though, no food to kill and gut, nothing obviously in need of repair. Margo was missing the weight of her gun, and had to lift the tension out of her shoulders. She said, 'I can help you do anything you need done around here.'

'I just can't believe you're here. Right here with me. Like a ghost. Like somebody from a past life.' The television was on. It had been on when Margo entered, and it seemed to grow louder as the minutes passed. 'You can stay here . . . ' Luanne said. 'I guess until about six o'clock Friday when Roger gets home. I'll make you an appointment with the doctor.'

Margo hadn't realized she was holding her breath. 'I went to the clinic today, but I left.'

'Why'd you leave?'

Margo shrugged.

'So tell me. Where are you living now?' Luanne asked. 'Your letter said you were only twenty-some miles away.'

'On the river.' Margo gathered herself. 'I trap muskrats like Grandpa taught me, and I sell their skins. And I fish. And there's this big black dog I love named Nightmare. He looks like the Murrays' dog Moe.'

'You skin animals?' Luanne slowly asked and then laughed. 'Your dad asked me to cook him a rabbit once. This was when you were little. So I boiled it with the hair on and the guts inside. I knew I was supposed to skin it and gut it for him, but I figured if I cooked it whole, he'd never ask me to do it again. I smiled when I served it to him.' Luanne left the room and returned with two cups of black coffee.

Margo tried to take a sip, but it was too hot. 'Dad always said you couldn't boil water.'

When her mother sat down again, she asked, 'Okay, you live on the river. What else?'

'This guy, Fishbone, taught me to skin a muskrat in two minutes.' She held up two fingers and repeated with emphasis, 'Two minutes. It was incredible.'

'It's almost Christmas,' Luanne said. 'I want to buy you a present. What would you like?'

Margo shrugged.

'Seriously. You must need something.'

'Socks,' she said. 'Ammo.'

'Maybe some nice underwear. That makes anybody feel better.' Luanne's smile was the one in all those photos. Only it no longer looked fake — it was her real smile. Luanne sipped from her coffee. 'Too bad it's not summer. You could swim in the pool. Come look at it with me.'

Margo pulled herself up and followed her mother to a side window. Luanne pointed out a big green rectangle between this house and the next. A few stray leaves littered the tarp, but there was no snow on it. 'We're planning to build an enclosure so we can swim year-round.

'Don't you swim in the lake?'

'Never.'

'Do you still lie in the sun?'

'God, no. I wish I hadn't done it all those years. They're saying now it damages the skin. You should be careful, too, wear a hat, if you want to keep from getting wrinkled. You think you're safe in the winter, but the sun reflects off the snow, and it's even worse. This has been a hard lesson for me to learn.' Luanne reached out and pushed Margo's hair behind her ear.

Margo turned away. As soon as it didn't seem rude, she shook her hair loose.

'How's Cal?' Luanne asked.

Margo shrugged. She sneezed. She didn't know what triggered it, her mother's perfume or all that sunlight reflecting off the snow and pouring through the windows. From where she was standing, she could see the house to the north, a white one-story structure with a steeply pitched reddish roof. The big lake was built up as far as she could see, one house next to another. Many of the yards had pontoon boats or speedboats too big for the river up on sawhorses in their yards, covered with tarps.

'Why don't you take a shower, and you can rest in the guest room if you like? I'll make a phone call before the clinic closes.' Luanne touched Margo's cheek again. It reminded her of the way Brian had touched her that first morning, as though she were made of clay that could be shaped. 'You don't use anything, do you? No mascara even?'

Margo had showered just the day before, but she wanted to use her mother's bathroom. It had two sinks and smelled like strawberries. The pink towels were thick and fluffy. The hot water never ran out, though Margo stayed in the shower for half an hour. As she combed her wet hair, she could hear the television from the other room, and the droning made her feel dopey. She wrapped herself in the towel and moved into the guest room. She lay on the bed, on top of the covers. Maybe soft towels were something she might want on her boat. She'd have considered stealing one if she'd had her backpack with her.

When she next woke up, the sky through the window was dark. She sat up and felt startled to be naked on a strange bed. She remembered where she was, at her mother's house, and convinced herself it was not a dream. The television still played in the next room. Her own clothes were not on the chair where she had left them, but had been replaced by a pair of women's jeans and a white button-up shirt like the one her mother had been wearing. Her army knife and her wallet were on the dresser. A green parka was hanging on the back of the door.

'It's sleeping beauty,' Luanne said when she entered the kitchen. 'You slept almost four hours.'

'I didn't mean to sleep so long.' Margo didn't usually even sleep four hours at night without at least waking up to feed the fire.

'You're talking to a woman who used to sleep all day. Do you remember that? That was a sign of depression, my doctor says. Look, I ordered us a pizza. I had them load it with everything. I remember that's how you liked it.'

Margo smiled as Luanne lifted the lid.

'You look good in my clothes,' Luanne said when they were sitting at the kitchen table, built into the corner, four times the size of the table on the *Glutton*.

'Where's my other clothes?' Margo said.

'I threw them in the washer and dryer, but maybe I should burn that jacket. Looks like something one of those Slocums would have worn. Oh, remember the Slocums?'

'That's Daddy's old jacket.'

'Well, it looks like it hasn't been washed since . . . in a while, anyhow. We'll see how it comes out of the dryer. I put another jacket in the guest room for you, a warm parka. You can have it if you like it. It makes me look dumpy. Do you want some wine?'

Margo shook her head.

'I don't usually drink during the week, but this day is turning out to be quite a surprise.' Her mother took a sip of white wine. 'Tell me something else about Murrayville. Anything.'

Margo swallowed and offered, 'A lady with a

340

mean dog lives in our old house. She smokes a
pipe. And Junior went to Alaska.'

'I'm glad to hear somebody else got out of
there.'

Margo hated how far away Junior was. She
swept that thought away and decided this was
the best pizza she had ever tasted. She devoured
the piece before her and took another.

'Did Cal . . . ?' At first Margo wasn't even sure
what she wanted to ask. 'Did Cal force you, Ma?'
She watched Luanne's face. 'Is that why you left
home?'

'Cal? Force me?' She laughed and put her
hand over her mouth. Her fingernails were
painted the same pearly color as the clinic
nurse's lipstick. 'You couldn't possibly have
known. You were so young. Cal and I were
. . . well . . . '

'What?'

'Cal and I were something. An item. Cal was
the great love of my life back then, not your
father, bless his heart. I can't believe I'm telling
you this.'

'You. Were with Cal? On purpose?'

'On purpose? I suppose you could put it that
way.'

'Did Daddy know?' This kitchen was bigger
than Joanna's kitchen. The surfaces were not
cluttered with containers, cutting boards, or
piles of dishcloths. Joanna had a whole row of
cookbooks under her cupboards, but Margo saw
none here.

'He knew after a while. And so did Joanna.
She promised she'd make my life hell if I didn't

341

leave. That woman is tougher than you think. Cal had said he would take me away from Murrayville, go out to California with me, but I realized he was never going to leave all that — his wife, his kids, his company. He had too much to lose. We had a lot of fun, me and Cal, but he would have thrown me under a truck to preserve his life as it was.'

'Daddy really hated Cal,' Margo said.

'Leaving you was the hardest thing I ever did, Margaret, but I had to go. I would have died otherwise or drunk myself to death. I never belonged there. The river stink drove me crazy. On the day I left, I found a blue racer snake curled around my damned clothesline. And the mildew. Every leather belt turned green, every leather shoe. It never bothered you or your father or the damned Murrays. I stayed as long as I could. You've got to give me credit for staying as long as I did. I waited until you stopped growing.'

Margo nodded so Luanne would keep talking, but the question must have shown on her face.

'Remember when you were fourteen and we measured you on that tree?'

'You left because I stopped growing taller?'

Luanne got up from the table and carried her glass and wine bottle into the living room. Margo followed, though she could have easily eaten more pizza.

'You didn't need me, anyway, Margaret. I didn't know anything about raising a kid when you came along. That's why I let you do whatever you wanted. I figured you knew better than I did what a kid needed.'

'I didn't mind if you didn't know.'

'Those Murray women minded plenty. They said I would raise a wildcat or wolf cub. But look at you! You're perfect.'

'A wolf cub? They said that?'

'Oh, I don't know what they said. I don't care about those people. I was crazy about Cal, though,' Luanne said and laughed. 'But don't worry, you are your daddy's child. No doubt about that.'

'You said in that note you left that you wanted to *find yourself*,' Margo said.

'Well, I figured out soon enough that *myself* wasn't who I was looking for. I was looking for somebody else, somebody who would take care of me.'

Margo looked behind her, out the living room window, at the lights giving shape to the darkness on the shore.

'Margaret, honey, look at me. You're not old enough to understand why I left, but sometimes a woman has to start over, make a whole new life to try to find happiness. I know it's selfish.'

'I worried that you forgot me when you went away.'

'Oh, Margaret, a mama doesn't forget her child. You have to know that. It's just that when I lived with your father, I dreamed of a house like this. Think how all three of us shared that one tiny bathroom with no tub, just a shower. Now I've got three bathrooms, four if you count the little one in Roger's photo studio.'

'Daddy quit drinking,' Margo said. 'Before he died, I mean.'

'I wish you could understand how I had to start over. A clean slate. Roger's a good guy, when so many of them are pigs.' She poured another inch of wine into her glass. 'How could you know? You're so young.'

Margo shook her head. 'I'm not that young, Ma.'

'It was dumb, what I did, to lie to Roger from the start,' she said. 'Do you think I should tell him the truth? See what he does? Take a chance on losing all this?'

'No, that's okay.'

'God, I just wanted to have some fun. I didn't mean to get separated from you this way. But things snowballed.'

'You did sleep a lot in Murrayville.'

'I was a depressed drunk. You didn't seem to notice, but everybody else did.'

'I just wanted to see you,' Margo said.

'You have every right to hate me for what I put you through, Margaret. Do you hate me?'

'No.' Margo tried to remember Smoke's words. 'You should live how you want.'

'You know, people think it's the worst thing to abandon a kid,' Luanne said, 'but I think there are worse things, like staying and ruining your own life and your kid's life in the process. And look how fine you turned out, how beautiful. Oh, how I love this show. Watch it with me.' Luanne picked up the remote control from the coffee table and turned up the sound. She lay back on the couch and stuck a throw pillow under her head. She had turned off for the night. The pillow pressed against Margo's leg.

344

They both remained on the couch without speaking for a long time. When Margo was sure her mother was asleep, she studied her face and figure. Her mother was very thin, Margo thought. In her life she had watched her mother sleep more than she had watched her do any other thing.

Margo hunted around the house until she found the washer and dryer in the basement and got her clothes. Then she went to bed in the guest room where she had slept earlier. She wondered if her mother might visit her sometimes, if they might sit on the deck of her boat and enjoy the river together. Margo fell asleep quickly, but then woke up after a few hours with her heart pounding. She was thinking about her father's ashes and how far away from them she was. She got up and raised the window, but it opened only an inch. At about four a.m. she woke up again and couldn't go back to sleep. She went into the living room, but found the couch empty. She ate two more pieces of pizza from the box in the refrigerator. Then she put on the parka, picked up some kitchen matches from the stove, and carried them outside. She gathered all the twigs she could find and made a little pile near the water as far as she could from the security light. She built a tiny fire on the frozen ground and crouched beside it. The fire was almost upon the water, and the reflected light warmed her.

She remembered how, at the Pokagon Mound Picnic Area and at her camp near the marijuana house, she had sometimes felt proud of getting through another day and night, of getting and preparing good food and keeping warm and comfortable. She felt a little that way now.

She lay back on the snow and stared at the three stars making up the man's belt, almost directly overhead now. The constellations she had seen with the Indian — the swan and the dolphin — were gone. She had heard someone once mention a dog star; she would have liked to know where that was. Margo should have asked what Smoke saw in the stars, but the two of them didn't tend to hang around outside at night. Margo already missed Smoke's breathy voice and his cursing, the way he cheered up when Fishbone's lanky figure appeared in the back yard. She missed the urgency of the river moving nearby. Compared to the river, the lake seemed almost dead.

'I'm not sure about this,' Margo said to her mother the following morning.

'You don't have to be sure. The first appointment is just an exam. They'll explain your options.'

'I was there already.'

'I told them you'd been there yesterday, but that you'd gotten nervous and left, and they let me make you another appointment. I'll come with you this time.'

Her mother was sitting at a little table in the bathroom adjoining her bedroom, looking at herself in the mirror. Margo was leaning against the doorframe with her own worn jeans on, army knife and wallet in her pockets. Luanne wiped makeup over her face and rubbed it around until it became invisible.

'Does anybody ever row on the lake?' Margo asked.

'The neighbor has a canoe. We have a pontoon boat, but it's in winter storage at the marina.' Luanne applied lipstick and blotted her lips on a tissue, then applied more and smiled at herself. 'I can show you how to do all this to your face. That's something I could do for you.'

Margo nodded vaguely and then went out to wait in the kitchen, and when her mother appeared, Margo thought she looked like somebody from TV. She wore a glossy black belt that accented her small waist. Her shirt was unbuttoned to show cleavage, and she wore a necklace, earrings, and rings with turquoise stones.

Margo walked behind her out to the car.

'What happened last night, Margo?' Luanne asked as she backed out into the road. 'I just listened to a phone message from my neighbor, saying there was a vagabond tending a fire in my back yard last night.'

'I couldn't sleep.'

'You can't really have a fire without a permit unless it's in a fire pit. Mr. Smith was afraid you were going to burn down his fence.'

'I was eight feet away from the fence.'

'Why were you outside so late at night, anyway?'

'I like to be outside at night for a while, to hear what's out there.' She had not heard any night bird sounds, only a raccoon scrambling on the neighbor's porch. 'I couldn't get the window in my room to open more than an inch.'

'Those are security locks. It's too cold to open a window.'

'Why don't you have a dog?'

'Roger doesn't want a dog.' Luanne sighed as she turned off the lake road and onto a two-lane highway. 'And I certainly don't want a dog. You know I never wanted a dog.'

Margo pressed a button that locked and then unlocked the door. She finally found the button that controlled the window, and she let it down a few inches. She didn't mean to be annoying to her mother, but everything was happening too quickly. When the houses along the road were no longer so close together, Margo saw a sign that read MAPLE SYRUP 4 SALE. Tied to the front porch of the house were two German shepherds. Margo watched them fall behind her.

'Are you glad you had me?' Margo asked. Her mother applied the brakes so that Margo was thrown forward slightly. She saw a car backing out of a driveway up ahead of them.

'Put on your seat belt,' Luanne said.

'Do you wish you hadn't had me?' Margo pulled the belt down over her shoulder and fiddled to attach it.

'Of course I'm glad I had you. Look at you. But I had a husband at the time who could help. I wasn't all alone like you are.'

'I'm not all alone.'

'Do you want to have a baby?'

'No. I don't think so.'

'Okay.' Luanne accelerated back up to speed.

Margo studied her mother's apparently flawless face.

'Why are you looking at me that way?' her mother asked and smiled.

'Whatever happens, Mama, I'll be all right.'

'Of course you will. It's not a complicated procedure.'

'Did you have one?'

'It wasn't terrible. Really. It was fine. It was a relief. Now, I'm going to have to run into the post office to drop something off. You go into the clinic and get the form and sit down, and I'll be there in ten minutes to help you.'

'I'm glad I found you,' Margo said. She would have liked to have a little brother or a sister. Maybe a sister Julie Slocum's age, someone whom Margo could have taught to fish and row and keep out of trouble. Maybe an older sister could have kept Margo out of trouble.

'I'm glad, too,' Luanne said and patted Margo's thigh. 'I'm glad I can finally help my girl.'

Luanne pulled up to the front door of the clinic and fished around in her purse. When a protester with a sign approached the car, Luanne rolled down both front windows and yelled, 'Go to hell, you freaks. I'll run your asses over. I've got mace.'

The protesters looked at one another and backed away.

'I appreciate everything you're doing for me, Ma,' Margo said. She liked seeing her mother ferocious.

'Don't think about all this too much. Just go

in. Tell them you're eighteen years old, you have no means of support. You don't even know the guy's name. They'll just examine you today, but they might give you some Valium to get you through until the procedure. Tell them you don't have to drive. You've got a ride.'

'Maybe I should wait another week.' Margo remembered the perfume smell of the clinic, the clipboard with page after page to be filled out, the small room with the high window. She would never have been able to explain to her mother, but she felt even more uneasy about it today than yesterday. She needed time to think.

'Trust your mama about this one thing.' Luanne turned to her with a resigned expression.

Margo nodded.

'I'll be back in a few minutes to help you with the form. I'll come into the exam room with you and talk to the doctor. We'll get through this together. Roger will be gone for three more days, so we'll see if they can't get you in for the procedure on Friday morning. That way I can take you . . . home afterwards. To wherever you're living.'

Margo leaned over and hugged her mother. Luanne's arms were easy and loose now, and Margo didn't want to pull away.

'Here's three hundred dollars in case they ask for it up front,' Luanne said, tugging free. 'It'll be the best three hundred dollars you've ever spent.' She pressed six fifty-dollar bills into Margo's hand.

'You did the best you could with me and Daddy. Don't feel bad,' Margo said as she opened the car door.

'Why are you wearing that ratty jacket under the parka?' Luanne asked.

'I didn't know if I'd be warm enough.' Margo had unzipped the parka because she'd been too hot in the car.

'I guess you feel sentimental about your daddy's jacket. I don't mean to suggest I didn't love your daddy, Margaret. He was a good man. I should have told you that. Just because I had to get away from him doesn't mean he wasn't good. Maybe if he would have taken me out to eat once in a while or dancing or even to The Tap Room, things would have been different.'

'I know.' Margo got out and waved. She entered the building and stood just inside looking out.

When her mother turned onto the road, Margo walked back out and listened for the trickle of water behind the building, the storm drain she had noticed on her first visit.

She hid around the corner of the building for ten minutes until she saw the car pull back into the parking lot. Relief flooded her body at the sight of her mother getting out of her car, walking toward the clinic. Margo hadn't known if her mother would really come back to help her.

She followed the flow of water in the storm drain down a shallow slope until it disappeared underground. She wandered around the area until she found the stream exposed again a hundred yards away. She followed that to a bigger storm drain that ran through a twenty-four-inch galvanized culvert and emptied into a brisk moving

351

creek, which, after a few miles, emptied into the river. The edge of the Kalamazoo was strewn with trash — broken glass, rusted cans, plastic bottles filled with green slime, old bicycle frames, car tires. Margo couldn't understand why people would let the river be treated so poorly. She walked along railroad tracks, around junkyards, past houses with small junkyards behind them. She walked past storefronts, small industrial buildings, a few bars with neon lights in their windows, through the edge of a golf course, until finally the houses were spaced farther apart. She walked miles along an undeveloped area on the south side of the river until she reached a road bridge in a small town that put her on the north side of the river, where she belonged. Despite the cold wind, she sweated. In the afternoon, the sun shone hard on her, and she carried her parka on her arm. It was dark when she reached her boat, and she kept on going. She opened the riverside door to Smoke's house without knocking, saw her rifle in his gun rack in the dimly lit kitchen. She entered and fell to her knees, exhausted, beside Smoke's wheelchair and ran her hand over Nightmare's ears. Then she laid her cheek against Smoke's bony thigh as she had never done before, and she cried. Smoke petted Margo's head in silence, stroked her hair the way a mother would stroke a daughter's.

21

Christmas Eve at dusk, Fishbone entered Smoke's kitchen without knocking. He removed his fedora, brushed the snow from it, and hung it on a peg over the forced-air vent, where Smoke never hung anything else. Margo did not understand how Fishbone's ears didn't freeze. She wore a stocking cap in this weather, and now that she had the parka, she sometimes also pulled the hood up and tied it tightly.

Because the kitchen table lamp hurt Smoke's eyes, the room was lit only by two Christmas candles. Nightmare growled gently at Fishbone and then relaxed.

'Merry Christmas,' Fishbone said and handed Margo four wooden stretching boards. Brand-new ones without bloodstains. 'I made these out of basswood. They'll be soft so you won't tear the hides.'

She thanked him and wished she had something to give him. He brushed the snow off the shoulders of his leather jacket and sat on Smoke's second kitchen chair, the one without any back. It occurred to Margo that in these last few months she had taken Fishbone's chair. Margo showed what Smoke had given her, four muskrat-sized body traps and three wool blankets, one of which was military-issue and had MESSER stenciled on it. Smoke had told her it was from his father's time in the military.

Fishbone accepted Margo's offer of a piece of black walnut cake she'd made with dried apples. He ate it slowly and swore it tasted as good as anything he'd eaten all year. When he finished, he pushed the plate to the center of the table. 'The farmer wants to speak to you, Margo,' he said.

Margo looked at Smoke.

Fishbone continued, 'I told George Harland you were a young lady who could take care of herself and not cause him any trouble. He said you didn't answer your door when he knocked on your cabin, after he saw you go inside.'

'You talk to him for her,' Smoke suggested.

'She's capable of talking for herself, Smoky. She's on his land. There's no reason to be afraid of the man.' Fishbone picked up the leather bag of lead type Smoke kept on the table and moved it from hand to hand as they spoke. It weighed about ten pounds.

'I'm on the water,' she said, 'not on his land.'

'And when you step off the boat, you're on his land. And when the water gets low, you'll be on his land. When you take drinking water from the hand pump in his barn like you do, you're on his land. Talk to him and he'll give you his permits next year.'

'I might not stay there. I might go somewhere else on the river.'

Fishbone shook his head. 'This whole situation is odd, don't you think, Smoky? A girl living out there alone is not normal.' He looked back at Margo. 'If you were my kid, I'd want you to finish school. You ought to be with your rich

354

ma on Lake Lynne.'

'Why do you care so much about normal?' Smoke said, sounding more forceful than Margo would have expected. 'It's hard enough to figure out how to live . . . without worrying about what the hell's normal. You keep your goddamned normal life to yourself.'

Margo felt a catch in her throat. She didn't want to be the source of more disagreement between them.

'This girl's going to have a baby,' Fishbone said and put down the leather bag heavily. 'It ain't just about her.'

'Look at her, sitting there. Really look at her, Fishbone. Look at that kid's beautiful face. She's got strong arms, splits her own firewood. You got all kinds of kids, Fishbone. I got none. My life ain't worth a shit, but I can help this girl live the way she wants to live.'

'Your life's worth plenty, Smoky.'

'Sure as hell doesn't feel like it these days.'

'Why do you have to swear all the time? You make every night a cuss fest.'

Margo was relieved when Smoke's temper quickly subsided. She retied a rawhide bootlace that had come undone. She smoothed her hands over her soft, worn jeans, just washed in Smoke's machine. She had left the top three buttons unbuttoned and wore the pants low because her belly was sticking out. She felt warm and clean and comfortable, despite the arguing, despite her uncertainty about the baby. She belonged with these men and Nightmare.

'Something doesn't smell right in here, Smoky.'

'The candles are cinnamon,' Margo said, but she, too, had been smelling something, a skunky odor.

Fishbone leaned close to Smoke and smelled around the collar of his work shirt. 'It's you. You feeling okay?'

'I'm fine.'

'You need to take a bath.'

When he was leaving, Fishbone put on his hat and patted Smoke on the shoulder and let his hand linger there. Smoke reached up and pressed his hand until Fishbone pulled away.

'Please take care of him,' Fishbone said to Margo. 'I would if I could, but I've got a house full of family and guests waiting on me.'

After Fishbone closed the door behind him, Smoke said, 'Like hell he would.'

'How come he's not cold with only that jacket and hat on?' Margo asked.

Smoke thought for a moment. 'That there is a man who decides how he wants to feel, and then that's how he feels. Temperature be damned.'

'Can you do that?' Margo put Fishbone's plate and fork in the sink and filled up Smoke's coffee cup again. 'Can you just decide how to feel?'

'Some people can,' Smoke said. 'Tell me something, kid, is he right? Do I smell bad?'

'Why won't you let the health aide help you wash like she's supposed to?' An aide from senior services was stopping by once a week, and Smoke only allowed her to tidy the house, change the sheets, and put away the groceries she brought. Margo leaned close and smelled the collar of Smoke's shirt.

'My body is none of them bitches' business. But it has been a few weeks since I've been able to bathe.'

'Let me wash you, Smoke, before you go to your niece's place tomorrow for Christmas. You don't want them to think you're not taking care of yourself,' she said. 'I told you I helped my grandpa when he was sick.'

Smoke nodded. Margo didn't really want to wash him, but she was the only one he would let near him. And Fishbone had asked her to take care of him.

Margo turned up the thermostat on the furnace and heard it kick on. Smoke unbuttoned his work shirt and revealed a dirty long underwear shirt. She pulled it off him and the smell was stronger. She helped him into the bathroom, and she put a milk crate in the shower and a folded towel for him to sit on. She washed his arms and chest with a washcloth.

Margo found a sore under his armpit that might be getting infected. She did the best she could in the low light of two candles — he wouldn't let her turn on the overhead light, nor would he take off his glasses. As she worked, he seemed to relax in her hands. There were swollen red areas on his back that emanated heat. 'What's this?'

'Pressure sores,' Smoke whispered and winced at her touch. 'I'm supposed to change position in my chair. And I'm supposed to sit up straight. I asked the doc how I'm supposed to do both at once.' He had another pressure sore on his tailbone.

Focusing on each part of his body made her forget the awkwardness and strangeness of what she was doing, and she found she liked caring for him this way. She emptied and refilled her pan of water a few times to keep it warm and clean. She let him wash his privates, which he did with care.

'I never washed anybody else before,' Margo said.

'I'd rather wash myself.'

Margo washed Smoke's thin legs, on which there were only a few wisps of hair. She had to be gentle in touching the backs of his knees, where there were more sores. His shins were scarred and marked with a variety of new and fading bruises. She washed his callused feet. Margo wondered if she would care for her mother in old age; maybe it would take her mother until then to need her.

She dried Smoke by patting him with a towel and helped him into clean long underwear and a work shirt with *Smoke* on it. They hooked his oxygen back up.

'My dad had shirts that said *Crane* on them,' Margo said. 'I wish I had one of those old shirts, but they belonged to the uniform service.'

'Thank you, kid,' Smoke said when they returned to the kitchen.

Margo poured him more coffee; it was astounding how much black coffee Smoke drank at all times of day. He said it helped keep his lungs and his bronchial tubes open.

'Fishbone is afraid he'll end up like this if he touches me. We're almost the same age, though you wouldn't know it.'

358

'How come you didn't get married, Smoke?'

'I did once.'

'What happened to your wife?'

'Lousy eight years for both of us, until she figured out to leave and go off with somebody else.'

'Why does Fishbone help you and look after you?'

'Why do you help me, kid? Why does anybody help anybody? Do you think we ought to just stay home and help ourselves? Is that how you want to live?'

Margo felt herself blush. 'Do you love Fishbone?'

'You're an observant girl. What the hell else have you managed to figure out after all these months of staring at me?'

'I mean, like loving a woman?' She said this hesitantly, thinking it might anger him.

'I wouldn't know,' Smoke said. 'I haven't ever loved a woman the way I love him.'

'But he's got a wife. And kids and grandkids.'

'So he does,' Smoke snorted. 'And I do not. That's why I have no one to take care of me in my old age.'

Margo nodded.

'Every person out there is a nut you can't crack,' Smoke said. 'That's what I've learned, kid. We can't even crack ourselves.'

'Well, I'll take care of you, Smoke.'

'You're a good girl. I'm sure even your crazy mama knows you're a good girl.'

———————

One clear, cold morning between Christmas and New Year's Eve, when Margo was in the cow pasture, halfway to Smoke's house, she could make out the sounds of saws and a big diesel engine. On the road were a dump truck and a huge backhoe. Margo stood behind a tree outside Smoke's house as two men in insulated coveralls cut into the old unattached garage that Fishbone called his river cottage. Then a third man operating the backhoe began working with the bucket, stabbing at the wall of the garage like a big yellow bird, punching through the wall boards. When the backhoe tapped the roof, the whole thing collapsed with a whoosh. With a few more artful gouges, the building was down, and the men on the ground began loading the bucket with debris, which was then dumped into the back of the truck. At this time, Smoke rolled his chair out onto the patio. Margo went inside to retrieve his coat and hat. She brought out the milk crate and sat on it to watch.

As the men lifted away chunks of wood, roofing materials, and window glass and deposited everything in the dump bed of the big truck, Smoke alternated puffs of oxygen and cigarettes. The men finished the job in a few hours, hardly offering a nod to her or Smoke. Neither she nor Smoke said anything much to each other, either, until, finally, all that remained was a square slab of pitted concrete between the patio and the fence line. While one potbellied man swept it clean with a wide broom, the other two negotiated the front-end loader onto a trailer. Then the three men got into the front seat

360

of the dump truck, and they hauled it all away.

'They'll send me a bill,' Smoke said. 'Wait and see. And you tell me if you see one damned rat.'

Margo saw no evidence of rats, but she knew that wherever there were people, there were rats, especially on the river. Nobody wanted the skins or meat, but Margo did not despise them the way everybody else seemed to. Rats were just creatures getting by on the river as best they could. People exaggerated the grubbiness of river rats the way they exaggerated the ferocity of wolverines.

'Do you see how people will take away your right,' Smoke said and paused to catch his breath in the cold air, 'to live the way you want? Remember this.'

Though she would not say so to Smoke, she would remember, as well, the pleasure of watching the demolition. Margo knew they should go inside, but she wanted to keep taking in the strange new landscape, the pitted slab, the length of fence she'd never seen from the patio.

'We could build a new garage,' Margo said, 'right on that same spot. Fishbone will help us. He says you know how to build just about anything.'

'I can't think about it.'

'I can imagine us all putting up wall studs and maybe a metal roof so we can come out and listen to the rain on it. As soon as the snow's off the ground.'

'Was nothing wrong with the old garage.'

'We should've fixed it up.'

'You know, Fishbone used to visit me.'

'He still visits you.'

'Now he comes to visit the river. He comes to get out of his house in the city, to get away from screaming grandchildren. He even comes to see you, I think. You know, I never told anybody what I told you.'

'Can I tell you something?' Margo said, and her voice began to warble. 'Something I didn't think I'd tell anybody?'

Smoke lit another cigarette and looked at her.

'You know how you joke about how I should kill you?'

'I'm not joking.'

'Well, I did once kill a man,' Margo said. 'Last year.'

'With that .22?' He sounded skeptical.

'A shotgun. I thought I had to kill him. He was hurting somebody I loved. For a while I thought I didn't regret it. But I wish I hadn't done it.'

'You going to turn yourself in?'

'Heck, no.'

Smoke laughed. 'Was he a lousy son of a bitch of a man?'

'Yes.'

'Then what's the problem?'

'He had little kids and a wife. They probably miss him. And thinking about you dying, and my dad and my grandpa dying. If I could undo it and make him alive again, I would.'

'If you could kill a man once, you can do it again,' Smoke said. He took off his glasses and squinted at her, but Margo, who was hugging herself against the cold, just kept looking at the empty slab.

362

The neighborhood Christmas lights came down after New Year's, and the winter trudged on through short days and long, cold nights. Margo took trips into town to get essentials for herself and Smoke, but she felt she was in a kind of semi-hibernation, a state in which she moved slowly and quietly and did only what she had to do. Her fake-fur-lined parka reached halfway down her thighs and more than covered up the fact of her slightly swollen middle to strangers she might come across, but whenever Smoke or Fishbone saw her taking off her jacket in Smoke's kitchen, they smiled at her belly as though she were bringing somebody prettier than herself into the room. Margo's body had always been her reliable friend, whether in handling a rifle, splitting firewood, rowing for miles, or keeping her balance despite physical strain, but now her body was becoming strange to her.

Fishbone was right that Margo had hidden from the farmer the first time he came to her boat; she had gone inside and curled up under her sleeping bags. She hadn't been ready to meet a new man, especially one who could ask her to leave. She didn't know if she'd be attracted to him the way she was to his brother Johnny. When he next came to her boat, in the middle of January, she couldn't hide. She was standing on a stepladder, raking the roof of her camper, dragging the snow off — it was something she had not thought about until Smoke mentioned it, that the weight of snow on the flat roof could collapse the structure. Margo climbed off the ladder and walked across her shoveled and sanded gangplank to meet the farmer. He was very tall and very thin.

'You must be Margo Crane,' he said. 'I'm George Harland.'

When he offered his hand, she stepped forward and shook it.

'Smoke's boat,' the man said and nodded. 'He tells me he sold it to you. Tells me I ought to go along with you anchoring it here on my property so his nieces don't get upset.' The farmer looked up and down the river and concluded, 'It's an odd sort of proposal. But here you are in person.'

She nodded. She liked his patient manner. When she had spied on him arguing with his wife, his slow calm had made him seem a little stupid. Margo wondered if that was how she seemed to other people. She focused on his right hand, which was missing most of its index finger.

'His *Pride & Joy*. He worked on it for years. Told me and my little brother that if a man was going to live on the water, he ought to have a boat that suited him.'

Margo glanced back at the cabin. Her rifle stood on its butt in the corner by the stove.

'Leon said I ought to give you my crop-damage permits this year. I'm cautious about who I let shoot on my property.'

Margo had a delayed realization of who *Leon* was. She looked at the man's hand again.

'I've given Leon the permits for years on Smoke's advice, but he only took two deer last

364

year. Both of them say you're a regular sharp-shooter.' The farmer nodded as though agreeing with Fishbone or agreeing with the universe. 'You're younger than I expected you'd be.'

She nodded along with him. She knew she should speak up, say something. The farmer's eyes were gray like Johnny's, but he did not have what his brother had, that raucous shine in his face, that dangerous scent.

'You must be about nineteen? Smoke says you're trapping. You got your license?'

She nodded.

'The crop-damage permit is for June through October to keep the deer out of my corn and beans. The deer eat thirty percent of my crop if I don't have somebody out here. And I'd like to have a few of the hides tanned. I can pay you for them if you'll skin them and bring them to me.'

She nodded again. She did want to stay here, at least for now, and she wanted the permits. It felt good to know what she wanted.

'And I'd ask you to tell me if you find a weasel or a mink or an otter down here. As much as the river has gotten cleaned up these last years, I'd put money on it that weasels are coming back. I might have to take more care with my chickens.'

Margo knew there was a bit of money to be made from these. She would talk to Fishbone about how to trap ermine and mink.

'Can you speak at all?' he asked and tilted his head.

'I'm not going to sleep with you,' she said. She felt her throat go unsteady, but her voice stayed strong. 'And not your brother Johnny, either.'

She had not meant that to be the first thing she said to the farmer, but she had to make clear she would not take in every man who showed up.

'So you've met Johnny, then. I was going to warn you about him.' He smiled, and when he showed his teeth, he looked a bit more like his brother. He said, 'I wondered if you were okay out here. I don't want to find a frozen woman when I come out in the spring.'

'I won't freeze.' She crossed her arms over her belly. There was no reason he would suspect her of being with child, no reason to think Fishbone or Smoke would have told him, though she was surprised he referred to her as a woman rather than a girl.

'What're you doing for heat in there?'

'Wood. Smoke had Fishbone check the stove for leaks. And there's a propane backup.'

He nodded. 'You can take any dead wood around here, but I'd ask you, don't cut any live trees out of my windbreaks.'

She'd already taken some dead wood.

'Go ahead and take any of that stuff behind the hay barn if you can split it. I let landscapers drop off extra wood there, but it's mostly stumps with roots. You can borrow my wheelbarrow from the barn, but be sure to put it back where it is now, on the lower level.' He paused. 'You really want to live out here on my land?'

'On the river. I might move somewhere else when I get a bigger outboard.'

'I'll mention it to the neighbors, tell them not to be surprised if they see you. A few years ago, I took pity on a fellow, let him spend the winter in my chicken shed. My wife was furious. He rigged up an old kerosene heater, burned the shed down.'

Margo nodded. 'I won't burn anything down.'

'My wife may not be crazy about this situation when she figures it out, but Smoke says you're a grown person. He thinks you know what you're doing. Leon says you're some kind of throwback. He admires you.'

Margo didn't know what *throwback* meant apart from fish too small to bother eating. She thought about all the things the farmer and his wife must have in their kitchen, all the pans and ingredients, the utensils, the rolling pins for piecrusts, stoves with coils that glowed beneath pots, windows that let in the sunlight, big overhead light fixtures for when there wasn't enough natural light. Those were the things Margo had given up for now, for her life on the river. She was sure the farmer's wife, like Joanna, had all kinds of cotton cloths for cleaning up messes in the kitchen and a washing machine to wash them in, chairs that scraped against wood floors when they were pushed out from tables, a chest freezer that could hold a whole deer. Maybe Margo was giving up too much to live out here on a boat, giving up too much for the freedom to travel away from here if she had any trouble. But for now she knew she would be giving up more if she tried to live any other way.

'I don't want to live in anybody else's house,' she said. She had four cooking pans that she loved, one from the Indian and three from Smoke, and they were sufficient for any meal she'd wanted to make so far. She had two propane burners plus the top of the woodstove. She loved the small, white-painted kitchen drawers with elegant handles into which her few utensils fit. Her dining table folded up against the wall, and the seats folded down to become her bed. The curtains over the window were a pattern of leaping fish in different colors. She'd washed the curtains and hung them back up. She couldn't imagine the fuel bills for a big house like the farmer's, all that waste heating room after room, indoor space that a person like Margo, who had the whole river for her home, didn't need.

'That's good,' the farmer said. 'I don't think my wife would like some unknown young woman living in her house. But you're right in thinking that if it got too cold, I'd feel I ought to invite you anyhow.'

'Thank you for the permits, sir, but please keep off my boat,' she said. 'No men are welcome here.'

22

'Less than two weeks,' Smoke told Margo one morning in early February. His voice had become rougher, and sometimes Margo had to lean close to make out his words. His speech was often fractured by long wheezing breaths. A family court decision was pending, and Smoke was certain he would not be allowed to stay in his house. Margo was fearful about other things, that Smoke would fall down or that he would cough so hard he would simply stop breathing. She reached out and brushed a toast crumb from his whiskered cheek.

Fishbone, who rarely stayed more than a few minutes at a visit now, before or after taking out his boat, insisted the nieces were taking Smoke's case before the judge because they cared about him and they couldn't stand to see him killing himself. 'They're harsh ladies,' he said, 'but they're your family, and they love you.'

'Save me from their fucking love,' Smoke whispered to Margo as soon as he could do so without Fishbone hearing. But Margo understood how his nieces might think he was not taking care of himself. She felt lousy about Smoke's deterioration, found that she could not stop worrying about him, whether she was with him or away from him. She felt helpless in the face of his pain and difficulty. She thought Nightmare, too, seemed haunted; for hours the dog would stare at his master, sometimes going most of the day without eating.

'I can stay with you, Smoke,' Margo said, as she poured him more coffee from the percolator, 'and your nieces will see I'm taking care of you.'

She sat beside him at the kitchen table, so they were both looking out at the river. A thaw had melted the ice and compacted the snow. Margo had shoveled the patio a few days ago, and it was still clear.

'You can't go back on a deal,' Smoke whispered.

'I won't do it,' Margo said, more loudly than she wanted to. Smoke's hearing seemed to be failing even as his voice grew more quiet.

'It hurts to breathe, kid.' The dog became agitated and stood up and went to the door. 'I can't even have real coffee in that place. They only got Sanka.'

'Maybe if they make you move, you could stay with one of your nieces.'

He shook his head. Margo, too, hated the thought. She let Nightmare out and sat back down. She spread on her toast some strawberry jam Smoke's sister had made. He said his sister had had brain cancer and had died in the nursing home within a few months of arriving. Smoke said his sister 'went off to that shithole like it was some goddamned party.' She had liked the nurses fussing over her, he said, treating her 'like a damned baby.'

'My neck aches,' Smoke said. 'From holding up my damned head.'

'It's better to be alive, Smoke.' Margo bit into

the toast and chewed, though her appetite was slipping away. 'We have to think about the consequences.'

'What about the consequences to living?' Smoke reached in his shirt pocket and pulled something out, pushed it into Margo's hand.

'What's this?' she unfolded five twenty-dollar bills.

'For the boat. It's what you gave me. And take my shotgun. It's yours. Fishbone's right. I need it like a hole in the head.'

'You already gave me too much, Smoke,' Margo said. She didn't know how to explain to him how having killed someone made it more important that she never do it again.

'What the hell am I going to do with a shotgun?' he said. 'You'll keep it clean, won't you?'

Margo arranged a piece of toast with jam, some scrambled egg, and a bite of sausage on her fork.

'I deserve to die, damn it,' he said. 'You need to respect that.'

'But I haven't figured out how to live yet.'

'You've figured it out as well as I ever did.'

'If you go, I've got no friends.' Margo heard Nightmare scratch on the outside door, and she got up and let him in, along with a blast of cold air. The weather was supposed to warm throughout the day because a storm was coming tonight. Nightmare lay down on a piece of rug between Margo and Smoke.

'Then you'd better start making friends,' he said. 'Nothing wrong with being a hermit, so long as you have friends when you need them.'

'I just want you.'

'I don't know if I would've made it without you these last few months, kid. Your company has almost made life worth living.'

Now that Smoke was getting sicker, it was harder for Margo to go home and leave him all alone. When she had come this morning at ten o'clock, Smoke had still been lying in bed. Margo had lifted him and helped him into his clothes and shoes.

'Fishbone will help,' Smoke said. 'After I'm gone, he's taking Nightmare. For protection for his wife.'

'Fishbone calls me *you people*. He thinks I should go live with my ma. He's always talking about me having the dang baby.' Margo's heart sank at the thought of Fishbone taking the dog away.

'Don't give up on your ma,' Smoke whispered. 'She might come around. And it doesn't look to me like you're putting any distance between yourself and that baby.'

Margo nodded. She went home that afternoon, checked her traps, and found them empty. She couldn't think about the baby, who was safe inside her for now, but only about Smoke, who seemed so weak. He also sounded more serious, spookier than ever before. If tonight's storm dropped a lot of snow, Margo was afraid she wouldn't be able to get through the field to his house in the morning to help him. She also wanted to tell Smoke that she was not giving up on her ma, not really, not the way he thought.

After dark, when the winds started picking up, Margo let her wood stove burn all the way down, and she laid another fire with newspaper and sticks, got it all ready, but didn't light it.

Margo locked up the *Glutton* and tramped back through the snow-covered cow pasture. The river sounded strange, as though glass were breaking all along its edges. Smoke's patio door was not locked, so she went in. She took off her boots and parka and walked quietly to Smoke's bedroom. Though the rest of the house was cluttered, his bedroom was sparely decorated and almost empty. She climbed into the double bed in her long underwear and lay beside Smoke. The housekeeping aide had changed the sheets the day before, and they felt clean. Margo had been putting off washing her own sheets, since she would either have to carry them down to Smoke's or wash them in her canning kettle and freeze-dry them outside.

'I don't want to lose you,' she said in a loud whisper. 'I don't want you to leave me.'

'I'm not your ma.'

'I know.'

'I'm a tired old man.' At first Smoke was rigid beside her, and then Margo felt him relax, as her grandpa had warmed and relaxed beside her on the sun porch. At the end, her grandpa had been weak and thin like Smoke, though he'd had lumps like tree knots on his armpits and neck and groin. Smoke's lumps were inside his lungs. Margo moved her hands across his shoulder blades. He shivered and then sighed. She lightly caressed his shoulders, his ribs, the small of his

373

back. Through his long underwear shirt, she felt the heat of his pressure sores.

She and Smoke lay that way for a few hours, neither of them quite falling asleep because of the strangeness and sweetness of being beside another person, until Smoke began to cough. He sat up on the edge of the bed and coughed for more than forty-five minutes according to the clock by the bed. The minute hand on the lighted clock face had moved slowly, but Margo didn't dare shift or speak or touch Smoke, for fear of making it worse. She knew she could put her arm around Smoke's neck and close his throat, stop his choking by stopping his breathing. Margo could bring Smoke peace, and if she pressed her thumbs over his windpipe, he would not struggle. She could end his pain right now, but she did not want to be his angel of death. Nightmare lay silent but awake on the floor. The dog's brown eyes glistened in the dark as he watched his master.

Smoke tipped up a bottle of codeine syrup to get the last drops. He readjusted his tubes and folded himself so his body seemed like a leathery shell surrounding his brittle lungs. After the coughing subsided, he breathed sharply through pursed lips. He disconnected his oxygen and lit and smoked a cigarette. He lit a second cigarette from the first, and finally a third. Margo saw how cigarettes were Smoke's slow-acting angels of death, the agonizingly slow hands of his strangulation. After putting out the third cigarette in the ashtray on the floor, Smoke lay back down, and Margo placed a hand on his shoulder. She leaned in and kissed his cheek.

'Smoke, you shaved. You're so smooth.' She took his hand in hers, and they fell asleep.

Margo awoke alone to the sounds of Smoke's wheelchair squeaking in the other room. She heard the door to the patio opening, wind roaring, and Nightmare whining. The door closed and she heard windowpanes rattling against the storm. These days she had a hard time pulling herself out of sleep, even to feed the woodstove, because the creature in her belly always tried to drag her back to dreams, sapping her consciousness until she'd gotten eight, nine, even ten hours of sleep. She shook off her exhaustion, dressed, and gathered together her things in order not to leave any evidence in case Smoke's nieces stopped by. A long time ago, back in Murrayville, she had sometimes awakened early like this from a dead sleep with a desire to hunt. Back then she had awakened fully with the abruptness of a light switched on. She'd dressed in silence, gotten her daddy's shotgun from behind his truck seat or out of his closet, and set out into the woods. Now when that feeling came — and she felt a ghost of it even this morning — she found she could simply imagine shooting a buck and the feeling would subside, or she could go out and check her traps for muskrats or coons.

Margo went into the kitchen and did not see Smoke, but found Nightmare sniffing at the door. The lighted clock read six-twenty. Margo checked the bathroom, but Smoke was not there. She had earlier dreamed he had growled into the phone, or maybe it had not been a dream. The predawn sky was brightened by the blowing snow, but Margo did not turn on any lights in the house, did not spoil her night vision. She put on her fake-fur-lined parka, picked her rifle off the rack in the kitchen, and hung it over her shoulder. Though Smoke had given Margo his shotgun, Margo had left it in the rack, worrying that taking it away would make him feel diminished. She did not let Nightmare out because he would run down to the water and howl at the wind, and she would have to wait for him to return before she could go to sleep again. If Smoke was out there, Margo would get him back inside in a matter of seconds.

She stepped outside into the swirling snow and found him sitting in his wheelchair at the edge of the patio, looking down the steep hill toward the water. He wore only his glasses, his long underwear, and an unbuttoned work shirt with his name on it. Snow was accumulating on his shoulders and bare head, and the wind must have been biting his face, but he didn't behave as if he were cold. Margo took one of his half-clenched hands in both of hers and warmed it.

'You shouldn't be out here in a snowstorm, especially without your jacket. And without your oxygen,' Margo said. 'Come back to bed.'

Nightmare barked.

'Sunrise in a few minutes,' Smoke whispered through puffs of breath, sounding stronger than he had the previous day. 'I think the neighbors are out of town.'

'You want to see the sunrise in a snowstorm? Pink sky in the morning?'

Smoke sighed, and Margo felt his gaze move from the river, to her, and to the river again.

'Come sleep a little more. The sun rises every day.'

'My jacket. My smokes,' he finally said with those quick puffs of voice. 'Don't let the dog out.'

Margo went into the house and tried to calm Nightmare. 'I'll get Smoke back inside, and we'll all go back to sleep,' Margo said. She grabbed the cigarettes from the bedroom, the jacket from the back of a kitchen chair. There on the table, she saw the note. She switched on the table lamp to read the heavy, neat print: *To my busybody nieces. I cannot go to All Saints. I will not go.* She stopped reading, dropped the cigarettes and the jacket, and after a brief struggle to keep Nightmare inside, she stepped outside into the storm. Smoke was gone.

Margo had not considered how close he had been to the edge of the patio. He must have pushed against the wheels with a burst of force strong enough to move him off the patio and to the edge of the hill. Once descending, it would have taken no strength to roll down the snow-covered hillside on the upstream side of the concrete steps and the dock. She followed the wheelchair tracks down the hill. In the pale light reflecting off the blowing snow, she thought she saw Smoke push his wheels once more. At the river's edge, one wheel caught in the gap between the lawn and the retaining wall, stopping the chair abruptly. Smoke, however, continued moving forward through the blowing snow and onto the river, breaking through the slushy ice on the upstream side of the dock. Margo's boots slipped out from under her as she was running down to help. She inadvertently kicked the chair forward, along with its oxygen tank, so it tumbled off the wall and into the water on top of Smoke's legs. The oxygen slid away and disappeared. The current dragged Smoke's body and the chair against some branches that had gotten caught under the dock. He was tangled in the debris there.

Moving with what felt like slow, clumsy motions, Margo crouched on the retaining wall and leaned down and tried to drag the wheelchair out of the water, but her position was all wrong, and she could not lift its weight. She slid her rifle off her shoulder and stuck its butt end into the snow. She wished she had left it in the house. She braced herself against the dock and the retaining wall and tugged at the chair again, but still she could not lift it off Smoke's legs. When she moved the branches, Smoke's head went underwater. Inside the house, Nightmare was barking.

Margo jumped off the retaining wall, through the slushy ice into knee-deep water, and her calves clenched at meeting the cold. She stepped into deeper water, up to her thighs, and her legs burned. She pulled Smoke's head and torso from beneath the water.

'I'll come visit you if you go to that place. I'll sit with you, Smoke. I'll sneak you coffee and cigarettes,' she said. 'Let's get you out of the water.'

Smoke's dark glasses had been swept away, and his eyes were closed. His legs were stuck under the wheelchair. They did not come free when she pulled as hard as she dared. Meanwhile the bottom of her parka floated around her and soaked up icy water.

Looking into Smoke's face, Margo felt foolish. She hadn't realized how much she loved him. What she felt was no less than what she'd felt for her grandpa, maybe even for her daddy.

'Let me go under.' Smoke tipped his head back and opened his red, raw eyes. The sky was growing pink and Margo saw snowflakes fall on his eyelashes, but he didn't blink. The current tugged at the soggy fabric of Margo's parka, making her whole body feel heavy. She should have left the jacket on shore with her rifle, so it would have been dry when she put it on again. Smoke seemed heavier than he should have been.

'I need to go get help.' Margo pressed her cheek against Smoke's cheek, spoke to him at such close range that their lips were almost touching. 'I need to get your other bottle of oxygen.'

'Please don't leave me,' Smoke whispered in a thinner voice. 'I don't want to die alone.'

'I have to,' Margo said, but she didn't budge. She knew the current would drag Smoke under, and he would drown before she could return. She held him above the surface. His shirt was waterlogged, but that didn't explain his heaviness in her hands. Margo pulled her feet out of the muck into which they were sinking, one, then the other. The cold of the river reached up through her and chilled her belly. Nightmare kept barking from the house.

'Let me go under.'

'I don't want to kill you, Smoke.'

He whispered into her cheek, 'This isn't killing, kid. You can do this.'

Margo felt the vibration of Smoke's mouth against her face, heard words flowing out of him, but she didn't know if he was saying them aloud. His face was growing purplish.

'Let me go under,' Smoke whispered again, and he took hold of her free hand with a fierce grip. The water beaded and fell from his thick silver hair, tinted pink by the light. His lips had gone colorless. She noticed then a leather thong tied around his shoulder and under one arm. She felt around him with the hand that was supporting him and found, tied to it, the bag of lead type he'd kept on the kitchen table. She tried to yank it off, but couldn't manage with one hand, and he still gripped her other hand tightly.

Margo kicked at the wheelchair again and it broke free from the branches and moved downstream under the dock a few inches. Margo saw how one of Smoke's feet was caught in it, and she thought maybe if she let go of him and wrenched her hand from his grip, she could possibly free his foot before he drowned. If he were still alive after that, maybe she could lift him onto the retaining wall. Maybe she could get him up the hill. If he were still alive when the paramedics came, he might survive another hour, or a day or a week in the hospital or nursing home, probably with pneumonia. His forehead was twisted with pain.

She looked at him one long, last time. She kissed his cheek and let go. He slipped below the surface. His coughing stopped and his chest convulsions slowed and stopped. Margo felt his tension and pain slip away, and his grip on her hand gradually loosened.

She wanted to lift Smoke's body out of the river and onto land, but she had to get out of the freezing water. She climbed onto the retaining wall and stood dripping, her teeth chattering. The blowing snow had already covered her tracks and the wheelchair marks. The water on her pant legs and parka quickly froze, and the snow stuck to her. Water beaded on the outside of her greased leather boots, but it had soaked in through her laces and into her socks so that her feet were blocks of ice. She looked up at the house and saw through the snow a thin man in a fedora walking across the patio. Then he was staring down at her, his arms crossed over his chest. She inhaled sharply, and it hurt.

Margo plucked her rifle from the snow, put the strap over her shoulder, not pausing to tap the snow out of the barrel, and moved up the steps. At the top, she stood before Fishbone and tried to say something, but his stony gaze stopped her from trying, and Nightmare's wild barking overwhelmed her. She made her way onto the porch, stomped the snow off, and moved inside. Nightmare followed her across the kitchen, agitated but silent. She grabbed her cloth bag from the kitchen, took the bottle of shampoo from the bathroom, two pairs of new socks from Smoke's bedroom drawer, a shirt with a label that said *Smoke* from the closet, and the rest of the jar of strawberry jam from the refrigerator. She grabbed the Remington from the gun rack and dropped two boxes of twelve-gauge shells into her wet pockets, where they weighted her like anchors. Before she walked out, she crouched and hugged the big dog and scratched his ears and his neck. 'Goodbye, Nightmare,' she said. 'I wish I could take you with me. I wish I could take care of you.'

She walked back outside. Through the blowing snow, she saw Fishbone's figure down at the water's edge. She clutched the shotgun in her bare hand — her gloves were in her pockets, soaking wet, under the shells. She set off on stiff legs downstream along the path toward the *Glutton*. For a long time, Margo heard the dog barking behind her. She wondered if the police might notice her tracks. Or was Smoke right when he had said nobody would care enough about the death of a sick old man to investigate?

Margo managed to slip through the barbed wire without snagging her parka. She slowed as she moved on her numb feet across the pasture, where no livestock were about. When she had almost reached the far side, she stumbled over something, maybe a frozen cow pie under the snow and fell to her knees. She crawled forward for a while, but had to rest before continuing on. She studied the river, could make out only gray and white blurs. The river was too cold even to stink, and according to last night's radio weather report, it might freeze again tonight after the storm. Her Marlin remained on her shoulder, but she had somehow dropped the shotgun into the snow. She felt around, but couldn't find it. She would rest for just a minute.

She was exhausted beyond anything she could remember feeling. She thought she had survived losing her father, but she had not yet survived it, nor any of her other losses. She pressed her cheek against the snow, felt the snow compress and melt slightly. Snow began to accumulate on her other cheek. She would lie there for a moment, until she was rested, until she understood what had happened this morning, and what had happened in her life. Her obligations had been met, and she was free, more free than she had ever been. Within minutes she was hardly feeling the cold. If she could return to her boat, she would start a fire to thaw herself out, or else she would remain right here, at rest.

She was awakened by a jolt, as though someone had kicked her from behind, but when she opened her eyes and looked around, she saw she was alone. The jolt had been as painful as an electrical shock.

After the sensation passed, Margo closed her eyes and returned her cheek to the snow, only to receive another blast of electricity so strong her eyes flew open. She rose to her knees and found she was beside a fence post near the water's edge, closer to the fence and to the river than she had thought. She pulled herself up to standing. She must have grabbed the electric fence with her bare hand and shocked herself, but she couldn't shake the feeling that the jolt had come from inside her own body. She continued toward the river, and she negotiated her way around the fence somehow without falling into the water. She made her way slowly to her boat through snow that now glowed pure pink from the rising sun. She was carrying her bag over one shoulder and her rifle over the other, and she was weighed down by her frozen parka.

Once inside her boat, she laid her rifle on the table. After breaking off two safety matches against the box, she lit the third and touched it to the balled-up newspaper she had placed there the previous day, beneath the teepee of dry kindling. Two small, dry chunks of firewood sat atop the stove. She stripped naked and wrapped herself in the scratchy wool army blanket, yellowed with age but very warm.

She wondered if Nightmare was still barking. She was envious of the dog for the simple way he would grieve for Smoke. She could grieve for him by cutting her moorings and heading down the river, but she knew that coming back up would be impossible with only her small and unreliable motor.

Soon the cabin was warmed from twenty degrees to fifty-five, according to the thermometer on the back of the door, and Margo dressed in dry pants, shirt, and socks. She fed a bigger piece of wood into the fire and continued listening for sirens, but there were no sirens. There was only her memory of the anger and sadness on Fishbone's face and the relief growing in her that the thing was done, that her debt to Smoke had been paid and he was no longer suffering. The sky was fully lit now, and the wind had calmed.

Throughout the last few months, since she'd stopped being sick every morning, the business in her belly had flowed with her movements, had drifted fishlike within her, had swum her like a river, but now, as the fire gradually warmed the boat's living space, the baby sloshed inside her like an angry bullhead in a bucket. After the fire warmed the room to sixty degrees, enough that Margo should have been comfortable, the baby twisted, pitched, and heaved, fought like a fish on the end of a line. This baby was furious, Margo thought, furious at her for almost killing it, furious at Smoke for taking them with him to drown in freezing water. Margo absorbed the creature's anger, and she found she no longer wanted it to slip away. It had been her constant companion these months, had endured wood chopping, roof raking, and muskrat trapping in the cold water. The baby had held on to her through all her trouble, and this morning, maybe it had saved her life. She had given the baby every opportunity to leave, but it had stayed, and she would not let it die now.

She put her hands on her stomach to calm the struggle. So many times she had gone to someone else, had begged at someone else's table, and now she had someone to take care of.

Margo would do at least as good a job as one of those wolves who raised human children. She could do as good a job as her own mother — and she would not abandon her child in a selfish effort to find herself. And maybe there would even come a time when Luanne would want to be a grandmother, if not a mother.

She tried praying to God, but it felt better when she put her hands on Crane's ashes and asked for his help. She also asked for help from Smoke, and from Grandpa Murray, and by the time the snow finally tapered off, she thought they had given her strength.

Her parka was still soaking wet on a chair by the stove, so Margo put her Carhartt jacket on her shivering shoulders, wrapped herself in the wool blanket, and trudged back to the pasture. She was unable at first to find the place where she had rested, but she kicked at the snow along the fence line until she found the shotgun. She brushed the snow off and stuck it under her arm.

Across the pasture, she saw a figure duck between strands of barbed wire and then wave in her direction. It was a tall man in a stocking cap. He waved again, eagerly. Margo thought she recognized him as the farmer. She didn't want to talk to him or anyone now. She began to walk away.

'Wait!' The voice was Johnny's. She turned to see him approach, almost at a jog, and she found her reaction time had slowed too much to run away, and so she stood like one of those cows in heat. Her grip tightened on the shotgun. She knew Smoke kept the thing loaded, with four shells in the magazine.

'Fishbone sent me. He told me to tell you that Smoke drowned in the river,' Johnny said. 'Looks like he did himself in like he always swore he would. I'm sure going to miss that old fart.' He was speaking in a subdued tone and nodding gravely, but Margo could feel excitement coming off his body in waves. He wouldn't let sadness hold him back. She was tempted to become a part of his fun, to lose herself in him for a while and let it dull her sadness. And then where would she be?

'Drowned,' she said and swallowed. Her eyes welled up.

'Why are you dressed like an Indian in that blanket?' he asked. 'Let me come back with you to Smoke's boat, Margie. We'll warm each other up.'

Margo recalled the jolt to her belly, willed it to come again to give her strength. She said, 'Stay the heck away from me.'

Johnny's eyes widened. 'Fishbone sent me to check on you. Don't you remember me? I'm Johnny. We met at Smoke's.'

'It's not Smoke's boat anymore. It's mine.' She raised the shotgun to her hip, stepped away from him. 'And if you step on the deck of my boat, I'll shoot you and dump you in the river.'

'Isn't that Smoke's shotgun?' Johnny reached for the barrel as though to take the weapon.

Margo stepped away. 'Smoke gave me this gun.'

She imagined how Johnny would feel pressed up against her, how his hands would feel on her breasts, how his hair and the back of his head would feel in her hand, how her cheek would press against his chest. His neck would smell sweetly of sweat.

'Here's your warning.' She racked the pump, which made a loud *ka-chung* sound. 'Put one foot on my boat and they'll find your body in Lake Michigan.' She was out of breath when she finished speaking those few words. There might come a time when she wanted what Johnny offered, but this wasn't it.

'I don't know what anyone has told you about me, but I'm a nice guy.' Johnny stepped away, but continued looking at her with those fine gray eyes. He managed to smile.

Margo turned away, walked to the river's edge, and made her way back around the fence on shivering legs, exhausted from freezing and thawing, exhausted from a whole life of holding herself up. She made her way back to her boat and spent the evening cleaning her guns by the light of the oil lamp, and her belly continued to settle. She rubbed linseed oil into the rifle's stock, into the carved squirrel. She polished the chrome until it gleamed. She ate a can of corned beef she'd found in the back of the cupboard, something Smoke had left in there. She decided that the next day she would shoot a squirrel and cook it in her pot on her stove. Or maybe a rabbit, and with that rabbit's skin she would start a new blanket. It wouldn't take many skins to cover a little kid.

23

After Smoke's death, the snow and ice storms continued, and the sun didn't come out for three weeks. On the morning the clouds finally lifted, Margo cooked a big carp on the woodstove. She was boning and processing it on the deck of the *Glutton* that afternoon when she saw a man coming down the path from the old barn. The slim figure approached, and Margo saw by the hat that it was Fishbone. She was cutting the fish into strips that she hoped she could smoke, dry, and store for later. The meat was shredding, though, and by the time Fishbone reached the riverbank, she was starting to question the wisdom of the project. She was wearing her father's Carhartt jacket because she didn't want to stink up her mother's parka, which she wore into town when she went to check her PO box and to buy potatoes and onions and tins of corned beef, for which she'd recently developed a craving.

Margo wiped her bare hands on a cloth wired to the table and grabbed the six muskrat hides she'd strung together with baling twine. She made her way across her gangplank. She held out the skins, clean and dry, all with perfect eye holes. Fishbone took a folded garbage bag out of his jacket pocket, slid the skins into it, and rested the bag near his feet. Margo thought she could feel the snow around them melting as they stood there. Fishbone stuck one of his little cigars into his plastic holder and lit it.

'I was curious about your rifle, so I looked into it,' he said. 'Presentation-model Marlin 39A. Five hundred of them made in 1960 with that squirrel and chrome. Marlin's ninety-year-anniversary rifle. You're probably the only person shooting with one. Everybody else keeps the thing in a box.'

Margo tugged on her jacket, pulled it down over her belly. Fishbone took a drag off his cigar. Snowbirds landed near the fire pit. The neighbor lady had given her a paper bag of seed and told her to see what kind of winter birds she could attract near the water.

'Smoky called me that morning, you know,' he said. 'Woke up my poor wife, scared her with his voice all wheezy. Now I think he was calling to say goodbye.'

'He said he didn't want to die alone.' Margo put her hands in her jacket pockets.

'After you left, I called the cops, and they found the note in the kitchen. No doubt about what it said. Cops asked me about suicide, and I told them Smoky'd talked about it plenty. His favorite topic.'

Fishbone was wearing his usual slim-fitting leather jacket over a thin wool sweater, and though he was more than three times Margo's age, he was not shivering the way she was. She had moved and reset her underwater traps this morning and had still not recovered. She would not be completely warm until this evening, when she would stoke the fire in her cabin. Sometimes she felt overwhelmed by the comfort she could create in her little home on the water, whether she was sitting up working or lying in her own bed reading with the woodstove blazing.

'You didn't come to the funeral,' Fishbone said.

'I walked into town. I even went into the building. But I couldn't stay with that many people. I didn't want to see him dead, anyway.' The gray-and-white snowbirds rose suddenly and took off upstream. A half dozen cardinals flew in and fell upon the seed.

'Farmer Harland was there, and his wife. Old customers from the print shop, too, people I knew. I wish you could have met him before the emphysema. He knew how to shoe horses, take care of sick cattle, build a boat, set type. He could do about anything.'

She nodded.

'He helped a lot of people in different ways. I still owe him money. He told me I owed it to you now.'

'You don't owe me,' she said.

'Yes, I do. I should've done more to take care of him. He took care of me whenever I needed it. But I just couldn't.'

'Smoke said you were a tough nut to crack.'

Fishbone inhaled deeply on his cigar, something he usually didn't do. He exhaled a rich stream of smoke and warm breath into the winter air. 'It's a great big wide world, isn't it, young lady?'

'Did you love Smoke?'

He paused as though he were going to say

something complicated, but said, 'He was a good friend.'

They were both silent for a while.

'I loved sitting and talking with you and Smoke,' Margo said. 'It was paradise to me.'

'Funny paradise.'

'I liked listening to the way you guys argued.'

She thought she might tell him how she'd tried to save Smoke, and how, in the end, it had been a relief to realize she had to let him go. She wanted to tell Fishbone how she'd dreamed that night about Smoke being with her in her bed, about how his ghost had climbed inside her with the baby, but she couldn't imagine how to get started saying such a crazy-sounding thing.

'Smoky made a new will. Did you know that? He put you in it.'

She squinted. 'What for?'

'For his house. He changed it right after you came back from your ma's. He had me take him to the lawyer. The house isn't worth too much.'

Margo didn't think Fishbone would joke with her about this, but she studied his face for a sign. She had missed his company.

'I've got a favor to ask you,' he said. 'Can I keep my boat at your place? You can use it anytime you want.'

'Smoke said you didn't visit him anymore. You came to visit the river.'

'I visited him, all right.'

'How come you want to be on the river?'

Fishbone snorted. 'I grew up on a river down in Ohio. We would have starved if not for hunting and fishing and trapping.'

'Why'd you leave?'

'I came up north to get a job, but it turned out I couldn't work in that auto plant. It would have killed me. Smoky saved me by giving me a job, and by letting me keep a boat at his place.'

Margo nodded. With Fishbone's boat she could row upstream or down and find the nearest heronry — every river had one, surely. And there would be a creek where she could find snapping turtles and watercress. She would practice moving the oars through the water without making a sound.

'My own kids had no interest in fishing or the river, grandkids neither, but maybe my great-grandkids will.' Fishbone looked at his half-burned cigar.

'I can help teach them to fish if you want. Are you sure about Smoke's house? I never thought.'

'Better place for a child than this boat. You glad now you're keeping that baby?'

She wouldn't try to explain why she was keeping her baby. It wasn't some point of principle — it was personal, between herself and the child.

She would cook something for Fishbone next time she saw him. She had flour and sugar from the store, and she would have raspberries in June, mulberries when she had a boat for getting across to the other side, wild gooseberries from the woods, and maybe wild strawberries, too. She would make a deal with the farmer to trade deerskins and venison for eggs year-round. She nodded, though she'd already forgotten what Fishbone had just asked her.

'Then stop splitting wood,' he said. 'Use the propane. That's why Smoky vented that propane heater out the side. I'll bring you another bottle of gas when you need it. I told Smoky I'd help you. And your ma will help. Have you gone to see her again?'

'Not yet,' Margo said.

'I don't know if Smoky was a good influence on you, always saying you should live any way you want. There's a lot to be said for trying to live a normal life.'

'You know a lot about little kids, don't you?' Margo asked.

'Oh, I got more kids and grandkids than I can count. And now great-grandkids,' Fishbone said. 'I wish you teenage girls could wait till you had a husband.'

'I've met the neighbor lady who lives across from the barn up there. I found her standing in her yard holding out birdseed, trying to get a chickadee to eat out of her hand.'

'Mrs. Rathbone?' he said.

'Rathburn, I think. She says she has baby clothes I can have. She said she'd watch the baby sometimes if I needed her to. She says she loves babies.'

Fishbone nodded.

'Her youngest daughter has a giant rabbit she takes for walks like a dog. Its ears are this long.' Margo flattened out her hands and made rabbit ears out of them.

'I don't suppose you told her what you usually do with rabbits.'

'No. But I could eat good on that rabbit for

two weeks.' Margo laughed. She noticed Fishbone had beard stubble today, something that was not usual for him.

'What's that you're doing with that carp over there?' Fishbone gestured with his chin at the table on the boat's deck. She was using her piece of teak boat as a cutting board. The asymmetrical curve of the thing made the juices run off over the words *River Rose* and through the bullet hole.

'Making jerky. I put too much salt on it, I think. It changed the texture. Maybe I should can fish in jars like tomatoes?'

'Maybe the venison would be better for canning.' He pulled some bills off a roll in his front pocket and paid her for the hides. He took his cigar out of his mouth and studied it one more time. 'I don't know if you're really trying to live like days gone by, but my ma used to can meat and fish. I can ask my older sister about it on the phone, see if she remembers how our ma did it. I think you've got to boil the jars under pressure. And my wife has pint jars she don't use. Smoky's got a pressure cooker somewhere, I'm sure. You're going to have to sort through all his junk.'

Margo nodded. She would learn everything she could from people who were willing to share what they knew. She would use the tools she was given to make her own kind of life. In one of the *Foxfire* books, she'd just read about how to make bootlaces out of woodchuck hide.

'My babies were born at home,' Fishbone said, 'but people don't do that anymore. You're going to have to go to the hospital.'

'I don't want to go to the hospital.' She could not imagine the people from *Foxfire* going to the hospital for their babies. Her Grandpa Murray had not been born in a hospital, and Annie Oakley was born at home, too.

'It doesn't matter what you want to do, young lady. You've got to get your baby his shots so he don't get sick. And if you don't take care of your baby, I'll call social services, and they'll take him away from you. If you put your child in danger, I'll take him away myself. That's the same as I told my granddaughter.'

Margo looked up at him in surprise.

'And you need to get a birth certificate at the hospital. Where else you going to get one?'

'You don't have to help me, you know.'

'I need a place on the river.' Fishbone squinted against cigar smoke going into his eyes. 'And maybe I've got a soft spot for a baby.'

'What about Nightmare?' Margo asked.

'I wanted to talk to you about that. He's in the truck.'

'Can I see him?' She held up her hands as if to show there was nothing in them.

'My wife wanted him for protection, but he just lies there, won't move. He growls all day and all night. I promised Smoky I'd take care of him, but he's lost fifteen pounds and his eyes are bloodshot like he's drunk.'

'He's a river dog,' Margo said. 'River dogs have to be on the river.'

'Let's say he lived with you. How would you feed him?'

'He can eat meat, same as me. I'll cook the muskrats for him. Take the glands out. And I'll get him dog food, too, if that's what he wants. I saw big bags at the grocery for five dollars.'

'Maybe you'd want to cook the muskrats outside. And you couldn't use the leg traps anymore. And he'd fill up that houseboat as long as you're staying there. You'd be stepping over him all day.'

'I've just been using the drowner line, and I live-trap the coons, toss the whole cage into the drink and drown them.' In fact, she'd never even set the leg traps Smoke had given her, for fear of catching up a stray dog.

'And he's going to bark and growl at every man comes around. And I'm not sure he won't bite a man who doesn't suit him.'

'He'll be happy living with me.'

'Are you sure you want this?'

Margo was more certain about the dog than she was about the house, which sounded like a fairy tale. Maybe she felt as much certainty about Nightmare as Luanne felt when she packed her bags and finally left Murrayville to make a new life. Maybe it was what Joanna felt when she swore at her wedding to honor and obey her husband, to forsake all others. Maybe when Smoke headed down that hill toward the river to drown he was as certain as Margo was about this dog.

Margo pushed the carp into a bucket with a tight-fitting lid, splashed some springwater from another bucket over the cutting board. She grabbed her rifle, slung it over her shoulder, and followed Fishbone along the trail to the barn. Nightmare was sitting in the driver's seat of the pickup. When the dog saw Margo, he put his front paws against the window. When Fishbone opened the door, Nightmare leapt heavily to the ground, bowed before Margo, wagged his massive tail, and barked once. He then turned back to Fishbone and growled.

'For crying out loud, dog,' he said and shook his head. 'I'm not your enemy.'

Margo hugged the dog and petted him. His ribs stuck out through his skin. 'Be nice, Nighty. We'll fatten you up.'

'I guess you're sure about this,' Fishbone said. 'With that tail he kept knocking everything off my wife's coffee table.'

Margo nodded. She had worried about Johnny showing up, coming along the riverbank. She had feared his scent was a key that could unlock her whole body, and it was his nature that he would try her. But not with this dog beside her, a barking and growling reminder that she wanted something more, that she had something worth protecting.

'Do you know anything about a dog star?' Margo asked.

'That would be Sirius. Your brightest star most nights.' He removed his burned-down cigar and put the holder in his pocket.

24

On the first hot morning in May, Margo woke up with the feeling that the river was fast rising from the previous night's rain. Not flooding, exactly, but coming up to meet her on the boat. She had awakened dreaming about her daddy. He had not been angry or disappointed this time, not even afraid for her. He had been sitting on a stump beside the Kalamazoo River sharpening a knife. Her sense in the dream was that he was her companion, as he had been before Luanne left, before all the trouble with the Murrays, and it made her feel at peace. She lay in her bed and listened to the high-pitched whispering and whistling all around her boat: a flock of cedar waxwings resting during their northern migration. She whispered and whistled back to them in their secret language. As far as she could tell, every language was a secret language, secret and manipulative and hopeful, starting with the nursery rhymes she'd been repeating lately because of the books Mrs. Rathburn loaned her. Sometimes Margo had been unable to find a language that worked for her, but she was pretty sure she was speaking one now.

Through the open window, Margo heard the meow of a catbird returned from wherever catbirds went in winter, and then the catbird changed its tune, began to whistle in imitation of the waxwings. The big dog on the floor whistled and wheezed in his sleep.

Through the window screens, Margo was feeling a warm wind, and for the moment she felt relaxed in her skin. Some nights now she lay in bed for hours pitching side to side, to the sound of critters chirping, trying to situate her expanding self. Last night, even without a fire in the stove, it was so warm she couldn't stand clothes or even sheets touching her belly, and she slept naked. Listening to a spring symphony of peepers, frogs, toads, and crickets was sometimes too much, but last night the rain banging on her tin roof had drowned out everything else, and she had slept so hard her eyes now felt swollen shut.

She could move into Smoke's house anytime she wanted, but she wasn't ready to leave this boat yet. Fishbone would come in a few days and together they'd drag the houseboat back upstream with the help of his aluminum boat and whatever else it took. He said he wished he had some mules like the ones that used to pull the barges up the river in Ohio when he was a boy. For the sake of the baby, she would move into the house — Mrs. Rathburn reminded her about the washing machine and running water so she wouldn't have to lug bottles — but Margo had grown happy on the *Glutton*, as happy as she could remember being. With her own safe and snug place on the river, she had been able to study herself the way she'd once studied the blue herons and the kingfishers, and the dogs and men she'd known. Nowadays she was able to puzzle through her troubles, not to solve them like problems, but to brood more deeply upon them to figure out what they could show her. She hoped Smoke was wrong about people being unknowable. She hoped that she could crack herself open like a nut and know herself, at least. Then she'd be able to start figuring out everybody else.

She swung her feet down onto Nightmare's rug beside her bed, patted the dog, and nodded good morning to her rifle on the rack by the door. She wrapped herself in a sheet, poured a bowl of dog food, and carried it out onto the boat's rubber-coated metal deck, which was warming up in the sun. She studied the churning surface of the river, which was running high, if not as dramatically as she had dreamed. Now that Crane's ghost was with her, he might someday tell her he'd like his ashes spread over the water. She wasn't ready to let them go yet.

The waxwings and some rowdy warblers were gathering in trees in the farmer's windbreak, descending from the sky and landing in branches, and then lifting off and settling again. When they alighted they became dark specks against a sky the color of heavenly blue morning glories, like the ones Joanna planted every spring at the river's edge. One waxwing after another flew down like a little masked bandit from its high perch to dip its beak in the spring water. The migrating birds would carry a bit of the Kalamazoo up north with them, maybe up to the Stark River, where they'd drink again before continuing their journey north, where they'd build nests and breed and possibly even see wolverines, who were not fouling traps or destroying camps, but just going about their business of finding food, shelter, and companions.

She heard equipment humming in a distant field. The farmer had survived the winter for a new season of work. She and he had been aware of one another all these months, but he'd not come to her boat until a few days ago, when he'd delivered the papers for the crop-damage permits. As soon as the farmer planted these fields, Margo was free to shoot all the deer she wanted, legally. She had finally met the farmer's wife when she'd been visiting Mrs. Rathburn, and the three of them had sat in the Rathburn kitchen and had coffee. Margo hadn't said more than a few words, but that was okay, since both those other women had plenty to say, and Margo enjoyed the music of their voices.

The catbird landed only ten feet from her, on one of the taut ropes tethering her barge to land. It wagged its tail to keep its balance, meowed a few more times, and then resumed its whistling mimicry of the waxwings. Margo wondered if the imitation was pure fun for the catbird, or if the bird learned something new with each borrowed note.

She crossed the gangplank and made her way barefoot along the riverbank and down to the water's edge. It was the first time she hadn't put on her boots before venturing off the boat. For the first time this year, for the first time ever, she felt the silt of the Kalamazoo squeeze through her toes. The fresh chill of it was electric. She walked to where the animals drank at the spring and left her footprints beside the four-toed signatures of songbirds.

Margo took off her sheet, wadded it up, and tossed it onto the deck of the boat. Only then did she think to look around and make sure no one could see her. She waded in up to her knees, and then to her thighs, felt the river weeds brush against her like a mother's long hair. Back in Murrayville her daddy had wanted her to wait to swim until the air was seventy degrees by the screen porch thermometer, but when he was at work, Luanne had let her swim as soon as she could brave the cold.

'All right, baby, welcome to the river,' Margo said. She stepped away from shore so the water went over the tops of her thighs, and before her feet could sink into the muck, she pushed off. The floor of the river gave way, and she submerged herself up to her neck. As her belly slid through the water, she felt a moment of uncertainty about her ability to swim. Her limbs didn't move right, didn't seem rightly proportioned for supporting herself in the water, and her head went under. She was being swept downstream. She struggled until she remembered to relax in the current, let it flow around her. She righted herself and began to sidestroke back upstream. She was lighter in the water — the river was a paradise for a girl swollen up the way she was. She buoyed herself with her belly and backstroked. She grabbed hold of an iron bar attached to the front of her barge and let

403

her legs float. Her naked belly stuck up and out of the water like the finest puffball mushroom in the river valley.

She had felt the baby startle at her contact with the river, had felt it jostle as she began to swim, and then the baby relaxed. As Margo floated, the baby floated with her. The black dog left his food bowl and jumped off the side of the gangplank, came splashing down into the river. He walked in up to his knees and lapped at the water. Smoke would turn in his grave to see his dog drinking from the river. Margo laughed and held on so as not to be swept away.

Acknowledgments

Thank you, Heidi Bell and Carla Vissers, Andy Mozina and Lisa Lenzo, for being smart and generous readers and fine writing friends. Thank you, Bill Clegg, for going above and beyond for this book. Thank you, Jill Bialosky, for your shaping, your fine tuning, and your plain good sense.

The following kind souls helped me by reading one or another draft of this novel: Gina Betcher, Jamie Blake, Glenn Deutsch, Godfrey Grant, Sheryl Johnston, Lindsey Kamyn, Mimi Lipson, Susan Ramsey, Diane Seuss, Melvin Visser, Shawn Wagner. Thank you Gary Peake, Master Bull's-Eye Shooter, for sharing your expertise and philosophy and for your exquisite attention to every shot Margo takes. I'm indebted to my grandpa Frank Herlihy of Red House Island, who lived long enough to know more than anyone else on the river, and granny Betty Herlihy, who knew plenty her husband didn't. And my dear Unca Terry Herlihy, who keeps a toe in the water.

Many people helped me with this book. A more complete list of acknowledgments appears on my website, www.bonniejocampbell.com.

Every person and place Margo encounters in this story is pure fiction. Even many aspects of the Kalamazoo River have been reimagined. *Once Upon a River* includes material from two short stories. 'Family Reunion' was first read aloud on WBEZ's *Stories on Stage* and first published at *Mid-American Review* and then in *American Salvage* (Wayne State University Press, 2009); 'Fishing Dog' was originally published in *North Dakota Quarterly* and then in *Women & Other Animals* (University of Massachusetts Press, 2000).

Thank you, Susanna, for always being there, and for being just the mother a writer needs.

Thank you, darling Christopher, for everything, always.

We do hope that you have enjoyed reading this large print book.

Did you know that all of our titles are available for purchase?

We publish a wide range of high quality large print books including:
Romances, Mysteries, Classics
General Fiction
Non Fiction and Westerns

Special interest titles available in large print are:
The Little Oxford Dictionary
Music Book
Song Book
Hymn Book
Service Book

Also available from us courtesy of Oxford University Press:
Young Readers' Dictionary
(large print edition)
Young Readers' Thesaurus
(large print edition)

For further information or a free brochure, please contact us at:
Ulverscroft Large Print Books Ltd.,
The Green, Bradgate Road, Anstey,
Leicester, LE7 7FU, England.
Tel: (00 44) 0116 236 4325
Fax: (00 44) 0116 234 0205

Other titles published by
The House of Ulverscroft:

GOLD

Chris Cleave

Kate and Zoe, elite track cyclists, are facing their last and biggest race: the 2012 Olympics. Devoted and self-sacrificing Kate, more naturally gifted but hampered by the demands of her personal life, is training fiercely; whilst her eight-year-old daughter Sophie dreams of the Death Star and of battling alongside the Rebels as evil white blood cells ravage her personal galaxy. Intense, aloof Zoe has always hovered on the periphery of real human companionship, and her compulsive need to win at any cost has more than once threatened her friendship with Kate — and her own sanity. Will she allow her obsession to sever the bond they have shared for more than a decade? Each wants desperately to win gold — and each has more than a medal to lose . . .

RIVER OF DESTINY

Barbara Erskine

On the banks of the river Deben in Suffolk lie ancient Anglo-Saxon barns. Their walls have secrets, which have lain buried for centuries. When Zoe and Ken move into one of the converted barns, they seem happy. But they grow more distant by the day. Meanwhile, the strange presence Zoe feels within their home, and the ghostly shapes she sees through the mists on the river, grow harder to ignore. Nearby, farmers are ploughing the land beside the river, and human bones are found. Are they linked to the Victorian tragedy the locals whisper about? What is the secret of the grassy mound, untouched for centuries? Its disturbance now seems to have devastating consequences. The river is ready to reveal its bloody secrets . . .

CALICO JOE

John Grisham

Thirty years have passed since eleven-year-old Paul Tracy watched his troubled father, Warren, a pitcher for the New York Mets, clash with his childhood hero, the Cubs' golden-boy Joe Castle, in a contest from which no winners emerged. Now the news that his father is dying brings the memory of that day flooding back. Deciding that it's time to face up to what really happened on that baseball field in 1973, father and son make their way to Calico Rock, Arkansas, where either redemption or rejection awaits them.

SHINE SHINE SHINE

Lydia Netzer

When Maxon met Sunny he was seven years, four months and eighteen days old. Or, he was 2693 rotations of the earth old. Maxon was different. Sunny was different. They were different together. Now, they are married, and Sunny wants more than anything to be 'normal'. But her husband is on a NASA mission to the moon, and a meteor is heading his way. Sunny wishes Maxon would turn the rocket around and come straight the hell home.

THE PRISONER OF HEAVEN

Carlos Ruiz Zafon and Lucia Graves

Barcelona, 1957. It is the week before Christmas in the Sempere & Sons bookshop. Daniel Sempere is happily married to Bea, and they have a son, whilst their partner Fermin is soon to marry Bernarda. Luck, finally, seems to be smiling on them. Then a mysterious person enters the shop, buys the most expensive volume on display — an illustrated edition of *The Count of Monte Cristo* — and inscribes in it the words 'For Fermin Romero de Torres, who came back from among the dead and holds the key to the future. 13'. Who is he? What does he want? The answer lies in a terrible secret, hidden for two decades ... a tale of imprisonment, betrayal, murder and love, leading back into the heart of the Cemetery of Forgotten Books.